PRAISE FOR
REKTOK ROSS

Rektok Ross offers "readers genuinely diverse characters, each of whom continues to grow throughout the narrative... Brace for impact readers, [Ross] holds little back."

—*Kirkus Reviews*

Rektok Ross has "inborn talent for the kind of narrative driven storytelling that makes for a compulsive page-turning read from cover to cover... Unreservedly recommended..."

—*Midwest Book Review*

"If you like action, suspense, and the horror real life can sometimes dish out, you can't go wrong... Rektok Ross delivers!"

—*Reader Views*

"[Ross] does a great job of making you care for [her] characters, keeps you guessing, and [gives] lots of chills."

—*Double the Books*

"Ross' thrillers are fast-paced and feature capable women in the lead. There's nothing to not like!"

—*Popverse*

"Ross crafts relatable, multi-dimensional characters and weaves together her signature recipe of thrills, chills, romance, and social commentary."

—*Temple of Geek*

PRAISE FOR SKI WEEKEND

*Winner of the WILLA Literary Awards, San Francisco Book Festival Awards, National Indie Excellence Awards, Next Generation Indie Book Awards, Independent Press Awards Distinguished Favorite Awards, Reader Views Literary Awards, CIBA Dante Rossetti Book Awards, Readers' Favorite Book Awards, American Fiction Awards, IAN Book of the Year Awards, and Firebird Awards!

*Named a Best Book of the Year by *Cosmopolitan, Entertainment Weekly, Yahoo!Life, Parade, Brit + Co., Book Riot, J-14, The Strand, She Reads,* and more!

"This is a suspenseful book that had me thoroughly hooked from page one... The emotional journey of *Ski Weekend* is relentless..."

—*Readers' Favorite*

"Rektok Ross delivers an absolute dynamic story packed with goofy teens, heart-stopping moments, romantic tension, and one adorable pup in this adrenaline-filled survival story."

—*BooknBrunch*

"Rektok Ross thrills readers with an electrifying winter tale that will have you wondering if that snow-filled adventure you've been planning is worth risking your life!"

—*Key Biscayne Magazine*

"A pacey thriller with moments of great tenderness—and spine-chilling horror."

—Lauren Kate, *New York Times* bestselling author of *Fallen*

"A nail-biter with some surprising moments. Recommended for high school and YA collections."

—*School Library Journal*

"Hand this to students who like thrillers and books about survival!"

—*Youth Services Book Review*

"*Ski Weekend* will hook you from the very start and keep your heart pounding long after you finish."

—Evelyn Skye, *New York Times* bestselling author of *The Crown's Game*

"Constantly twisting and emotionally relentless, *Ski Weekend* is a story of survival, friendship, and family… Alternately heartbreaking and hopeful—a chilling, thrilling read."

—Laurie Elizabeth Flynn, bestselling author of *The Girls Are All So Nice Here*

"This book will send so many chills up your spine, you'll feel like you're alongside the snowbound characters. The only time I don't recommend reading this book is right before bed. You won't be able to sleep, and you won't want to."

—Jeff Zentner, award-winning author of *Rayne & Delilah's Midnight Matinee*

"All the intensity and thrills of *The Hunger Games* packed into one car over a snowy weekend. Secrets, lies, strong characters, and twists will keep readers turning pages. If you've ever wondered how far you would go to survive, you need to read this book."

—Eileen Cook, author of *You Owe Me a Murder*

"Ripped from the headlines, *Ski Weekend* is so real you'll be shivering with the characters, fighting the elements, and asking yourself—what would you be willing to do to survive? Forget Netflix and chill. Binge this book."

—Sorboni Banerjee, Emmy Award–winning journalist and author of *Red as Blood*

"Ross weaves a stirring tale where each of her characters wrestle with choices that could result in life or death—some survive, and some don't."

—Paul Greci, award-winning author of *Surviving Bear Island* and *The Wild Lands*

"This pulse-pounding story of survival mirrors all the highs and lows of the hit reality TV show *Survivor*. In my case, I knew I could quit any time, but these kids aren't so lucky. Buckle up—this is one wild ride!"

—Corinne Kaplan, two-time *Survivor* and *Amazing Race* player and reality TV star

PRAISE FOR SUMMER RENTAL

"[A] masterpiece! Deeper than just a chilling horror story… it's also a beautifully crafted work that expands on marginalization, vengeance, and bullying."

—*Readers' Favorite*

"*Summer Rental* keeps the reader's riveted attention from the first page to last… more plot twists and turns than a Disneyland roller coaster!"

—*Midwest Book Review*

"A fun and scary slasher thriller!"

—*Kirkus Reviews*

"Harkens back to '90s slashers and to *Mean Girls*!"

—*The Hollywood Reporter*

"Rektok Ross delivers yet another impossible-to-put-down young adult horror page-turner with Summer Rental… a must-read for *Scream* and *Mean Girls* fans."

—Perri Nemiroff, *Collider*

"[*Summer Rental*] delivers chills and suspense… [A] quick and compulsive read which makes for a good summer beach read."

—*Fresh Fiction*

"A fun, fast read and fans of teen slasher films will find it reads like a '90s thriller!"

—*Youth Services Book Review*

SPRING HARVEST

ALSO BY REKTOK ROSS

Ski Weekend

Summer Rental

Spring Harvest

The Pop Star and the Devil

*

See all of Rektok Ross's books and find where to get them on her website at:

www.RektokRoss.com

*

NEVER MISS A RELEASE.

Get exclusive giveaways, review copies, and enter to win free gifts and more by subscribing to Rektok Ross's newsletter:

www.RektokRoss.com

SPRING HARVEST

A THRILLER

REKTOK ROSS

Ic13
BOOKS

Ic13 Books

Sam,
See you at
the harvest!
RR

Published by Ic13 Books

Wilmington, Delaware, USA, 19808

www.Ic13Books.com

Ic13 Books name and the Ic13 Books logo are trademarks of Ic13 Books or its affiliates.

Published 2024

Printed in the United States of America

Print ISBN: 978-0-9882568-6-6

E-ISBN: 978-0-9882568-5-9

Library of Congress Control Number: 2024905962

Cover Design by Dane Low and team

For those that rise above fear to become the heroes of their own epic stories.

Even the darkest night has its dawn.

—*Ancient Proverb*

PART ONE
THE AWAKENING

CHAPTER 1
DAY 1: 3:45 P.M.

60 miles to Allium Valley, Oregon

The gas station appears out of nowhere.

A flickering neon sign hangs out front, spelling out an ominous "WELCOME" in blood-red letters that seems more warning than invitation. The cracked asphalt parking lot is empty. Two rusty old pumps stand outside, weathered by time and neglect. The place looks like some harbinger of evil straight out of a bad horror movie. If we weren't almost out of gas, I'd make Logan keep going, but our RV camper is surviving on fumes alone at this point.

The five of us have been driving for hours, taking turns behind the wheel. Me and my best friend Zoe, her boyfriend —and my nemesis—Chad the douchebag, our sorority sister Jenny, and Logan, my sweet but bitter ex.

There'd been plenty of places to stop and refuel along the way when we first left Nevada State University early this morning, but we haven't passed a building, or even another car, for miles now. No telling when we'll see another gas station.

If only Logan had listened to me earlier instead of being so stubborn. I'd told him to fill the tank back at the rest stop at the Oregon border, but he'd ignored me, just like he's been doing the entire drive. Like he's been doing for days. I guess I shouldn't be surprised he still isn't talking to me. I *did* break his heart, after all.

At least that's what Zoe says.

Last night when we were packing for our trip, Zoe made one of her silly jokes about the "Ice Queen" striking again. Ice Queen is her nickname for me on account of my ruthless dating history. She says I go through boyfriends like other women go through lipstick.

Zoe Danvers and I have been best friends since junior high. Right from the start we shared a special bond, both of us being beautiful and knowing what it's like to have people hate us because of it. Zoe's much nicer than me, though. Sweet. Thoughtful. Always trying to make everyone happy.

Not me. I don't waste time worrying about the feelings of others, though I admit I feel bad about hurting Logan.

We were together for almost a year—my longest relationship by far. Golden boy Logan Ward is undeniably handsome in that all-American, blue-eyed way, with a sweet smile and muscles for days. He's Southern to the core. His family owns those Bass Haven Outfitters wilderness stores all over the south. He has a heart of gold, too. And smart. Top of his ROTC class.

Logan is perfect on paper. There's just one tiny little problem: last Saturday night, at the Alpha Delta Sigma Spring Fling party, he told me he wanted to marry me.

Of course, I had to break it off after that.

The real bummer is that he sprung it on me just days

before our spring break. Now, I'm forced to sit mere feet away from my pouting ex-boyfriend in the RV camper his dad loaned us for our trip to the Garlic Groove Music Festival. And it isn't just the ten-plus hour drive to Oregon I'm worried about. Once we get there, we'll have to survive each other's company for the entire weekend.

"Hey—you're going to miss the turnoff!" I shout from the back of the RV when it looks like Logan is about to drive right past the gas station. "Go right!"

"I see it, Alix," he says, jerking the wheel to the side. "Relax, okay?" His expression is frozen into a scowl in the rearview mirror. Well, as much of a scowl as perennially good-mannered Logan is capable of.

"Yeah, you don't have to yell at him." Chad turns around in the front passenger seat with a patronizing look on his stupid weaselly face.

"I wasn't yelling," I mutter, even though I guess I was.

Logan is already ignoring me again, turning the volume up on the radio to blast another Taylor Swift revenge break-up song.

Oh well.

At least he's sort of talking to me again?

Zoe catches my eye across the RV dinette table where we sit. There's a certain elegance about my best friend. Zoe's got that old Hollywood glamor thing going—sculpted cheekbones, full lips, radiant glowing skin. She's like a young Halle Berry, even when, like now, her perfect face scrunches up with amusement and she's trying desperately not to laugh at my discomfort. Zoe finds my messy love life hilarious.

"Not funny," I mouth to her and slink into my seat. I knew I should've stayed home.

Okay, yes, so I am kind of an asshole, but I'm not heartless. I already felt bad enough breaking up with the guy; I didn't want to ruin his spring break, too. I just kept hoping he'd snap out of it.

"Don't worry, babe." Zoe leans in to squeeze my hand, her favorite gold hoop earrings jangling against her cheeks. A birthday gift from Chad. "He'll get over it. He's just hurt," she whispers. "He told Chad you're the first girl he's ever fallen for."

"Not making me feel better," I say dryly.

"Well, you can't be totally surprised he's upset, can you?"

She pulls back, giving me *the look*. It's the one she always gives me whenever this sort of thing happens. It's the look I got when I broke up with Jeremy Pittman after he bought me roses on Valentine's Day and a plane ticket home to meet his parents. I got the same look when I dumped Billy Roseman after he tried to "lavaliere" me. He showed up at our sorority house to give me some ugly pendant with his fraternity letters; I showed him the door.

"Hey, I offered to give my pass away," I say, crossing my arms over my chest, jutting my chin out. "Logan insisted I come. He knows how much I love music festivals." I smirk. "Well, the fashion, at least."

Zoe arches a brow. "Or maybe it's because he's still hoping you'll change your mind…"

"I won't."

Maybe I am an Ice Queen, but at least I know what I want. I don't waffle around like some people do, indecisive, afraid to make tough choices. We never know how much time we're going to get in this life, and I plan to make the most of mine.

Jenny starts to snore loudly on the RV couch beside us, her mouth agape. Her mushroom haircut that she thinks is so stylish, but isn't, is smashed comically against her face.

Garish purple eyeshadow, caked on too thickly, smears across her cheeks.

With a grin, I fish inside my designer tote and pull out a bag of SkinnyPop popcorn. I toss a few pieces at Jenny, seeing if I can land one in her mouth.

"Al, stop!" Zoe grabs my wrist, giggling. "You're going to choke her."

"Only if we're lucky."

I'm joking, mostly. I'm not the biggest Jenny fan. Not like Zoe is. Zoe adores her little sister in our sorority.

Zoe rolls her eyes at me and rips the popcorn from my hand, stashing it away.

The RV engine groans into silence as Logan puts it in park and strides toward the pump with that sad puppy dog look on his face. From this safe distance, I can't help but admire his physique. A simple white tee clings to his long, muscular frame as he brushes a lock of blond hair from his eyes. He sure is nice to look at. Shame he couldn't let things be easy.

My cell phone chirps shrilly in my lap.

Can't wait to see you, Alligator! Counting down the days!

"Is that your dad?" Zoe asks, reading the incoming text over my shoulder. "Aw, he's the cutest. Tell him I say hi!"

My heart warms as I think of visiting Dad next week. While the rest of the group is going to Vegas for a few days after the festival to keep the party going, I'm flying home to Austin to see him.

I text back, confirming my flight details, and then nag him about scheduling his annual physical. Sometimes I worry about him being all alone.

After Mom died my senior year of high school, I'd almost rescinded my offer at NSU to stay home, but Dad wouldn't hear of it. Studying fashion design had always been Mom's dream for me. She'd wanted to be a designer, too, but her parents pushed her into teaching. She named me Alix Ford Summerlin after her favorite designer of all time—Tom Ford.

Our plan was for me to get my degree and then move to New York City to work for a major fashion house and live out the dream for both of us. Mom was going to be there cheering me on every step of the way. Except then she went and broke her end of the deal.

Mom died on Christmas Eve. She never should've been at that damn mall, but I'd been a brat, complaining that our local boutiques didn't carry any cool clothes. As she was getting back on the highway, her car filled with holiday gifts for me, a stupid cat ran into the road. Mom swerved and hit a tree. The hospital said she died on impact.

"I'm gonna get more brewskies," Chad announces, pushing the RV door open.

"I think we're set." I scoff and nod toward the kitchen counter where he's already stacked up enough beer for a frat party.

"Good thing no one asked you," he says and turns to Zoe. "You comin', babe?" He flashes her his big mega-watt smile. His always too-white teeth gleam in the late-afternoon sun. The dude has an unhealthy addiction to bleach and hair gel.

I don't understand what Zoe sees in him. I guess he *is* conventionally attractive, and he does have perfect bone structure, but his personality really sucks. The only reason I even tolerate him is because Zoe loves him so much, only God knows why.

"Come on, you two," Zoe says, eyeing us both. "Can't we all just get along this weekend?"

"Hey, don't look at me. I'm not the one who absolutely decimated poor Logan," Chad says, smirking as he turns to face me. "Brilliant move dumping him right before the festival, Alley Cat."

"Oh, shut up, you asshole. And don't call me that!"

I stomp past Chad and step outside, marching toward the rustic little gas station to put distance between myself and his judgy glare. I know he's just being overprotective of his frat brother, but Chad always gets on my nerves.

As I step inside the gas station, the overwhelming scent of something musty and old greets me. Flickering fluorescent lights reveal a worn linoleum floor at my feet, peeling and stained, and rows of dust-laden shelves. I stop in front of the candy aisle, stomach rumbling.

I try my best to eat healthy so I can fit into all my cute clothes, but Mom had a serious sweet tooth, and it's another thing I inherited from her. She always used to say, *there's nothing so bad in life that a little chocolate can't make better*. If I'm going to survive this weekend, I'm going to need a shit ton of chocolate.

I reach for a six-pack of dark chocolate bars when Jenny pops up behind me, so close I can feel her lips on my ear. "Straight for the sugary stuff, huh? Samesies!"

I jump back, heart nearly flying out of my chest.

"Jesus, Jenny! Where'd you come from?"

Jenny is always sneaking around, like a shifty little rodent. To be fair, it might just be that she's so good at fading into the background you rarely notice her. She kind of resembles a rodent, too, with her mousy brown hair and pointy nose... though even I have to admit she's sort of pretty in her own peculiar way.

"Sorry. Didn't mean to scare you." She reaches around me to grab a bag of Sour Patch Kids and rips it open, passing it to me. "Want some?"

"Ew. No." I push her hand away. "I don't eat junk food."

I hate grape-flavored candy. The gritty taste has always

bothered me. Truth be told, Jenny Holloway bothers me too, even if there's nothing truly objectionable about her. She's cute enough, smart enough, funny enough—just not a standout. Totally and completely average.

Plus, I don't love how she's such a suck up.

"You don't eat it?" She tilts her head, pointing at my chocolate. "But then what's that?"

"God, Jenny. Get a clue!" I snap. "This is *dark* chocolate. Barely any calories, and it's got antioxidants. It's practically a vegetable," I say, wiping away the sweat gathering at my brow. I can't believe how hot it is here, and it's only spring. Must be a heat wave or something.

"Need one?" Jenny asks, pulling out Kleenex from the pastel purple fanny pack strapped around her waist. She never goes anywhere without her ridiculous bag of supplies.

"Sure. Thanks." I snatch some tissues from her, and we head to the counter together.

"Here, let me get this. My treat," she says and takes the chocolate from my hand as we walk. She's always buying Zoe and me things on her daddy's Am Ex credit card. "This weather's so strange." She fans at her face. "It's never this hot."

Jenny's from Oregon. She's actually the one who told us about Garlic Groove, better known as the Allium Valley Garlic Groove Music and Food Festival. The three-day-long event is supposed to be even better than Coachella. Less crowded. Better access to the stage. More obscure indie bands. There's also a huge selection of garlic-infused foods like world-famous garlic fries Jenny claims are to die for. Jenny's aunt and uncle are farmers who live in Allium Valley. We'll be camping on their family land for the weekend.

"Uncle Jimmy says they're having major issues with the

spring harvest," she continues. "Barely any garlic's growing. It's the worst drought the town has ever seen."

"Isn't harvest a fall thing?"

Zoe and I took a girl's trip to Napa last October to celebrate our birthdays. I vaguely remember somewhere between drinking copious amounts of wine and stuffing our faces with cheese and crackers that people were crushing grapes at the wineries.

"Not for garlic," Jenny says. "It's planted in fall and harvested spring to summer. Uncle Jimmy calls it a *'long-maturing crop'*." She makes air quotes as she says the term. "Had to start even earlier this year with winters coming sooner. Everyone's blaming global warming."

"What a bunch of horseshit!" Chad says, coming up behind us with Zoe and Logan at his sides. He carries a case of beer over his head. "Global warming isn't real. It's just something those idiot Dems made up to scare voters."

I suppress a groan. Chad is the head of the Young Republicans Club at school. He thinks he's going to be the next great American president.

"What're you talking about, man? 'Course it's real," Logan says. "Didn't you see *Avatar?*"

Chad sneers. "Oh, you mean that over-stylized piece of garbage that panders to the masses, created by a bunch of Hollywood libtards?"

"You're nuts." Logan shakes his head, laughing. "That movie was great!"

"It's totally my *favorite!*" Jenny gives Logan an eager grin, batting her eyes at him. "I just love virtual video game characters, don't you?" she asks, making it clear she's never seen the James Cameron movie, which is about aliens. Logan made me watch it with him. It was no *The Devil Wears Prada,* but it was okay.

"Who cares?" I shrug. "It's not like global warming will affect any of us."

Logan's eyes lock on mine. "That's right, Alix. As long as it hurts someone else, just not you, right?"

Ouch.

"Geez, Logan. Chill out," Zoe says. She reaches for my hand and squeezes my thumb twice. It's our secret language we made up as kids. *I'm here,* she says silently with her touch. *I got you.*

I feel a twinge of guilt, but it's quickly replaced by anger. Why should I feel bad about ending things? It's not my fault Logan is a silly romantic that fell too hard. We're only twenty-two. What did he expect—a white picket fence, 2.5 kids, and a home cooked dinner every night?

That's not me. Never will be.

"I'm sorry." Logan looks down, scuffing the floor with the toe of his combat boots. "I shouldn't have said that." He attempts to give me an apologetic smile, but it doesn't go all the way to his eyes. "Let's just get to Allium Valley, okay?"

I nod. Even if his smile looks pained, I suppose it's progress.

"Did y'all say you're goin' to Allium Valley?" the gas station attendant asks from behind the counter. He's a slightly grizzled, balding man with an unkempt beard. He looks old, like a grandpa—a hickish, toothless, grandpa.

"Yes, that's right, sir," Logan says politely, handing the attendant his credit card for the gas. He grabs the food from Jenny and pays for that, too. Always such a gentleman.

"That's a bad idea." The attendant hacks loud, wet, coughing sounds. "Y'all be best to avoid Allium Valley right now."

"What do you mean?" Logan asks, leaning in.

"Well, it's too damn hot, for one thing," the attendant says. "Too hot means no spring harvest."

Chad snorts. "We're here for the festival. Who cares about some stupid harvest?"

"You should care, boy!" The attendant starts to stand, leaning heavily on his wooden cane. "No harvest means trouble's comin'…"

We all wait for him to say more, but that's all he says.

"Uh, okayyy…" Chad circles his pointer finger around his temple. "Looks like someone's about three fries short of a Happy Meal."

Zoe elbows him in the gut. "Chad!"

"Oh, come on, babe!" He laughs. "The old geezer's clearly crazy."

"Who you callin' crazy?" The attendant's freckled, gnarled hand reaches underneath the counter. My stomach twists with alarm. What is he reaching for? *A gun?*

"Please ignore him, sir. He forgot to take his meds today." Logan flashes his most charming, dimpled grin—the one that can disarm even the most hardened individual—and the old man relaxes slightly.

Zoe hands Chad's beer to Logan and hooks her boyfriend by the ear, her face red with embarrassment as she escorts him out the door. I can tell she's giving him a mouthful. Not that it will help. Chad is unredeemable, completely incapable of positive change. Zoe should be with a guy who has manners and knows how to behave in public. A guy like… well, I guess like Logan.

Logan signs the credit card slip and drops twenty into the tip jar with another apologetic grin. As we exit, the bell above the door jangles eerily, and a raspy murmur from the attendant catches my ear.

"… *beware of the night* …"

The back of my neck prickles. I pause, trying to make sense of his strange words while Logan and Jenny head for the RV, oblivious.

"Did you hear that?" I ask Logan, a sense of unease settling over me.

Logan shrugs. "Just some old man rambling. Forget it."

But I can't.

Beware of the night? What the hell did that even mean?

I glance back one last time and see the attendant's silhouette haunting the doorway, his words an ominous warning echoing in my head long after we drive away.

CHAPTER 2
5:30 P.M.

Garlic Groove Festival Campgrounds

W e get off at the exit for Allium Valley with about two hours before the first night's opening act is supposed to come on. Through the bug-splattered windshield of the RV, I spot a little sign ahead that reads *"Welcome to Allium Valley: Population 3,000."*

As far as the eye can see is a patchwork of vast withered fields and dusty farmland, no doubt a testament to the relentless heat. We're really in the backwoods boonies now. I even spot a few scarecrows staked in the fields, just off the sides of the quiet country road.

Jenny told us about the town's history on the drive up. There were a few cool parts, but it was mostly boring— though to be fair, Jenny is mostly boring, so it could just be her storytelling.

Apparently, Allium Valley is one of the oldest farm towns in the Northwest. It was founded hundreds of years ago during the Gold Rush. Kind of like in California, Oregon had its own mini-Gold Rush when the discovery of gold there led to an influx of people from around the world seeking their fortunes. It wasn't as famous as California's, and though the people that settled Allium Valley got little gold, they realized fast that the rich soil and favorable climate made it a great place to farm. Garlic, especially, grew well. That's how the town got its name.

Another thing Allium Valley had going for it—water. A large, flowing river divided the town right down the middle. It was a boon for the early farmers, but not without some downsides. Every few months, something bad would happen near the river.

Young children would tragically drown. Otherwise healthy-looking animals like deer and coyotes were found dead at the riverbanks. Some people who ventured too close to the water would inexplicably vanish or become lost in the surrounding woods. The townspeople called it the Devil's River and the name stuck.

Logan hits a pothole, and we bounce out of our seats as he steers the RV toward Jenny's family's farmland. Her aunt and uncle's place is one of the designated campgrounds for the weekend, conveniently within walking distance of the festival grounds. We're greeted by a makeshift community as soon as we drive through their tall wooden gates.

Rows and rows of colorful RVs and cars and tents nestle together under the blazing sun amidst desolate farmlands. Fellow festival-goers dressed in bright costumes twirl and sing in front of their vehicles, music blasting. A few have set up campfires to cook their dinners, though I don't know how they can stand the fire in all this heat.

Logan finds an empty spot toward the middle of the campgrounds and parks the RV. We all step outside, stretching our arms and legs from the long drive, checking things out. Two pretty girls with space buns wearing brightly colored bikini tops and sunglasses walk by, arm in arm. Unlike the rest of the fun-loving crowd, they have worried frowns on their faces.

"Caroline, Caroline!" The taller brunette calls out.

The other girl, the shorter one with bright blue eyeshadow, stops in front of our RV. "Have you seen our friend Caroline?" she asks and holds up her cell phone, showing us a picture of a scantily clad, fun-looking girl dressed in a neon raver outfit. "She never came back to camp last night."

"No, sorry," Logan says, and the girls move on to the next RV.

"Kinda wish we had seen her, though," Chad says to Logan with a wolfish grin. "Caroline sure looks like a lot of fun."

Zoe pinches his arm. "Hey! Watch it, Mister!"

"Oh, relax," he says and scoops her in for a big wet kiss. "You know I'd never trade my smokin' Hot Chocolate for another woman."

I snort. I can't believe he actually calls his gorgeous Black girlfriend "Hot Chocolate," but Zoe just giggles, kissing him back. She thinks it's adorable.

"Hey, guys, look!" Jenny points to a farmhouse on the outskirts of the campgrounds. "That's where Uncle Jimmy and Aunt Karen live."

"Neat," Logan says, his smile gracious.

The house is the ugliest thing I've ever seen.

Witch grass and weeds grow tall and wild in the front, unkempt and begging for a good lawn service. The home itself is in dire need of a facelift. It's huge and sagging, two stories of weathered wood rising up from the field with paint chipping along the sides and a roof that's missing more than a few shingles. On the far side of the main house stands a massive, fire-engine red barn, its rusty doors yawning open, as if inviting visitors. A weathered silo sits behind like a sentinel, its metal cylinder towers rusted and peeling. The place is seriously giving *Texas Chainsaw Massacre* vibes.

"Let's go say hi!" Jenny says, taking an eager step forward.

I yawn. "Pass."

"Al, don't be a jerk," Zoe says.

"I'm not!" I smile innocently, like I wasn't being intentionally rude. "No time. I still have to get ready."

"It's all right," Jenny says with a little shrug. "I guess I can go alone."

"I'll come with you, Jen. I'd love to meet your family and thank them," Logan says. "Sure is nice of them to let us camp here for free."

"Really? That'd be awesome!" Jenny beams, batting her stubby little lashes at him. "You're just the sweetest!" She gives him a flirty giggle and grabs onto his hand, leading him away.

It's so sad. Everyone knows the poor thing has a massive crush on Logan. If she wasn't such a nonentity—and if I actually cared—I might be annoyed with her fawning all over my ex, but Jenny isn't a threat to me. Hell, maybe it'll even help. If Logan goes for Jenny, maybe he'll stop sulking and actually be fun again.

"You think they have a bathroom there?" Chad asks, curiously eying the farmhouse. "I could use a shower."

I groan. "You do realize we have our own bathroom in here, right?"

"Yeah, but it's the size of a matchbox," he says, voice filled with disdain.

"You're such a prima donna."

"Takes one to know one." He winks and grabs his enormous toiletries duffle bag—which is almost as big as my own —and chases after Jenny and Logan.

"Hurry back!" I call out to Jenny before they can get too far. "I still need you to do my hair—just like I showed you on Instagram, got it?"

"Of course, Alix," she says sweetly, her ponytail bouncing as they all walk away. "I packed all my supplies. I even got new hair clips for you. You're gonna look so hot!"

"Hmph." I huff. "I'd better."

Once they're out of sight, I pull out my makeup bag and spread out at the RV living room table. I make all sorts of exaggerated, annoyed sounds as I open bottles of foundation and contour palettes and lipsticks and organize them, so Zoe will know I'm irritated. Jenny usually does both my hair and makeup. For someone with no style, she's surprisingly good at it.

"Do you always have to be such a bitch to her?" Zoe asks, taking a seat next to me.

"Oh, come on." I laugh. "She lives for this stuff. Doing things for us literally gives her life purpose." I pull out my makeup mirror and plug it in. It's oversized and has lights all around the sides, so I feel like I'm getting ready to walk the fashion runway every time I use it.

Zoe groans. "You're ridiculous, you know that, right?"

I grin back. "Yeah, but you love me, anyway."

She chuckles and kisses the top of my head before reaching past me to grab my favorite chunky holographic glitter. With a practiced hand, she applies it to the apples of her cheeks. Zoe has the absolute best cheekbones.

We turn on some music and blast Britney Spears, drinking beers and helping each other apply our cute festival makeup. We use bright colors like neon greens and fluorescent blues and hot pinks. Lots of glitter and shimmer, too.

"Ugh! It's like a sauna in here!" I fan at my face. It's so

hot, even with the air conditioner on full blast. My eye makeup is melting in creases and corners it's not supposed to melt in. "We're going to sweat our asses off tonight," I say, closing my eyes and dousing myself with setting spray.

"Good thing we'll hardly be wearing any clothes." Zoe grins deviously as she changes into the matching outfits I picked out for us: glitter bralettes, cut-off shorts, fringe boots, and a sparkly headband and dangling earrings I found on Amazon to complete the look.

My outfit is the same, just in a different color. She's purple, I'm pink. I got the idea after scouring old Coachella photos on Pinterest.

We've just finished getting dressed when there's a knock from outside the RV. Zoe peers over my shoulder as I open the door, my half-empty beer in hand, to find an attractive Asian guy standing on the steps. He looks to be a few years older and has a cute baby face with tousled brown hair and big thick glasses that give off Clark-Kent-undercover-hottie vibes.

"Can I help you?" I lick my bottom lip flirtatiously.

There's serious potential here, though his sense of fashion could use some work. From the waist down, his camo shorts and khaki-colored tactical boots look like something straight off a military base. Not great, but not completely offensive on their own. Unfortunately, he's paired them with a beat-up tactical utility vest covered with bulging pockets over a faded *Grateful Dead* T-shirt and a tie-dye bandana around his neck. He looks like a color-blind hippie G.I. Joe.

"Well, hello there," *Grateful Dead* says. His eyes widen with admiration as he ogles Zoe and me up and down. "I'm Ethan Park, but everyone calls me Frog. I'm camping next door." He points to the big orange tent pitched to the right of us.

"Frog?" I raise a brow. "Kind of an unusual name, no?"

"I'm kind of an unusual person." He grins and holds up an enormous bong like an offering. "Just wanted to come by and say welcome to the neighborhood. Wanna hit?"

"Ohhh, thanks! Love to!" Zoe says, pushing past me to snatch the bong from him. She takes in a long rip, the unmistakable smell of pot mingling with the scent of dry earth.

"So where're you guys from?" Frog asks.

"We go to school near Reno. At NSU," I say, grabbing the bong from Zoe and taking a hit. I sigh happily as the warm, familiar feel of marijuana hits me. I'm not a big pot smoker, but I'm up for a party when the time is right.

"What about you?" Zoe asks him.

"I'm a local," he says. "Did my four years at Central Oregon College right up the road. Got a BA studying Folklore and Mythology with a minor in Herbalism." He gives us a cute smile, his nose crinkling as he steps closer. I notice he's got freckles. Adorable.

"Cool. Maybe you can show us around?" I twirl my hair around one manicured finger, flirting even though he's nerdier than my usual type.

With the exception of golden-blond-all-American-beefcake Logan, I tend to go for tall, dark, and handsome. The mysterious, bad boy type that always play the lead on those angsty dramas on Netflix. But this weekend is just for fun, and with enough beer and a little pot, this guy will do the trick.

"Sure. I could do that," Frog says. "Believe it or not, we have some pretty amazing hikes on the northeast side of town, over by the gorge. Devil's River gets a lot of action, too." He chuckles. "Terrible name, I know, but great fishing."

I hate fishing.

Dad used to take me as a kid. He was born and raised in West Texas and loves all that "living off the land" crap. He never had a son, so he forced me to learn things like how to hunt, and fish, and start a fire. I always went along with it, faking excitement on our wilderness trips because they made him so happy, even though it wasn't my thing. I've always been far more comfortable shopping at the mall than roughing it in the great outdoors.

"Of course, tourism has died down recently..." Frog adds, swallowing uncomfortably. "We haven't had a lot of hikers since the attacks."

My ears perk up. This sounds interesting. "What attacks?"

He hesitates.

"Uh, nevermind."

"Come on!" I beg. "Tell us!"

"I don't know..." He rocks back onto his heels and smiles nervously. "Not sure I want to scare off the prettiest girls I've seen all day."

"Don't worry, we don't scare easily." I assure him with a little wink.

"Yeah, we love a good spook," Zoe says.

"All right, if you're sure." He shrugs. "About two weeks ago, a group of hikers came in from Portland. Seniors at their college hiking club." He takes another hit of his bong, coughing as smoke fills the air. "After they missed a few classes, their parents got worried. Local police started searching the trails. Found all four of them by Crimson Bluff —way over on the other side of town—*dead.*"

I yawn loudly.

"Oh, is that all?" I sit down on the RV stairs and stretch out my long, tanned legs. "The way you said it, I was thinking it was something really messed up—like a crazed serial killer or some satanic cult sacrifice." I take another sip of my beer. "It was a bear attack, right?"

Dad once took me to Yellowstone National Park for one of our father-daughter bonding trips. The area we camped at in Montana was known for bears and even the rare grizzly attack. Besides our guns that Dad brought along for target practice, he also bought bear spray and special whistles that he made me carry everywhere—even just to go to the bathroom. After all that, we didn't even see a bear. Not even a stupid black bear. Not that I had a death wish or anything. I just thought it might be cool to see them in their natural habitat, from a safe distance, of course.

"Don't think it was a bear..." Frog shakes his head, a strange expression on his face. "Nope, no way."

"Really? Why not?" I ask.

"'Cause their bodies were discovered miles from where they were supposed to be hiking. Completely mangled. Throats and wrists all torn up." He grimaces. "Gruesome stuff."

"Whoa..." Zoe's eyes widen. "That's messed up!"

A shiver creeps up my spine as we exchange anxious glances.

Jenny's shrill, annoying laughter breaks through the silence, and our friends come into view a moment later. Jenny is being super clingy, giggling, hanging all over Logan. They both have huge, boozy grins on their faces. Chad follows behind them, swinging a half-empty handle of vodka over his head.

"We come bearing gifts," Chad says, stumbling past Frog without even saying hi. He heads up the RV stairs and rushes straight for the bathroom. Guess it's not too small for him to take a piss in.

Logan disentangles himself from Jenny's grasp. "You

look really pretty, Alix," he says, his eyes lingering on my face before turning to Frog and introducing himself.

"About time you got back," I huff at Jenny and glance down at my phone. It's almost seven o'clock! Jenny is starting to piss me off. She should be waiting on me, not the other way around.

"I'm so sorry, Alix," she says. "Logan and I were just having so much fun, we totally lost track of time." A blush sweeps across her puffy chipmunk cheeks as she gazes over at Logan dreamily. "But don't worry, I can still do your hair," she adds, hastily.

"You better," I say and push her inside the RV. "Or else…"

She looks almost scared of me even though I'm obviously joking.

"Just ignore her." Zoe smiles at Jenny, wide and comforting, and Jenny's panicked expression relaxes.

"Well, it was nice to meet you," I say, turning back to Frog. "We'll see you at the festival later, right?" I flash him a glittering smile.

"Hell no." He shakes his head. "I'll be holed up with a good manga comic and some cheap whiskey. And my munitions, of course," he says, patting at his overstuffed vest. I can't tell what's in all those deep pockets, but I think I see a throwing star poking out of one, like the kind ninjas use.

"You're not going? Why not?" I ask with a hint of disappointment. He's a little strange, sure, but cute, nonetheless.

His voice turns serious. "Now's not a good time to be out after dark," he says and then gives a little wave goodbye, heading back toward his tent. "Be careful, okay? And if anything happens tonight, you know where to find me."

Logan watches Frog's retreating figure with a puzzled look on his face. "Huh? What's he talking about?"

"No clue." I shrug, trying to shake off the sudden feeling of unease.

Zoe grins and pantomimes someone smoking. "Pretty sure he's been hitting that bong all day," she says, and bursts into giggles.

I join in the laughter, but it feels forced.

What did Frog mean, warning us to be careful? We're in the middle of Hicksville. Careful of what? Eating too much garlic?

Chad starts handing out shots of vodka. When he gets to mine, he adds some squeezes of lemon and a dash of cranberry juice. "I know it isn't one of your fancy drinks, but it's the best I can do, Your Highness," he says, handing it to me.

I swallow it down in one big gulp.

"Hell yes!" He claps a hand on my shoulder, nodding his approval. "Thatta girl!"

I salute him and smile back, wiping away the excess liquid with my hand. Chad is obnoxious as hell, but the guy sure knows how to party. Then I take a second shot to quell any sense of foreboding still lingering from our conversation with Frog.

I don't want to think about strange attacks on hikers, or why it could be dangerous to be out after dark, or why an otherwise normal-seeming cute guy would be running around with ninja weapons on him. The festival is about to start. Excitement is supposed to be in the air, not fear.

Still, I can't help but notice Frog's tent while we head off to the festival. It stands zipped up and locked down, as if bracing for a storm, his odd warning looming over me like a dark cloud as we walk away.

CHAPTER 3
7:45 P.M.

Garlic Groove Festival

We arrive at the festival entrance thirty minutes before EcoEcho is supposed to come on. Unlike big festivals that have multiple performers each day, Garlic Groove only has one stage, featuring an opener and major act for the evening. EcoEcho has recently gotten popular, so I'm not surprised they're headlining, even though I think they suck. They're a bunch of whiny emo guys that pluck at guitars and sing about climate change and saving trees or the elephants in Asia or whatever the hot cause is right now. My plan is to be so shit-faced by the time they start playing, I won't be able to tell if it's EcoEcho on stage or a bunch of monkeys.

The festival grounds are already packed as we walk through the gates. Throngs of people stand in long lines at the food and beverage stalls and in front of the rows of porta-potties set up for the event. A huge lit-up Ferris wheel spins off to one side, surrounded by typical county fair games. Ring Toss. Shooting Gallery. Whack-a-Mole. Dozens of players await their turn.

The casual concert-goers—the families and big groups of friends—lie sprawled out at the back of the fields, lounging on blankets and striped lawn chairs brought from home. Closer to the stage are the hardcore fans. They're crammed in like sardines: girls in tiny outfits sitting on their boyfriends' sweaty shoulders to get a good view. There must be a few thousand people here—far more than I expected at a small-town festival.

Who knows? Maybe it's the garlic food, like Jenny said.

We stroll past the concession stands first, and I'm amazed by the sheer number of garlic-flavored offerings. Garlic ice cream. Garlic cake. Garlic kettle corn. Garlic beer.

"They're already out of garlic fries?" Chad cries, distraught. He whirls on Jenny with an accusing look. "You said there'd be plenty here!"

"There usually is!" Jenny scans the festival midway in confusion. The only visible garlic fry stand has a big red "Sold Out" sign hanging in front, just like almost all the other stalls with garlic-infused offerings. "This is so weird. It must be the drought?"

"I'm sure they're just restocking," Zoe says, patting at Chad's arm comfortingly. "Why don't you get the regular fries for now, babe?"

"Because I don't *want* the regular fries, Zoe!" He pulls his arm away. "I *want* garlic fries!" He stomps his tasseled loafer shoes into the dirt like a little baby, and turns, cheeks red and puffy as he scowls at me. "This is all your fault. You're the one who made us late with your ugly hairdo."

"I think her hair looks nice," Logan says softly, smiling at me.

Chad snorts. "She looks like Medusa."

"You're clearly deranged. I look amazing." I smooth down my braids, which turned out even better than I'd hoped after I added glitter and colorful ribbons to them. "Besides, you're one to talk," I say. "Whose idea was it to go off and raid Jenny's uncle's liquor cabinet? If you'd been back on time, we would've been here hours ago."

"Well, good news." He smirks. "Now none of us are getting any delicious garlic food, but at least you can turn your enemies to stone with one look. Hope it was worth it, Big Al."

I grit my teeth.

Who the hell does Chad think he's talking to?

"Oh, you wouldn't know style if it jumped up and bit you on the face!" I grimace at his feet. "You're wearing boating shoes at a music festival, for Christ's sake. How are you not embarrassed?"

"Okay, guys. Let's take this down a notch, okay?" Zoe chuckles and attempts to pull Chad away, but he digs his hideous shoes into the dirt. His face scrunches up angrily and he steps closer until I can smell his sickeningly sweet spearmint-gum-meets-vodka-and-beer breath.

"At least I'm not some stupid, superficial bimbo only concerned about looking hot on the outside 'cause her insides are so damn ugly."

The air whooshes out of me all at once.

He did not just say that.

My hand tightens into a shaky fist. That's it. I don't care how much my best friend may love the jerk. I'm going to punch that smug expression right off his douchey face.

"Okay, that's enough!" Zoe steps in between us, giving her boyfriend a steely glare. "Let's go, babe. You need to cool off." She yanks hard, pulling him in the opposite direc-

tion from me, and the two of them vanish into the crowd
seconds later.

Logan and Jenny shuffle their feet into the dirt and peer
over at me, like they're embarrassed for me. "You okay?"
Logan asks, a sympathetic expression in his warm eyes.

"I'm fine!"

He swallows hard, blinking, and I worry I've hurt his
feelings. Again.

"Sorry." I force a weak smile. I don't want to be an
asshole to Logan, but I don't need his pity. Or Jenny's. What
I need is to get away. "I'll be right back," I say, eyeing one of
the booths with a flashing BEER sign.

"Alix, wait—" Jenny calls after me, but I'm already gone,
making a beeline for the beer stand.

The line is ridiculously long, but I'm grateful for the time
alone. I take a hot pink bedazzled bandana out of my back
pocket and wipe the sweat from my forehead and chest. The
heat is unrelenting, even with the sun long gone. This must
be some kind of record heat wave.

I spritz my face with my Evian atomizer and confirm my
makeup is still in place with a quick check of my cell phone
camera. *Perfect as usual,* I smile at myself and then squint into
the crowd, searching for my friends. I figure I'll have to
rejoin the group eventually, so it wouldn't hurt to keep tabs
on them while I wait in line.

That's when I see *him*.

He leans up against the condiment table, alone, far away
from other people. He's dressed in all black. Black tee. Black
shorts. Black boots. More than a little unusual in this blistering heat, but it isn't just his strange choice of color that
catches my attention. Even with dark sunglasses on, I can
tell he's strikingly handsome.

His nose is straight, angular. Strong jaw. Thick sexy
lips. Skin pale as porcelain next to a shock of dark hair. He

has the kind of face you see on the pages of a fashion magazine. He's got that aura about him, too—that head-turning charisma that makes me wonder if he might be with one of the bands. Hell, he looks so good, maybe he *is* the band.

Except, no, I'd read through the Garlic Groove lineup a bunch of times when we booked our trip. Tall, Dark, and Handsome definitely wasn't on the list.

There's something else about him, too. Something about the intense way he scours the crowd, searching. Poised. Calculating. The muscles of his forearms are tight and clenched. He looks strong but lean. Like he could run really fast if given the chance. Then it hits me.

Now I know what he reminds me of...

Logan took me deer hunting last semester with his family in Tennessee. He'd been pleasantly surprised to see I knew my way around a gun. I was by no means an expert— I didn't even enjoy it—but there were all those trips with Dad where he'd taught me the basics. I knew shooting live animals would be different than target practice with my dad, and I wasn't sure I could do it, but I never got a chance to find out. It turns out we weren't the only ones hunting that day.

The second Logan spotted the mountain lion, he rushed me out of the forest. I'll never forget how that big cat looked right before it attacked the deer. Its gaze trained on its target. Body stiff with purpose, ready for action. It's exactly how the guy in front of me watches the crowd right now— like a predator, sizing up his prey.

He turns suddenly and catches me staring. My body warms as our eyes connect. I hold his gaze and smile invitingly in a way I know men find irresistible. Then I wait for him to come over like they always do.

For a fraction of a second, he matches my gaze, but

unlike me, he isn't smiling. He looks completely disinterested before turning back around again, almost dismissively.

I stare at his backside, stunned.

Well… this is new.

I've never gotten that reaction before after smiling at a cute guy.

My cheeks heat, almost painfully. It takes me a moment to recognize it's embarrassment, an emotion I rarely feel. I've always taken my ability to attract men as a given. A gift. After all, what's better than being seen as pretty? It's the hallmark of how important you are; how powerful.

I pull out my cell phone camera again, feeling a rare bout of self-consciousness as I double check things. Do I have dirt on my face? Something in my teeth?

But no, I still look perfect. My lips are pink and plump. Skin is spotless, tanned and contoured. Blonde hair silky and shiny. And my cornflower blue eyes are clear and bright as usual—my best feature, according to my high school senior class who voted me for "Best Eyes" along with "Most Beautiful."

My ego still feels a bit bruised when I get to the front of the line, so I order two beers instead of one. I'll admit, it makes me feel a little better when the pimply-faced guy behind the counter gives me my drinks and even throws in a pretzel, saying, "No charge, on the house."

When I get to the condiment table, Mr. Tall, Dark, Handsome, and Uninterested is still there. Even worse, he's standing right in front of the mustard dispenser, blocking it. I ponder skipping the mustard to save face but then realize I'm being ridiculous. Why should my delicious pretzel go mustardless simply because one guy isn't falling all over himself to get my attention?

Besides, something else was probably on his mind. Maybe he also got into a fight with his best friend's insufferable idiot boyfriend. Maybe he's gay? Whatever it is, it's definitely *him*, not *me*.

I decide I don't care what the reason is. He's just another good-looking guy. They're a dime a dozen.

"Excuse me. You're in my way," I say to him.

He turns and lowers his sunglasses, staring at me with sexy dark eyes. The frown from earlier is gone, replaced by a lazy grin that sits on flawless lips. It's even worse than I feared. He's not just handsome—he's the handsomest person I've ever seen in my life.

"I could move," he says, in a confident—and slightly arrogant—voice, "but then I'd be depriving you of this view."

I snort. "Somehow, I think I'll live."

He moves aside, chuckling, and picks up the dispenser, squeezing mustard into a small plastic cup and placing it onto my cardboard tray for me. Now, I'm certain I made the whole thing up in my head. He's being perfectly polite, even a bit flirty.

I grab some napkins and when I look back up, he's still there, watching me. A shock of electricity runs through my body.

Damn, he's so attractive. It's really throwing me off my game. For the first time since I can remember, I'm practically at a loss for words.

"So, uh, good band, huh?" I stammer, sounding like an idiot.

He grimaces. "I hate indie rock."

I can't help but laugh. "You're kind of in the wrong place then, no?"

"Good point," he says with a little grin.

I take a bite of my pretzel. "So what's a guy who hates indie music doing at an indie music festival?"

His face darkens. "My ex-girlfriend dragged me here."

Oh.

Well, damn.

Now that explains it. That's why he looked all bent out of shape before. As I suspected, it had nothing to do with me. He must be having issues with his ex, like I am.

He leans away from the condiments, stepping one foot to the side. It appears he's about to leave, which would be a shame. I don't want our conversation to be over already.

"I'm Alix, by the way. And you are?" I ask to keep him talking.

"Kade," he says.

"Cool name."

"Yep."

He takes another little step away, and I start to get annoyed. I'm not used to having to do all the work; usually guys are the ones bending over backward to have conversations with me. What's wrong with this guy? Doesn't he at least want to ask for my number?

"So, um, have you tried the garlic fries? They're supposed to be amazing, but they just ran out," I say, and then cringe inwardly.

Holy shit. Did I really just ask him about garlic fries? Could I have brought up a less sexy topic?

"I'm afraid I don't like garlic much, either."

He's laughing at me now; I can see it in his eyes. They're such an unusual color. So dark, they're almost black.

"There you are, babe!" Zoe throws her arms around me, a bit drunkenly. "We were looking everywhere for you! Weren't we, Chad?" she asks her boyfriend who is now studying a pile of dirt on the ground like it's the most interesting thing he's ever seen. *"Weren't we, Chad?"* she repeats, elbowing him.

He groans out loud. "Sure were."

"Well, I've got to get going. Enjoy the festival," Kade

says and then gives me a little wink as he walks away. "And good luck with those garlic fries."

Before I can say anything else and stop him, he's already making his way back into the crowd, probably never to be seen again. Sigh.

Zoe's fingers lace through mine. "Chad has something to say to you, Al. Don't you, babe?" she asks, her brow raised in his direction.

Chad whispers something unintelligible, the sound getting lost beneath the twang of guitars and throbbing bass as the opening band starts their encore.

"Louder," Zoe demands. "So she can actually hear you."

"I'm sorry, Alix!" he yells above the blaring music and cheering crowd. He even looks sort of apologetic, too. Go figure.

Zoe pivots towards me next, expectantly, her features bathed in a kaleidoscope of light as the stage's yellow, purple, and red beams dance across her face. "Al? Do you have anything you want to say to Chad?"

I suppress a groan. It doesn't take a genius to figure out she wants me to apologize back, even though I didn't do anything wrong.

"How about it, Big Al? Friends?" Chad asks, his lips quirking upward.

"Whatever." I shrug. "Sorry I said you have ugly shoes."

"Yeah, and your hair does look kind of cool," he admits.

Zoe gives a joyful yelp and throws her arms around us both. Chad's knuckles meet mine in an awkward but firm fist bump. Even if Chad is beyond obnoxious, I guess he's not the worst person in the world, especially when he's like this—an almost halfway decent human being. And he really does love Zoe.

Zoe first met Chad Harrington III freshman year in her

Race and Ethnic Relations class. Zoe is a Social Work major and wants to change the world, but Chad only took the class because his counselor said it was good for students with political aspirations. Zoe wound up tutoring him the entire semester.

They've only broken up once in four years. Last year, Zoe thought Chad was flirting with the vice president of the Young Republicans Club. Chad swore the girl was the one coming on to him and not the other way around, but Zoe broke up with him, anyway. Chad was so devastated, he came to me of all people, begging, tail between his legs. He was so pathetic, and Zoe was so sad, I didn't have a choice. I had to help get them back together.

As we push our way to the front of the stage, Logan and Jenny join us, and EcoEcho begins their set. The evening becomes a blur. We sing and dance like maniacs, sweating buckets as we party the night away. I'm still on a high as the festival ends and we exit, shoulder to shoulder, through the entrance we came in earlier.

Sudden panicked shouting shatters my euphoria. People start pushing, shoving each other in a rush to get to the parking lot. "Move, move!" someone yells up ahead and then yellow-shirted security guards sprint past us, faces set, determined.

Logan reaches out, trying to grab one. "What's going on?" he asks, but the guards are already gone, swallowed up by the crowd.

Paramedics race by next.

"It's probably some tweaker," Chad says. "There's always some idiot at these things who can't handle his drugs."

Someone shoves me hard from behind, and Logan reaches out, steadying me so I don't fall. I feel a sharp sting and look down at my left hand.

Well, that's just great. My perfect bubblegum-pink acrylic nail is now broken.

Then I see it. The stretcher. The body. A man, huge, and his neck…

God, his neck is a gaping, bloody mess…

The paramedics move too slow with the sheet, and I can't unsee it. A wave of shock and then disgust rolls through me. "Is he *dead?*" I whisper, clutching onto Logan's shoulder.

"Don't look." Logan tucks me close to his muscular chest, guiding me past the crowd and away from the horror. Behind us, I can hear the other festival-goers speculating as we flood the exit. Was it a fight? Drug overdose?

"Suicide," a girl says next to me with a knowing look. "Same thing happened at Bonnaroo."

I shudder. It sure didn't look like a suicide. Who slashes their own neck at a music festival?

Finally, we're at the parking lot. The crowd starts to dissipate and things calm down now that the emergency is over. I glance around to get my bearings and am surprised to find Kade, the hot guy from earlier, staring back at me.

I wiggle out of Logan's arms—wouldn't want anyone getting the wrong idea—and give Kade a small wave. He saunters over, and I start to smile and say hi, when he leans down so close I can feel his cool breath on my cheek.

"If you're smart, you won't come back tomorrow," he says, his voice low, almost like a threat. It catches me off guard, making me feel a bit light-headed, but I force a flirty grin.

"But I saved my cutest outfit for tomorrow," I say, batting my lashes and pouting.

"This isn't a joke!" He grabs my wrist, almost desperately. His touch sends a shiver through me—equally thrilling and alarming. Those obsidian eyes fix on me in a way that makes me slightly uncomfortable but also a bit excited. I can't turn away.

"If you come back again, you'll regret it," he whispers, his words sounding like a promise. Then he gives me one last long imploring look before disappearing into the night.

CHAPTER 4
DAY 2: 4:00 P.M.

Garlic Groove Festival Campgrounds

The dead guy with the slashed throat from last night is all anyone can talk about the next day. Turns out he was a local. Some said he was getting over a bad breakup, doing a lot of drugs at the festival, and decided to end it all. Others said he was a troublemaker known around town that had picked a fight with the wrong guy and gotten slashed by a beer bottle.

No one knew for sure, but the one thing everyone agreed on? It was a freak incident and nothing to get bent out of shape over.

Even the festival organizers didn't have much to say about it other than an email blast to all ticket holders reminding them of the "no weapons policy" and a warning to expect longer wait times tonight as all bags and persons would be "thoroughly searched" before entry.

"I love your top," Jenny says, gazing at me in admiration as we get ready for night two of the festival.

It's just us girls in the RV. The guys left a few hours ago to walk around town and explore. Logan heard about some hunting and ammo store and wanted to check it out. Chad went with him. Apparently, there was an old beer brewery downtown, too, and Chad never passes up an opportunity to drink more beer.

"Right? Isn't it so cute?" I grin at Jenny and straighten the straps of my pink rhinestone bodysuit, watching it sparkle and glitter in the mirror.

I created the top for one of my couture sewing projects in design class last semester. It took me days to painstakingly sew each Swarovski crystal by hand, but the bodysuit glimmers like a thousand stars sparkling in the night. Definitely worth the effort.

I paired the sexy top with micro booty shorts, knee-high Louboutin flat boots, and my mom's favorite dangly pearl earrings. Dad gave them to me after she died, so I could always have a piece of her with me. They're beautiful and classy—just like Mom was—and go with everything. A hot pink rhinestone cowboy hat finishes off my Disco Barbie look. Not a lot of women can pull this off, but I've got something special. And no, it's not just good looks. It's confidence.

"You always look so great, Alix." Jenny's eyes fill with envy as she watches me primp. "I could never wear anything like that."

"Thanks." I fluff my glossy blonde hair, smiling at my reflection.

"What about me? Do I look okay?" she asks, attempting an awkward twirl.

She's draped in a ruffled Pepto-Bismol pink dress that swishes above her knees, cinched at the waist with her bulky fanny pack. On her feet are white lace-up boots, a style that hasn't been cool for decades. Oversized plastic yellow lightning bolts are in her ears, and her hair is teased into a high ponytail, secured with a matching neon hair scrunchie. Jenny always looks like she's stuck in some bad '80s rom com. The poor thing truly has no sense of fashion.

"Uh huh." I swallow. "That dress is really… something."

"You really think so?" Her face lights up as she adjusts her boxy shoulder pads. "Thanks, Alix!"

Zoe catches my eye, quirking a brow as she applies sparkly gloss to her lips. She knows I'm full of shit but is too nice to say it out loud and hurt Jenny's feelings.

"You look super cute, Jen," Zoe says.

Unlike me, Zoe means it.

Zoe, of course, is stunning, per usual. Her crisp white romper flatters her glowy dark complexion, the material hugging her in all the right places, but it's the candy apple red platform boots I picked out for her that take things to the next level. She's a total knockout.

The thing is, Jenny could look good too—if she knew how to dress. Style. Some people have it, some people don't. Having a pretty face or a great figure is nice, but it's not the most important thing. Anyone can look hot with the right clothing and attitude. That's why I'm so passionate about fashion design. I love how the perfect outfit can completely transform a person.

"Actually, here," I say, with a rare burst of generosity, pulling out one of my extra outfits from my luggage. It's a glittery tube dress in Jenny's favorite color—purple. The form-fitting bodice will flatter her body type far more than that baggy dress she has on. "Wear this."

"Really? You don't mind?"

"Not at all." I shrug. It's not like I was going to wear it, anyway. When I pack, I always throw in alternate outfits. It's important to have options. But with only one day left of the festival, there's no chance I'll need the dress. "It'll match your purple belt bag, too," I add, feeling especially magnanimous.

"Wow, Alix! This is so awesome of you!" she squeals, snatching the dress from me.

"Sure, just hurry up. You need to start curling my hair, ASAP."

About an hour later, the guys return. Logan shows off a new hunting knife and a slick-looking crossbow he found at the hunting store. Chad is already drunk off some special crafted garlic-infused beers he bought from the local brewery. He got the last few left before they ran out.

He passes a can around for us all to try as we get ready to leave. It's got a strong smell—kind of spicy and pungent. Still, I've drank far worse at frat parties. I hold my nose, and Zoe and I finish it all.

On the way out of the campsite, I look for Frog, our friend from yesterday. I wouldn't mind a little flirting and male attention. Unlike Mr. Gorgeous and Aloof from last night, at least Frog showed some interest. Plus, I could use a few hits from his bong to take the edge off Chad's weird garlic beer aftertaste.

Unfortunately, Frog's tent looks empty and he's nowhere to be found.

Going through the festival's main gate takes twice as long tonight. It doesn't help that the crystals on my outfit set off the metal detector. After we finally get past security, Logan makes us race over to the main stage. His favorite band in the festival lineup—the Blue Moon Outlaws—are coming on soon.

As soon as we push our way near the stage and get settled, Zoe and Jenny offer to get drinks for everyone. Zoe makes Chad go along to help carry everything, leaving Logan and me alone for the first time since our breakup.

Neither of us talks. To say it's beyond awkward is putting it mildly. He keeps his eyes glued to the stage while I wipe sweat from my cheeks and forehead and sway around to the music.

A few rowdy, aggressive-looking men in Western boots and cowboy hats keep staring at me, slowly inching their way closer. Logan moves to my side to block me from their path. He smells like he just stepped off the pages of an *L.L. Bean* catalog: clean, woodsy, and a little bit preppy.

He clears his throat. "So, uh, you having fun?"

"Sure!" I shout over the music. "Aren't you?"

I risk a direct glance at him and immediately wish I hadn't. His puppy dog eyes are big and sad as he stares at me.

"I miss you, Alix."

Shit.

"Logan." I sigh. "Not now. Let's just have a good time tonight, okay?"

"I can't help how I feel," he says, biting at his lower lip. "I'm not like you. I can't turn my emotions off and pretend I don't care, like some kind of robot."

"I'm not a robot!" I jerk back, stung by his words. "Just because I don't sit around and mope about my feelings doesn't mean I don't have them." I cross my arms over my chest. "It's just a breakup, Logan. Get over it already."

I hear a whoosh as the breath goes out of him, and he deflates like a boat with the wind gone from its sails.

"I'm sorry—that's... er... that's not what I meant." I regret my words instantly. I don't want to hurt Logan. He's such a great guy. It's just bad luck that he fell for me. "I care about you—*truly*—but it's like I told you, we don't want the same things. Can't you try to understand that?"

"Yeah, I can, but I only said I wanted to marry you *someday*. I was caught up in the moment, I guess. I didn't ask you to walk down the aisle tomorrow or pick out names for our kids or anything."

"Yet."

He takes a step back, blinking angrily.

"What's that supposed to mean?"

"Oh, come on, Logan." I let out a sigh of frustration. "That's what you want, isn't it? Just like your mom and dad, right? Engaged straight out of college, married thirty years. Life on the Navy base and then home to Knoxville to work at your dad's stores. A gaggle of kids and some hunting dogs, weekends at the lake house, and homemade apple pie on Sundays."

"Well, so what?" His cheeks redden. "Is that really so bad? My parents are the happiest people I know."

"That's great, Logan—*for them*. It's a beautiful life, really," I say, trying my best to stay patient. "It's just not what *I* want."

"You don't want to get married?" His voice rises with disbelief. "*Not ever?*"

"I don't know, Logan." I pinch the bridge of my nose and take in a shaky breath. "Not right now, that's for damn sure."

I'm not sure if I was ever like other girls that dream of their prince on a white horse and a big, beautiful wedding, but if I ever did that before, it stopped after Mom died. I don't know if I believe in happily ever after anymore.

"Look, Logan, you're a great guy." I touch his arm gently. "You're going to find someone amazing. One day, you'll be with this gorgeous, incredible girl, who loves you as much as you love her, living the life you deserve. Trust me, you'll forget I even existed."

"I don't want another girl," he whispers. "I want you."

Whoosh.

His words stab me like an icicle, right through my cold little Ice Princess heart.

"Oh Logan…" I sigh sadly.

For a second, I start to crack. His arms go around me, and I lean into him, the warmth of his body spreading into mine. He really is incredible. Any sane woman would be over the moon for a guy like him. So why aren't I?

"If we care enough about each other, we can make this work," he whispers into my hair. "I know we can."

If only he was right. If only the life he wanted was the life I wanted, and I could have him. But it would never work. I know myself too well.

I could never give up my dream of New York, of a career in fashion and making a name for myself, of building the future my mother and I always wanted. And no matter what he says, no matter how much he thinks he wants me now, Logan would never be happy with that life. He'd want to go back to his family and to Tennessee and to all the things he grew up believing life was about. Eventually, he'd resent me.

Even if Logan is amazing and devoted and wants with all his heart to make me happy, it isn't enough. We're just too different.

Besides, what's the point of love if people can be ripped away from you at any moment?

Just look at my dad. He'd loved my mother. They were also high school sweethearts—just like Logan's parents. They used to talk about how they were going to grow old together. They'd retire in Florida and live in a cottage on the beach and read books and watch sunsets together.

But that wasn't how it turned out in the end. Mom died in that awful car accident, and Dad was left heartbroken. I don't know if he'll ever be happy again without her. So why the hell would I want that?

Love makes you vulnerable. It only causes hurt and pain. Better to cut things off with Logan now, while I still can.

"We're back!" Zoe shouts, bouncing in beside me. "Did you miss us?"

I startle and break away from Logan's embrace, glad for the interruption. Things were getting way too intense there.

"Oh snap!" Chad singsongs behind Zoe, swinging his drink carrier full of beers. His eyes narrow at Logan and me, the tension between us palpable. "Are Barbie and Ken heading for a reunion?"

"Shut it, babe." Zoe pinches his side and passes me a drink. I resist the urge to throw it in his face because, hey, why waste a perfectly good beer?

Jenny appears an instant later, carrying a pizza box close to her chest as she elbows her way through the crowd. She stops in front of us and flips the top open, revealing a cheesy expanse of pepperoni and olives. The strong smell of garlic whiffs toward me as she grabs the largest slice, her eyes gleaming with delight as she shoves it in her mouth.

"Must be nice not to care about what you eat." I let out a little scoff, my lips twisting into a smirk, even if I do feel a little twinge of envy. I love pizza too; I just like being a size two more.

"I only got one slice!" she says defensively, cheesy goo dripping down her chin. "The rest of the pizza is for Chad!"

"Hey, no judgment here." I hold up my hands, feigning innocence. "You eat all the carbs you want, sweetie."

Zoe frowns at me and reaches for a slice. "Well, *I* think it looks amazing. Thanks so much, Jen. You're the best!" She takes a big bite of pizza, moaning with ecstasy. "Mmmm, delicious!" she says, and her teasing eyes flicker toward me. "The garlic stuffed crust really melts in your mouth."

My stomach grumbles loudly.

"You *sure* you don't want any, Al?" She laughs knowingly and tilts Jenny's heavenly-smelling pizza box in my direction, baiting me.

Well, damn. It really does look amazing, all gooey and melty, and I've never had a garlic bread pizza before. It would be a real shame to come all the way here to the garlic capital of the northwest and not try it…

"Fuck it," I say, snatching a piece. "I'll go for an extra-long hike in the morning."

By the time the Blue Moon Outlaws take the stage, I've had two slices of Jenny's pizza and am on my third beer, feeling tipsy and deliciously full. I forget all about Logan's broken heart as my best friend and I shake our asses, laughing and singing along to the music. Sweat drips out of every pore.

Chad keeps trying to cut in to dance with Zoe, but I keep shoving him away, pushing him into Logan. I deserve a few hours of girl time without him constantly in the way. Every now and then I catch Logan sneaking furtive little glances at me, but I ignore them. I won't make the mistake of being alone with him again.

"That hot guy over there is looking at you!" Zoe giggles, pointing to the left of the stage.

When I glance over, I spot Kade staring at me. I don't know how it's possible, but he looks even better than yesterday. He's dressed in all black again, even in the heat. Another polo, shorts, and sneakers. Yet, unlike me and my friends, I don't see a single drop of sweat on him. It appears he's alone again, too.

I try to catch his eye, but he's got that indifferent, unsmiling look on his face again.

I can't figure this guy out. He seems to run hot and cold. Mostly cold.

"That's Kade," I say. "I met him yesterday at the concession stand. I don't think he likes me."

She snickers. "Every guy likes you. If I didn't love you so much, I might hate you."

"Oh whatever. Like you have any problems whatsoever in the guy department."

"You're right." She grins and wiggles her hips, sexily. "I don't." She giggles again, harder. "Damn. He's still looking at you."

"Stop staring!" I hiss.

"I can't. He's gorgeous." She lets out a lustful groan. "Seriously, Al, if you don't go for this guy, I will. Screw Chad!"

Against my better judgment, I turn again to see if Kade is still looking at me, but he's gone. A smidge of disappointment mixes with relief. Mostly relief.

Guys like that are trouble. He's far too handsome. Not to mention the fact he isn't racing over to hit on me like other guys do. It makes him interesting. Exciting. Like some sexy hot enigma. He's the kind of guy that can make you lose control, and I don't like to lose control.

A flicker of memory comes back to me, and I hear his words again from last night as we were leaving the festival. He'd warned me not to come back here. I'd almost forgotten all about that.

What a weird thing to say…

The crowd goes quiet then and people raise their cell phones in the air. Hundreds of lights shine in the darkness as the Blue Moon Outlaws play the hauntingly beautiful opening chords of their most popular hit—*Tough Girl Like You*.

I'd first heard the love ballad when Logan played it for me while we sat around a cozy campfire. He'd taken me away for the weekend to this cute little place called the

Mount Sierra Lodge up in the Sierra Nevada mountains. He'd wanted us to go skiing, but I'd refused. I'd just read about a group of high school kids that died after getting stranded in a blizzard during a ski trip there, and it'd freaked me out. He treated me to a massage and facial at the spa instead.

It was a great trip. Logan had been fun and sweet. Carefree and not at all clingy. If only things could've stayed that way. If only he hadn't gone and ruined everything...

Before I'm able to stop myself, my gaze strays toward Logan. He's already staring at me. Judging by the wistful look in his eyes, I can tell he's thinking about our trip, too.

He takes a tentative step in my direction and reaches a hand toward me. Warmth floods my veins as he beckons me closer for a dance.

I know I should turn away. I don't want to lead him on, but I wasn't lying when I said I still cared about him. I do. Slowly, as if they have a brain of their own, my feet start to move in his direction.

But then, a blood-curdling scream pierces the air and shatters the moment between us. High-pitched. Terrifying. The crowd surges backward in a tidal wave of panic. People start pushing. Shoving. Security staff in their over-sized neon yellow shirts race toward the stage.

"What's happening?" Zoe asks, reaching for my hand, her sweaty palm gripping mine.

"Something's going on up front," Logan says, shifting his position, trying to get a better view.

Jenny gets on her tiptoes. "I can't see anything. Is someone hurt?"

My heart pounds a frenzied, frantic rhythm. I crane my neck but only see an ocean of bodies. Sweat rolls down my back.

Something's wrong. Very wrong.

Then the band stops playing.

Silence followed by more screams and cries. All around us is a savage smell that I sense, but not with my nose—with my gut. It's the scent of terror. Of death.

Logan sees something ahead that makes him stop in his tracks. He turns to us, his eyes wide with fear. "We have to get out of here!" he shouts. "RIGHT NOW!"

CHAPTER 5
9:00 P.M.

Garlic Groove Festival

The air is thick with panic as the frenzied festival crowd becomes a living, heaving, deadly entity. People press against me from all sides. A relentless, overwhelming tide of desperation and panic. The ground beneath my feet trembles with the stampede.

Bodies are everywhere, pushing, shoving. Screams— sharp and terror-stricken. The stench of sweat and tears and garlic mingling with sheer horror. Heavy. Suffocating.

An elbow slams into my gut and knocks the wind out of me. I gasp, struggling to stay upright.

"I got you." Logan's voice is in my ear, strong and steady. "Stay close," he orders, clasping my hand and shoving the stranger away from me.

He scans quickly, then moves. Fast. Herding all of us toward a fence left of the stage.

I glance back, just once, to make sure that Zoe, Chad,

and Jenny are still behind us. The festival lights, once a beacon of celebration, now cast eerie shadows everywhere. Faces become masks of hysteria. I squeeze my eyes shut and tuck my head into Logan's back.

"What's happening?" I ask, heart racing.

"People fighting up front. I saw blood…" Logan breathes heavy. "It's *bad*."

We get to the fence. A momentary reprieve from the crowd, but it won't last. Already, others flood toward us in droves.

"I'm scared!" Jenny pushes close to Logan, starting to sob.

"What do we do? Where do we go?" Zoe shouts.

"We need to get out of here! We'll get crushed if we don't move!" Logan yells back.

"Move?" Chad repeats. "Through *that*?" His eyes ping-pong from the fence to the exit. It seems far. Too far. Hundreds of people lie between us and the gates. "Are you insane?"

The press of bodies around us is overwhelming. Someone shoves against me and sharp metal cuts into my bare arm. I turn, trying to get space. Metal digs into my back instead.

"We have to try! Hands in front, like this." Logan demonstrates how to use our arms to make extra space for our lungs to expand. "Slow breaths. Don't waste energy."

I position my hands, mimicking him, and he starts to move us through the crowd. Chaos swirls around us. All my senses are on high alert, every nerve strained to breaking as we're helplessly swept up in the frenzy. For a moment, I can't breathe. I feel like I might die…

My mind flashes back to a memory. Years ago. Our annual vacation to Palm Key Island in Florida to see Mom's family. Playing near the surf. The ocean turning treacherous in an instant. A rip current catching me, pulling me under. Water crushing in from all sides. Deadly. Unyielding. Gasping for breath, certain each one would be my last. Fighting a losing battle with nature's unforgiving force.

I died that day.

It was only for a few seconds. They revived me, but I've never forgotten the terror. Never stopped wondering what it might feel like the next time, when no one is around to save me. Or how soon that day might come…

Is it today?

Bodies surge around me, an unstoppable current of flesh and bone. Each shove, each jostle, is a new wave crashing over me. I'm drowning on land, the crush of the crowd as suffocating as the ocean…

"Keep going! Faster!" Logan pulls me forward.

Carnage is all around us. People on the ground, crying for help. The crowd mows over them, mercilessly. Some bodies stop moving entirely.

Are they… *dead?*

No, this can't be happening. Not here, not at a garlic festival in Small Town, USA!

"How much further? I can't breathe!" Jenny sobs, her dirt-streaked face next to me. She latches on to Logan, clinging to his other side.

I freeze in place, spinning around.

Zoe?

Chad?

I don't see them anymore.

"Where are they?" I ask, icy fear twisting around my guts. I'd been sure they were right behind us.

"Who?" Jenny asks.

"Zoe!"

Logan tugs me forward. "Keep going! We'll find them later!"

Desperation surges through me, and I wrench away from his grasp and turn around. I eye the crowd with determination. I'll fight every single person here if I have to. Zoe's out there. She needs me.

I have to find her!

"Logan? Please!" Jenny cries, yanking on Logan. "We can't stop. We need to keep going!"

He tears himself from Jenny's grip and reaches for me again. "Alix—no!" His grip is like iron. "*You're not going back there!*"

I struggle to free myself, but it's useless. He's too strong.

"She's okay. She's with Chad," he says, urging me along. "We'll find them after."

I try to resist once more, to go back for Zoe, but it's not just Logan. The crowd fights me, too, surging behind us with renewed energy. We get caught in the next wave of panic. A wall of steel is at my back. Crushing, forcing us onward.

Jenny screams for us somewhere in the distance. I scan the crowd and spot her, just up ahead. She's being swept away from us in the opposite direction. Away from the exit.

"Jen!" Logan grips me fiercely and pushes us through the throngs of people to get to her. "Hold on! We're coming!"

"Logan! Please!" Her arms reach for him, eyes wide and terrified. *"Please help me!"*

And then she's gone, engulfed by the crowd.

We stumble forward, herded like cattle. Elbowed and stepped on. A girl falls in front of us, and Logan picks her up, probably saving her life. His only thanks is a frantic kick to the shins.

When we eventually get to the exit gates, the parking lot is a chaotic mess. Reunions. Tears. Pale faces. Some bloodied. Paramedics and bodies on stretchers. A few local police run around like chickens with their heads cut off. Conversations buzz all around us, but no one seems to know what happened.

What caused the eruption of panic?

What happened at the stage?

We're all fucking clueless.

Logan leads me over to a quiet, empty spot near the far side of the gates. I fall to my knees, taking in big, great, gulping breaths of air. I've never been so happy to feel my lungs expand again to their proper size.

Logan continues holding on to me and I realize, with a shock, that his hand is shaking. He'd seemed so controlled and focused inside the festival, so determined to get us out of the stampede in one piece, it didn't occur to me he might have been as terrified as I was the entire time.

"Are you okay?" I ask, my eyes raking over him with concern.

"I'm fine."

Together we slump down onto the pavement, still holding hands, and wait for our friends to show.

My brain still can't comprehend what just happened.

How can civilized people push and shove at each other like that, without any care as to the consequences? Without even noticing they're hurting—*killing*—people? How can human beings turn so savage, so quickly?

The screams continue behind us, muted, off in the distance. The terror keeps going. Somewhere in the festival fields, other people are still trapped inside and trying to get out.

I scan the parking lot and keep watching the entrance gates, searching anxiously for any signs of Zoe. Of Jenny. Hell, I'd even be glad to see Chad, as long as he's with them.

Minutes tick by. The amount of people stumbling out of the exit starts to thin and still no sign of our friends.

Worry and fear course through me, threatening to over-whelm me.

"What do we do?" I ask Logan. "Where's Zoe? Why aren't they here yet?"

He squeezes my hand. "They're coming."

"What if she's hurt? What if she needs our help?"

Zoe has to be okay. I can't lose her, too...

I'm shaking so hard Logan wraps an arm around my shoulders.

"It's going to be okay, Alix. I promise."

Moisture gathers in the corner of my eyes, my breath coming in jagged and raspy. I have a hard time getting air. My heart thrashes so hard against my chest I think I may be having a heart attack.

Logan holds me, stroking my hair gently while I tremble in his arms. I let him comfort me like that until I'm able to pull myself back together a few minutes later. The instant my senses return, my cheeks heat with embarrassment from my emotional outburst, and I scoot away until we're no longer touching. I wipe dirt and tears from my face and fix my outfit, straightening my crooked top and smoothing down my shorts.

I remember my cell phone then and pull it from my pocket, attempting to call Zoe. I dial her number a few times, but nothing goes through.

I try Jenny and Chad next, but my phone keeps making that weird beeping sound like when too many people are calling at once and the system is overloaded. I switch to my socials instead to see if Zoe has sent me a DM, but I can't get online either.

"Do you have service?" I ask, shaking my phone around, hoping it might help.

"Nope."

He shows me his phone. Zero bars.

With nothing else to do, the two of us sit together in silence on the hot concrete, waiting for our friends to show up.

Ten more minutes go by.

Then twenty.

Then thirty.

Eventually, the trickle at the exit stops completely. It seems like everyone who was inside the festival grounds has made their way outside the gates and to the parking lot—well, everyone who can, has.

"Where the hell are they, Logan?" My lower lip starts to tremble.

"They must've gotten out before us. They probably went back to the campgrounds." He stands, brushing the dirt off the back of his khaki cargo shorts, and reaches out a hand, helping me up. "Let's go look for them there, okay?"

"Zoe wouldn't do that." I shake my head. "She wouldn't leave without me."

I know my best friend. If the situation were reversed and she'd gotten out first, she'd sit here and wait for me, like I'm doing for her. I'm certain of it.

But then, where is she? Why isn't she here yet?

A lump hardens in my throat.

"Logan…" My voice catches as I think of the unimaginable. Hot tears start to burn the corners of my eyes. "Zoe isn't… You don't think—"

"Al—there you are! We were looking everywhere for you guys!"

Slender arms hook around my waist, and I smell the faint trace of Zoe's expensive floral perfume. She buries her head into my neck, hanging onto me so tightly that I can't breathe again, just like in the stampede, but this time I don't mind at all.

"Oh my God, Zoe!" I cry. "I was so worried!"

"What a shit show, huh?" Chad says, trailing after Zoe.

Zoe and I pull apart, unable to stop smiling at each other. My eyes widen as I take in her wrecked appearance. Her cute white jumper is covered in dirt and her right knee is torn up, skinned. Blood drips down her leg.

"Are you okay?" I ask. "What happened?"

I bend down to get a closer look and check the broken skin, making sure it's nothing serious. Thankfully, it's just a few superficial scratches. Nothing some rubbing alcohol and bandages won't fix.

"I'm fine." She bats me away. "Some asshole shoved me, and I fell." Her eyes go wide and terrified. "Oh, Alix, it was horrible! One minute we were right behind you, and then I was on the ground. People started trampling over me. I couldn't breathe. I was screaming, but Chad couldn't get to me. I thought I was going to die!" A tremor courses through her slender body. "But then—remember that hot guy? The one who was looking at you?"

I blink. "Um, yeah? Kade?"

"He showed up out of nowhere!" Her voice goes all breathy and soft. "He got me to my feet and helped me. He saved my life."

Chad groans in annoyance. "It wasn't that big a deal. I would've gotten you out, babe."

"And then," she continues, her voice rising, "before we had a chance to thank him, he turned around and disappeared into the crowd again. He went right back inside to help more people. Can you believe that? He's so brave—" She stops mid-sentence and peers around. "Hey—where's Jenny?"

I fidget, fiddling with the crystals on my top. I was so excited to be reunited with Zoe, I forgot all about Jenny for a moment.

"Uhhh… we sort of lost her," I say.

"What do you mean *you lost her?*" Zoe's mouth hangs open.

"It wasn't my fault, Zoe. She—"

"Alix!" She cuts me off with a horrified look. "How could you?"

"*I* didn't!" I bristle at her consternation, crossing my arms over my chest. "*She's* the one who left *me!*"

Logan puts a hand on my shoulder and gives Zoe an earnest look. "We really did try, Zoe. There wasn't anything we could do."

The flame in Zoe's eyes dims slightly, his words calming her. She may not believe I wasn't careless with Jenny, even if it's true, but she trusts Logan implicitly.

"And for your information, I even tried calling her cell already," I say to Zoe, "but the phones are down."

"I'm sure she's fine," Logan says.

"Yeah, you're probably right. I bet she just—*Oh, hey!*" Zoe's face lights up. "Hey! Over here, Kade!" She jumps up and down, waving her arms overhead.

I turn just in time to see Kade striding out the front gates. He pauses for a second, glancing around for whoever is calling his name, and then spots us. He freezes. His eyes lock on mine and my heart jolts.

"Kade!" Zoe yells again, louder.

He gives a little shrug and proceeds to walk all the way over.

"I'm so glad you're okay!" Zoe says, throwing her arms around him. "I don't know how to thank you for what you did for us!"

"It's fine," he says, looking embarrassed as he disentangles himself from her embrace. "It's no big deal. Really."

"Right, that's what I said." Chad slings a possessive arm over Zoe. His eyes narrow in Kade's direction as he pulls her in closer to his side.

"Everyone all right?" Kade asks, looking directly at me. His stare is bold, assessing. His gaze rakes up and down my body, as if assessing for injury. I swallow tightly, pretending not to be affected by the way those intense dark eyes make me feel.

"Yeah, man. We're fine," Logan says in a gruff voice and rests his hand lightly on my waist. Apparently, it's now his turn to get territorial in front of the good-looking new guy.

"Did you see our friend inside by any chance?" Zoe asks, peering past Kade, toward the exit gates. "Short brown hair, purple tube dress, white boots?"

"No, sorry." He shakes his head. "I don't think many people are still in there."

"We should go back to the campgrounds," Logan says, looking past the parking lot toward the path we walked earlier to get here. "I bet she's at the RV or her aunt and uncle's house. There's probably phone service there, too. We need to get away from the crowds."

"Well, good luck to you guys." Kade starts to inch away. "I'd better be going…"

"That's probably a good idea," Logan says, looking slightly relieved.

"Yeah. See ya, dude." Chad gives Kade a mock salute.

"No—wait!" Zoe grabs Kade's wrist, stopping him. "Come with us."

Kade's eyes widen with surprise. "I really don't think I should."

"Of course, you should! You're all by yourself, aren't you?" Zoe asks. "We can't let you wander around alone, not after how you saved our lives."

Chad groans. "C'mon, babe. Leave the guy alone, would you?" Annoyance peppers his voice. "I'm sure he's got places to be."

Another eerie scream cuts through the night air. This time it sounds like it's coming from somewhere else, somewhere besides the festival grounds behind us. Like whatever was wreaking havoc inside has now made its way outside. It makes the hair rise on the back of my neck.

"Maybe we should stick together a bit longer?" I ask. It's not that I care if the hot guy comes with us—I don't—but we can't be certain if the danger has passed. "We still don't know what caused the stampede." I hesitate, surveying the surrounding area with a wary gaze. "Maybe it was just crowd panic, but maybe it was something else? Something… *worse?*"

Logan's shoulders stiffen, body alert. "Yeah, that's a good point," he says. "It could be any number of things, and we have no way of telling if the threat's been neutralized." He sighs and turns back to Kade with a small shrug. "Guess you probably should join us… at least until we know it's safe."

CHAPTER 6
10:45 P.M.

Garlic Groove Festival Campgrounds

All the streetlights seem to be out, and with little light other than our cell phones and the moonlight, we're forced to walk slower than usual to get back to the campgrounds. Logan leads the way. Zoe and I follow behind, our arms locked together at the elbows, with Chad at Zoe's heels. Kade hangs back a few feet, bringing up the rear.

The entire way, Chad prattles incessantly about his own crazy right-wing theories for what might have caused the chaos at the festival. Terrorist attacks. Weak immigration borders. QAnon conspiracies. I groan and do my best to tune him out.

It takes us almost an hour to get back. When we arrive at the campgrounds, things seem very different from when we left earlier in the day. Before, the campgrounds had been ablaze with action. Headlights from cars and campers, along with lanterns and campfires, had all cast light around the fields. Music had been blasting. People dancing and drinking, bouncing from group to group.

But now, the fields are almost pitch-black other than a full moon and stars overhead, and things are eerily silent. Many of the RVs and tents are already gone. Discarded trash and tread marks linger in their wake, as if people departed in such a hurry they didn't have time to bother cleaning up. The vehicles and tents that still remain appear deserted or like the people inside are staying quiet. No one in the windows or lounging around the front porch areas. Lights off, doors and zippers shut tight.

I'm surprised by how fast the place has emptied out. I guess after what happened tonight, there won't be a Sunday event, but still, it's late. Almost midnight. People have been drinking all day. You'd think most of them would at least wait until the morning to drive home?

We use our cell phone lights to illuminate the path ahead as we walk through the fields to find our RV. It's difficult with so many already gone. There are no roads. No parking signs. Many of the weekend's self-erected landmarks we'd gotten used to are no longer there, like the yellow double-decker bus someone outfitted for the festival, or the bachelor party from California that had set up a mini golf area in front of their Airstream.

"Where is everyone?" Zoe asks, eyes darting around the grounds.

"People are freaked. They must've taken off." Logan shrugs. "Hell, I wouldn't mind taking off, too, once we find Jenny."

"But the Velvet Patriots are playing tomorrow!" Chad whines. "We gotta stay."

Kade makes a deep grumbling sound behind us. "Trust me. You don't want to stick around here."

"Sorry, man, I don't think anyone's playing tomorrow."

Logan scratches the back of his neck, giving Chad a sympathetic look. "Not after what just happened."

"It's okay, babe." Zoe gently squeezes Chad's arm. "We can go see them another time."

As we search for our RV, our shoes slosh and squish like we're stepping in mud. The ground is spongy and uneven, as if damp from the rain, even though it hasn't rained for as long as we've been in town.

"What the hell?" I lift my boots, eyeing the bottoms with my phone light. A mixture of dirt, old grass, and something liquidy and red coats the soles. "Ugh—gross! What is that? Ketchup?"

Logan inches in close and kneels down to inspect my boots. His throat catches and he blinks, as if caught by surprise.

"That's weird. It looks like blood?"

Chad snorts. "Ha ha. Very funny."

"I'm serious." Logan stands back up, his light brow wrinkling. "That's how Grandpa's boots look after he comes hunting with us. He's real old and his eyesight sucks, so he's not the best shot anymore. Sometimes he'll fire a whole round into a stag to make sure he doesn't miss, and then he winds up shuffling around in the remains."

I swallow. "That's pretty… um… graphic, isn't it?"

"How horrible! That poor deer!" Zoe cringes beside me.

Kade's voice becomes more urgent. "You really should get to your car and get the hell out of here."

"Relax, dude." Chad rolls his eyes. "It's probably just paint or something."

I shiver, despite the warmth of the night. I don't know whether Logan is right, but the idea of someone's blood on my shoes is unsettling, to say the least. Plus, the general creepiness factor of all these dark fields and a mostly abandoned campsite doesn't help things.

Logan quickens his pace. He's super athletic and has long legs like a sprinter, so the rest of us have to almost jog to keep up with him.

As we get deeper into the camp, we eventually come across a few stragglers. Tired, weary-looking festival-goers that wave goodnight to us from closed-up windows as we go past. I let out a sigh of relief, feeling a little less alone. At least we're not the only ones still here. I was really starting to wonder for a second...

Finally, we spot our RV.

"There it is!" Zoe takes off into a jog, pulling me along. "Now all we have to do is find Jenny."

"Told you we'd be fine," Chad says, strolling behind us, taking his sweet time.

Logan arrives at the RV an instant before us. He lets out a long hiss and drops to a knee, getting down next to the two front tires.

"Fuck!"

"What is it? What's wrong?" I ask, rushing over.

He shines his phone flashlight toward the RV, revealing a chilling sight. The two front tires, once robust and ready for the open road, now sag almost down to the ground. Each has a gash in the center, like a huge gaping wound.

"Shit—how the hell did we get *two* flats?" Chad asks. "Did we hit an entire bed of nails?"

"It's not a flat." Logan's jaw tightens in disbelief. "Someone slashed our tires."

Zoe gasps. "No way. Who would do that?"

"Someone who doesn't want us leaving," Logan says.

"You sure?" I shoot a curious glance at the surrounding woods at the edges of the dusty campground. Instead of lush greenery like I'd expected to see in Oregon, rows and rows of desiccate-looking trees stand muted in a palette of brown and gray, their leaves dulled and curled at the edges like old paper. The drought has leeched much of the life away, though it still appears hospitable enough to house at least some wildlife. "Couldn't it be something else? Like wild animals?"

Nervous laughter escapes Zoe's lips. "Yeah, maybe wild animals with tire-slashing tools?"

"'Fraid not." Logan shakes his head and points to the jagged punctures in the rubber. "Those are razor marks. A knife or a blade, probably?"

"Whatever it is, you better patch it up fast and get out of here," Kade says, sliding in next to me. I gasp at his nearness. He moves so quietly, I didn't even hear him approach.

"It's too big to patch without the right tools. We need to call for a tow." Logan holds his cell phone up toward the sky and shakes it around. "Damn. Still no reception. Anyone else?"

We all glance at our phones and double check them, but they're still not working even in a new location. It's looking like the entire town must be having some sort of electrical issues.

"Let's just go inside the RV and wait for Jenny and the phones to start working again." Zoe yawns, stretching her arms overhead. "I'm exhausted."

"Now's not a good time for a nap, Zoe." Chad's face pales, his eyes still fixated on the vandalized front tires. "We should walk back to town. Catch an Uber or a taxi or whatever and get the hell out of Dodge."

I smirk. "But I thought you wanted to see the Velvet Patriots tomorrow?"

"That was before Freddy Krueger murdered our tires," he says, swallowing hard and inching away from the RV, looking completely freaked out. Gone is the cocky, cavalier Chad I'm used to. "Now I think I'd rather see my twenty-third birthday."

Zoe laughs, grabbing Chad's hand and weaving her fingers between his. "Don't you think you're being a tad dramatic, babe?"

"Nope," he says. "Didn't you hear what Logan said? Some crazy maniac is running around with a knife, vandalizing cars. There's no cell service, no electricity, not to mention the bloodbath on the ground, whatever the fuck that was."

Zoe shrugs. "Logan doesn't know for sure that was blood."

"Not the point, babe!" Chad snaps.

The night air thickens with tension as we all exchange nervous glances, realizing that what was supposed to be a fun-filled carefree weekend has just taken a rather unexpected—and unwanted—dark turn. It occurs to me then that if whatever went down at the festival isn't yet over, our secluded campground would be a perfect place for the perpetrators to go next. It's within walking distance from the festival and is filled with potential new victims. It would make a fantastic hunting ground.

"We should go to Jenny's aunt and uncle's house. It's closer than town," Logan says. "She might be there. Maybe her family can help us."

Logan and Chad guide us toward the Holloway farmhouse, as they've already been there. It doesn't take long. The sagging porch creaks underfoot as we approach the house and walk up the weathered and rotted wooden stairs. A tire swing to my left sways in the night breeze as if animated by a presence unseen. Wind whispers beside us, rustling the golden stalks of grass surrounding the farmhouse.

"What's that?" I ask, pointing to a wizened, strange-looking wreath clinging to the front door. It appears to be made from what smells like dried garlic, cloves strung together with twine.

Kade steps in front and touches the wreath. "It's an ailmentbane."

"An ailwhat?"

"It's a talisman to ward off evil," he explains. "It's just something superstitious older folks do around here. Like all the scarecrows you see when you're driving into town."

"I thought scarecrows were to protect crops from birds," Logan says, reaching for the rusty, wrought iron door knocker.

"That too." Kade shrugs. "But in Allium Valley, people also think they protect the land from supernatural harm."

Chad makes a face. "This town is fucking weird. I don't care if they do have good garlic pizza, I'm not coming back next year."

We knock a few times, but no one answers. Everyone must be asleep already. Luckily, the door is unlocked. Logan twists the knob and motions for the rest of us to follow him inside.

It's dark and quiet in the foyer. Logan flicks a switch, but it doesn't seem to work. The electricity must be out here, too.

He calls for Jenny's aunt and uncle, but no one responds, so he leads us down the hallway. Logan's phone light combined with the glow of the moon through the open door and the windows helps to illuminate things enough for us to see our way around.

The farmhouse has an open layout with a kitchen that bleeds into a combined dining room and living area. I don't see anything unusual inside except for the hideous furniture. An old couch in an unfortunate plaid pattern. Some chairs missing a leg.

Logan makes his way up the stairs while the rest of us

hang downstairs and wait. He disappears into the bedrooms, checking things out. Moments later, a loud clattering noise sounds from above, breaking the silence and startling us. It sends my pulse skittering.

"Everything okay?" I call out to him.

Logan appears a moment later at the top of the staircase.

"Sorry." He grins apologetically. "I ran into a lamp."

"Any sign of Jenny or her aunt and uncle?" Zoe asks.

"There's no one up here. Place is empty," Logan says, walking back down the stairs. "Maybe they went out for dinner?"

"At midnight?" Chad's brow wrinkles. "I doubt it. They're old."

"I'm sure they'll be back soon," Zoe says.

"We're wasting time." Kade runs a hand through his hair, clearly agitated. "We need to get going."

The front door flies open with a loud whooshing sound, and a middle-aged woman bursts inside the farmhouse. Her disheveled hair is a bright red hue that Mother Nature doesn't provide, and she wears a ratty old *Vampire Weekend* band tee and studded biker shorts covered in dirt. Her makeup is running. Heavy mascara clumps under her eyes, and bright lipstick smears her chin.

"Hello?" Logan calls out. "Can we help you?"

The woman staggers toward us like a drunk person who's been over served. Her arms are wide and open. "Please… my friend… outside!" she cries, stumbling to the floor.

"Whoa, are you okay?" Logan rushes forward, helping the woman back to her feet. Her knees are skinned and raw. Blood drips onto the hardwood floor.

Chad snickers next to me. "Looks like someone's been partying a little too hard."

"Don't be an ass," I say, shoving him aside and approaching the woman. Being that drunk is no fun, especially without your friends around. She doesn't need Chad mocking her. What she needs is food to soak up the alcohol and a safe place to sleep her high off.

But as I get closer to her, it becomes abundantly clear that something is wrong. More wrong than just a few too many shots of liquor. The red in her clotted and clumped hair is not just from dye. It's blood. A huge gash runs across her forehead. The skin's been torn open and hangs in meaty slabs above her brow.

"My friend—" The woman stops mid-sentence and turns, her eyes darting back outside, wild with panic. "Please, you have to help her!"

"Slow down." Logan puts an arm on her trembling shoulder. "What are you talking about? Where's your friend?"

"They're going to kill her!" The woman points frantically past the front door.

Logan flashes his phone light, illuminating the porch. My gaze follows the beam to find a small, slight figure lying sprawled on the dusty ground a few yards away from the house. A woman. Unmoving.

Two large, bulky, menacing-looking men surround her. They circle her body like coyotes closing in on prey.

A low growl erupts behind me.

"Get away from the door!" Kade yells.

A second later, the men pounce.

What comes next seems like it's happening in slow motion. We watch from inside the house, horrified, as the men tear the woman's body apart. Blood spills to the ground. Bone crunches and breaks.

I can't believe what I'm seeing. It almost looks like...

"Oh my God! Are they... *are they eating her?*" Zoe gasps, terror lacing her words.

Logan lurches in my direction, but Kade is closer and faster. He grabs me by the waist and yanks me away from the door and whatever horrors are happening outside. "Get back!" he says, maneuvering me behind his body. "Stay behind me."

My heart races with fear. I burrow my head between his shoulder blades and squeeze my eyes shut.

Oh God. What the hell is happening?

Footsteps pound in the distance, heading for us. Closer and closer. Then the floorboards creak, and I can tell they've made it to the farmhouse stairs. My stomach clenches into a ball of panic as I realize the horrifying men must have finished with the woman outside and are now coming for us—

But no, that's not it.

When I look up, I see it's the guy we met last night— Frog. He emerges from the shadows, wearing head-to-toe camouflage, like a soldier. An ammunition belt is slung across his body and a deadly-looking rifle is in his hand.

"What the fuck is going on?" Chad shouts.

"No time for questions." Frog darts inside the house and slams the door shut behind him, locking it. "Follow me if you want to live."

CHAPTER 7
DAY 3: 1:00 A.M.

The Holloway Family Farm Silo

We move quickly and quietly, following Frog through the Holloway farmhouse and out the screened patio. He shines a flashlight ahead, directing us through the darkness and toward the silo out back.

The red-headed woman whimpers, crying about her dead friend as she trails behind our group. The rest of us who never met her friend are way too rattled to be sad like she is. The only thing we can think about is getting as far away from those men as possible.

Frog swings the door open and ushers everyone inside the silo. A cool hush envelops us, a stark contrast to the punishing heat outside. The atmosphere is still, the kind of quiet that feels almost tangible, a soft pressure against the eardrums.

It's empty inside—a cavernous cylinder that I imagine

was once filled to the brim with corn or garlic or some other local crop, but now stands as an unintended monument to the drought.

It feels secretive and secure.

There are no windows for anyone to see inside, and the metal around us acts as a conductor. It conceals any sounds to the outside world, like our breathing and even talking. Plus, it's not exactly the first place you'd look for people if you were some kind of crazed psycho killer.

We sit in a circle on the floor, cross-legged, in shock and riddled with fear. Logan is on one side of me, Kade on the other, both effectively sandwiching me in. I try to listen for any signs of life outside in the fields but hear nothing. No footfalls or chatter. Everyone has either gone into hiding—or worse.

Frog double checks that the door is closed up tight and then sits down. "We'll be safe here. For now, at least," he says, putting his flashlight in the center of the silo so we can see things better. "Everyone okay?"

"Hell no, we're not okay!" Chad barks, his voice ricocheting off the metal walls. "Did you see what happened to that chick? What *the fuck* is going on?"

Frog waves a hand, motioning for Chad to lower his volume. "Calm down, dude," he says. "Panicking isn't going to help things."

"Don't tell me what to do, bro!" Chad stands and charges toward Frog, looking like he wants to slug the guy. "I'll do whatever I want!"

"I said, *you need to calm down,*" Frog repeats and though he doesn't seem to do it in an overly threatening way, it is lost on no one when the rifle's barrel turns in Chad's direction.

"Sit down, babe," Zoe says, catching Chad's eye.

"Okay, okay." Chad holds up both hands and backs

away from Frog, sitting back down next to Zoe. "So what—we just hang tight and wait for the cops to show?"

"Don't count on it," Frog says.

"What do you mean?" Logan asks.

"I mean cops aren't going to do shit." Frog scoffs. "This is way beyond that."

"I don't understand," I say, my heart still beating at an unnaturally fast pace. "But if the police aren't coming, then what are we supposed to do?"

"We wait here and try not to die." Frog lowers his rifle.

Oh God…

My hands shake at my sides.

Logan had been right.

It wasn't ketchup on my shoes. Wasn't ketchup at all…

Kade touches my knee, so softly I almost don't feel it at first. "It's okay," he says. "No one's going to find us here. They'll be too busy with whoever's still walking around outside."

"Hey, I know you!" Frog says, cocking his head in Kade's direction. "You're Kaden Black. We went to school together."

Kade blinks. "Did we?"

"Sure did! You were a year above me. Everyone knows the Black Family Farm. Your fields are a mile or so from ours." Frog's eyes are wide and openly admiring. "'Course, why would you know me? Our little ol' place isn't anything like the agricultural empire you guys built, but then, the Black family has been in Allium Valley longer than almost anyone. Suppose you got a head start farming, huh?"

"Guess so," Kade says with an indifferent shrug.

The red-headed woman moans across from me. "She's dead!" she wails, putting her head in her hands. "I can't believe Lisa is dead!"

Zoe leaves Chad's side and walks over to the other end of the circle, taking a seat next to the woman. She puts an arm around her, patting at her shoulder and making little soothing sounds.

"I'm sorry about your friend," she says. "So very sorry, Ms. uh—"

"Margie." The woman rocks back and forth on the ground, shaking and sobbing. "My name is Margie…"

"What the hell were those men doing to her friend?" Logan asks, turning to Frog.

"I think the term *men* is debatable," Frog says.

"Screw semantics!" Chad snaps. "If you know what's going on, just tell us already!"

"Wait—are you saying those weren't people?" My hands tremble in my lap. They sure looked like people. Savages maybe, but people, nonetheless.

"There's not really a good name for them. Not that I've ever heard, at least." Frog shrugs. "I suppose if you want to call them something, vampire is probably as good a word as any."

"Vampire?" I ask, waiting for the punchline. "You're joking, right?"

I don't know why he would be screwing around at a time like this, but he can't be serious. I'm not sure what was attacking that woman, but one thing I'm certain of— vampires don't exist.

I peer closer at Frog, examining him a bit more carefully: the weird camo vest with throwing stars, the ammo belt, the gun. I think I even see nunchucks sticking out of his back pocket.

I start to wonder if we've somehow stumbled upon a creepy conspiracy theorist or crazed cult member. I'm still not sure what the hell is going on outside the silo, but I don't know if hiding inside with a nut job is any better.

"Sounds like all that pot has gone straight to your head, bro." Chad gives Frog a condescending look before turning to the rest of us. "Why are we sitting here listening to this loser, anyway?" He huffs. "Let's just find a car that works and get the hell out of here."

"I'm not going back out there," Margie whimpers as she continues rocking back and forth on the silo's floor. "Outside is only death. Monsters everywhere…"

"Lady, you don't know what you're talking about." Chad rolls his eyes. "There's no such thing as monsters. It was probably a bunch of freaks hopped up on bath salts."

"Drugs don't make people feed on other people," Frog says.

"Sure they do," Chad says. "I saw it on YouTube. Some guys in Florida ate a bathtub full of homemade drugs and ran around eating people's faces."

"It's not drugs. That's not what's going on here." Frog shakes his head adamantly. "I'm trying to tell you—"

"Oh right," Chad says, cutting him off with a conde- scending laugh. "I forgot—it's *vampires*."

"Babe, be quiet. Let him talk," Zoe says through clenched teeth.

Frog's posture goes rigid with barely contained anger. "You think you know what's happening? You think you've got all the answers, cool guy?" he asks Chad, a mocking edge to his voice. "Well, I'm telling you right now, you don't know *shit*, buddy. Call them whatever you want, but there are flesh-eating-throat-ripping-blood-sucking-looking-to-eat- you-the-fuck-up-vampires out there," he continues, voice rising. "So, unless you want to be next, maybe you should shut up and listen to someone who actually knows what's going on."

There's a long moment of silence while we try to digest Frog's words.

I'm not ready to believe in something as insane as the existence of vampires, but I can't deny that some really messed up shit is happening. The more we sit around fighting about it, the more time we're wasting. Our best chance of making it out alive is to move past the denial phase and get straight to the survival phase.

I swallow hard. "Okay, so, let's say we believe you. How do you know all of this, anyway?"

Frog looks indignant. "You think I'm just some yokel local idiot that gets baked at campgrounds?"

Zoe shrugs. "Well... you did get us stoned yesterday."

"That's just a cover. I've got a higher purpose." Frog's grin is a bit smug. "Although I do enjoy a good toke every now and then. I mean, who doesn't?"

"A higher purpose for what?" Logan prods impatiently.

Frog puffs out his chest and straightens up proudly. "I'm part of a secret elite force that watches over Allium Valley. There's a group of us—the families that know the truth about this town and have pledged to keep it safe from the vamps.

"We learn the stories as kids." He gives a short, sharp cough to clear his throat. "The way my grandparents tell it, it all started in the 1800s, during the Gold Rush when everyone was heading west. There was gold here, too, and Oregon was less crowded. Less competition. Not to mention, the Sierra Nevada Mountains got a bad rap after that whole Donner Party cannibalism disaster." His face twists into a grimace, the mention of cannibalism and death perhaps a little too on the nose given our current predicament. "But I digress. The point is, people came here and loved it. The weather was good. Not too cold, not too hot—"

Sweat drips down my temple. "I'm not so sure about that last part."

"We'll get there," Frog says. "As I was saying, by all intents and purposes, Allium Valley seemed pretty damn hospitable. Nice weather. Plenty of farm land. Fresh water from the Devil's River."

"Yeah, still don't love that name," Zoe mutters.

"It was the perfect place for the settlers to drop their flag and build a new home," Frog continues. "They started to get comfortable. Sent out word to their friends and relatives back home to come join them. It was like paradise." He lifts a knowing brow. "Paradise with just one small itty-bitty problem… The townspeople suddenly started dying."

Frog lets his words sit for a moment.

"Dying how?" I ask, though I'm starting to get an inkling.

"They were being drained," Frog explains. "Bodies would show up, bloodless. Throats slashed. Wrists torn open. Something was hunting them." He swallows, his Adam's apple bobbing up and down. "At first, the townspeople thought it was an animal. A night watch was formed. They called themselves the Order of the Clove. They meant well, but in the beginning, they were fucking clueless. They set up barricades and traps, hoping to catch whatever was doing it. Wolves. Bears. Mountain Lions."

"Those animals don't drink blood," Logan says with a furrowed brow.

"Exactly!" Frog points his finger and shakes it in the air. "Nothing the Order did stopped the killings. Men. Women. Children. Even house pets. No one was safe."

"If it was so bad, why didn't they just leave?" Chad asks.

"And go where?" Frog frowns at him. "They risked their lives to travel across the country. Most of them spent everything they had. And how did they know another place would be any better? How did they know whatever was killing them wouldn't just follow them to the next town?" He shakes his head. "No, there was nowhere else to go. They'd made their stake in Allium Valley, and they'd just have to make it work.

"So they doubled down," he continues, flexing his knuckles. "Built homes. Infrastructure. Created aqueducts for the river. Planted crops. They mourned their dead as the bodies piled up, but they pushed through the grief and did their best to survive." Frog pauses and looks around the silo somberly. "By winter's end, they'd lost more than half the town.

"But then, spring came, and a funny thing happened. The killing slowed. A few families, in particular, were completely spared. At first, everyone thought it was luck, or coincidence, until they figured out it was all the houses that were growing garlic. And not just the garlic farmland, but any homes up against the riverbanks were also largely unaffected. That's when they realized what was going on."

"What was it?" Zoe asks, on the edge of her seat. "What was keeping them safe?"

"It was the garlic itself. It was repelling the vamps," Frog says. "And something about the Devil's River."

"I don't get it. Was there holy water in the river?" Logan asks, cocking his head.

Frog snorts. "That's just in the movies. It's got nothing to do with the church. Running water is a natural force that has the power to purify and remove evil; that's what scared them off." His voice swells with excitement. "The townspeople planted more garlic, and the next year it was everywhere. Every family was stocked. They kept it around the house, in their pockets, in their horse-drawn carriages and buggies. That was the first spring they had no deaths. With hard work and a little bit of luck, they'd solved their little ol' vampire problem."

My friends and I stare at each other uncertainly across the circle, not sure what to make of Frog's strange story. As my gaze flickers toward Kade, I realize he's the only one in the silo—besides Frog—who doesn't look completely unnerved by this conversation. It occurs to me then that he's also been awfully quiet ever since Frog began speaking.

Why *is* he so quiet?

Just like Frog, Kade also grew up here. Shouldn't he know about all of this, too?

Why isn't he saying anything?

"What do you think?" I pivot, facing him head on.

"About what?" he asks, arching a brow.

"Well, you're a local too, right?" I ask. "Didn't you hear these stories?"

"Yeah, sure. Everyone in town knows them." He shrugs. "It's a local legend, passed down from generation to generation. Like Sasquatch in Northern California or the Loch Ness Monster in Scotland."

"And?" I prod.

"And what, Alix?" His voice takes on a slightly annoyed edge.

I let out a frustrated sigh, glaring at him. "And do you think the stories are true or not?"

It almost seems like he's being purposefully obtuse, like he's hiding something and doesn't want to tell us what he really thinks about the situation. Except, that doesn't make any sense.

"So what if they are true?" Logan asks. "What's that got to do with what's going on now?" He steeples his hands in front of his chin and looks toward Frog. "You said the villagers got it under control, so then why is it starting up again? What's changed?"

Sweat drips into my eyes, and I wipe it away with the

back of my hand, disgusted. Even this late at night, even with all the cool metal around us, we still can't escape the heat. It's brutal. Insufferable. It's—

"Oh my God." Goosebumps pepper my skin. "It's the drought, isn't it?" I ask, turning to Frog. "That's why they're coming back, right?"

He gives me a chilling look. "This is the worst garlic harvest we've had since the town was first settled."

"The downed power and the phones? That's them too, isn't it?" Logan nods along to himself as if he's just realized something important. "And they must be the ones who slashed our tires."

"But why?" I ask. "What are they trying to do?"

"It's a siege." Logan looks around the circle slowly and deliberately. "They're cutting off our lines of communication and supplies. They want to isolate us—so we can't fight back. It's Electronic Warfare Strategy 101."

The air inside the old silo hangs heavy with the scent of dust and fear. I find myself instinctively huddling in closer to Logan, my legs pressing up against his. A shiver traces the length of my spine at the cold realization that the creatures of nightmares are not just confined to folklore like I always believed.

Real monsters do exist.

The revelation is a suffocating mist, seeping into the marrow of my bones. Panic rises like a bitter tide as my reality shifts. The mundane world I once knew fractures, revealing a terrifying new unknown.

"So what's the plan?" Logan asks Frog, his hands balled into fists at his sides. "If this is real, how do we strike back? Besides garlic and the Devil's River, what else hurts them? Crosses? Mirrors? Daylight?"

"Garlic and running water, yes." Frog nods and then lets loose a derisive chuckle. "But the rest are old wives' tales.

And they don't sparkle, either, like those cute little fictional *Twilight* vampires in Washington. Unfortunately, Oregon got the bad ones."

"Okay, well, do they bleed?" Logan ignores Frog's poor attempt at a joke. "Can we stab them? Stake them?" He nods toward the rifle at Frog's side. "You've got that gun for a reason, right?"

Frog guffaws. "Theoretically, yes, they bleed, but good luck trying. They're faster than us. Stronger. Just as smart, too," he says. "Guns and other weapons can help if you're in a bind, but I wouldn't bet my life on them."

Kade turns to Logan, eyes narrowed. "You should forget about trying to fight this, whatever it is," he says. "Focus on just trying to survive."

"And how are we supposed to do that?" I ask him, still not totally sure I believe he doesn't know more than he's letting on about what's happening.

"We should sit tight. Stay hidden." Kade continues to stare down Logan, his gaze cold and calculating. "And we definitely shouldn't go looking for trouble."

"And then what?" I ask. "We can't sit here forever."

"Tomorrow morning, when it's light again, we can find a working car and get out of here," Frog says.

"No, please!" Margie's sobs are hushed in Zoe's arms. "We can't go outside. They're still out there!"

"Why morning?" Logan asks Frog, ignoring the hysterical lady's panicked mutterings. "I thought you said daylight doesn't hurt these things?"

"It doesn't. But I'd rather see what's in front of me and not risk falling over and breaking a leg—wouldn't you?" Frog yawns and stretches his arms over his head. "We should get some sleep. We'll need to be at full strength tomorrow."

Zoe's eyes find mine across the circle. "Do you think Jenny's okay?"

"I'm sure she's fine."

There's no point in Zoe getting all worked up and stressing. There's nothing we can do for Jenny, and if there really are bloodsucking monsters running amok, there's not much we can do for ourselves, either.

"Besides, you know Jenny's prepared to handle any crisis with that belt bag of hers," I joke, trying to lighten things.

Zoe's eyes fill. "I'm just so worried about her."

"She's probably with her family, hiding out somewhere, like us," Logan says, giving Zoe a reassuring look.

We all stretch out for the night, trying to get comfortable in the silo. I don't know how anyone will sleep after everything we've witnessed today, but it's important to try. We can't afford to be tired or slow tomorrow. Not with whatever is outside trying to kill us.

Frog dims the light on his flashlight to conserve the battery, and we agree to take turns watching the silo door to make sure no one gets in while we're asleep. Frog walks over to the door, taking the first shift, rifle in hand. Kade lies down near him, body at attention, even though his shift isn't until much later.

Logan spreads out next to me, positioning himself so he's blocking me from the doorway. The sides of our bodies touch in the darkness, and I find I'm grateful for his warmth and nearness. I close my eyes and try to forget the terrified scenes from the festival and what I saw on the porch, even though I'm fairly certain those images are permanently burned inside my head.

Eventually, the stress of the day starts to catch up with me, and I begin to drift in and out of consciousness. When sleep is just a few moments away, the memory of the old attendant at the gas station flashes in my mind again.

It turns out he wasn't so crazy, after all. He'd been trying to warn us all along.

Beware of the night.

The night. Of course…

That's when the vampires first attacked.

PART TWO
THE SIEGE

CHAPTER 8
7:30 A.M.

The Holloway Family Farm Silo

I'm the first to wake in the morning.

Well, Kade and me.

As I open my eyes and stretch my arms overhead, I'm shocked to see he's already wide awake—watching me. He stands in front of the silo door, his body at attention and on high alert. His fists are gripped at his sides, prepared for anything.

"Did you get any sleep?" I whisper, but it's not because I'm particularly altruistic or overly concerned about some stranger's health. If he didn't sleep well, he'll be tired. And if he's tired, that will slow him down. And that makes him a risk, not just to himself, but to my friends and me.

"I'm perfectly fine, thank you," he says in a crisp tone that makes it clear he knows exactly why I'm asking, and that I should mind my own business.

Well, okay then…

I glance around the rest of the silo to survey the situation. Everyone else is still fast asleep, except for Frog who appears to be missing—along with his rifle. He left his flashlight behind, though. It's still lying in the center of the circle, dimly illuminating the silo.

I wonder where he went?

I suppose I could ask Kade about it, but he's made it clear he's not the chatty morning type. Besides, if it was something to worry about, I'm sure Kade would've woken us up to tell us.

Frog returns a short while later, just as the others slowly start to awaken. It turns out he'd decided at daybreak to go searching for a car we could use but found nothing helpful. The vehicles that still remain at the campgrounds have slashed tires like ours or he couldn't find any keys. He didn't see any people outside, either. It wasn't a total bust, though. He did find some supplies.

We huddle together in the dim light of the silo, the air thick with tension, while he shows us what he got. Some medicine, waters, and other supplies, pilfered from Jenny's aunt and uncle's house. An extra shotgun. More ammo, too, which I hope we don't need but is good to have.

He urges us to leave right away. The sooner the better.

Even though the daylight isn't a deterrent for the vampires, he figures they still need to sleep like any other animals do. Since they were up all night, slaughtering God knows how many people, there's a good chance most of them are sleeping now. Frog thinks they could even be nocturnal, like bats or coyotes. There are no guarantees, of course, since no one has dealt with them in hundreds of years, but it's a real possibility we should try to take advantage of.

"Our safest bet is to head for Devil's River and seek shelter there," he says, pacing back and forth, the sound of his boots echoing against the silo flooring. "It's just under ten miles away, so it shouldn't take too long. A few hours, maybe. We just have to get there before dark. We don't want to be running around when these things wake up."

"We should stick by trees and vegetation," Logan suggests. "That'll help camouflage us."

Zoe fidgets on the floor, looking uneasy. "What if we need to stop to, uh, you know?" she asks, her cheeks flushing.

"TMI, babe." Chad makes a grossed-out face, and Zoe swats him on the shoulder.

"Don't worry. We'll figure it out as we go," Frog says, looking down, checking the guns to make sure they're fully loaded and ready, his movements precise. "We'll need to be quiet out there. No shouting. No unnecessary shooting. We don't want to attract attention."

Logan perks up. "That reminds me," he says, standing and stretching out his long legs. "I've got some weapons back at the RV. Let's swing by there first."

"No way." Kade shakes his head. "We need to get to the river as fast as we can."

"We only have two guns for seven people." Logan frowns. "That's not enough firepower to protect a group this big. We're going to need everything we've got."

"What's at the RV?" Frog asks, head cocked, his interest piqued.

"A brand new Ravin R29X Sniper, for starters."

Frog's eyes light up. "With premium arrows? Noise dampeners?"

Logan chuckles. "You know it."

"Unless it's a bazooka, it won't help." Kade looks unimpressed.

Logan flashes a rakish grin and flexes his fingers high

overhead, cracking them loudly. "You haven't seen me with a crossbow, dude," he says.

"It's true. He's an insane shot," I agree, and Logan beams back at me.

Frog nods. "Yeah, let's grab it. It's on the way, anyway."

"This is a mistake," Kade growls, clenching his fists. His frustration is palpable. "Every second counts right now."

Chad stands, facing Kade with a sharp glare. "If Logan says we need more weapons, then we need more weapons. If you don't like it, leave."

"Relax, babe," Zoe says, grabbing Chad's hand. "We're all in this together. Kade's just trying to help."

Chad looks incredulous. "We don't even know him, Zoe! Why should we trust anything he says?"

"You shouldn't." Kade shrugs, nonchalant. "But about this, I'm right."

Frog raises his hand in the air. "I vote more weapons. More weapons, better odds."

Logan looks over at Kade and offers a peace-making smile, wide and friendly, despite their disagreement. "Your call. Stay or go," he says. "We'd like you with us, but it's your choice."

Kade doesn't return the smile, but he doesn't bolt out the door or do anything drastic, so I guess that means he's decided to stay around. At least for now.

The red-headed woman, Margie, silent until now, starts to whimper again. She rocks on the floor, holding herself. "I don't want to go. I want to stay here," she cries.

"Please, Margie, you have to come with us," Zoe says, coaxing the woman to her feet. "You can't stay here by yourself."

Margie's eyes go wide around the edges. "But I'm scared…"

"Me too," Zoe says, squeezing the woman's shoulder.

Frog grabs his gear and rifle and passes the extra shotgun to Logan. "Everyone ready?" he asks, placing his hand on the silo door.

A chorus of yeses answer him even though there is no real "ready" for this kind of thing. We have no idea what's waiting for us outside. Will it be a bloodbath? Dead bodies everywhere?

Will it be Armageddon?

I brace myself, heart seizing, as Frog pushes open the door. Zoe moves to stand beside me. She grabs my sweaty hand, holding on to me for dear life.

I squeeze her thumb twice. *I got you,* I say silently. *Don't be afraid.* Then we step outside together.

The first thing I notice is how bright it is. Blindingly sunny and brutally hot again. It's still early, but I can already tell today is going to be another scorcher. I have to blink a few times to clear my vision and then shield my eyes with one hand to scan our surroundings.

The next thing I notice—how quiet it is. No chatter. No music. No footsteps or movement in the fields or any other sounds of life at all. No screams, though I take that part as a good thing.

That leaves three distinct possibilities: either the people who were still outside in the campgrounds last night have escaped or found a safe hiding spot like we did, the vampires have stopped trying to kill them, or the people are all dead.

I guess we'll find out soon enough which one it is.

Sweat pours from my brow and temples as we leave the safety of the silo and begin our trek past the Holloway farmhouse and to the RV. Frog and Logan take the lead, holding their guns at the ready, looking like zombie-hunting characters from *The Walking Dead.* Zoe, Chad, and I follow. I'd prefer to be up front with Logan, in charge, but even I understand that would be foolish without a weapon. You always put your best offense at the front. Dad taught me that.

Margie shuffles along behind us, glassy-eyed, shaking like a leaf. If I'm being honest, she doesn't look long for this world. Kade, of course, is at the back, as far away from everyone else as he can get.

We quickly pass the Holloway farmhouse and are back at the camping area again. While the few remaining vehicles and tents we'd seen last night still appear to be in place, the once bustling fields now seem to be devoid of any other humans besides us. It's so empty. Unnervingly so.

Where are all the people?

Zoe and I exchange glances, and I know she's thinking the same thing.

They can't *all* be dead, can they?

Besides, if they are dead, wouldn't there be more bodies? There's blood, yes. Now that it's daylight, I can see what I couldn't last night when we were walking home from the festival. Little puddles of red everywhere, like what remains after a light rain shower. A minor inconvenience to be stepped around.

But that's the only sign of something amiss. No human remains. No torn limbs or body parts. We don't even see any ripped-off clothing or missing shoes. If it weren't for the blood puddles, I might be questioning whether yesterday even happened.

Well, other than the fact the place is totally deserted...

We keep our footsteps light and soundless as we make our way through the campground to the RV. Each of us does our best to stay as quiet as humanly possible. I can feel the unease pouring off our group. Nostrils flare with heavy breath. Heads swivel in all directions. The back of my neck is damp with sweat, my clothes soaked through from a mix of the heat and also my ragged nerves.

A few minutes later, we reach the RV.

Logan opens the vehicle and urges us inside, closing the door quietly behind us. He's fast and precise, like a platoon leader, as he gathers up the weapons from the RV and hands them out methodically.

He takes the crossbow for himself and then passes me Jenny's uncle's shotgun. After Frog and him—who are both now armed with serious weapons—I'm the next best equipped to use the shotgun. Chad and Zoe have never even held a gun before. As for Margie, she's such a wreck she probably shouldn't be trusted to carry a butter knife. And Kade, well, I'm not sure if he can be trusted at all.

Of course, Chad throws a fit, wanting the shotgun for himself, but that's a nonstarter. He doesn't even know how to fire it properly or aim using the sights. He gets Logan's new Benchmade hunting knife instead.

After that, the only other weapons left in the RV are some kitchen knives in the drawers. Margie shocks us all with a sudden burst of energy, swiping the biggest and sharpest one—the butcher knife. That just leaves a pile of smaller steak knives for Zoe to choose from.

I almost say something and take the butcher knife back because, well, who the hell does Margie think she is? We don't know her. Why should she get to pick before Zoe?

But Zoe doesn't seem to care. Besides, I'm not sure it makes much of a difference. Somehow, I don't think knives, no matter how big, will help much with whatever is hunting us.

Plus, Margie is such a terrified pathetic mess. Scared of everything, even her own shadow. If carrying a butcher knife is going to make her feel even a little bit better during our journey and get her slow ass to move faster, that's a good thing.

Once we're done with weapons, we pack a few supplies

from the RV to take with us. Waters. Granola bars. Chocolate. Trail mix. Band-Aids. Soap. Napkins. Tylenol. Towels. Trash bags. Some of the vodka because Frog says it can be used as a disinfectant as a last resort. Chad—the moron—wants to take the beers, too, but Logan stops him. There's not enough room in our packs for everything, and beer is the least important.

Frog's backpack is already full of medicine, ammo, and supplies from the Holloway farmhouse, so we fill up Logan's pack with all the food and then Chad, Zoe, and I use our bags for the remaining supplies and waters. Once we've taken everything we can, Zoe and I quickly change out of our grimy festival outfits in the back of the RV and put on comfortable clothes and running sneakers. Then we all trudge back outside.

This time, with my sturdy shotgun in hand, I forge ahead with Frog and Logan. I feel so much better at the front. I'm always more comfortable when I'm in control. The straps of my heavy backpack dig into my shoulders as we push forward and head for the campgrounds exit.

We haven't gotten far when a twig snaps loudly in the distance. We all stop dead in our tracks, freezing in place.

CHAPTER 9

9:30 A.M.

Garlic Groove Festival Campgrounds

I scan the deserted festival campgrounds, searching for the source of the noise. A sweaty finger finds the shotgun's trigger, poised and ready for action. My heart drums in my chest as my body tenses, bracing for a fight.

Frog puts a finger to his lips. *Don't make a sound,* he says silently with his eyes.

Did something hear us?

Is someone coming for us?

Out of the corner of my eye, I think I see something move off in the distance. I whip around toward the tall trees that line the campgrounds, but there's nothing there.

We wait for what seems like forever, barely breathing, pulses racing. Time drags on. Minutes feel like hours as we trade looks back and forth, unsure what's out there and what to do.

Do we run? Stand our ground?

Eventually, when nothing comes for us, we decide we're safe for the time being and resume our journey.

On the way out of the campgrounds, we pass by a row of porta-potties that were set up for the festival crowd. Margie doesn't say anything to the rest of us as she takes off, racing toward the first open stall. She obviously has to go to the bathroom—badly.

Zoe and I peek at each other and shrug. Now is as good a time as any for this. Unlike the guys, it's not as easy for us to just go in a field, and I doubt there will be many other civilized bathrooms along our way to the river.

We follow after Margie while the guys go to the bathroom behind an empty camper a few yards away. We catch up to the older woman just as she reaches the nearest porta-potty. She swings the door open and lets out a guttural scream, backing up so hard and fast that she almost knocks Zoe and me to the ground. I throw a hand over her mouth to squelch her cries. The smell hits me a moment later.

It's a putrid, sour stench that assaults my senses, thick and suffocating, drenching me in foulness. My stomach churns violently, a gag reflex triggered by the sheer intensity of the odor, and that's even before I see the body.

What once was a woman sits on the toilet seat, slumped over. Bite marks ravage her broken neck. The rest of her body has also been brutally mutilated. Missing chunks of flesh reveal muscle and bone. Dried blood cakes the floor.

Margie's eyes roll backward, and she begins to heave while Zoe and I trade panicked looks.

Another dead body?

Up until this weekend, I'd never seen a dead person in my entire life. Now it's almost becoming commonplace. What the hell is happening?

My heart hammers wildly, drowning out all other

sounds. For an instant, my body is frozen in place, paralyzed by my revulsion and fear.

And yet, just like I quickly realized in the silo last night, I don't have time to sit around and dwell on my emotions the way I normally might be able to. That's a luxury I can no longer afford. In this new normal, all I can do is swiftly process horrible, sickening things and move forward, focusing only on survival and next steps. So that's exactly what I do.

Like nothing has happened, I try the other porta-potties, covering my nose and mouth as I check to see if they're usable. Thankfully, besides the horror show we just witnessed, the rest appear to be perfectly fine. Still, Zoe makes me stand guard outside the door of her porta-potty while she uses it. Once we've all taken our turns, we leave the campgrounds for good.

We stay close to the road at first. I don't like being out in the open. It makes me feel vulnerable, like a walking target. I'm on high alert the entire time, fingers twitching, muscles tensed, but there's nowhere else for us to go.

All around the route are empty fields. Frog explains that wheat and barley are grown on this side of town, but they require a lot of water. The drought has made it impossible for those crops to thrive this year.

After a mile or so, Frog points out a woodland of large Douglas fir trees up ahead. We rush to take shelter under their sparse canopy. The drought has taken its toll here too, leaving the branches scantily clad with brittle, brown needles that rustle dryly above our heads. Although not the lush, leafy hideaway I'd prefer, the parched undergrowth still offers some much-needed cover. And not just from whatever is out there preying on humans, but also from Mother Nature and her deadly heat. We're getting close to midday now, and it's hotter than I ever thought possible.

Frog and Logan make sure we take little sips of water as we walk, staying hydrated. We have a few bites of granola bars for lunch. Whatever we can get down while still moving along. There's no time for stopping. We're already going too slowly, though it's not for lack of trying. Most of us are athletic enough, but Margie is really holding things up.

The woman looks half dead as she stumbles along at an agonizing pace. Her shoulders hunch forward, limbs swinging with a certain lifelessness. Her gaze is vacant, fixated on nothing in particular, as if her eyes have long lost the ability to focus. The worst part is, I can't even yell at her to hurry up or threaten to leave her behind because we have to be so damn quiet.

I eyeball my phone again, hoping there might be reception now that we've gotten to a different part of town, but it's no use. Still no bars.

It's scary and unsettling to be so out of touch. Before this weekend, the longest I ever went without my cell phone was during a Pilates workout class. With no access to the outside world, I wonder how far this attack has extended. Is it just here in Allium Valley or have they already hit the next town over? Have they made it to Portland yet?

What about bordering states like Washington or California or even other countries like Canada?

I'm so caught up in my own thoughts, I don't realize the others have stopped walking. Logan grabs me by the shoulders, pulling me back, holding me in place.

Frog raises his hand. *Wait!* he mouths and points ahead.

An aged and weathered rectangular building looms in front of us, casting sinister shadows that dance across the sunbaked earth. The structure bears the scars of neglect and abandonment. Its walls are constructed from timber that's taken on an ugly, grayish hue over time. Patches of moss cling to the sides. Large, boarded-up windows with jagged edges and a corrugated metal roofing, now rusted by the elements, hint at a utilitarian past.

Adjacent to the building sits a red barn, with rows and rows of outdoor animal pens and empty feedlots. Big gaping water troughs sit in the overgrown grass, unused. Enclosing it all is a towering, industrial-sized chain-link security gate.

I shiver, fixated by the sight. The place evokes a sense of menace and foreboding, as if the timbers and nails hold whispers of misery that have unfolded within.

Something rumbles off in the distance. An incoming vehicle is approaching.

My chest tightens, nerves tensing, as we duck under the closest trees and watch silently as a cattle truck lumbers into view. Its red paint is faded and rusty, the sides constructed with vertical slats for livestock. I can see shapes moving within the cages. It looks like animals are in there.

Horses? Cows?

I can't tell from this far away.

The truck approaches the metal swing gate, and a hulking, muscular man appears. He unlocks the latch on the gate and waves the truck inside. Worn and weathered tires kick up clouds of dirt as the vehicle rumbles forward, leaving a dusty trail in its wake.

"That's the old cattle farm and slaughterhouse," Frog whispers. "I don't understand. It's been closed for years." He tilts his head, a hand shading his eyes as he scans the horizon and then inches closer for a better look. He takes a few steps forward and peers around the trees cautiously.

"What is it? What do you see?" Logan asks, his voice low and taut with anticipation.

Frog's body suddenly stiffens, his breath catching in his throat. *"Holy shit!"* Surprise etches across his face as he whirls around to face us, his words coming out in an excited rush. "There's people in the truck! They're getting out!"

"Odd time to reopen a cattle farm, isn't it?" I ask.

"I bet it's some kind of CCP!" Logan's eyes light up with excitement.

Zoe's brow wrinkles. "Huh? What's that?"

"A Casualty Collection Point," Logan explains. "It's a first aid triage spot, like a hospital. When there's a mass casualty event, the local government finds a place to triage and treat survivors. They do it in war, too, when they need to provide urgent care to the troops."

"Really?" I stare at the building, puzzled. "And you think they'd pick an old cattle farm? Isn't there some kind of medical center that would be better suited? Or even a school?"

"Actually, it makes a lot of sense," Frog says. "Plenty of open space and shelter."

Logan steps forward. "I'll go check it out."

I shrug. "Yeah, okay. Me too."

Kade grabs my wrist, holding me in place. "That's a bad idea."

"Hey! Watch it!" Pain flares up my arm, and I yank myself free, rubbing at my wrist.

"Shit. I'm sorry," he says, looking so apologetic I let it slide. I can tell he didn't mean to hurt me, but *damn*, he's strong. "But you're not going in there."

Logan steps in closer, getting in between Kade and me. His eyes narrow at the taller guy, shooting him a warning look. "I'm sure you're just trying to help, man, but we don't need your permission," he says.

Kade's gaze locks on mine, tinged with warning. "Please. It isn't safe."

"Why not?" Zoe asks. "Logan says it's a medical center."

"He doesn't know that," Kade snaps. "He has no idea what's going on there."

Logan reaches for me. "Come on, Alix. Let's go," he huffs, pulling me forward.

Kade exhales loudly, his frustration obvious. "Fine, but I'm going with you," he says, his gaze capturing mine with an intensity that sends a little flutter through me. "You shouldn't go alone."

"She isn't alone." Logan tightens his grip on my hand. "She's with me."

Chad shoots a worried glance at Logan. "We don't all have to go though, right?" he asks. "Can't the rest of us stay here while you scope it out?"

"I'm not going." Margie shakes her head, digging her motorcycle boots into the ground. "I don't like cattle farms."

"Yeah, you can stay," Logan agrees. "We'll be faster and less noticeable in a smaller group, anyway. I just want to get close enough to see what's going on."

"Nothing good," Kade mutters.

Logan ignores him. "We'll be back soon," he says to the rest of the group and turns to Frog, the only other person besides us with a useful weapon. "You stay here and hold down the fort."

"You got it." Frog salutes him. "Good luck."

Logan and I drop our bags, leaving them with the group so we can move faster.

"Ready?" Logan glances down at me and squeezes my hand. "In and out as fast as possible. Got it?"

I nod my understanding and tighten my grip on my shotgun.

Then we make a run for it.

CHAPTER 10
1:00 P.M.

The old Allium Valley Cattle Farm

The three of us trod cautiously through the tall, weed-like grass until we get to the imposing gate that encloses the factory farm. We scan the perimeter but don't see any people, not even the big guy who was manning the gate earlier. The truck we saw from afar is long gone by now.

It's quiet. Too quiet.

It sure doesn't sound like you'd imagine a busy triage center would sound—outtake attendants checking folks in, doctors and nurses running around, patients calling out for help, that sort of thing. But then again, we're still pretty far from the actual buildings.

Kade shakes his head, still looking pissed to be on this scouting mission, while Logan tries the latch to see if he can open the gate. No such luck. It's locked tight with a sturdy padlock that won't shake loose. It looks like the only option is to scale it.

My mouth goes dry as I stare up at the formidable barrier of steel and wire mesh. It's a monolithic structure, easily over fifteen feet tall. A daunting height meant to keep out trespassers. It's not that I'm afraid of heights—I'm not —but I've never climbed something like this. The closest I've gotten to doing anything even remotely similar was back in high school when I had to get to the top of the cheerleading pyramid at our varsity football games. And I didn't climb that myself; I was lifted up by my squad.

As we reach for the metal bars, Kade warns us—yet again—to be quiet and careful. That we don't know who or what is behind the gate, and we should assume they aren't friendly until proven otherwise. He's a bit of a broken record, and I can tell Logan—kind, sweet, easy-going Logan —is starting to lose his patience.

Kade, though gorgeous, is turning out to be a downer, a real glass-half-empty kind of guy.

Before we start our climb, Logan slings his crossbow over his back and takes my shotgun from my hands to make things easier for me. He goes first, skillfully maneuvering over the first level of chain link, showing me how it's done. I suck in a big breath, say a little prayer, and then scramble after him. Kade follows last.

The gate groans with our weight, a sound that seems to echo through the air, amplified by the stillness around us. We cast worried glances at each other and hold our breath, pausing, hanging in place.

Has anyone heard us? Will we get in trouble for trespassing?

When no one comes running, we continue our ascent. My fingers grasp each rung, every movement a deliberate challenge against gravity. Up and up we go.

Suddenly, my hand slips. I start to fall, heading for the ground at a rapid pace. I cry out, arms flailing, grasping nothing. Adrenaline pumps through my veins as I brace myself for impact.

But then a strong hand flies to my waist, steadying me and stopping certain disaster. I sigh with relief and glance over my shoulder. Kade is below me. His handsome brow is wrinkled with exertion, sweat dripping down his temple as he supports the weight of my body with one hand.

"Thank you," I whisper gratefully.

"Be more careful," he grumbles back, but I notice he doesn't let go of me until I've got a good grip on the gate again. And even after that, he stays right by my side, glued to my heels. He's barely an inch away from me at all times.

Finally, I get to the top and swing my legs over to the other side. Getting down is far easier, and I land seconds later with a soft thud. My body fills with joy, ecstatic to be on solid ground again. Logan hands me back my shotgun, and I watch as Kade hops down beside us with the grace of a big cat. I thought Logan was a great climber, but Kade makes him look like a total novice.

We clear the front pasture next and are close to the slaughterhouse building's doors when the smell hits me. I gag, choking. It's the most nauseating scent—like sweat, excrement, and something nasty and decaying all mixed together.

"What is that…?" I ask, holding a hand over my nose.

"Must be the cattle," Logan says.

Kade gives us a strange look. "There hasn't been any cattle around here for years."

We get to the front of the slaughterhouse, and Logan places a hand on the hulking double doors. Kade grabs his arm. "I really don't think we should go in there," he says. "We have no idea what's inside."

"Listen, man. I'm getting a bit sick of this," Logan says through clenched teeth. "If you're scared, you can wait here for us. We won't be long."

"I'm not *scared*," Kade hisses. "I'm just not some idiot who goes around barging into places I don't know anything about."

"Now wait a second." Logan flinches and his fists clench next to his thighs, balled up tightly. "Who're you calling an idiot?"

I suppress an eye roll. This is just what we need right now. An alpha male showdown.

"Relax, Logan." I put a hand on his shoulder. "He's just being careful."

My touch seems to calm him, and his fists loosen at his sides.

"Yeah, I get that." The angry lines on his face soften just a bit. "I just think he can be 'careful' out here by himself. No one's making him come inside," he says. "We don't need him, Alix."

Kade's eyes fix on my hand, resting perhaps too comfortably on Logan's arm. A shadow flickers across his face, his eyes darting between the two of us as the pieces fall into place. A hint of something—disappointment, maybe?—passes through his eyes before he schools his expression back into one of cool indifference.

"Ah, I see now," he says, taking a small step backward. "Look, man"—he glances over at Logan—"I'm not here to step on any toes between you and your girl." He gestures at me vaguely with a flick of his wrist. "I just don't want to see anyone get hurt, okay?"

"Oh no." I jerk my hand away from Logan in a swift, reflexive motion, my words tumbling out in a fluster. "He's not my boyf—"

"I couldn't care less," Kade says, cutting me off. "Your

dating status isn't important to me. What *is* important is no one getting killed. So how about we scope things out before we crash the party, yeah?"

"What are you suggesting, exactly?" Logan asks.

"Let's check things out first. Walk around some." Kade points behind the building and around the sides. "Look for windows or openings. Peek inside. Eyeball the barn. Pens and paddocks, too. Get a lay of the land."

The hard, defensive expression on Logan's face smooths out further. "We call that an R&S threat assessment in school," he says, nodding. "It's smart, actually, but it takes a lot of time. Time we don't have." His gaze turns up to the sky, worry etched across his face. The sun has lowered from the midpoint and is beginning its descent downward. It must be close to two o'clock now, from the look of things.

"Fair enough." Kade shrugs. "Forget all that then, but let's at least investigate the slaughterhouse. That work?"

"Yeah, sounds reasonable," Logan agrees, and the three of us back away from the front entrance.

We circle around the sides of the slaughterhouse first, like Kade suggested. All the doors and windows we encounter along the way are boarded up with wood and nails, preventing us from further investigation. It's a bit strange, but perhaps to be expected since the factory farm was abandoned years ago.

As we approach the rear of the building, the wailing surrounds us. Low, muffled sounds seeping through the building's walls. It's almost like people are crying.

Or screaming.

I stop in my tracks and steady my shotgun. "What's going on in there?" I ask, feeling a tightness in my chest. "That doesn't sound right, Logan."

"A triage center always has hurt and sick people inside. Probably badly injured too, judging from what we saw last night," he says nonchalantly. "Just keep going." He urges me forward with a wave of his hand.

With every step, the groans and cries intensify, raising my guard further. Regardless of what Logan believes, it doesn't sound like people are being medically treated and cared for inside these walls; it sounds like they're being tortured.

But what do I know?

I've never spent time in a hospital treatment ward or triage center. I don't even like to go to the doctor's office.

"Hey, what's that?" I ask, pointing to a small opening near the bottom of the back of the building. It looks like a window, but it's so close to the ground, not at all where you'd expect to typically see one. It's also barricaded, like the other windows we've seen, but a small hairline crack runs through the center of its wooden shutters. It's like someone has tried to break the opening from the outside, kicking through the plywood.

I kneel into the dirt to get a closer look.

"Careful," Logan says, grabbing onto my shoulder. His fingers dig deep into my muscles.

I push him away, grinning.

"Of what? I thought you weren't worried?" I tease.

I peer through the opening. I was right, it is a window.

The glass is old and dusty, the corners crusted over with dark brownish mud streaks, obstructing much of the view. I take the edge of my shirt to wipe the streaks away before realizing the streaks are on the inside—not the outside. And they're not brown. They're dark red.

Red like blood.

I bend down further, so close my nose is pushed up against the glass, and get my first view inside the slaughterhouse.

The window appears to lead to some kind of holding

room. A pen, perhaps. Dozens of people stand upright. For some reason, they all seem to be crammed together on one side. It's like they're trying to evade something in there with them. Their faces are terrified. Mouths open. Screaming.

I blink and my vision clears further to reveal what's on the other side of the room. It's a man. He lies on the ground, neck ripped open, blood gushing out. His skin is gray, tinged purple. Eyes glossed over, seeing nothing. He's dead, I think.

I hope.

Not long dead, though, judging by all the blood and the screaming.

But that's not even the worst part. It's the woman crouched above him, her legs straddling his chest.

From this angle, I can only see her profile, but I can tell she's beautiful. Glowing, bronzed skin. Long shiny hair the color of polished mahogany. Slender, ski-slope nose with an upturned tip. Her body is fit and toned in a matching teal workout set, the cute, trendy kind they sell at Lululemon or Alo. She could be a model—one of those gorgeous women on the glossy pages of a fitness magazine—except for all the blood, of course.

It drips down her long, swanlike throat as she guzzles at the dead man's neck. Then she moves onto his chest. She rips it wide open, chewing eagerly on muscle and human grizzle.

Suddenly, she turns and looks right at me. She must have seen me in the window reflection or sensed me staring somehow. Her sculpted arched brows go back, as if surprised for an instant, and then she smiles.

It's the scariest smile I've ever seen.

CHAPTER 11
1:50 P.M.

The old Allium Valley Cattle Farm

I recoil from the horrifying sight in the slaughterhouse window, a scream rising in my throat. It's like I'm stuck in a nightmare. I can't move; can't speak. Nothing computes in my brain except for those two sharp canines. Long as knives. Blood dripping down and splattering onto the grimy slaughterhouse floor.

"What is it?" Logan asks, instantly at my side. He grabs my elbow, pulling me away from the window. "What's wrong, Alix?"

"We have to go! *Now!*"

Logan doesn't require any further explanation. The two of us take off at full speed, Kade trailing behind, a few yards back.

A part of my brain registers confusion. Why isn't he keeping pace? Is he injured? Hurt?

But I don't have time to turn around and check. I can't think about anything else but getting out of there.

Oh my God... That woman...

What in God's name was she doing to that poor man?

My breath is ragged and urgent as we run. I extend all my energy, every muscle firing, every sinew straining. Faster and faster. I've never run like this before in my entire life, not even during track and field regionals.

An agonizing stitch in my ribs begs me to stop, but I ignore it, pushing through the pain.

Then we're at the fence.

Logan takes my gun from me again and scales the metal gate. He's already up and almost at the top by the time I grab the first rung.

I'm barely a foot in the air when someone grabs me from behind. Logan screams a warning, but he's too late. A forceful yank, so hard it feels like my ankle snaps, and then I'm on the ground. A knee mercilessly presses against my chest, holding me, but it doesn't feel like just a knee. It's like the force of a thousand pounds slamming down on me.

A man.

Protruding cheek bones. Sharp hawk nose. Mean eyes. Teeth.

Holy hell... Those teeth...

Long and sharp as a tiger's, they point right at my neck.

I kick and scream, but the man has arms like a vise. He squeezes so tightly, I can't move. I can barely breathe. If I had my shotgun I might have a fighting chance, but it's on the other side of the fence with Logan. Useless. Unreachable.

I'm trapped.

A gun cocks behind me. Logan readies his shot, but the supernaturally strong man, the *vampire*—whatever he is—is already lowering his fangs to my neck.

A scream catches in my throat. I squeeze my eyes shut, bracing for death. There's nothing left to do but pray it at least comes quickly.

And then I hear a guttural roar. Loud. Strong. It reverberates throughout my entire body.

Kade!

I don't know how but he's there, ripping me from the edges of death, pulling me from the monster's grasp. He shoves me toward the fence. To freedom.

My fingers clutch metal and I gasp, one hand flying to my throat. My fingers examine the warm skin there, as if in disbelief. My neck—it's still intact.

I'm still alive!

I stand paralyzed; in shock. I can't believe how close I was to death. I'm unable to make my hands or legs work. Unable to even attempt to climb the fence and get away.

In front of me, Kade growls with rage and charges at the vampire. His fine-featured face is white, cold with fury. A killing light illuminates those dark eyes. His entire body emanates pure anger and menace as both men go flying to the ground.

"Alix! Run!" Logan screams at me, but I can't do anything except watch in horror as Kade battles with the vampire.

It doesn't seem like it should be much of a fight.

The vampire is larger than Kade. Taller. Bigger. Sharp fangs snap in Kade's direction. Yet somehow, Kade holds his own.

They trade powerful punches. Kicks. Throws. Miraculously, Kade gets his arms around the vampire's beefy waist and pins him to the ground.

"Go!" he yells at me, his face red with exertion. "I can't hold him for long!"

That's when it all clicks.

Finally, I understand why Kade has always trailed after us, always walking behind at the back of the group. It's not that he dislikes us or wants to keep his distance, like I thought. Not even close.

This whole time, he's been playing defense. Protecting us. Watching. Waiting to confront anything that might ambush us from the rear.

"Alix—GO!"

The terror in Kade's voice frees me from my temporary paralysis. I race over the fence, fast as a spider monkey, and rush into Logan's waiting arms on the other side.

Logan reaches for my hand, urging me forward, but I can't help it. I have to look back.

On the other side of the gate, Kade still struggles with the vampire. His forehead is bloody, a nasty gash above his right temple, but he's still on his feet. That's good. But he's unarmed and outmatched. His luck won't last forever.

And once he's dead, that vampire is going to come after us. The only hope for Logan and me is to put as much distance between us and the vampire now, while he's distracted with Kade, and hope it buys us enough time to escape.

But instead of running—as any rational person would—I grab my shotgun from Logan. My hand shakes, sweat dripping into my eyes as I point the barrel between the gaps in the mesh metal fence. I grit my teeth. Steady my aim. I don't have time to over-analyze things. I just hold the gun steady and pull the trigger, like Dad taught me.

Bang!

My jaw drops with shock.

Bullseye.

The bullet goes clean through the attacker's head on my first try. Blood splatters. Vampire brains go everywhere. The man stops moving and slumps over dead.

"Damn..." Kade stares at me, half stunned, half admiring, and lets out a low whistle of appreciation.

I can't help grinning. "I know, right?"

But we don't have time to sit and mull over my apparently awesome shooting skills because someone else is coming out of the factory, heading straight for us.

Fast as lightning, Kade climbs the gate and lands next to me. Together, the three of us race for the woods.

When we finally reach our friends, the wave of endorphins evaporate and I'm left with nothing but exhaustion. My legs buckle beneath me, and I collapse onto the forest floor. Dirt and dead leaves dig into my palms as I keel over, wheezing, each breath a battle.

"Oh my God! Are you okay?" Zoe rushes to my side, dropping to her knees. Her hand finds mine, her grip a lifeline.

Chad hovers over us. "What happened?"

I don't even have enough energy to answer. I'm too tired for words. Too sweaty. Too sore, all over, in muscles I didn't even know existed. I just lie in the dirt and pant like an old dog.

"I was... wrong," Logan says, breathing heavy, head hanging between his legs as he tries to recover. "Not... a... triage... center..."

"What was it then?" Frog prods. "What's going on over there?"

"Vampires..." Logan pauses, taking another shaky breath to steady himself. "And they're... they're keeping people."

"Keeping people? What do you mean?" Zoe asks.

I see that monstrous woman's face again in my head, ripping into that man's body. Shivering, I curl my knees into my chest like a baby. "Like cows," I whisper, finding my voice. "To *eat*."

"I knew it!" Margie sobs, shoulders shaking. "There's nothing here anymore. Nothing but death…"

It's so much more horrible than I ever could have imagined. Worse than my worst nightmare. Nothing could have prepared me for this. All the books and movies in the world —it's nothing like what I just witnessed. These vampires aren't the stuff of romance, and they don't sparkle in the sun. They're hungry. Bloodthirsty. Deadly.

We barely made it out of the cattle farm alive, and that was just one of them. How many more are there running around this town? Five? Ten? A dozen?

Hundreds?

I uncurl from my little ball and scan the woods, heart clenching in my chest. Did we escape? Or are they still after us?

Hell, they probably are.

Of course, they are. Can't let a warm dinner get away, right?

Branches snap a few feet away. I gasp, jerking around in fear, but it's only a rabbit.

"You don't look so good, Al," Zoe says, helping me back to my feet. I lean against her, slumping into her side.

"She'll be okay," Kade says, his steady gaze meeting mine, giving me a reassuring nod. "We just have to get to the river."

Zoe's still watching me, eyes wide with concern. "Maybe we should take a minute. Let her rest." She snaps her fingers at Chad. "Babe, get her some water!"

Chad hands me his drink, and I gratefully take a few sips before passing it back to him. "I'm fine," I say, gritting my teeth and wiping off blood from my skinned knees. "Kade's right. We have to move before they catch us."

Chad glances around, confused. "But I don't see anyone—"

"Just fucking go!" I yell, still so shaken, I forget we're supposed to be quiet.

Something stirs again in the woods behind us, but this time I don't bother to turn around and look. I take off running.

I run.

And run.

And I don't stop.

CHAPTER 12
3:30 P.M.

Four miles from the Devil's River

Eventually, we get to a spot that seems like a safe distance away from the cattle farm. We slow our pace down to a brisk walk. We pause. Stretch. Take time to catch our breath.

I'm light-headed. My entire body is exhausted and weak, like overcooked spaghetti. So tired from all the running and the fear. It probably doesn't help that I've barely eaten anything all day besides the granola bar earlier. After what happened at the factory farm, we've all been too scared to stop long enough to eat more.

Even Margie has managed to keep pace with the rest of us somehow, though I notice that she's starting to limp. With the adrenaline slowing down, it's beginning to take its toll, and not just on her, but on all of us.

The sun starts its descent behind the trees. We've got just a few remaining hours of daylight left to get to the river.

The trek from one side of town to the other has taken far longer than Frog told us it would. In a car, the trip would probably only take twenty minutes. But, today, on foot—anxious and tired and in this damn heat—it's taking forever.

At this point, I'm so spent I don't even care about being in control anymore. I lag somewhere in the middle of the group, biceps aching as I drag my shotgun along behind me. Frog and Logan remain at the front, but Kade has given up his usual position at the rear to walk beside me instead. Every now and then, I catch him sneaking little sidelong glances my way, as if reassuring himself I'm okay. It's like he now feels some sort of responsibility for me after rescuing me from that vampire.

I'm not mad about it, though. He's basically saved my life at least twice now—first at the Holloway farmhouse and then at the cattle farm—and we're only two days into the vampire apocalypse. In other circumstances, if things weren't so totally and completely messed up, I might be flattered by all his attention. I just wonder what's behind it.

Your dating status isn't important to me...

His harsh words from earlier echo in my head. He's made it pretty clear he has no romantic interest in me whatsoever. So what then? Why does he seem to care so much if I live or die?

It's a mystery.

Kind of like Kade himself, I guess.

Behind us are Zoe and Chad. I can hear him whisper funny little things in her ear as they walk, making her giggle, distracting her from the horror of our circumstances. Sometimes, when I turn to check on her, I catch a glimpse of him reaching for her hand and holding on tightly.

He presses her fingers into his skin, as if making sure she's still alive. He kisses her cheeks. Her forehead. Coaxes her to drink more water and massages the back of her neck and shoulders when she complains of muscle cramps. As much as he gets on my nerves, I have to admit he's good for my best friend. It's obvious how much he cares about her. It doesn't fully redeem him, but I guess it makes him a little bit less of a douchebag.

Margie is the last of us.

Her limp is getting worse, and she has great difficulty keeping up. Her skin has turned an ashen, pale shade. Lips white and crusty. Sweat pours off her in waves, soaking through her clothes. I'm no doctor, but she doesn't seem well. She looks sick, like she might have something bad, and it might be spreading.

No one would ever accuse me of being particularly nice, but if I had more energy, I might go back there and check on her. Help her keep up and encourage her to keep going. That's how bad I feel for her; that's how awful she appears.

Unfortunately, I'm barely able to put my own two feet in front of each other. This is survival of the fittest now, and I can't spare my energy on a stranger—especially one that seems like she's so close to death already.

It's silent around us as we forge onward, the only sounds are our heavy breathing and the light crunching of our shoes against dirt and dry leaves. Sometimes I hear snippets of faraway noises, like screams or cries of people or even gunshots off in the distance, but I ignore it.

We all do. We act like we don't hear them.

There's nothing we can do about it, anyway. We're at half capacity. We can't help anyone. We can barely help ourselves.

Margie starts to cry softly behind me. She blubbers about how there's no hope; no way to escape the monsters. I know I should feel bad. It's so sad and pathetic watching her spiral. But all I can think about is that she's making too much noise and is endangering the rest of us with all her nonsense. I wish she'd either shut the hell up or fuck off. Her tears, and the racket of all her sobbing, are an indulgence that'll get us killed.

Of course, Zoe is like an angel to the woman. She takes pity on her, ignoring Chad's eyerolls as she leaves his side and drops back to keep Margie company. She grabs Margie by the arm and pulls her along, shushing her gently and patting at her hand.

Zoe is such a good person. A better person than I'll ever be, that's for sure. Too bad being good has nothing to do with survival. In a life or death situation, being nice can get you killed. Just look at what happened to my mom, trying to save that stupid fucking cat.

I give Zoe a warning glare and motion for her to leave Margie's side. I don't like Zoe being all the way at the back of the group where I can't easily keep tabs on her.

Zoe pretends like she doesn't see me and continues to help the woman, which only slows her down, too. Now both of them are falling behind the rest of us.

I groan and double back to join them. At least if I'm there, Zoe and I can both drag Margie along faster.

With Zoe's caretaking and cajoling, Margie's sobs eventually slow and become just pitiful little hiccups. It's an improvement, but it's still too much sound as far as I'm concerned.

I just want to be done with all this already. I want to get somewhere safe where I can lie down and rest. I want to sleep and sleep. Maybe if I sleep, I can pretend the last twenty-four hours have just been one bad dream.

I feel like Alice in Wonderland. I've fallen down the rabbit hole and popped up in some insane, imaginary, deranged world. A world where vampires are real and one of them almost killed me.

I grimace, still seeing those terrifying fangs coming for

my neck. And then I see the slaughterhouse… For as long as I live, I'll never be able to get the horrific image of that woman eating that man out of my head.

I dig my fingernails into my palms painfully until they make crescent-shaped little indents. Then I curl and uncurl them, just to test and make sure I can still feel. That I'm still here and alive. That this isn't all one horrible hallucination.

"You all right?" Kade asks, dropping back so he can keep walking with me.

"Just peachy," I whisper.

I peer over at him. The gnarly gash above his right temple from his fight with the vampire, the injury that looked like it would need stitches, is already starting to heal. It's not even bleeding anymore. I guess it wasn't as bad as I thought.

"You feel okay? Does it hurt?" I ask, reaching out to touch the cut.

"I'm fine." He pushes my hand away.

"Okayyy…"

He stares down at me intently as we move side by side, as if he's some kind of examining doctor and I'm his sick patient.

"Here—have some," he says gruffly and hands me his plastic water bottle.

I don't even mind the bossiness. I rip the drink from his hands and gulp it down greedily. I didn't realize until this very moment how thirsty I am.

I empty it all, finishing the entire bottle and then wiping away the excess moisture from my lips, wishing I could drink that too.

"Sorry," I say, even though I'm not sorry at all.

"Better?" he asks.

I shrug. Better is a subjective term right now.

"Got any more?" I ask.

He gives me a crooked smile. "Take it easy, Sniper. You don't want to overdo it."

"Whatever." I wave him away, not really in the mood for his unsolicited advice, even if he is right.

Back in my track and field days, coach always lectured us about the dangers of excessive water intake. So yeah, I'm well aware it's best to avoid too much water after physical exertion so you don't get hyponatremia, but all I really want is to guzzle more of it. I'm so tired. So dehydrated. So—

I stumble over a tree branch jutting out of the ground. Before I can go tumbling into the tangled underbrush, Kade catches me. He grips my elbow, anchoring me until I get my footing again.

"Careful!" he warns.

"I got it. Thanks." I jerk my arm away, embarrassed.

What is wrong with me?

Clumsiness like this is out of character for me. I've always been athletic. In high school, I was the girl who lettered in three varsity sports—track and field, volleyball, and cheer. It's not that I was so much into athletics, but sports looked good on college applications, and I couldn't leave anything up to chance. Mom was counting on me to get into a good school. As for cheer, all the popular girls were cheerleaders at my high school, so that was a given.

When I got to NSU, I wasn't good enough to make the Division I teams, but I kept in shape. I traded the outdoor track for a treadmill at the gym, and I still use my pom-poms on my sorority dance team. We've won the Panhellenic Greek Week competitions four years in a row.

Normally, a day hike like this wouldn't even make a blip on my radar, but that close brush with death and all the running today is seriously making me drag ass.

Kade's eyes narrow as he continues watching me.

"You don't look so good."

"Gee. Men usually tell me the exact opposite," I say sarcastically. "If this is your way of flirting, you should know you suck at it."

"Maybe you should take a quick break?" he suggests.

"Maybe you should mind your own business."

I keep plodding on ahead.

Even if I wanted to, I can't stop now. Not when we have to get to the river, and the sun is dropping so rapidly in the sky.

As I continue onward, I feel the weight of my backpack lift from my shoulders. Spinning around, I find Kade smirking at me. My bag is now slung effortlessly over his side.

"Excuse me?" I snap, surprised and a bit irritated. "What do you think you're doing?"

"Helping you out, obviously," he says. He raises an eyebrow, his smile widening. "You're welcome, by the way."

I make a grab for my backpack, but he sidesteps my attempts with the grace of a cat.

"I'm not some silly damsel in distress," I huff, placing my hands on my hips. "I can carry my own stuff, thank you very much."

"I don't doubt that for a second," he drawls, scanning me up and down with an amused glint in his eyes. "But let's be honest, I can carry it better, and if we want to see the river before nightfall, you might need to pick up the pace." He reaches for my shotgun next. "May I?"

I grip the gun to my chest. "Back off, Sticky Fingers."

The backpack is one thing. Truth is, I already feel a thousand times better without it. But not the gun. Not after what happened at the cattle farm earlier. I won't be caught by surprise like that again.

He chuckles softly, a sound that's both infuriating and a little bit charming. "As you wish. Just remember, I offered," he says and gestures me forward with a cocky tilt of his head. "After you, Sniper."

It's unreal. I'm still huffing and puffing, sweating up a storm, even without the pack anymore, but Kade has no problems at all. The guy is barely out of breath as he strides along. He's clearly in amazing shape.

I think back to the fight earlier. He'd fought off that monster—that vampire—I still don't know how. Frog said that vampires were stronger than humans, though I guess he never said by how much. I'm not sure if these blood suckers are supposed to have superhuman strength or just the same strength as a really, really strong person. If all the other vampire lore doesn't apply, like the holy water or daylight being deadly to them, then I don't know if anything else I've seen in movies or TV is true or not.

Still, even if that vampire didn't have crazy supernatural powers, he was a big dude that would've been difficult to take on in any circumstances. Yet, Kade had done well fighting him. Very well, in fact.

Kade may be a tad arrogant, and aloof, and resistant to my considerable womanly charms, but I realize we're lucky to have him with us. He's strong. Fast. Smart. And he's got great instincts. He'd been right about the slaughterhouse, even when everyone else had disagreed with him. Who knows what would've happened back there if he hadn't been with us and kept warning us not to go barging inside those front doors...

"How much longer until the river?" Zoe asks, watching the sky with a worried look. It's almost dusk. We have maybe another hour, tops, to get to this magic river that's supposed to protect us.

"Almost there," Frog says. "Just another mile or so."

Chad groans. "You said that an hour ago."

"Walk faster then!" Frog barks.

"I'm hungry," Margie says. "When do we eat dinner? You said we could eat soon."

Frog rolls his eyes. "Would you rather eat, or would you rather be eaten?"

"But I'm so hungry. Please…"

God, will she ever shut up?

I rub at my temples. My whole body is beginning to throb like one massive migraine.

"Surely, we can eat and walk, can't we?" Zoe asks, rubbing gently at Margie's shoulders.

"Please, can we?" Margie begs. "Just a little something to hold us over?"

Frog and Logan agree to divvy up our provisions as we keep moving. I watch as they split up the food in Logan's backpack, figuring out what we can eat now and what to save for the days to come.

It seems that they both have experience with the best ways to ration food in situations like this. Logan from his ROTC Field Training classes and Frog—well, I don't know how he knows these things… I guess from whatever doomsday survival prepper shit he's obviously into?

In their combined "expert" judgment, they agree everyone in the group should get a few handfuls of trail mix and a maximum of one bottle of water. Even though we're almost to the river, we still have to conserve our current water supply until we have time to gather firewood and boil the river water to purify it.

I think about complaining. We've walked for miles without much food or water all day. Surely, a couple of nuts aren't enough nutrients to hold us over. I'm fucking *starving*!

Besides, even worst-case scenario, we already know there's game in the woods like the rabbits we saw earlier. Logan and I can hunt. We can fish. I bet Frog can, too. He has that look. And we can scavenge houses for food as well, if we need to. We've got plenty of options. There's no need to panic.

But in the end, I'm more tired than I am hungry. I simply don't have the energy to argue, so I take my nut mix with a smile and finish it all in one big gulp.

"Alix, you need to chew!" Logan says, a concerned expression on his face as he watches me. "Eat slowly so you don't choke."

I roll my eyes and gulp down another handful of trail mix. Then I drain my water bottle. "Good news," I say with a little burp. "I'm still alive."

"Can't we eat more?" Chad asks, frowning. He's already finished his food, too. "This is barely enough calories for a toddler."

"Me too. I need more," Margie cries.

Logan shakes his head. "We need to conserve to be safe. We don't know how long we'll be stuck at the river."

Margie's eyes water. "Please—I'm so hungry!"

"It'll be okay." Zoe rubs Margie's back soothingly. "Logan's being smart. It's just for a little bit," she says as she takes tiny pecks at the nuts and raisins in her hand like a bird.

I admire Zoe's restraint. In hindsight, I wish I'd eaten my food slower, too. My stomach is already grumbling something loud and painful, begging for more nutrients, but I've got nothing new to give it.

Margie stops in her tracks.

"Wait a second, this place looks familiar…" She tilts her head, eyes darting around the forest. Her fingers snap, crisp in the quiet. "Now I remember! We were here the other day, hiking. Lisa wanted to see the river before the festival." A gleam lights up her eyes, her tone pitching higher with enthusiasm. "There's a shortcut right around here. It's not far at all!"

Frog looks confused. "Are you sure? I remember the river being at least another mile or so…"

Margie shakes her head, a shadow crossing over her features as the sun temporarily ducks behind some cover. "No, no. I'm certain of it. It's just around the bend," she says, stepping forward, beckoning us onward with a smile that doesn't quite reach her eyes. "Follow me."

CHAPTER 13

5:45 P.M.

One mile from the Devil's River

For the first time all day, Margie leads the way, hobbling ahead through the parched and brittle canopy of forest that is both oppressive and liberating. Logan and Frog flank her sides at the front while the rest of us follow behind.

Despite her limp, Margie moves faster now than I've ever seen her move. She seems to have gotten a second wind —or a first one. Perhaps it's a burst of energy from the food or the urgency of the situation. The day is almost over. We don't have much longer now to make it to the river and to safety.

The sun continues dropping below the tree line. Its farewell rays struggle through the foliage, casting shadows that stretch and merge, morphing the forest's beauty into something a bit more sinister. The scent of pine and dusty earth fills my nose. It's a pungent, grounding aroma that now seems tinged with the metallic hint of danger.

The closer we get to nightfall, the more alert, the more on edge I become. Every sense now is heightened. I'm keenly aware of each crackle and rustle in the underbrush as we walk, every sound magnified in the growing silence. Even the trees themselves seem to make noises, their dry leaves whispering secrets. A chill seeps through my clothes, despite the heat.

Kade moves with a quiet assurance beside me, his gaze alert and vigilant as he scans the forest path ahead. I can feel the tension in him, like a coiled spring ready to unleash. He, too, seems to be getting more anxious as we get closer to sundown.

"Are you sure this is the right way?" Frog's deep voice breaks the silence. He cocks his head to the side. "I could swear the river is the other way," he says and points to the right of us, in the opposite direction. "Don't you think so, Kaden?"

"Not sure." Kade shrugs. "Never spent much time by the river, to be honest."

"No, no. It's just up ahead," Margie says, her voice ragged with heavy breathing. Her skinny, sinewy arms pump up and down as she pushes ahead. "Keep going. We're almost there."

"This is ridiculous," Chad grumbles. "How much longer is this going to take?"

"Relax, babe." Zoe links her elbow with his. "We'll be there soon."

"We better be."

Chad's lips thin with irritation as he glares at Margie's back. Zoe just shakes her head at him with an amused grin and drags him along.

Up ahead, Margie stumbles over a tree branch and her sharp, pained cry pierces the air.

Logan reacts instantly, rushing to her side. The rest of us

catch up a moment later and then hang back a few feet, letting Logan handle things and giving him and Margie space.

"Are you okay?" Logan asks her, concern etching his features.

He extends a hand to help her up, but she refuses, shaking her head as she rocks back and forth on the ground. She clutches desperately at her ankle, pain contorting her face.

"I think I twisted it!" She gasps. *"Oh, it really hurts!"*

"I'll get the Tylenol!" Zoe says and starts to rummage through our bags for the pain meds.

"Deep breaths," Logan says, giving Margie's shoulder a comforting squeeze. "You're going to be all right." He leans his crossbow and backpack up against the nearest tree stump to free his hands and then drops to his knees to examine her. "Let me see it," he says softly, reaching for Margie's injured leg.

That's when it happens.

Margie's expression shifts, the pain on her face vanishing like a light switch turning off. In one swift motion, she pulls out the butcher knife from behind her back—*our* butcher knife, the one we gave her at the RV because we felt bad for her—and uses it to stab Logan in the shoulder.

She plunges the blade in so hard, so viciously, he tumbles over in shock. His cry of pain cuts right through me.

"Logan!" I scream, lunging forward.

My heart clenches with fear and then anger as my finger finds the trigger on my shotgun. I line up the barrel and lower my gaze to the sights, aiming. I'm going to *kill* this bitch!

Frog curses, swinging his rifle around toward Margie as well, but the woman is fast, faster than we ever suspected. Before either of us can get a shot off, she's already got

Logan's backpack and is disappearing into the shelter of the trees. She flees to the right of us, exactly in the direction that Frog kept saying the river was.

I sprint to Logan's side, a cold shiver of dread racing down my spine. His face is ghostly pale, a stark contrast to the bright crimson blood oozing from the gash on his shoulder. It soaks his shirt, a growing stain that seeps into the forest floor. I press my hands against the wound, applying pressure to stem the flow of blood.

"You're okay, Logan," I say, keeping my voice steady despite the panic swirling inside me. "It's going to be okay."

Chad takes a step in the direction where Margie took off, ready to give chase, but Kade grabs him roughly by the shoulders and holds him in place. "Get off me, bro!" Chad yells, thrashing around, trying to shake free.

"Don't!" Kade hisses.

"That bitch stabbed Logan! And she's got our food!"

"It could be a trap," Kade says. "Let her go."

Zoe edges over, trying to catch Chad's eye. "Please, listen to him, babe," she says, reaching for Chad's hand, trying to calm him down.

While Kade and Zoe deal with Chad, I attend to Logan's stab wound. I rip a piece of fabric from the bottom of his shirt, fashioning an impromptu bandage for him, and carefully wrap it around his shoulder. Just tight enough to hold the dressing in place but not so tight as to cut off his circulation.

Thank goodness, the wound isn't all that deep—it's already stopped bleeding. His body shakes while I clean things up as best as I can, but I sense it's more a physical reaction to the shock and betrayal than to the actual injury.

"Thanks, Alix," he says, his voice strained but steady. His eyes meet mine, filled with a mix of pain and gratitude.

"It's not too bad. You're going to be fine." I squeeze his shoulder and try to sound as comforting as possible.

His face fills with disbelief. "I can't believe she *stabbed* me..."

"We have to keep moving," Kade says, urgency lacing his words. He scans the surrounding woods, eyes sharp and calculating as they flicker about anxiously. "There's no telling what else that woman is capable of. She may not be working alone, either."

"Sun's setting, too," Frog says and points to the darkening sky, now a canvas of deepening blues and purples. "We need to get to the river—while we still can."

Kade bends down in a swift motion and secures Logan's crossbow, slinging it over his shoulder. Then he reaches out a hand to help Logan up.

Logan takes it, his grip hesitant at first. I can see the clench of Logan's jaw, the way his pride fights against his need for support. But survival trumps all, and he allows Kade to pull him to his feet, steadying him.

"Thanks, man," he grunts at Kade.

Frog leads us away in the other direction this time, the way he originally said we should go before Margie tricked us all with her made-up short cut.

As we hurry along, the forest seems darker to me, the shadows longer. Margie's deception is a reminder of the world we now live in. A world where survival is the only currency and trust needs to be earned, not just freely given away. Not everyone is what they seem.

Margie fooled us all.

She was never the helpless victim she pretended to be. I don't even know any more if that limp was even real or fake. It's unclear if she'd been playing the long game and this had been her plan all along, or if something changed after we discovered the cattle farm and realized the vampires' real plans for us.

Did something inside Margie snap when she heard about how bad things were inside the slaughterhouse?

I suppose we'll never know why she repaid our kindness with a stab in the back. Why she stole all our food, leaving us in grave danger, after we'd saved her life. The only thing we know for sure: she wasn't a feeble, pathetic lady, after all. She was a ruthless snake in the grass, just biding her time to strike.

I feel so stupid for falling for her act. I promise myself right then and there that I won't be tricked again. Not by anyone.

Margie's treachery won't be the end of me and my friends, but it is a wake-up call. It's yet another hurdle in this twisted game of life and death that we've all been thrust into.

And this is a game I'm not about to lose.

CHAPTER 14
7:00 P.M.

Devil's River

We get to the Devil's River just in time.

Overhead, the sun is almost gone as the sky threatens to turn black with the approaching night. The only light comes from the twinkling stars above and the moon as it takes its position overhead, casting an ethereal glow over the river's gentle ripples. Silver beams of moonlight dance on the water's surface, creating a play of shadows in the night.

There's still no signs of life anywhere else. No lights on buildings or houses off in the horizon. No sounds except for the river rushing, a soft echoing melody, interrupted only by the occasional hoot of an unseen owl and the chirping of crickets gathered by the banks.

Frog lets out a wild yelp of joy.

No longer worried about being quiet, he races to the river's edge and gets on his knees, laughing like a maniac as he cups water in his hands. He splashes it all over his face and body. Eagerly, he motions for us to join him.

After the rest of us make our way down, I kneel beside my friends and take off my shoes, dipping my toes in the river's edge. The fresh water is cool and refreshing, like salve against the heat. I wash my face and hands, cleaning away the sweat and grime of the day. Water seeps through my dirty fingernails—broken and cracked. The sparkly pink manicure I'd been so proud of for the festival weekend is long gone and ruined.

I catch a glimpse of my reflection in the water, and it startles me. I barely recognize myself.

My skin is sunburned. Red, flaky, and a bit crusty on my chin and cheeks. Strands of greasy, clumpy, dirty blonde hair hang drably around my face. The feature everyone always compliments me on—my cornflower blue eyes—are bloodshot and weary. I spot a small ugly bruise below my left eye, though I'm not sure how it got there. With my fingertips, I trace the blues and purples and am surprised to find the skin is tender and swollen.

I guess a vampire apocalypse isn't exactly good for your looks.

I snort softly at my own lame joke, the sound barely more than an ironic scoff. But soon, I'm collapsing, laughter overtaking me with such force that I'm sprawled out on the river's muddy edge, my sides aching as tears cascade down my face. It feels so good. It's like all the stress and fear I've been carrying around since yesterday lifts right off my chest. I can breathe again.

For once in my life, I find that I don't care that I don't look beautiful. I don't care that I didn't wear sunscreen and got burned today, probably earning me a few wrinkles. I don't even care that the bruise on my cheek is going to get bigger and turn black, and I have no makeup to cover it up.

I'm still here.

I'm *alive*.

That's all that matters.

"I've never seen you like this before," Logan says, taking in my muddy and torn clothes and my worn-out, ragged face as he stands next to me. I, Alix Ford Summerlin—the most-wanted, most stylish, most admired co-ed at NSU—look like a complete dumpster fire.

I grin. "Me neither."

"I kind of like it," he says, and then laughs along with me as our eyes lock. The way he looks at me makes me feel like I'm being wrapped up in a warm, cozy blanket. It's nice.

Maybe more than nice.

After everything that's happened today, it feels like exactly what I need.

As we settle in for the night, Frog takes out towels from our bags and spreads them around on the grass of the riverbanks so we can lay down. He picks a spot so close to the water, our feet are practically in it. I curl up next to Zoe, and Chad and Logan take the empty spaces on either side of us, blocking us in, guarding us.

True to form, Kade makes camp far away from the rest of us, up the slopes of the riverbank. He turns away, facing outward. He wants a clear view of the forest and any threats that might come our way. I understand his logic but find I'm a little disappointed. I was kind of getting used to having him close by, keeping an eye on me.

"How long do you think we'll be stuck here?" Zoe asks, yawning as she snuggles in beside me. "Do you think the police are on the way? Or the Army?"

"I wouldn't count on it," Frog says. "Local police are probably all dead by now—or hiding. And the chances of anyone outside Allium Valley knowing about this yet are slim. It's only been a day. It'll take time before they start to suspect things."

"Okay, but we're safe for now, right?" Chad asks. "We're by the water like you said? So that's good, isn't it?"

Frog nods. "For now, yeah."

I glance down at my cell phone. The battery is almost dead, and still no bars, even in this new part of town. I guess cell service isn't working here, either.

"Phones are still out," I say.

"We should turn them off, if you haven't already," Logan says and reaches over to power down my cell phone for me. "Best to conserve the battery until this all blows over."

"You really think it'll blow over?" Zoe asks with a hopeful note.

"I mean, it has to," Logan says. "It's just a matter of time."

Frog snorts. "Not necessarily."

"Yeah, necessarily," Logan insists. "Even if those things —whatever they are—have managed to temporarily shut off the power and phones here, eventually people outside Allium Valley will realize something's wrong. And when they do, someone will come for us."

Frog bolts upright, his face turning red and blotchy. "Buddy, with all due respect, I'm not sure you understand what's going on here," he says. "Every day, those *things* are getting stronger. They're multiplying. They'll take over more land and kill more people until there's no one left to fight." His voice rises, trembling with urgency. "If something doesn't change, and fast, they'll take over this entire planet, and we'll all wind up some distant memory like the fucking dinosaurs."

A suffocating silence descends on us, as deep and as dark as the river at night. We all exchange worried glances, unspoken fear flickering in our eyes. Chad, paler than I've ever seen him, breaks the hush with an audible gulp that seems to echo in the tense air.

"Well, that's fucking bleak, bro…"

The ghost of a smile plays on Zoe's lips as she looks over at Chad. "It does seem a bit over the top," she agrees, curling in closer to him, resting her head on his shoulder. "I know things are tough, sure, but even at our lowest, we've still got to stay hopeful."

"Couldn't agree more," Logan says. "It's about mental toughness as much as firepower, that's the ROTC way." He slides one hand behind his head, nestling into the riverbed's uneven embrace, and elevates his wounded arm on a pillow of tangled grass and dirt. "Seriously, man, I think you watch a little too much TV." He gives a big yawn in Frog's direction. "This isn't some crazy alien invasion movie. This is real life."

"Who's talking sci-fi?" Frog's face pulls into an affronted frown. "This is history. It's called colonization, and it's been happening on this planet for hundreds of years."

"Dude, what are you even talking about?" Chad asks.

Frog clasps and unclasps his hands, visibly struggling to contain his irritation. "Ever heard of Christopher Columbus? Look what happened to the Native Americans," he says. "Hell, look at how we treat livestock. Cattle and pigs and chickens. Branding them, and putting them in cages and slaughterhouses."

Logan scoffs. "I'd like to see those vampires colonize a team of Navy SEALs."

A chill crawls up my spine as the horrific memories of what I saw inside the factory farm play in my head again. I hate to believe it, or even just think it, but Frog has a point. It seems like the vampires have already started their colonization of the human race right here in Allium

Valley. Who's to say they won't keep spreading like Frog suggests?

"Frog is right." I shiver. "You didn't see what I saw in that slaughterhouse, Logan. It was *horrible!*"

Logan reaches for my hand in the dark and squeezes. "I don't doubt it was, but it's nothing a good ol' fashioned bullet to the head won't fix." He grins at me. "You saw to that, Alix."

"No, I just got lucky…"

Zoe turns, tilting her head in my direction. "Lucky how?"

"Back at the factory, Alix took out one of those things all on her own," Logan says, a note of pride in his voice. "Shot the bastard right in the head!"

"Whoa! That's my girl!" Zoe goes to high-five me, but I shake my head and pull away from her.

"No, it wasn't like that. The vampire had me pinned down and helpless. I only shot the thing after Kade had it distracted." I swallow hard, feeling a little shock of terror as I think about my close brush with death. "I almost died."

Logan's jaw clenches, his muscles taut like coiled springs beneath his skin. "I was coming back for you," he says.

You would never have gotten there in time, I think, but I don't say it out loud. No reason to hurt his feelings.

"Okay, but the point is, these things can be shot, right? Am I hearing that correctly?" Chad's eyes spark with a surge of adrenaline. "So we don't have to stake them through the heart or burn 'em or chop off their heads like they do in the movies?" He turns to Frog with a smirk on his face. "Because you kind of said before that wasn't possible. Looks like you were wrong."

"That's not what I said." Frog frowns. "I never said it couldn't work. Bullets to the head or heart do the trick fine. What I said was, these fuckers are strong and fast and can be pretty hard to kill. Between guns and running, I pick running every time."

I'm a bit puzzled by Frog's words. It's not that I think he's wrong, but it's not all making sense to me, yet. I *saw* Kade on the ground, fighting with that vampire. Saw it with my own two eyes. Who knows what would've happened for sure if I hadn't killed the thing, but Kade seemed to last for quite a while, just fine minus the split brow, even without my intervention.

"Are you sure about that?" I ask Frog. "Because before I shot that vampire, Kade had him pinned on the ground. He seemed to handle himself okay."

"Yeah, I saw that, too." Logan nods. "Maybe the vampires aren't so strong or fast, after all."

Kade makes a strange chuckling sound up by the riverbank slopes. He's been so quiet this entire time, I didn't even realize he was listening to us.

"He was plenty strong. Trust me," he says, his voice soft, mocking.

"I suppose it could've been a Stage I vamp." Frog's brow furrows in deep contemplation. "That would explain things."

"A stage what?" I ask.

"You know." He shrugs. "Stage I, Stage II, Stage III."

"No, I don't know," I say sarcastically. "We didn't all grow up being groomed to join some secret vampire killing cult, okay? Spell it out for us."

Frog temples his fingers below his chin. "The easiest way to explain it," he starts, voice raised above the rush of the river, "is to think of vampirism like a genetic disease. The vamps aren't foreign monsters from another planet. They're humans—like us—but with this vampire-gene-thing that activates under certain conditions.

"It's similar to how genetic mutations increase your risk

for diseases like heart issues or cancer. If you never smoke cigarettes maybe you never get sick, but if you smoke, then that gene can get turned on, increasing your chances," he continues, his gaze piercing in the darkness. "Not everyone with the gene turns into a vampire, and it's hard to tell who will. Some folks believe the founding families that first settled Allium Valley have an increased predisposition. The original population here was small, obviously, with a limited gene pool."

"It sounds like *The Vampire Diaries*," I say, shifting around, trying to get comfortable as the soft, lumpy ground moves beneath me. "The original vampires were the oldest family —the most evil and most powerful."

"Yeah, though, who knows if that part's true." Frog shrugs. "So many new people have moved here over the years, marrying locals, diluting bloodlines. Either way, the transition seems to only occur in younger people. Once you hit a certain age, you can't change. Must be too hard on the body."

"What's the garlic part, though? Why does that affect them so much?" I ask.

Frog stretches his arms overhead and lets out a yawn that seems to ripple through the still, hot air. "Think of garlic like chemo or radiation treatments for cancer or statins for heart disease. Garlic treats vampirism—it suppresses it. But now," he continues, locking eyes with each of us in turn, "without the garlic, the genes are getting activated again."

"And the stages?" Logan prods. "What's that about?"

"There are stages of vampirism, like a disease," Frog says. "Someone with less of the disease in them or someone that just turned is a Stage I. That means they aren't that strong or fast; they don't have all their powers yet. Kaden must've been fighting a Stage I." He strokes at his chin thoughtfully. "I suppose you could go up against a Stage I and survive, especially if you're a good fighter. Like me, I'm a black belt. Hell, maybe you could even survive a Stage II. But a Stage III—no way." He grimaces. "No human can fight a Stage III and live."

"Okay, so how many Stage III vampires do you think there are around here?" Zoe asks, her hands shaking next to mine. "Like, opposed to the easy kind, the Stage I kind?"

Frog gulps. "Guess we'll find out soon enough…"

After that cheerful discussion, no one wants to talk anymore. We all close our eyes, trying to fall asleep. Logan reaches for my hand, tucking it tightly within his own. I surprise myself by allowing it, not pulling away this time. The warmth of his skin against mine is comforting. After all we've been through these last two days, I find myself grateful to have him near.

Within a few moments, he drifts off. His breathing slows as his muscular chest rises up and down peacefully.

On my other side, Zoe starts to snore softly. I watch over her for a bit, my half-empty stomach grumbling with frustration. Between the fear and my hunger, it's difficult for me to fall asleep as fast as my friends have. My mind swirls with questions.

Even if we're safe now by the river, how long can we stay? Won't we have to leave this place soon to get more food and water, especially after Margie took Logan's pack?

What will happen to us then?

And if what Frog says is true, if the vampires are multiplying and getting stronger every day, what hope do we have to stay alive?

CHAPTER 15
DAY 4: 8:00 A.M.

Devil's River

The gentle lapping of water against the riverbank nudges me awake. My eyes flutter open to the soft hues of dawn painting the sky over the Devil's River.

The air is hot, stifling, even this close to the flowing water. Heat rises up from the ground beneath my body on the grassy bank. My hand feels warm, and I turn my head to find Logan, still asleep, his fingers intertwined with mine. His handsome face is relaxed in sleep. Innocent. Almost childlike.

Zoe stirs beside me. She blinks open her eyes, and a smile forms on her lips as she glances over at Logan and me.

"He's still holding your hand," she whispers, her voice barely audible over the sounds of the rushing river.

I stare down at our entwined fingers, feeling a mix of comfort and confusion. Logan's touch is familiar, yet distant, like a memory from another life.

"He clearly still loves you, Alix." Zoe props herself up on one elbow, her gaze thoughtful as she watches us. "He'd do anything to protect you."

Her words hang in the air, heavy with unspoken questions. I sigh and release Logan's hand gently to avoid waking him.

"I know."

"Okay, well, how do you feel about him?"

"I'm not sure anymore…" I fidget with a small pebble from the ground, rolling it between my fingers as I grapple with my tangled feelings. "What's wrong with me? Shouldn't I know that? I always know."

She smiles and places a comforting hand on my shoulder. "It's okay to be confused, Al. Just make sure you're not letting go of something really special. True love is worth fighting for, even when the world is falling apart."

As the others around us slowly awaken, I find myself lost in thought. It's so unlike me to be unsure of things, but these last few days of life and death are making me question everything I thought I knew—including my feelings for Logan.

He's so steady and strong and brave, and he loves me so much. I always knew he cared about me, but to see his true feelings in action, to see him actually risk his life for me over and over, to want to protect me even in the worst-case scenario possible, is something else entirely.

Even an Ice Queen has to thaw at a certain temperature. Those are the laws of nature. I worry I may be getting dangerously close to my melting point.

Did I make the right decision?

Or was breaking up with Logan a huge mistake?

Beside me, the river babbles and whispers, its continuous flow a symphony of unrest. It offers no answers, only echoing my own uncertainties.

"I'm fucking starving," Chad says, rubbing sleep from his eyes.

"Me too." My stomach rumbles loudly in sympathy.

We haven't eaten anything since yesterday's trail mix, before Margie made off with Logan's backpack and our food.

"That bitch," Chad mumbles. "I hope the fucking vamps got her."

Logan sits up, groaning, as he stretches out his injured arm and shoulder. He rubs the area around the stab wound and winces sharply, like he's in pain.

I grab Tylenol from one of the backpacks and hand it to him. "You doing okay?" I ask, nodding toward his shoulder.

"Just a flesh wound, thankfully. I'll be all right," he says, swallowing down the pills with his water, and then he turns to the group. "We're going to have to find more food soon."

"Okay, but where?" Zoe asks. "Do we go into town?"

"Town's too far," Frog says, getting to his feet and surveying the woods surrounding the river. Then he nods to himself, as if seeming to come to a decision. "We should try the forest."

"Hell no! We can't leave the river." Chad shakes his head, eyes round with panic. "We just got here—it's safe here."

"Won't be safe if we starve to death," Frog mutters.

"Won't be safe if we leave and get captured, either," Kade says sarcastically. "What's the rush? Let's just wait and see if anyone else shows up with food or supplies."

Logan frowns. "Playing defense isn't the right strategy in a siege. We need to go on the offense."

My stomach sinks. I'd thought we were safe, at least for a few days. That we could stay by the river, rest up, gather our strength, and strategize our next steps. But now? It seems like we're back to square one again, thanks to Margie. Here we are, scrambling once more to come up with a new way to survive the day—and fast.

"What about fish?" Chad eyes the river hopefully. "Can't we eat that?"

"Seriously, Chad? Do you have sawdust for brains?" I ask. "You see any bait around here? How about fishing tack?"

"Alix." Zoe gives me a look, but I shrug it off. I'm not going to feel badly for saying the truth. Chad is a total idiot sometimes.

"Can't we just, uh, catch them with our hands?" Chad asks.

Dear Lord. He's actually being sincere. Not a note of irony in his voice.

Logan glances at Chad, nodding along. "Actually, it's a good idea."

"No, it's not!" I snap. "It's ridiculous."

"Not the hand fishing, obviously." Logan grins at me. "But if I can get the basics, I can catch enough fish to keep us fed for weeks."

"Hey, man, I like the enthusiasm, but that's not going to work," Frog says.

"Why not?" Logan lifts a challenging brow. "I'm a champion bass angler."

"I'm sure you are." Frog's lips curl up with amusement. "I'm pretty handy with a rod, too, but the nearest tack shop is in Orchard Valley—all the way over in the next town. We'd never make it that far on foot, not before nightfall catches us. Or something worse."

Logan blows out a frustrated breath and stares off into the surrounding forest, just a few yards from the riverbanks. With his good arm, the uninjured one, he reaches for his crossbow at his feet.

"Guess we're going hunting then," he says.

"Another terrible idea," Kade says, a deep scowl marring his otherwise perfect face.

"Listen, *Mr. Cool Guy*, I'm getting kind of sick and tired of you always disagreeing with me," Logan says, his voice as edgy as Logan is capable of. "If you don't like it, don't come. I can catch enough food for all of us."

"I bet you can," Kade says. "It's not skill you're lacking."

Logan's jaw sets tightly, the muscles at his temples flexing visibly. "What's that supposed to mean?"

"Relax." Kade flashes a charming grin. "That was actually a compliment. All I'm saying is we can't afford to be impulsive. Going on the offensive, like you say, doesn't work anymore."

"Oh yeah? How come?"

Kade sighs, and I can see he's frustrated more with the situation than with Logan. "Don't you get it yet, man? You're not the Apex predator anymore. *They* are," he says, gesturing toward the woods. "You can't keep thinking like a shark. You're the minnow now."

"I would actually kill for a minnow right now," Zoe says ruefully. "That's how hungry I am."

Her corny joke breaks up the tension, and we all laugh.

"Okay, I hear you," Logan says to Kade, the tense expression on his face relaxing somewhat. "We won't stray far from the river, all right? We'll be quiet. Careful. And if we hear any sign of danger, we'll hightail it back here. But sitting around idle isn't an option anymore."

Kade grits his teeth and says nothing.

"I'm going with you," I say, standing and wiping grass and dirt off my legs. I reach for my shotgun, grateful I still have it. At least that bitch Margie left our weapons. Not that I have any notions she was doing us a favor. She probably just couldn't carry anything else after loading up on all the food.

"Me, too," Frog says.

Zoe grabs Chad, pulling him up. "So are we."

"We are?" Chad's mouth drops. "But we don't have any weapons and——"

"We're going," she repeats, elbowing him hard in the ribs.

Chad sighs forlornly but gets to his feet.

We pack up our belongings and sling our packs over our shoulders, heading for the woods. Kade joins us, silently. I'm surprised to see him come along after he made it super clear he thinks this is a huge mistake, but I don't say anything that might stop him. I want him there. I can't explain it, but I feel safer with him around.

As soon as we're at the entrance to the trees, Logan raises his crossbow at eye level, and Frog follows to the right of him at attention. Between the two of them, I'm sure we'll find game, if there's game in here to find. I follow behind them, cocking my shotgun and making sure it's ready to go ——just in case.

Behind me, Chad stumbles on a rock and cries out loudly. Zoe helps him back to his feet while we all remind him he has to stay quiet. Not only because we don't want to scare the animals away, but because there's also a chance vampires are out here with us, somewhere. Hopefully they're sleeping, mostly nocturnal like Frog believes. But if they are asleep, we don't want to wake them because of Chad's clumsiness.

I feel kind of bad, but I can't help wishing Zoe and Chad had stayed back at the river. While I appreciate Zoe's willingness to pitch in, her knife shakes in her hand and I'm more worried she'll accidentally stab herself—or one of us ——rather than anything we'd want to eat. I really don't think she should be carrying a weapon.

Still, Zoe with her kitchen knife is miles better than Chad who has somehow already lost the hunting knife

Logan gave him back at the RV. So… Chad's basically worthless. Which I already knew. I guess if he can manage to stay out of our way and not cause trouble, that alone will be a win.

The muscles in my face tighten, my pace quickening as we climb a few hills and head deeper into the woods. We're in luck. The forest is teeming with life—much more than I expected.

I spot some rabbits skittering off a few feet away from us while tree squirrels run between the tree branches overhead. Though neither sounds particularly tasty, beggars can't be choosers. Even though I've never killed a live animal before, never had to, I think I can do it if we need the meat to survive. As long as it's a quick death and we eat it all, so nothing goes to waste. Anything else would be barbaric and cruel.

I've never understood the concept of pure trophy hunting. Before Logan, I'd met a guy freshman year who told me he was a hunter. I went back to his fancy apartment after our dinner date where he proudly showed me a picture of his family smiling next to a poor dead elephant. His dad took him and his brother once a year to Africa where they paid thousands of dollars to shoot protected animals. They didn't eat the meat, either. It went to waste. It wasn't for food or survival or any of those things. They just wanted to kill something exotic.

Obviously, I dumped his ass.

"Watch out," Kade says, coming up quietly beside me. He grabs my elbow and steers me clear of a branch hidden beneath a pile of dead and decaying underbrush.

"Thanks," I whisper back, smiling lightly as we tread through the dense woods, leaves crunching underfoot. "It seems like I'm always thanking you for something, doesn't it?"

He shrugs. "It's okay."

"No, I mean it." I pause, my grip tightening on my gun. "Really—thank you. You've saved my life more times than I can count now."

A smirk tugs at the corner of Kade's mouth, a playful glint in his eyes. "It was just a tree branch. Pretty sure you would've survived."

"You know what I mean." My gaze drifts off, lost in thought. "And Zoe, too. You saved her at the festival. I have no idea what I'd do without her. She's been my rock since junior high. We've been through everything together."

"Friendships like that are rare," he says. "Zoe's lucky to have someone who loves her as much as you do."

"No, I'm the one who's lucky."

I close my eyes for a second, the feelings of panic and fear coming back to me as I remember how it felt when Zoe went missing that night at the festival.

"I was so scared. I kept trying to get to her." I gulp, swallowing back the awful memory. "How'd you even find her in that crowd? It was total chaos."

He glances away, and I'm unable to see his face anymore.

"Actually, I was looking for you," he says almost reluctantly, his voice low and cautious.

"Really?" I blink. "Why?"

"I saw the crowd surge and… I got worried."

My heart skips a beat.

He was worried about me?

The thought sends an unexpected warmth through my body.

"So are you, like, my personal guardian angel now?" I ask in a teasing tone.

A half smile plays on his lips, softening his usually stoic and guarded demeanor. "Something like that," he replies, his gaze lingering on me a bit too long. Then he laughs. "Mostly, I was afraid for your pretzel. Figured you probably had another one that might get smashed."

I slug him in the shoulder. "Jerk."

We smile at each other, and it feels like something is shifting, a silent acknowledgment hanging in the air. Something new. Something exciting and unexplored.

But as quickly as it comes on, it's gone again. Kade quickens his pace and pulls ahead of me, the mask of indifference he wears so well sliding back into place.

"Let's keep moving. We need to stay alert," he says gruffly.

Just then, a fat white-tailed rabbit dashes in front of us. Logan looks back at me, raising a brow. I nod back my understanding. Rabbit, it is.

We don't need words to communicate with each other for this. Logan and I have always been in sync as far as the physical stuff goes. It's the emotional part that screwed us.

By late morning, we take down two rabbits together. I'm much better at hunting than I ever thought I would be. I guess all those wilderness trips with Dad are really paying off.

Kade isn't half bad either. Even without a gun, he somehow winds up with a bird that looks like some form of wild turkey. Anyway, whatever it is, it seems plenty edible to me. Plus, Frog spots some berries that have managed to grow despite the drought. He fills his pockets to take back to the river.

We make out well. No signs of vampires, or even other natural predators you might encounter in woods like these, like cougars or bears. Either they're not here or they're avoiding us—or something else. I try not to think too much about the latter possibility. Either way, it makes things a lot easier for our group.

My spirits rise as we start our short trek back to the river. We've been lucky to secure plenty of game and edible vegetation, too. Hopefully, we can survive on this for a while.

We're almost to the edge of the forest when I hear it.

Snap!

The sound of a branch breaking nearby. I look around the group to see who misstepped, but everyone seems as confused as I am.

Snap! Snap!

Sweat pours down my backside as I continue scanning the trees for the source. It sounds like... *Is someone else walking around in these woods with us?*

The noise appears to be coming from somewhere to my right. It gets closer and closer until I'm certain.

Yes.

It's definitely feet.

Someone is nearby, moving along very, very fast in our direction.

In one swift motion, I turn and bring my gun to firing position. I spot her right away. Less than fifty yards from me is the female vampire from the cattle farm, striding through the forest.

CHAPTER 16
11:30 A.M.

Allium Valley Forest

My pulse skyrockets and I duck behind the nearest tree, making myself as small as possible behind its trunk. I don't think the female vampire has seen me or my friends yet.

Thank goodness.

My breath comes hard and fast. My shotgun levels in front of me, ready for anything.

After a moment, I dare a peek from beneath the protection of the tree. Kade, Frog, and Logan now lie on the ground, bodies flattened against dirt, but Zoe and Chad are still in the same spot they were standing seconds ago.

A suffocating wave of horror washes over me. I don't understand.

Why aren't they hiding?

And then I realize what they must be seeing: a beautiful woman, walking alone in the woods. Nothing to be scared or panicked about. A survivor, like us. Someone hunting, as we are. Or maybe someone who's lost and searching for help.

Never mind the fact we're all supposed to be on high alert for anyone or anything, especially strangers. And we all know by now that vampires look exactly like regular humans and might be roaming around anywhere, at any time.

Chad—the dumbass, always a sucker for a pretty face— lifts a hand to give her a welcoming wave. He opens his mouth to call her over, and I spring from my hiding spot, but Kade beats me to it. He clamps his hand down over Chad's mouth, pinning Chad's arm behind his back.

Kade points at the woman and mouths, *"Vampire!"*

Finally, my friends get it.

Zoe and Chad freeze in place, terrified expressions on their faces as Kade yanks them both behind a tree.

My stomach churns with icy fear as I wait for the vampire to leave. I pray from within the shelter of my own tree—to God, to the Universe, to anyone that will listen— for some miracle that we somehow escape. Unlikely, but what else is there to do besides hold my gun and pray?

At first, it appears to work.

She continues down a different path, walking further and further away from us. Then she's fifty yards away.

Then seventy-five yards away.

Then even further until I can't see her anymore.

My muscles relax with relief. I sag into the tree, lowering my gun. It seems we've finally caught a break…

And then Chad, stupid fucking Chad, starts to cough.

This time Kade isn't fast enough. The sound echoes like a gunshot in the silent forest. The woman's footsteps stop, pausing. I hold my breath, panic surging through me.

Please, please, let her keep going…

When the footsteps start again, I can tell she's heading right for us.

Moments later, she comes back into view. She walks with the slow, careful gait of a predator as she scans the woods. I can spot the exact moment she finds us. Her eyes—a preternaturally shade of deep violet—light up, and a cruel grin spreads across her face. She lifts the old-fashioned hunting bow in her hand.

Then a flash of motion.

Chad lets out a strangled yelp and goes crashing to the floor. An arrow sticks out from his chest, brightly colored feathers marking the end.

Zoe rushes to his side and reaches over to pull it out.

"*No!*" Logan and I scream in unison.

If she pulls that arrow, Chad will bleed out. She'll only kill him faster that way.

"Okay, okay!" Zoe cries out. She holds up her hands, panicked. "What do I do?"

Chad begins to gasp like a dying animal. It's like no sound I've ever heard before—a half-swallowed, sickening shriek.

A loud snapping noise sounds again in the distance. The vampire, with an unsettling calm, reloads her bow, her movements deliberate, almost ritualistic.

She takes her time, in no rush at all. She's clearly savoring the moment, confident that her prey—*us*—have nowhere to go. Powerful arms draw the string back and she begins to hum softly. Part of my brain recognizes the familiar pop song.

Just days ago, we danced to it at the Alpha Delts' frat party, Zoe and I wearing matching togas I'd sewn for us. Swirling and twirling around Logan and Chad. Not a care in the world. Now, we're seconds from death.

"Get to the river!" Frog takes off at breakneck speed. He

doesn't even attempt to use his rifle and shoot the vampire. He just flees.

I burst from my hiding spot, now useless, and race toward Zoe. Desperately, I grab at her arm and try to pull her away. There's nothing to be done about Chad.

"No!" She rips herself from my grasp, turning back to her boyfriend. Tears stream down her face. "We have to help him!"

"He's already dead," Kade says without emotion.

"Zoe—come on! We have to go!" I beg.

"Please..." Chad sputters. Blood seeps out of his mouth, trickling down his lips. *"Please don't leave me..."*

Then Logan is beside us.

Chad screams in agony, crying, as Logan and Zoe attempt to pick him up. As much as I don't like Chad, have never liked Chad, I'm filled with pity. A suffocating sensation tightens my throat, my stomach rolling with nausea. Chad's not dead yet, but he's close, and it's not an easy death, either. I wouldn't wish this upon anyone.

I raise my shotgun and turn back to the vampire, but she's already a step ahead of me. She aims her own weapon low and fires again.

A thwump sounds loudly, like a broken guitar string as an arrow glides through the air. One blink. A flinch. And then it embeds itself right into Chad's heart. With a final shudder, all the life leaves his body. He slumps over and falls to the ground.

Dead.

Zoe stares at the hole in his chest and then glances, dumbly, at her own hand. Blood runs between her fingertips from where she'd been holding him only seconds ago. Bits of his muscle and sinew splatter the grass at our feet.

The vampire whistles softly, and two men appear, magically, as if she's crafted them out of thin air. They flank her sides. Taller. Bigger. Even more menacing than she is.

Three vampires.

Holy shit.

My head spins. I've never been more terrified in my life.

Zoe's eyes go wide with raw fear, and she stumbles backward, falling to the ground, limbs flailing. Her body is riddled with shock as she attempts to crab-crawl away from them.

I grab her by her armpits, my hands locking underneath, and rip her back to her feet. "Run!" I command, pushing her ahead of me.

We race for the river—our only hope now—with Logan and Kade right behind us. We're a whirlwind of panic, legs pumping as we dodge and weave through the trees and leap over gnarled roots. My bag scrapes against outstretched branches, slowing me down.

I rip it off. Throw it to the ground.

I run so fast and hard my sides ache, but I won't stop. Can't stop. Stopping now means death, and I'm not ready to die.

"Keep going!" Logan shouts. "We're almost—"

His words are cut off by screaming, and then something heavy hits the ground.

I shouldn't stop to look, but I can't help it. I have to know if he's okay.

My heart squeezes with despair when I see Logan lying on the forest floor. Unconscious. A dart jutting from his neck. Tears stream down my face as I watch, helpless, while one of the male vampires tosses my big, beautiful exboyfriend over his shoulder like a sack of potatoes.

I hate myself for what I do next, but I turn away from Logan and keep running. There's nothing I can do for him now. I have to focus on Zoe. I have to get her to safety.

Then we're at the clearing.

The river appears, like a flowing, sparkling miracle. Our salvation. It's so close I can practically taste it.

We're only a few yards away from safety when something sharp stabs me in the leg. I cry out and go crashing to the ground, my leg aching, throbbing, consumed with pain. I look over, horrified. A hunting dart has impaled itself in my calf muscle.

The air whooshes next to me, and then Zoe is down, too. She yells my name, her cries piercing straight through my heart.

I don't even worry about my own life anymore. My only thought is getting to Zoe. I crawl toward her on my hands and knees. I *have* to protect her...

"Do NOT move!"

Kade's hand is on my mouth. His strong arms yank me backward, pulling me behind a nearby bush. Hiding me. Protecting me.

I struggle, trying to free myself.

"Zoe!" I croak pitifully through his fingers.

"You can't help her. She's theirs now," he says, voice in my ear, his grip like steel.

I watch as Zoe slumps over, unconscious. A moment later, the woman and her foot soldiers approach and collect Zoe's body, too, just like Logan. I watch it all happen, my body consumed with despair, and something even worse.

Heat, like sickness, pulsates through me.

My eyes water from the pain and I blink, staring down at my leg in both shock and terror. The dart. Something... something *very bad*... is in that goddamn dart...

And then I pass out.

CHAPTER 17

Time passes in a cloud of darkness and confused thoughts. My brain is a dense fog. I exist, but that's about it.

No sound. No smell. No sight.

No sense of anything, really.

Death or dream, I'm not sure, but if I had to guess, I think I'm still alive. I don't think there's pain like this in Heaven.

My body heats with a constant fire that goes all the way from my inner core down to the tips of my toes, head aching like a thousand nails from a gun puncturing into my skull. Every time it gets to be too much, and I'm certain I can't survive another minute, *he's* there.

I sense his presence, and something about it calms me. If I'm dying, at least I'm not dying alone. Not like my mother did on that wet road on Christmas Eve years ago. The thought that someone is with me, that I won't leave this world all by myself, comforts me.

Eventually, I begin to sense more. Solid bits and pieces

of my current existence. I no longer just float in the nether land; I start to experience little slivers of life.

Sipping water he gives me.

Swallowing pills from his hand to cool the flames on my skin.

Eating bits of bread that he brings.

Listening to stories he reads to me. Familiar stories that make me smile inside.

Then, falling asleep. Again.

And again.

And then one day, just like that, I'm fully awake.

When the fog lifts for good, the first thing I notice is pink.

Pink walls. Pink pillows. Pink sheets. Pink stuffed animals. A warm, soft pink comforter, faintly smelling of strawberries, envelops my body. Even the canopy bed I'm lying in is pink. My favorite color, it instantly reminds me of my childhood bedroom. I feel safe, despite having no idea where I actually am.

Across from me, early evening light seeps through a large bay window and casts the room in a golden glow. It must be dusk. Centered beside the window is a rocking chair with a pillow and blanket thrown over it, like someone has been sleeping there. A table nestles next to the chair and a kerosene lamp sits on top beside a worn-looking copy of Percy Jackson's *The Lightning Thief.*

I recognize the cover right away. Growing up, my mom and I used to read all the Percy Jackson books together. No wonder the stories had sounded so familiar to me...

A closet with mirrored doors is on the other side of the bedroom. My reflection stares back at me, and I sit up, shocked by my haggard appearance.

My skin is paler than I've ever seen it, even paler than during finals week when I don't have time to spray tan. Hair

mats against my damp neck like a rat's nest, dark bags
residing beneath my eyes. My lips, dry and crusty, are in dire
need of plumping balm. I go to wipe the crud from my
mouth, and something clinks beside me, banging against the
side of the bed. A glance to my right reveals a plastic tube
attached to my arm. At the other end is a bag of clear fluid,
hanging from a metal hook.

It takes a moment to take it all in: the fact that I look like
a corpse brought back to life, that I'm hooked up to some
kind of IV stand, and that I'm dressed in a way-too-small
frilly pink nightie that barely covers what it needs to. Clearly,
someone has been taking good care of me while I was
unconscious and helpless—but who?

Where am I?

What's happened to me?

I throw the covers off to investigate further and find
thick, rolled bandages wrapped around my leg where the
vampire's dart hit me. Leaning over, I touch the gauze with
the pads of my fingers and wince. A jolt of pain rushes up
my body.

That's not good.

Still, I can bend my leg back and forth and curl my toes
upward. I take that as a positive sign.

Next, I test my upper limbs, raising my arms overhead
and stretching. No problems there. That part of my body
seems to be doing just fine.

Thunk-thunk-thunk.

Floorboards rattle below me. Heavy boots clunk around,
footsteps heading up what must be stairs. The sound grows
louder as they approach my room.

I straighten my nightie. I'm not exactly worried—more
curious. Maybe I don't know all the details of what's going
on, but I feel safe. If this person wanted to hurt me, they
wouldn't have brought me to a cozy bed, nursed me back to

health, and read me bedtime stories while I was passed out and vulnerable. It would be crazy to think I'm in some kind of danger.

Which is a very good thing, because if I was in danger, I'd be totally screwed.

My gun is nowhere to be seen, and any hope for a quick getaway is highly unlikely. Not when I'm hooked up to an IV and, even worse, unsure if my injured leg would even support me standing, much less running. The bandage down there appears to be pretty damn serious.

The door swings open with a loud, creaking sound and he steps inside. Dusty black hiking boots. Black shorts. Another black polo shirt that clings to his well-muscled frame. Those dark, intelligent eyes rake over me inquisitively.

"Good," he says, a smile ruffling one corner of his mouth. "Sleeping Beauty has finally woken up."

"Kade!" I croak. My throat is dry and scratchy from lack of use, like sandpaper. "What's going on? Where am I?"

"My little sister's room."

He takes a seat in the rocking chair, pushing aside the blanket and pillow to make more room. His elbow rests on his knees and long, graceful fingers brush away a few locks of dark hair from his forehead. A sliver of memory flashes, and I can see those same fingers with a wet washcloth, cooling me down, helping with my fever. Wiping my head. My face. My exposed collarbone.

"Oh." I peer around. "And, uh, where is she?"

"Gone."

"Gone?" I repeat, not certain I understand. "Gone where?"

"I don't know." A muscle clenches in his jaw. He bends down to his boots, rubbing a spot of dirt from the tip. "Place was empty when I got you back here."

"Ah, well, I'm sure she's okay. They must have gotten away…" I stammer, even though I'm not sure of this at all. But what else do you tell a guy whose entire family seems to have disappeared?

"How are you feeling?" he asks, changing the topic. He studies my face, searching for signs of pain or discomfort.

"I'm not sure."

I'm alive, so there's that, but it's hard to judge the full extent of damage to my body while I'm lying in bed like this.

"What happened? I don't remember much of anything after that dart," I say.

"It was some kind of tranquilizer drug."

"Drugs?" I gasp. "Why are vampires using drugs?"

He leans out of his chair and reaches toward the dresser, opening the top drawer and pulling out a dart. He holds it up high so I can see. It's about the size of my pinkie and has a long metal cartridge with a rear component made of what appears to be red tail feathers.

"It's like how they use tranquilizers in zoos," he explains, rolling the dart around between his index finger and thumb. "They're rounding people up. Stunning them and taking them back to the factory." He glances over at my bum leg, pointing at the bandages. "Got you good, too. You took three darts to that leg. That's why you were so sick."

A twinge of pain shoots through my temples, exploding between my ears. I groan, raising a hand to my head.

"How long was I out for?"

"Almost a week. It was touch and go for a while, but you're a fighter." A hint of admiration lights up those dark eyes. "Sorry about the pain. I tried to get something stronger, but all I could find was Advil." He gestures to the stand that I'm hooked up to. "I was lucky to get IV liquids at the urgent care. The place was ransacked when I got there—"

"You went into town?" I gape. "For me?"

Frog had said town was far away from the river. I can't believe Kade took such a huge risk like that for me.

"I couldn't just let you die." In the dim light, his brow furrows, deep lines etching across his face. "You were in bad shape. I was worried you wouldn't make it."

"Well, I'm sure glad I did." I smile lightly.

He laughs. "Me too."

I raise my arm, the IV tube clanging against my sore bicep. "Pretty impressive, by the way. How'd you know how to do this?"

"My dad." He coughs. "He was... uh... sick for a while. The doctors showed me how. He didn't want to go to the hospital."

"Wow, that must've been hard."

He flinches and looks away. "Yeah, it was."

My heart seizes as I remember what he said earlier, about coming back home to this empty house. He's also lost family he loved, just like me. It seems we have a lot more in common than I realized.

There's a long moment of silence before he speaks again.

"So, um, can I get you anything?"

"I'm okay."

I sit up higher in the bed and look around, scanning the room for signs of the others. Zoe. Logan. Even Chad. Frog, too. Backpacks or clothes. Something that would tell me they're here somewhere.

"Where is everybody?" I ask.

His eyes widen with alarm. "You don't remember?"

"Remember what?"

He pauses and his shoulders hunch up as if a silent

weight is pressing down on them. Sadness flickers across his face. He's so quiet it starts to scare me.

"Kade?" I prod. "What is it?"

"We're the only ones that made it out of the forest, Alix."

In a horrible flash, it all comes back to me.

Frog running away. Chad lying in a crumpled bloody mess on the floor, dying. Zoe and Logan crying out as they went down in heaps to the ground. The vampires converging in on them, picking up my friends' limp bodies one by one, like bags of trash.

"Okay, but where are they?"

I know Chad is dead, but I can't believe the others are, too. They can't all be gone…

Kade shakes his head mournfully, and I realize I already know the answer.

To the factory.

The vampires took my friends to the factory.

Bile rises in my throat. I gag, nauseous, as I imagine Zoe and Logan imprisoned in cages like the other people I saw through the slaughterhouse window. Enslaved. Terrified. Fighting to stay alive.

"You need water." Kade jumps to his feet. "Let me get you something to drink."

Pulsing white hot anger courses through my body.

"I'm not thirsty!"

My friends, kept as prisoners in that horrible place! Trapped with those monsters! Sitting around helpless, waiting to be slaughtered, like a bunch of fucking cattle. Just waiting to die, unless they're already dea—

"How long…" I gulp, swallowing down my revulsion and then continuing. "How long do you think they keep people trapped there before they… you know?" I can't finish the sentence, the idea is too horrific to put into words.

A chill black silence fills the air.

"Kade?"

"I don't know." He doesn't meet my gaze, eyes averted. "Could be hours. Days."

"But it could be longer, too, right? Like weeks?" My voice reverberates in the quiet bedroom, high and whiny. Desperate. Begging for a shred of hope. "I saw inside the window. There were tons of people and not many vampires. It could be a long time before they need them all, couldn't it?"

He sinks down into the bed beside me, eyes sad. "I'm so sorry, Alix."

"But it could be, right? They could still be alive, couldn't they?"

"I don't know." He shoves his hands deep into his pockets and shrugs helplessly. "I'm really sorry."

"Stop saying you're sorry!"

Anger surges through me. I know it's displaced—that this isn't his fault, that he's also grieving people he loves— but I can't help it. I'm furious at everyone and everything. At the world itself. Even at Kade.

I don't want his sympathy or more apologies. What I want are my friends back. What I want is for none of this to have ever happened.

But then, after a while, the anger begins to fade, and a wave of deep despair takes its place. It's sadness like I haven't felt in years. Not since Mom died.

We sit in silence in his sister's bed—alone, but together —until night comes. Neither of us says anything as the room darkens for the evening. Eventually, my sorrow dampers enough that I feel ready to speak again.

"It's one of my favorites," I say, pointing to the Percy Jackson book lying next to the rocking chair.

His face brightens. "It was my little sister's favorite, too."

"She has good taste."

"She's a bossy little shit, is what she is." He laughs, loud and genuine, without holding back. I realize it's the first time I've ever heard him really laugh. When he laughs, the right side of his mouth goes slightly higher than the left, and he doesn't look mysterious or broody or guarded, like usual, but like he's actually having fun. It's incredibly endearing. My heart tugs just a smidge.

"You two probably have that in common." I grin and peer down at the pretty pink quilt covering me. The image of a beautiful and sweet little girl—though maybe a tad precocious, not unlike her occasionally aggravating older brother—pops into my head. A girl with black eyes and raven-colored hair like Kade's.

"I hope I get to meet her one day."

He turns his head, jaw clenched, eyes locking onto something in the distance, something I can't see.

"Me too," he says softly.

"Thank you for taking care of me." I reach out, laying a hand on his arm, feeling the muscles tense beneath.

He glances down at my hand, a flicker of something—duty, care, maybe even a hint of affection—crosses his features before he stands up, pulling away from my touch.

"Enough talking for today. You need to rest."

He props up my pillows and helps me ease back into the bed. I think about all that has been lost already, for both of us, and feel like crying. Exhaustion is heavy in my bones, the throbbing pain in my leg a constant reminder of the danger still lurking somewhere outside.

The room dims further and my vision blurs, not just from the night, but from a threatening migraine clawing at my temples.

"Do you think Frog made it?" I whisper.

"I'm not sure. I hope so."

As the seductive pull of sleep promises relief from the lingering pain, one solitary question claws its way through the fog of my mind.

"Kade…" I murmur, trying to hold on to the thought before I fall asleep because I know it's important. "Have you seen anyone else since the forest?"

If he's been into town, searching for medicine, perhaps he's run into others like us. People that are free.

We can't be the only ones left that aren't dead or trapped in the factory farm, can we?

"You mean humans? No." He shakes his head. "If they are here, then they're hiding good, like we are."

I don't ask the other important question—maybe the most important question—whether he's seen any vampires.

I don't want to know the answer.

CHAPTER 18
DAY 11: 6:30 P.M.

The Black Family Farm

I awake the next day around dinner time.

This time when he comes to my room, he has soup he made using a gas stovetop downstairs and some matches. The soup has big thick noodles and chunks of chicken and carrots and smells absolutely heavenly. I can't help but think of how my mom used to make me the same kind of chicken noodle soup whenever I would get sick.

It didn't matter what I had. Flu. Cold. Menstrual cramps. A bad day at school. Mom's answer was always a big heaping bowl of soup. She always said chicken noodle soup made everything better, and she was right. Except it was Mom, not just the soup, that made me feel better.

I smile to myself. I'm not sure if I believe in the afterlife or signs from the universe, but if those things exist, this feels like one of them. It's not too hard to imagine Mom watching over me right now, protecting me. I can't think of a better explanation for why I'm still here when so many others are dead or captured.

Kade lights the kerosene lamp in the corner by the rocking chair and then helps me sit up. He perches on the corner of my bed, watching me while I sip my soup. It's the way you look at someone who's sick, making sure they do everything correctly and don't hurt themselves. It's surprisingly sweet. And not only the soup-eating-watching-thing, but the way he's been taking such good care of me, giving me food and medicine and making sure I'm okay.

Unfortunately, his soup is not very good.

It must have come from a can somewhere, not made from scratch like Mom used to do. Still, I smile up at him, thanking him as I finish it all. Considering this is basically the Apocalypse, I can't afford to be picky.

I reach for my cup next and the pitcher of water he always leaves for me atop the nightstand. Beneath that, concealed within a drawer, lies the loaded pistol he's entrusted to me—for emergencies. Beside the pitcher is a cluster of plastic horse figurines. Horses of all different colors, dressed in pretty saddles and matching bridles, sit there as if waiting for his sister to come back any minute and play with them.

Kade sees me staring.

"Those are her favorite." He swallows hard and corrects himself. "Were her favorite, I mean."

"Don't say that!" I snap, my tone sharper than I intend. I just don't want him giving up hope yet.

He sighs sadly. "Why not? Pretending doesn't make it better."

"It's not pretending—it's called optimism. We don't know for sure that they're gone, so what's the harm in being hopeful?"

He pauses for a moment, as if considering.

"Okay, Alix. Whatever you want."

I reach over to pick up a horse. There are no tubes in my arm anymore. Sometime while I was sleeping, Kade took the IV out. I grab the horse closest to me and spin it around to face us—it's pink, of course.

"What's her name?" I ask, petting the horse's soft mane.

"Bubblegum."

"Your sister." I laugh. "Not the horse."

"Ah. It's Jolie."

"Pretty name."

"Funny enough, that's what it means," he says. "My mom was obsessed with Paris. Always wanted to go there. Jolie is the French word for pretty, and you can bet Jolie used to remind us of that *all the time*." He smiles to himself, thinking about his family. "You have any siblings?"

I shake my head. "No, it's just Dad and me. I think Mom always wanted another kid, but it never happened, I guess." I pause, a lump forming in my throat. "She died a few years ago."

I expect him to stammer and feel sorry for me like everyone else does when they find out about my mom, but he holds my gaze steady. A look of empathy on his face.

"I'm sorry."

"It's okay." I shuffle beneath the sheets. "It was a while ago."

"It's not okay, but I know what you mean." His voice is soft and strangely comforting. "It never gets better, but it does get bearable."

"Yeah, I suppose it does."

"Grief is the price we pay for love. The greater the love, the greater the pain," he says. "My dad told me that. Me—I'll pay that price every single time."

His words remind me of Zoe. She said something similar right after my mom died: That once the painful, drowning grief passes, you're left with beautiful memories, and someday you'll smile at them again. Love makes it all worth it.

I don't know. It's a nice sentiment, but some days, when I think of Mom, I don't feel like the pain will ever really go away.

"It must be hard for you, being the only one your dad has left," he says.

I shrug. He doesn't know the half of it.

I think of Dad all the way over in Austin, hundreds of miles away from all of this, and pray he's still safe. Surely the vampires haven't been able to infiltrate all the states that lie between Oregon and Texas in this short of time. Hopefully, they haven't even gotten to the next town yet.

After we finish dinner, Kade removes the tray and sits down on the edge of my bed. The proximity sends a jolt of awareness through me. I'm acutely conscious of every inch of space he occupies, every movement he makes. His fingers brush against my skin, setting my body off like a live wire as he begins tending to my knee. I watch, fascinated, as he deftly unwraps the bandage. The bruising on my leg is starting to fade.

"You heal fast. Must be all that stubbornness," he says with a teasing lilt.

"Yeah, I'm just full of surprises."

"That you are, Sniper." Amusement flickers in his eyes.

I attempt to keep my breath steady as his hands linger on my leg a bit longer than necessary to clean my wounds. I try to focus on anything but the warmth of his touch.

"You're lucky. It could've been much worse." His tone is matter-of-fact, but there's an undercurrent of something else —concern, perhaps?

I nod, unable to break eye contact. "I... thanks for taking care of me."

I'm not used to being on this side of the equation—the side where I'm in need of help from someone else, especially a man. I'm used to being able to take care of myself.

"Even the strong need looking after sometimes," he says, shrugging, but his voice carries a trace of tenderness. I can hear the subtle acknowledgment of my discomfort, like he knows how hard this is for me and understands.

He finishes his work and his hand pauses on my knee in a touch that feels more intimate than medical. The air between us crackles. For a moment, I think he might close the distance between us and give in to the tension that's been slowly building ever since that moment in the woods, but then he pulls away. The mask of indifference slams back in place.

"There—all better." He pats my leg and straightens up before disappearing into the hallway.

He returns a moment later and presents me with a walking stick he's made. It's rigged together using branches from some trees outside. A belt is tied around the tops of the sticks to secure them and give me a little handle.

The next day, he helps me practice walking. It's just for a few minutes, just long enough to get my feet working and blood pumping. He won't let me walk up or down any stairs, though. He insists I'm not ready yet. My body isn't fully healed. Even when I complain how sick I am of being cooped up in bed and how much I want to see the rest of his house, he doesn't cave. He carries me downstairs instead.

The house is unexpectedly beautiful. Yards of plush ivory wall-to-wall carpets. High vaulted ceilings with fancy chandeliers. Huge plasma TVs everywhere. He even has a Sub-Zero fridge, which sets you back a pretty penny. One of the rich playboy types I dated last year wouldn't stop bragging about his.

"Whoa!" My eyes widen as I take it all in. "And I

thought you were just a simple-life farm boy."

I attempt a few laps around his living room with my cane, working on my coordination. His eyes follow my every move, ready to spring into action if I stumble or trip.

"Why would you think that?" he asks.

"Isn't that how most farmers are? Modest, salt of the earth people?"

"How many farmers do you know?" His mouth curves into a teasing grin.

I laugh. "Good point."

"Some farmers are like that, sure, but my family has been doing this for generations," he says. "We have the biggest garlic import/export company in the country. That much garlic can buy you a lot of nice shit."

"Clearly."

At nighttime, we sit down on the sumptuous oversized living room couches and stare out the windows as the sun sets. He makes sure we arrange ourselves so we can't be seen by any potential intruders. I'm sure before the drought it was all very beautiful, but currently his front yard is just a whole lot of dirt and dead plants. Brown, lifeless, undulating earth. Trees yellowing and wilting from dehydration.

He makes us two steaming mugs of bedtime tea using the gas stove in the kitchen and brings me his sister's hairbrush so I can untangle the knots in my hair. After he helps me brush out the parts I can't reach, he joins me on the couch, sitting so close I can feel the heat from his body against my legs.

He cracks open his well-loved copy of *The Lightning Thief*, the spine creased from use, and begins to read me another chapter. His voice is a soothing timbre, rich and deep, and I find myself leaning into the sound as much as the words from the pages.

I find I enjoy the time with him more than I probably

should. It's weird to have happy moments when so much is wrong, but Kade says doing things like this keeps us sane. Sometimes, like now, it's almost too easy to forget all the bad things and only focus on the moment when I'm with him.

I forget about everything except how comfortable and cozy Kade makes up the couch for me, fluffing up pillows under my injured knee. Or how nice it is to have someone read me a story again like Mom used to. Or how adorable he can be, putting on different voices for each character and trying his best to make it entertaining for me. Part of me knows this is all one big distraction, but I like it, all the same.

Still, it's not like I've forgotten about my dad or my friends or the looming threat outside, but there's nothing I can do about any of those things. Not yet, anyway. Not until I'm fully healed.

He closes the book, finishing our chapter for the day, but I'm not ready yet to go upstairs. I don't want our time together to be over.

"I'm surprised you stayed here. Why is that, exactly?" I ask, hoping to delay things but also wanting to find out more about him. He's so mysterious; I can't quite figure him out.

"You thought I'd leave you all alone to fend for yourself with a busted leg and poison in your veins?" He leans back, a dark brow arching in mock offense. "What kind of guy do you think I am?"

A laugh escapes me. "No, not that," I say, playfully nudging his shoulder with mine. "I meant before the festival. I don't understand why you were living here of all places?"

"Where else would I be?"

"You just seem like the kind of guy who would be in a big city or something—like New York. You have that look."

"It's all the black clothes, isn't it?" he asks, a corner of his mouth tilting up with a teasing grin.

I swat at him. "You know what I mean."

Why *was* a guy like him still hanging around Allium Valley when he could be so many other places? He's smart. Capable. Brave. Resourceful. Caring. Rich, clearly. Not too hard on the eyes, either. So what in the world kept him here in the middle of nowhere?

"Actually... I was in Manhattan for a while," he admits.

"I knew it!" I laugh. "That's where I want to go, too! My dream's always been to move to New York City after graduation."

"It really is magical," he says, a wistful note in his voice. "I was there getting my MBA and interning at Schwartz Capital—they specialize in agricultural technology and agribusiness investments. It was pretty great, actually."

"So what happened? Why'd you come back?"

Sadness flickers across his face. "Dad got sick. My family needed me."

"Oh shit. I'm sorry."

"That's all right. It's not your fault," he says, shifting uncomfortably on the couch. "I moved home to be closer and help out with the farm. Felt like the right thing to do."

I bite my lip, hesitating. I don't want to ask the next question, but I know I should.

"Was he... was he okay?"

"Actually, yeah. He got better."

"Wow. That's amazing." I blink, surprised.

I was expecting the worst, but maybe that's just because of everything I've experienced in my own life. I'm already starting to forget that not everything is always dire and filled with death. Sometimes there are happy endings.

"Yeah, it was a miracle. We'd just gotten the all clear right before... " He grimaces. "Before, well, you know..."

There's a long, hard pause and then he continues his story, almost shyly. He starts to open up, telling me all about his life *before*.

He was planning to return to Manhattan as soon as his father was strong enough to manage the farm on his own again. His five-year plan was to get his MBA and then snag a full-time job at the investment banking firm he interned at. He wanted to learn everything he could about ag-tech and agribusiness investments before one day taking over the family business.

His ex-girlfriend Lillith, the one he mentioned that first night at the festival, had been living with him in New York. He'd known her since junior high. They'd dated all through high school and were crowned the King and Queen of their senior prom. She'd gone off to Manhattan with him to model and dance. The modeling hadn't taken off yet, but she'd landed a few off-Broadway gigs in chorus lines. After his dad got sick, she'd decided to stay in Manhattan without him.

She loved the city and wasn't close with her family, not like he was. They'd broken up after he left, but she wanted him back. That's why she'd been in town for the festival.

We don't discuss what happened to her after that, but I have my suspicions. I have a bad feeling she'd been one of the first to disappear at the festival, like Jenny had; probably one of the first to be killed by the vampires. Otherwise, I'm sure he would've left us at some point to go find her.

We talk about my life *before*, too. Kade seems most curious about my relationship with Logan. I tell him I care for Logan, but it's complicated, and I sort of leave it at that.

He lets me. He doesn't want to pry.

We finish our conversation before it gets too late. Kade has a rule about that, too—no kerosene lights or candles on downstairs after dark. So even though it's nice and comfy downstairs, as soon as we need more light, we head back up the stairs.

We quickly settle into a routine.

Kade leaves each morning to do a security check around the perimeter and to scavenge the area for more food and supplies. His home is already stocked with plenty of water and canned food—especially lots more of the below-average-tasting chicken noodle soup. Lucky me. He isn't worried about starvation anytime soon, but he says it's important for us to have fresh protein and produce. We have to keep our strength up.

He's never gone for long and doesn't stray far from the house. He wants to be nearby in case I need him. Without electricity and cell service, mobile phones have become a thing of the past. The only way to be in touch is to stay close and check in often.

That means there isn't a lot of opportunity for hunting, but he does the best he can. Bass fish one day, wild berries the other. When he surprises me with real honest-to-God deer meat a few days later, I find I no longer have an appetite for it. Something in me has started to change. The idea of eating another mammal, cutting its life short to serve my own needs, doesn't sit right with me anymore.

Still, he seems so happy about his bounty, I don't have the heart to tell him this after he went to so much effort. I don't want to seem rude after all he's done for me. Instead, I pick my way gingerly through the deer burger, hoping he doesn't notice I'm hardly eating, before allowing myself to gorge—without guilt—on the homemade fries he's made. They're crispy and salty perfection. I'm impressed.

"Where'd you get the potatoes?" I ask in between delicious mouthfuls.

"One of the neighbor's houses." He finishes his own burger in one big bite. "I've been going door-to-door when I can. Turns out the Anderson's have a pretty stocked pantry."

"Well, these are amazing." I shove another fry happily into my mouth. "You're a good cook."

"I'm okay," he says. "My dad is the real chef in the family. I learned a lot helping him out." His eyes get sad again and he goes quiet for a moment. "Lillith always liked my cooking."

Oh right. Lillith—his ex.

I'd almost forgotten about her.

"Maybe she got out? She could be okay?" I say, trying to cheer him up.

He looks away. "She's not okay."

I don't ask for more details. It's clear the topic is upsetting and based on his reaction there are only two likely possibilities, just like I'd already suspected: either she's dead or she's at the factory and will be dead soon.

I reach for his hand and squeeze gently. "Vampires suck, huh?"

It takes me a moment to realize the irony of my statement.

"Oh God, I'm sorry." I throw a hand over my mouth, heat shooting up the back of my neck. This poor guy has probably lost his entire family and his ex-girlfriend, and I'm making terrible puns. "I'm such an idiot."

His face twists into a half smile.

"Yeah, but they really do suck, don't they?"

I giggle, relieved he isn't mad. If I only have one friend left in town, I can't risk alienating him.

After dinner, I limp into the kitchen, leaning on my walking stick. "Want some help?" I ask as he steps up to the sink to hand wash our dishes.

He gives me a lopsided smile, eyes gleaming with roguish charm. "You sure? I wouldn't want to be accused of exploiting the injured."

I groan. "You've been taking care of me for days now.

Playing bed nurse. Hunting. Cooking. It's time I start pulling my own weight." I set aside my walking stick and roll up my sleeves. "I'll have you know, I'm a pretty fantastic dishwasher."

Together, we tackle the pile of dishes. The clink of plates and the swish of water create a rhythm as we move in sync. Our arms brush occasionally, sending unexpected shivers down my spine. Each touch is like a spark, reigniting that something between us—whatever it is.

Kade hands me a soapy plate. "You know, I usually prefer solo missions, but working with you isn't completely terrible."

"Oh no?" In a sudden, impulsive move, I flick a handful of bubbles in his direction. "How about now?"

I meant to just sprinkle a few suds his way, but I wind up soaking him. Dishwater goes everywhere: his hair, tee-shirt, even his eyelashes are dripping wet. He looks so shocked, I can't help myself. I burst out laughing.

Surprise gives way to a devilish grin. "Two can play at that game," he warns, scooping up his own sudsy ammunition.

We dissolve into a fit of giggles as we fight each other with bubbles. Mid-battle, Kade reaches out his fingers to brush away a rogue bubble that gets a little too close to my mouth. His touch is gentle, revealing a tenderness he usually keeps hidden.

"Careful, I might start thinking you've got a soft side," I tease, locking eyes with him.

"Don't tell anyone." He winks. "I have a reputation to protect."

We both grin at each other, warm and genuine. Kade is still an enigma, but in moments like this, he feels less like a mystery and more like someone I'm slowly getting to know.

CHAPTER 19
DAY 17: MIDNIGHT

The Black Family Farm

The next evening, I'm unable to fall asleep. I feel feverish and sick with worry.

Nights are always the hardest for me. Sometimes, I toss and turn for hours. Visions of the vampires and what they did to my friends torment me. I can't stop thinking about it, or what they might do to my dad—and to the rest of the world—if given the chance.

For some reason, my throat is unusually dry tonight. Even after guzzling down the water Kade sets by the bed, I'm still thirsty. He doesn't like me using the cane to go down the stairs alone and prefers me to call for him, but I hate needing someone's help. Besides, he already does so much for me. I'm not an invalid; surely, I can manage this one tiny thing by myself.

On my way down the hall, I hear a strange noise coming

from his bedroom. I pause, my ears pricking. It sounds like people are talking?

Confused, I take a few more steps down the hallway toward his room.

"You can't be in here! Get out!"

Softly, yet clearly, his words float toward me in the otherwise silent house.

Who in God's name is he talking to?

Who—or what—is in this house with us?

My breath catches. For the first time since I was shot in the woods days ago, I'm scared. The facade of false security we'd created here in Kade's house shatters into a million little pieces.

I'd convinced myself we were safe in this little cocoon home. It'd been so quiet; no sign of anyone except Kade and me and a few rabbits and squirrels. I'd known the danger still existed outside—somewhere—but it'd felt so far removed from us.

Now, I realize, it's never been far at all. It's been here all along, watching and waiting for the right time to strike.

My cane shakes in my hand as my mind runs over options. I could go downstairs. Run out the front door. Save myself. Part of me seriously considers this option, too.

But no, not after all Kade has done for me.

I can't leave without finding out who he's talking to. Is it someone he knows or has one of those vampire monster things come to kill us? What if he needs my help? I have to make sure he's okay.

My first thought is of the knives downstairs in the kitchen. I could use one of those, perhaps, but I'm not sure I can get down and back up fast enough. Not if someone is already in Kade's bedroom. Besides, we still don't know how effective knives are. Neither of us have tested one out yet.

Then I remember the gun Kade gave me, tucked away in my nightstand drawer. I've shot a vampire before and killed him, although maybe that was a fluke? I have no idea if Kade's handgun will help or not, but it's the best idea I've got.

Moving as stealthily as I can with my cane—fast yet quiet—I make it back to my bedroom. As soon as the gun is in my hand, I feel better. Its cool, heavy metal comforts me. Makes me believe I have a fighting chance.

I creep back through the shadows and toward Kade's room, gun in hand. As I place one hand on the door, my belly turns to lead, terrifying memories of vampires invading my thoughts.

Cold, fathomless eyes.

Long, sharp white teeth.

Blood spattering on the ground.

"I SAID GET OUT!"

There's no question about it. Kade now sounds scared.

If Kade—brave, strong, stoic Kade—is scared, I don't know if I can handle whatever is inside that room with him.

My hand starts shaking. My gun wavers, pointing downward instead of straight ahead where it should be.

I'm afraid.

Jesus… I'm so afraid.

Fear paralyzes me.

I wish that I'd never come here. That I'd stayed back home at school for spring break or gone straight to Dad's house in Austin. That I'd done anything but come to this godforsaken, cursed town…

And then I hear high-pitched, oddly sweet laughter coming from his bedroom. It sounds like… like a woman?

But why would a woman be inside his room?

"Stay back! I'm warning you!" Kade yells like he's afraid for his life.

I shake my head and steel my shoulders. No matter how

much I'd like to, I can't wish this reality away. This is happening. I can either jump in with both feet and do something about it, or I can watch the only person I care about still alive in Allium Valley die. And then I'll probably be next.

I cock the gun and place my finger on the trigger. Then I throw the door open, ready to blast whoever is in this house with us. I'm going to take this son-of-a-bitch out, or I'm going to die trying.

Except when I step inside the room, the only person I see is Kade.

He stands by the window, bare-chested, dressed in his black sweatpants. His back is turned away from me, muscles knotted with tension, as he stares out into the darkness. He breathes hard and heavy, the sound filling the quiet night air.

I glance left and then right, but sense nothing amiss. We're all alone in the bedroom.

"Kade?" I lower the gun barrel and take a tentative step toward him. "What's going on?"

"*Alix?* Is that you?"

He turns around. His face is paler than usual, eyes wide and dazed like he's just seen a ghost.

"Um—yeah. Of course, it's me." My heart is still pounding so loudly I can hear it in my ears. "Are you okay?"

I glance past him toward the large open window. A warm breeze blows into the bedroom, causing the curtains to flutter in a way that seems almost ominous. There's something about it that unsettles me, though I can't quite pinpoint why.

"What are you doing in here?"

"I heard voices," I say, hobbling with my cane over to the window, peering outside. I scan the landscape curiously, but there's nothing to see except empty fields and the deep, shadowy night. "I thought I heard you talking to someone?"

"Voices?"

"Yes!" I snap, impatient. "You sounded scared. Who was in here with you?"

I slam the window shut, the pane banging against the frame, and then, impulsively, I lock it. All of a sudden, I've got a bad case of the jitters. Something is seriously wrong here. I *know* I heard him talking to someone. So why is he acting like this? Like I'm crazy?

What the hell is going on?

"Oh right. That." A fleeting hesitation lingers in the lines of his expression. A tiny, momentary break in his usual calm demeanor, almost like he's trying to think of an answer. His eyes—those dark pools that hold such depth—betray a faint flicker of uncertainty before regaining their composure. "I'm afraid I may have been sleepwalking."

"Sleepwalking?" I echo, skepticism sharpening my tone.

His lips curve into a practiced smile. It's a blink-and-you-miss-it shift, but it's enough for that knot of suspicion in the pit of my stomach to grow just a little bigger.

"Yeah, I used to do it as a kid," he says, almost sheepishly "Walk around. Talk to people who weren't there. Really freaked my mom out."

"But it wasn't just your voice. I heard someone else. A woman…"

He shakes his head. "You must be confused—there's no one here but us."

I can't stop staring at that damn window. Even closed, something about it continues to nag at my brain, refusing to go away. It's large enough to be an entrance or an exit. Could he be sneaking someone in and out of the house?

No, that isn't possible.

We're all the way on the second floor, and this is a large

farmhouse with high vaulted ceilings. There's no way someone could get through that window—not without a ladder or some kind of help.

Except, maybe... maybe whoever Kade was talking to doesn't need help getting up the second story of a house?

The thought is so absurd, I dismiss it outright. I don't even know where it came from. The idea that someone can —what? Fly? Scale a house wall dozens of feet high? It's impossible.

Isn't it?

"Let's get you back to bed, okay?" Kade clasps my elbow and takes the gun from me.

I allow him to steer me back to my room and tuck me into the bed. I sink into the pillows, exhaustion washing over me. My brain feels foggy, overcome by the strong urge to sleep.

I'm not so sure what I heard anymore. Sleepwalking sounds like a logical explanation, and it's quite possible I imagined the other voice. Perhaps my mind is playing tricks on me. Given the circumstances and all I've been through recently, it's only natural I might hear strange sounds or imagine things that aren't there.

"You sure you're all right?" I peer over at him once more.

"I'm fine," he says and pulls the covers over me, making sure I'm comfortable. "Sleep tight, okay? And next time call for help—don't get up without me." He flashes me a teasing, mischievous grin. "Unless, of course, you're sneaking into my bedroom in the middle of the night for another reason?"

"In your dreams!" I blush, heat rising to my cheeks.

I can still hear him chuckling down the hall after he leaves my room.

Once I'm alone again, the tiredness engulfs me and pulls me toward slumber. My mind starts to succumb to the foggy haze, clarity fading into a dreamy blur. There's just one nagging thought that won't leave me. It jars in my gut, setting off little alarms in my head.

Despite how handsome he is and how charming he may be on occasion, despite how many times he's saved my life, I'm not sure I can fully trust Kade, no matter how much I may want to. The truth is, Kade is still a stranger.

Not that I'm now afraid of him. Rationally, I understand that if he wanted to hurt me, he would've done so. He's certainly had ample time. No, I'm not scared of Kade...

But maybe I should be.

CHAPTER 20
DAY 18: 1:00 P.M.

The Black Family Farm

T he following day, an unexpected knock shatters the
eerie silence of Kade's house. The door creaks open,
revealing Frog standing on the porch.

Frog is alive! He's here!

Joy floods through me, mingling with surprise.

He still wears the same military-style camo clothes I
remember from the woods, but they're now disheveled and
smeared with dirt, no doubt from days spent evading death
in the forest. His hair is a tangled mess, and there's a wild,
desperate look in his eyes that speaks of horrors seen and
narrowly escaped. He grips a gun, a newer, sleeker rifle he
must have found somewhere since we last saw him.

Kade and I usher him inside the house, and Frog sinks
into the large recliner chair in the middle of the living room.
His eyes are weary, body tense. He appears less like the
confident vampire hunter I remember and more like a deso-

late survivor, clinging to the last threads of resilience. We give him food and water, and then his gaze becomes distant as he recounts the harrowing tale of what he's been up to since we parted ways in the forest.

After escaping the vampires in the woods, he hid by the river for days, surviving on sheer will alone. With no supplies or weapons, his only option was to hole up there until things calmed down and he was certain the vampires were no longer hunting in the nearby woods like they'd been doing the day they found us. As soon as he could, he went searching for food and weapons and then for us.

Assuming we'd been taken to the factory farm, he started there first. The sight that greeted him was like something out of a nightmare. Hundreds of people were now being held at the cattle farm, caged like animals, awaiting their grim fate. And not just inside pens in the old slaughterhouse building where I'd seen them days ago, but also in the overflow area, spilling into the outside paddocks behind the slaughterhouse building, too.

The vampires, once just a handful, appeared to have multiplied. From what Frog's been able to ascertain, there are at least a dozen of them now. They roam the streets at night, scouting the town and hunting down any survivors still left. In the first few days, he would hear screams and cries in the middle of the night as people were captured and ripped from their hiding places, but it's been a while since he's heard anything like that.

"But how did they take over so quickly?" I ask, my heart pounding against my ribcage.

"It was the blackout," Frog says. "They knew exactly what to strike first—our lifelines, our technology."

A cold realization dawns on me. Frog had said vampirism was like a genetic disease. That meant the vampires were normal people first, with human knowledge and skills. Some of them probably worked for places like power and phone companies before all this. They knew our weaknesses all too well and how to best take advantage of them.

Frog's next words hit me like a physical blow.

"Alix, your friends... Zoe and Logan. They're at the cattle farm."

My heart leaps with a mixture of hope and terror.

"Alive?" The word bursts from me as I seize onto the sliver of hope like a lifeline.

Frog nods. "It was three days ago when I saw them, but yeah. They were trapped inside one of the slaughterhouse pens."

A muscle tightens in Kade's jaw. "Don't even think about it, Alix."

"But I have to!" My hands ball into fists at my sides, a surge of energy coursing through me. Now that I know without a doubt my friends are still alive, the path ahead of me is crystal clear. "I have to save them!"

"It's too dangerous." Kade shakes his head, his expression darkening. "Think about your dad and the rest of the world. We need to focus on them—on saving more than just a few. We have to be logical."

"Screw logic!" I explode, my frustration boiling over.

"Alix—"

"I don't need your permission, Kade!"

I turn to Frog, seeking an ally. I know he likes me. I've seen the way he looks at me. And even if it's a lot to ask of him, he *is* a vampire hunter. Order of the Clove and all that secret society nonsense. This is what he's supposed to do, isn't it?

"You'll help me, won't you, Frog?" I ask, desperation creeping into my voice. "You already know the way. You can

take me back there, can't you? We can save them
—together."

Frog shakes his head sadly. "It would be a suicide
mission, Alix."

"Please, Frog. We have to try…" I beg.

Frog rises from the chair. He thanks us for the water and
food and our hospitality. Then he crosses the room to where
I'm seated on the couch, each step deliberate, weighted with
a finality that tightens my chest. His hand extends
toward me.

"I'm leaving town, Alix. This place… it's lost," he says, a
quiet resignation in his tone. "Come with me."

Before I can react, Kade is there, a solid barrier between
Frog and me.

"She's not going anywhere," he growls.

Frog hesitates, assessing Kade. His eyes narrow slightly,
recognizing the challenge but not deterred by the towering
figure Kade presents. His shoulders straighten, not backing
down, even though Kade is several inches taller and
broader.

"She's free to choose," Frog says, meeting Kade's
commanding glare with one of his own. "You can't stay here
forever. They'll find you eventually."

Kade crosses his arms over his chest, a defiant, cocky
look in his eyes. "Let them try."

Frog's hand drifts to his rifle, his finger traveling toward
the trigger in a subtle display of readiness. "What's it gonna
be, Alix?" he asks, his voice firm, yet with an undercurrent
of urgency.

Kade edges closer to me, resting a possessive hand on
my shoulder. The air crackles with tension, and a hint of
danger, as both men trade looks back and forth.

Old Alix would've been excited about the prospect of
two good-looking guys fighting over her. She would've sized

them both up and picked the best one—the most handsome, most successful, most desirable. But me now? New Alix? She only cares about saving Zoe and Logan. Her only concern is which guy is best suited to help achieve her sole objective of rescue.

Kade is the one staying in Allium Valley. Allium Valley is where my friends are. It's a no brainer.

After Frog says his goodbyes and leaves, I feel renewed with energy. I plan to stay at Kade's house only as long as I need to. I'll focus all my attention and time on getting better and then, when I'm ready, I'll go to the cattle farm and save my friends.

I'm determined and resolute with my new plan and decide there's no time like the present to begin. With an initial test, I attempt to stand without leaning on my cane. Bracing one hand against the couch's arm, I gingerly push myself upright. A lance of pain shoots up my leg, so sharp and sudden that a cry escapes me.

In an instant, Kade is at my side, his concern barely masking his frustration. "What the hell is wrong with you?" he asks, pushing me back down onto the couch. A vein pulses in his forehead. "Your leg is just starting to heal!"

"What do you expect me to do—just give up on my friends?"

To my relief, the pain from my leg is already beginning to pass. It's replaced by a dull throbbing that, while distracting, is somewhat manageable.

"You can't fight, Alix. You'll get yourself killed."

"Then teach me!" I shout, my voice laced with anger. "Teach me how to fight!"

"This is madness! Your friends are probably dead by now," he says, a brutal look on his face. "Just like my family."

Tears sting my eyes, but I blink them back fiercely. I

don't understand how he can be so sure of this if he hasn't seen it with his own two eyes.

"They aren't dead." I lift my chin. "You'll see."

"No, *I* won't see because *I'm* not going back there. And if you want to stay alive, you won't go back there, either!"

Our eyes lock in a silent, angry stare down. Neither one of us is willing to give in.

"Stop being naive." Kade's frown deepens. "Do you have any idea how many of them there are now? A lot more vampires than you can handle—even if you are a crack shot, Sniper."

"I'll find a way," I insist.

"You'll die, Alix!" he hisses between gnashed teeth.

"It's better than being a coward. Better than watching everyone I love die."

"I said NO!"

There's something sad and desperate in his eyes. It makes me soften, just a bit.

"Kade—"

"I've already lost my family." His words hitch, caught on a surge of emotion. "My friends. Lillith. I've lost everything that matters to me." He glances down and then back up, his gaze catching and locking with mine. "I can't lose you, too…"

The way he's staring at me makes my brain buzz, giddy with a strange heady energy. A tingling sensation spreads from the tips of my toes all the way up my legs before embedding itself directly in my heart. Something is happening between the two of us. There's no denying it anymore. It's more than just friendship. More than just a bond of convenience between two people forced to work together to try to stay alive.

"Kade, please—"

"Listen, here's how it's going to be," he says, his voice

hardening again, his eyes dark and storming. "You're going to do *exactly* as I say for the next few days. No arguing. No trying to get out of bed alone and injuring yourself worse. No crazy plots to save the world. And absolutely no more talk about leaving and going to that fucking factory—"

"You can't tell me—"

"And then," he cuts me off, stabbing a finger in my direction, "only if you agree to all my terms—will I agree to help train you."

I blink, shocked. "You'll do it? You'll help me?"

He raises his hand, silencing me. "And then, *only* once you're healed and ready, will I let you leave here. After that, I suppose you can go anywhere you like, though I hope by that point you'll have come to your senses." He snatches the walking stick from me and lifts me from the couch, enveloping me in his arms and carrying me upstairs to my bedroom. "But until then, you're not leaving this house. No matter what."

I don't think he means them to be, but his words almost sound like a threat. I know I should be grateful for all he's done for me and that he's just trying to keep me safe because he cares, but part of me does start to wonder. More and more, Kade's protectiveness is starting to feel like a cage.

A chilling thought crosses my mind. Am I a patient recovering under Kade's care, or is something more nefarious going on here...

Am I being kept as his prisoner?

CHAPTER 21
DAY 19: 7:45 A.M.

The Black Family Farm

True to his word, Kade begins helping with my physical therapy the next day.

We discover his dad's medical books in the library downstairs. I guess living so far out in the country means you have to know a few things about medicine and home care. We pore through the books for research, and Kade puts me on a "physical therapy" routine to get my leg back in shape.

At first, everything is difficult.

I can get around by myself now with the cane he made for me, but when I hand it to him and force myself to balance on my own two feet, walking around the living room and up and down the stairs, the pain returns. It shoots up my leg like daggers. Then the headaches start. I almost pass out a time or two because it hurts so bad, but Kade is always there to catch me just in time.

Soon I'm up to two hours of walking and stretching

each day. We use old weights he has in the garage for strength training. Curls. Bench presses. Squats. Dead lifts. Crunches.

Training with Kade is so much harder than any workouts I've ever done before. We train twice, sometimes even three times a day. It makes my prior gym routine—which mostly comprised of me putting on cute outfits and prancing around from the treadmill to the smoothie bar—look like a joke.

He pushes me until my muscles cramp, and I don't think I can go a minute longer. Then he makes me go some more.

He does all of this somewhat reluctantly. I think he'd prefer to keep me hobbled and hidden away upstairs if he could. He's worried about what will happen to me when I'm healed enough to leave.

Every day I get faster and steadier on my feet. I fight through the pain, determined to get back to normal. Hell, *better* than normal. I have to be strong enough for what's next.

I ask to go hunting with him, but he won't allow it. Says it's too dangerous. That I can't run yet. If we were to stumble upon a vampire, there'd be no way for me to get away. I'd have to shoot—and hit my target on the first try—or I'd be toast.

Instead, he agrees to let me trail after him in the mornings when he leaves to hunt, at least until the end of his property line. While he's gone, I forage, grabbing whatever sparse crops are growing nearby this time of year and in these dry conditions. Some wilting leaf lettuce and spinach. Radishes that haven't matured yet. A few hardy raspberries and currants. There isn't enough, but I pick what I can, so he can kill less.

Eventually, I'm able to walk everywhere without my crutch.

Then I can jog.

We work on other things, too. Fighting things.

In the garage, his family has a collection of guns. Hand-guns. Shotguns. Rifles. We practice shooting them and perfecting our aim. Since we have to be quiet and careful not to attract unwanted attention, we resort to exercises like dry firing to work on the motions of shooting without ammunition. We practice pulling the trigger and aiming at targets in a safe direction.

He's also got a silencer for one of the small-caliber rifles. It muffles the sound of the gun's discharge, making it hard to hear from a distance. We fire that one on rare occasion, midday, when we're most confident any nearby vampires would most likely be sleeping.

He teaches me target visualization and other techniques that use the mind to mentally practice aiming and help improve accuracy. He fits lasers on the barrels of a few rifles. They emit a laser beam when the trigger is pulled, allowing us to aim at specific targets and see where the shots would land. My aim is pretty good, but it's nothing compared to his.

I've never met anyone as skilled at shooting as Kade. He's even better than Logan and my dad, and that's saying something since Dad's an ace huntsman. Kade plays it off. He claims surprise. Says he hasn't been shooting since he moved away to New York, and it must be muscle memory and luck.

We train with other weapons too, like knives and even our fists. Kade isn't sure how effective anything other than a bullet will be in combat with the vampires, but he says it doesn't hurt to be prepared.

It turns out I'm not too bad with the knives, either. It's kind of thrilling. I can throw them straight and often hit the target. It's probably thanks to all the volleyball I used to play; both require a lot of hand-eye coordination. Kade says I'm a natural.

My hand-to-hand combat needs work, though. No matter what we try, I'm not very good at it. I'm not strong enough. Not fast enough. Not cutthroat enough. It's frustrating to be forced to do something I don't excel at, but Kade makes me keep going.

We wrap our hands in towels, so we don't injure each other, and practice our punches. Kade sets up blankets and pillows on the ground, just in case, but he's careful to make sure I don't fall. I'm not particularly muscular, so Kade shows me how to use the muscles I do have to my advantage.

Soon, I start to improve and am acing all our shooting and combat training sessions. My leg doesn't even bother me anymore when we spar in the garage, and I'm able to get myself to a full sprint when we jog around the fence perimeter. I'm at full capacity again.

Actually, I'm better than I ever was before, thanks to Kade. It's obvious to us both that it's almost time for me to leave the farm, but I can tell he's still not ready to let me go —even if he doesn't say it out loud.

One night when we sit down together for dinner, he brings it up. On our plates are the radishes I dug up in the fields earlier that day, canned green beans from his pantry, and some rabbit he caught yesterday. I have to force myself to eat a few bites of the rabbit. More and more I find myself disliking animal meat, but there aren't a lot of alternative protein sources around right now, and I need all the strength I can get for what's to come next.

"So walk me through this," he says, chewing on his food thoughtfully. "Tell me what your plan is for getting inside the factory and rescuing your friends."

I raise a brow. "You sure you want to talk about this?"

He nods.

"You *really* want to know?" My eyes narrow. "And not just to try and talk me out of going?"

He hesitates, almost shyly. "I was thinking I could help?"

I lift a hand to his forehead. "Are you feeling okay?"

He laughs, brushing me away. "Look, I'm not an idiot. I know you're almost ready to leave, and if there's nothing I can do to stop you—"

"There isn't—"

"Then let me at least help." His voice is firm yet tinged with something softer, something more. "If you really have to go, I want you coming back to me alive afterward."

Our eyes lock and a surge of warmth floods through me. There's an intensity in his gaze, a fervent, almost palpable desire for my safety that ignites a flutter in the pit of my stomach. It's a look that more than hints at the deep, unspoken connection that exists between us.

I cough, clearing my throat.

"Okay, here's what I've come up with so far," I say. "I'm going to find a map to the factory in your dad's library, you're going to loan me some guns and knives, and then I'll follow that map, kill some vamps, find my friends, and save the fucking day." I smile weakly at him from across the table. "How's that for a plan?"

As far as search and rescue operations go, it's more aspirational than finely tuned. Even I know that. But it's all I've got.

"Don't take this the wrong way," he says with a slight smirk, "but that doesn't sound like a very good plan, Sniper."

I sigh despondently. "I know…"

He's not wrong, but that doesn't mean I'm going to change my mind. I'm finally recovered, and it's time for me to leave like I always said I would. Still, I can't help feeling

more than a bit remiss that I hadn't studied something in
college more useful to my current circumstances, like, say,
military strategy. Fashion is important and great for a lot of
things, but fighting vampires isn't one of them.

"That's good, actually. That you realize that." His eyes
twinkle with amusement. "At least you're not completely
insane. I was starting to wonder…"

I stick my tongue out at him. "I thought you said you
wanted to help? When is the helpful part coming?"

"Right now."

He gets up from the kitchen and disappears down the
hall, back toward the garage. A few moments later, he
returns with a double-knotted black trash bag in his hands.
He drops it down in front of me with a big grin on his face.

Confused, I untie the bag and pull out its contents.
Inside, I find a treasure trove of vampire-fighting supplies
that he's put together for me. There's a book on lock-picking
that must be from his dad's library and what looks to be
pocket-sized lock-picking tools to go along with it. An
expensive Swiss Army knife with a bunch of handy attachments. His dad's binoculars. A tiny vial of garlic oil mixed
with some kind of flammable liquid. A lighter. Small leather
sheaths to wear inside my shoes and under my tee-shirt to
conceal a knife or a handgun.

Lastly, he's included a hand-drawn map with directions
to the cattle farm. He's made three large Xs on it. One X is
for the slaughterhouse where I need to go. One X is for the
Devil's River, in case I have to take shelter. The last X is for
his house, should I come to my senses and realize the whole
thing is way too dangerous and I want to come back here.
He says this is my home now, too, for however long I need.

"I can't believe you did this for me," I say, touched by his
thoughtfulness. My mind whirls with emotion, heart
swelling, as I stare at all his gifts.

"It's no big deal." He glances down at the table, focusing on the weapons, readjusting them with unnecessary precision. "It was all just laying around here anyway."

"It's a *huge* deal." I reach out and grab his hand, a little jolt of electricity traveling up my arm at the contact. "The fact you did this for me, even knowing how much you disagree with me?" I swallow back the emotion that threatens to overwhelm. "I just… thanks, Kade. It means a lot."

"I still don't want you to go." He looks up, his eyes deep pools of turmoil. "But I know that's not who you are."

In his gaze, I find understanding, a recognition of my true nature. Kade sees me—really sees me—for who I am.

"So here's what I think your best plan is," he continues, his voice hardening, taking on a tone of reluctant resolve. "You need to be quick and silent. The factory farm is probably going to be more heavily guarded at the main entrance since that's where they come and go, so you should avoid that." He points to a section of the map, tracing a path with his finger. "Look for a smaller, less protected entry point. Scan the fence and the perimeter for openings. That's your best shot at getting in unnoticed.

"Frog said your friends were in the slaughterhouse pens, so check there first," he continues, leaning back, the chair creaking under his weight, his eyes never leaving mine. He scans my face, ensuring I'm absorbing every word. "Once you're inside, stick to the shadows. Move swiftly. Carefully."

"Yeah, okay." I nod along. "And then what?"

"Then you get your friends and get the hell out," he says. "You may need to create a diversion. Use the garlic oil and the lighter." He gestures to the table where they lie. "You can set off a small explosion. That should distract the vampires long enough for you to get your friends and escape."

Kade's plan is clear and concise, but it's also fraught with danger. Still, it's a chance, a flicker of light in this dark nightmare. Instead of worrying about all the risks, I cling to the slim thread of hope he's offered me.

"I can do this," I say, more to convince myself than him.

"Just... promise me one thing." He pauses, taking a deep breath. "Promise me you'll be careful."

"I will," I say. "Thank you, Kade. For understanding. For this." I nod over at the gifts he's given me. "For everything, really."

"I just wanted you to know how I feel about you."

A dizzying current rushes through me, the very air around us turning electric.

"And how... how do you feel about me?"

He hesitates for a moment, and my heart hammers madly in my ears.

"I feel like..." He pauses a beat. "Like even though it hasn't been very long, I care about you more than people I've known for years. More than people I've known my entire life, even. You've probably already figured out I'm a bit of a loner. I don't let people in. But you..." He takes in a deep breath, shrugging. "You've somehow snuck inside. I don't understand it, but I feel closer to you than any friend I've ever had." A flicker of uncertainty crosses his face, like he second guesses what he's saying. "Does that sound completely crazy?"

All the air leaves my body, like a wilted and deflated balloon.

Friend?

Is that all?

I don't know what I expected from Kade; some sort of romantic declaration now that I'm leaving, and we may never see each other ever again?

But no. Why would I get that?

This is Kade, after all.

Stoic, cold, infuriating, mysterious Kade. For all I know, this *is* how he really feels. Perhaps he only cares about me the same way he cared—cares—about his little sister Jolie.

He stares at me expectantly, like he's waiting for me to say something back.

I groan inwardly. Even if I'm disappointed, I can't tell him that, not when the gesture is so damn sweet. It's not his fault he's a cold-hearted moron.

I smile, my teeth grinding together on the inside.

"Not at all, Kade. I feel the same way about you."

CHAPTER 22
DAY 28: 6:15 P.M.

The Black Family Farm

Dinner on our last night together is a quiet affair.

You'd think we'd talk a lot since we may never see each other again after this evening, but I'm too worried and anxious to make much conversation. I think Kade must feel the same. Instead, we focus on eating and drinking since this might also be my last real meal for a long time.

Maybe forever.

He finds the nicest bottle of wine in his dad's cellar. It's a fancy red Cabernet with a name I can't pronounce. I recognize it from a Michelin-starred restaurant one of the rich, show-offy guys I dated before Logan would take me to.

He opens it up and we drink a glass together and then another. It's a little weird to act like this is some kind of celebration when we both know what's coming tomorrow, but since I have no idea what's going to happen to me after tonight, I figure I might as well enjoy the time we have left.

If this is my last night on Earth, I plan to go out with a bang.

After we finish our dinner, he walks me back upstairs to my bedroom. A backpack is already filled for my journey and sits by the door, waiting for the morning.

I've packed light.

The bag contains the tools and map Kade gave me, medicine from his house, waters, enough food for a day or so, ammunition, and a large hunting knife. Any more than that will slow me down and be too difficult to carry for long. It's enough to get me to the factory farm, but not much further than that. If I'm successful there, I figure I can always get more supplies afterward. And if I'm not successful, well, then I suppose there's no need for extra supplies anyway.

Propped up next to the bag are my two guns—a shotgun and a handgun Kade gave me to tuck into my waistband—plus two more small knives and the leather sheaths.

I've been preparing for this for days now, so there isn't much left to do tonight except get ready to go to sleep. I change into pajamas and slide into bed while Kade heads over to his reading chair across the room. He grabs the dog-eared copy of *The Lightning Thief* off the table. He wants to read the last chapter of the book to me before I leave. We've been saving it for tonight, kind of like a farewell party.

"No, sit here," I say, patting a spot beside me in bed. I want him close.

He nods and drops down, wordlessly. His body presses against my side, his free arm just grazing my bare legs, but never fully touching. The room is warm, like it always is, even with the window cracked open a bit to let fresh air in. But tonight, the heat of our bodies so close together makes it even hotter than normal. It's a good hot, though, one I don't want to end.

He reads slower than usual, as if hoping to draw things out.

I understand.

I want the night to last as long as possible, too.

But before I know it, he finishes the story and reluctantly closes the book. He places it on the nightstand next to the bed and blows out the lantern beside me, casting the room in shadows.

"It's late," he murmurs. "We'd better get some sleep. Big day tomorrow."

He starts to stand.

"Come with me," I whisper.

"Alix—"

"Please, Kade." I clutch his hand. "If you're really worried about me, come with me. Make sure I don't do anything dumb. Please... don't make me go alone."

I promised myself I wouldn't do this—wouldn't beg him to go with me—but now that the moment is here, I can't help it. I try to play tough and act like I don't need anyone, but the truth is I want him with me. I've grown attached, and now I can't imagine being outside these fences without him. I can't envision him not being there by my side after tonight.

"I'm sorry." His sigh is heavy and sad. "I just can't."

He pulls away from my grasp. In the dim light, I watch him wrap his arms around his legs and rest his chin on his knees. He stares out the bedroom window forlornly, looking almost lost.

"You think I'm wasting my time," I say to his handsome profile. "You think they're all dead. Your family, too. That's why you won't come, isn't it? You're too scared to go with me and find out for sure."

"Maybe I am."

"But wouldn't you rather know the truth?"

He shrugs. "Sometimes ignorance is better."

My eyes prick with wetness. I'm disappointed by his words, but mostly, I'm just hurt. If he really cared about me, he would never let me go alone, would he?

"*Please*—I don't want to do this all by myself!" I cry, my voice a desperate whisper.

His presence engulfs me as he leans in, his cool breath skimming across my cheek. Fingers tender, yet commanding, tilt my chin upward, compelling my eyes to his. Inches apart, I'm caught in the storm of his gaze. Regret and sorrow war with his resolve.

"Try to understand." His voice cracks, a raw edge of grief slicing through. "You're not the only one who's lost people they love. I know you're sad about your friends, but I lost my entire family. My mom. Dad. My little sister—she was only twelve, for Christ's sake!" he chokes out, his face a canvas of stark, undisguised anguish. "I know you're hurting, but you don't have a monopoly on pain, Alix."

"I... I never meant—" I blink hard, stumbling on my words. "That's not what I—"

"Do you really not get why I can't go with you?" he snaps, his eyes crackling fiercely. "I can't stand to lose another person I care about. The thought of you, in danger, it's unbearable!" His voice softens to a plea. "Do you really not see how I feel about you?"

His hand trails to my cheek, a whisper of a caress that sets my skin ablaze. My body hums at his nearness. His face hovers so close, his lips almost touch mine. I can't stop staring at them.

I'm mesmerized.

And then I decide I don't want to wait for him to make a move anymore. I've never been the kind of girl who waits around anyway. I'm the girl who knows what she wants and takes it.

I close the gap and kiss him.

The air crackles with electricity as our lips meet. For a moment, time seems to pause around us. The only thing that exists is the soft warmth of his lips against mine. His touch is tender, almost sweet, yet I sense a fierceness behind it, too. It ignites a fire deep within the pit of my belly, and I force myself to pull away. I feel like I might lose all control if it goes on for even a second longer.

Heat flames my face. A rush of conflicting feelings threatens to overwhelm me, leaving me breathless and yearning for more. That was the best kiss of my entire life, but I have no idea how he feels about it. I basically jumped his bones. Did he want it too, or did he only kiss me because I made him?

He blinks, surprised.

"Why did you do that?" he asks.

"I'm not sure." I duck my head, uncharacteristically shy. I never get insecure around guys, but there's just something about Kade that gets me all flustered.

I sneak a peek.

He's still staring at me.

"Why? Did you like it?" I grin hopefully.

"Yeah." He licks his lips, his eyes full of a heat and intensity that holds me transfixed, unable to look away. "Very much so."

He cups my face in his rough, calloused hands. Just his touch alone turns my legs to jelly, making me weak. It feels as if the entire room—the entire world—is holding its breath along with me. And then he draws me back in and his lips close on mine.

This time, he presses his mouth against mine with such emotion, such passion, it sets my whole body on fire. My heart slams in my chest, need surging through me like light-ning. I push in closer, until there's not an inch of room between our bodies. I want to feel him touch every part of me. I want his hands all over. I can't get enough of this.

Of him.

I can feel his body answer back, hot and urgent. Insistent. He slides his fingers through my hair, and I gasp as his tongue slips into my mouth. Slowly and sensually, he explores me.

My breath catches in my throat. I feel strange and dizzy, like I might implode and explode all at the same time. He kisses me and kisses me with such desperate intensity, like it's the last kiss either one of us will ever have. He kisses away all the fear. All the desolation. All the loneliness inside us both.

For just a moment, cradled in his arms and high off the feeling of him, I allow myself to dream of a different life. Of a life where Kade and I live happily ever after in this great, big, beautiful house. Just the two of us, holed up here together for a lifetime, never to be discovered by anyone else.

Happy.

Safe.

Our bellies full with vegetables and grains from his farm and the surrounding fields. Getting drunk on fancy wines from his father's cellar. Enjoying a perfect little life where he reads to me in bed every night, and kisses me until I can't breathe, and vampires don't exist.

But then... I wake up.

PART THREE
THE RESISTANCE

CHAPTER 23
DAY 29: 6:30 A.M.

The Black Family Farm

The next morning, he wakes me with a warm, home-cooked breakfast in bed. After we eat our last meal together, it's time to say goodbye.

He doesn't kiss me again though I wish he would. He just pulls me into his arms and holds me so tight it's hard to breathe for a minute. Then he wishes me well, and we walk outside together, past his fence and to the road ahead. He goes one way; I go the other.

As far as final goodbyes go, it's anticlimactic. There were more tears when my high school boyfriend and I split up to head to different colleges. It makes me second guess everything from last night. Maybe he doesn't really care about me at all—at least not the same way I was starting to care about him?

I wonder if last night for him was more about being with a woman—any woman—than it was about being with me.

This could be End of Days, after all. The idea makes me a bit sad since I was beginning to develop real feelings for Kade, but I don't have time or energy to dwell on it. Right now, I have bigger things on my mind than romance. Besides, since I may never see him again anyway, it's probably easier this way.

Instead of letting my thoughts linger on what might have been, I do my best to think of our time together fondly and try not to make it out to be more than it was, no matter how my heart may feel. What matters is that Kade kept me from dying. He helped me when I needed help the most. He fed me. Protected me. Got me healthy again. And then, he taught me how to fight back. Those things are far more useful to me than any declaration of love could ever be.

As I start my journey down the road, I triple check again that all my guns are loaded and ready to go. The shotgun is in my right hand, handgun on the holster at my hip. My knives are easily accessible: one small knife tucked near the gun holster, the second small knife hidden in my boot. The third knife, the larger hunting knife, sits in the outside pocket of my backpack.

Before long, I arrive at the woods that run parallel to the road and head for the trees. It will be safer to get off the road and continue my journey there. Even the sparse cover provided by dried, dusty branches is better than nothing, offering at least some shield from the searing morning sun and protection against being spotted. According to Kade's map, the factory farm is about two miles away. I should be there in less than an hour. The goal is to get there with as much daylight left as possible and hope it gives me some small advantage against the vampires.

I keep myself moving, foregoing stopping for anything other than a few sips of water, so I don't dehydrate. No time for snacks. No resting breaks. Time is of the essence.

Go, Alix, go, I pep talk myself.

The sun beats down on me relentlessly. It's so brutal. Almost unbearable. Sweat coats every inch of my body. The clothes Kade loaned me for the trip cling to me: a pair of his mother's biker shorts, a tank top, and her best hiking boots. I've got my hair tucked into a ponytail in his New York Yankees baseball cap—black, of course—to keep the sun out of my eyes.

Soon, my bad leg starts to ache. It's nothing too terrible yet but feels like it has the potential to get worse. I pause for just long enough to grab the Advil that Kade made me pack, grateful for his foresight, and swallow down two pills with a big gulp of water. I'm hot, sticky, and achy, but it doesn't matter. Nothing matters except getting to my friends.

After about a mile, the western path I follow veers to the south, almost converging with the nearby road that runs parallel to the woods. According to Kade's map, this is the major interstate within Allium Valley. He told me they built the road back in the heyday of the factory farm when they had to move cattle and meat products around the state. Theoretically, there could be traffic from out of town here. Kade said I should be watchful and keep my eyes peeled, but I don't see any cars go by. Not a soul in sight, just me standing alone in the silence.

It makes me wonder.

Most—all?—of the town's residents are probably trapped inside the factory farm by now, or dead, but what about the neighboring towns? Why isn't anyone from outside Allium Valley driving in?

The most logical answer is this is just not a high traffic area to begin with. A small farm town like this, all the way out in the middle of nowhere, probably doesn't get a lot of outside visitors.

Or perhaps the vampires have blockaded the entrances,

closing the main road in and out of town. Made up some kind of reason for folks not to come here. A gas leak? Hazardous material spill? Health quarantine? Road construction, even?

A quick and disturbing thought comes to me—I *really* hope it's not because the other neighboring towns have already been taken over, too...

Finally, the factory farm comes into view.

As soon as I catch sight of the massive, ominous compound of horrors, the full impact of what I'm about to do crashes over me like a tidal wave, almost knocking me down. Once again, I'm assaulted by memories of horrific vampire carnage. Long canines—white and deadly. Sharp as knives. Dripping blood.

What would it be like to have those razor teeth pierce my skin? Rip open my neck?

How would it feel to be drained of all my life?

A chill runs through me, despite the blistering heat. It's so overpowering that I have to lean against a nearby tree and brace myself. For just a moment, I allow myself a brief surrender to the terror, giving in and languishing in it. My entire body turns cold, my pulse pounding in my ear like a thousand speeding freight trains.

But then, I find a silent resolve from somewhere deep within and reign it all back in. I straighten my shoulders, tossing away the shroud of paralyzing feelings like last year's trendy "It" bag. Courage is the new black. I have a job to do, and I won't be distracted by fear now that I've come this far.

Above me, the sun is almost at the highest point of the day. I've made good time.

Through Kade's binoculars, I peer at the front gate and at the compound's perimeters to get a better look at the security detail. Kade thought the main entrance would be the most heavily guarded, but I don't see anyone obviously patrolling or watching things. Not that I know what I was expecting to see, anyway. A vampire in uniform, holding a rifle? That seems kind of absurd.

These things don't need guns to control humans.

Still, just because I don't see what seems like guards, doesn't mean they aren't there. For all I know, they could be right inside the paddocks or in the slaughterhouse, just chilling and looking like "normal" people. I might not even recognize one until it's too late and they're after me.

Kade thought finding a small opening around the perimeter would be my best chance of getting inside undetected, but not knowing what the enemy looks like is a big problem no matter what entrance I try to breach. I have no idea who is friend or foe here, and by the time I can figure it out, it could be too late.

But I already knew that was a problem.

After that awful day in the forest with my friends, I'd seen first-hand the dangers of not being able to recognize the vampires fast enough. That's why my new plan, the one I thought of late last night, is my best chance of success.

I'd been unable to fall asleep after Kade left my bedroom, so I stayed up reading the book he'd given me, plotting and strategizing more ideas on the best way to infiltrate the factory farm. I wasn't sure until now. I needed to be here with the binoculars to see it first-hand, but now that I've confirmed things, I'm even more confident of the final plan I came up with.

There's only one way to get inside this place and not risk getting caught too early. Only one thing I can do to ensure entry while keeping the vamps oblivious to my scheme.

I have to be taken in voluntarily... as one of their prisoners.

CHAPTER 24
11:15 A.M.

The old Allium Valley Cattle Farm

I hide my guns and my backpack with the large hunting knife in a ditch as close to the cattle farm gate as I can get them without risking being seen. I certainly can't bring them inside with me. The guns especially will blow the cover story I've come up with to get inside. At least this way, I'll have easy access to them once I escape with my friends, if all goes as planned.

The other two smaller knives I keep on me; the one still safely tucked inside my boot and the other underneath my shirt within Kade's leather sheath. I've also got hidden within my pockets the lock-picking tools Kade gave me—the hook pick and the tension wrench and even the mini pry bar —names I learned reading his dad's book last night.

Also in my pocket is the Swiss Army knife with the handy attachments: blade, scissors, screwdriver, pocket flashlight. Tucked deep inside my sports bra, close to my heart, is the tiny vial of garlic oil and the lighter. If all goes to hell, I figure I can at least use them to distract the vampires and get away.

My plan hinges on the vampires not being suspicious of me, seeing as I'm going inside voluntarily. The hope is they won't even think to check me for weapons upon my arrival. After all, who would be crazy enough to try to breach a vampire lair so openly and all by themselves? I can't imagine anyone else left in Allium Valley would have such an unconventional plan as mine. The vampires will have no reason to suspect me of anything, other than being a total imbecile. They'll have no idea I'm going Trojan Horse on their asses.

Funny enough, I got the idea from the Percy Jackson books. When I was brainstorming last night, I thought of Percy and all the Greek heroes and legends and how they'd won battles against insurmountable odds. It made me remember something I learned back in school about the Trojan War.

The Greeks, unable to penetrate the fortified city of Troy to wage war there, constructed a wooden horse. They presented it as a gift—a symbol of their surrender—and offered it to their enemies. But then, in secrecy, they hid their soldiers inside. That's how they got into Troy and won the war. If it worked for them, why not me?

My third time scaling the cattle farm's gate feels old hat by now. I get up and over it almost effortlessly. Then I put a big smile on my face and walk straight to the front door of the slaughterhouse and knock.

What they will see: a petite, innocent-looking blonde woman in her early twenties, with a smudged face, dressed in sweaty workout clothes. She's from out of town. Her car broke down a few miles back. She's been walking, searching for help, lost and worried, until stumbling upon this old cattle farm. She's thrilled. Totally oblivious to the fact that she's just walked into a death trap.

They'll have no idea what my real purpose is, or what I'm capable of. For once in my life, the stereotype of dumb blonde should work to my advantage.

The handsome vampire who opens the door towers over me, muscles rippling under the tight fabric of his dark shirt. There's a predatory glint in his icy blue eyes, and his cruel mouth hints at malice, though it currently curls into an ear-to-ear grin, as if he can't believe his luck.

I beam back my most charming smile and greet him happily.

He asks my name. Am I hurt? Would I like to come inside?

He could kill me in two seconds, drain me of all my blood right here in the middle of the slaughterhouse door-way, but he's having too much fun toying with me. This one likes to play with his food.

He takes my hand and escorts me inside, wearing that fake-ass disarming smile all the while. My insides run cold at his touch, the hair on the back of my neck standing straight up. It's like holding hands with a deadly reptile. Every nerve in my body is on high alert, telling me I'm in mortal danger. That I should run.

Instead, I follow him further down the hallway.

The first thing I notice is all the lights. They must have an alternative source of power running inside here. A generator, maybe?

Johnny—that's his name—makes small talk while I pretend to be interested and engaged as we walk past a big empty office on the left. All the while, I'm checking out the situation.

How strange. I don't see anyone else around the place.

I wonder if the rest of the vampires are off sleeping or

resting or whatever they do during the day? Perhaps only a few are needed inside to keep things under control. Especially now, when almost everyone in town is either locked up in here or dead.

The entire time, Johnny keeps his facade up and I keep mine. He's perfectly charming, maintaining his polished veneer. That is, until he heaves open the massive double doors—doors that are both grand and formidable, thick enough to muffle the sounds of the world within them.

We've finally arrived at the area of the slaughterhouse where all the indoor paddocks are housed. That's when everything changes.

I pretend to scream and cry as soon as I see the people trapped inside. I act terrified and put on a good show. I give him everything he wants—the sadistic fucker—as he shoves me, laughing, toward one of the caged pens. Only after he locks me up and leaves do I reach down to stroke my hidden knives through my clothes. I smile to myself, taking comfort knowing they're here with me.

I can't believe it.

I'm inside! My plan worked!

I scan my new surroundings, taking note of as many details as possible for future use. I've never been inside a slaughterhouse before. I have no clue if this is what they all look like or if the vampires have made changes for their own specific needs.

There's one long hallway that runs down the center of the building that dead-ends into yards of fenced-in pens. That's where the cattle are kept. The cattle here, of course, are people. The vampires have trapped what looks to be the entire town, like a twenty-four-seven all-you-can-eat smorgasbord.

Inside each pen seems to be at least a dozen or so humans all squashed together, wearing various types of attire. Some appear to still be in their clothes from the Garlic Groove Festival, weeks ago. Once sparkling sequins and tassels and colorful fringe are now tattered and caked with dirt and splatters of blood. Some people are in nightgowns, like they were snatched right out of bed. Some are in work uniforms. I suppose they're all still wearing whatever they were captured in. The only thing they all have in common: a big orange tag hanging from their ears.

Confusion grips me for a split second, the surreal scene warping my senses. Then, the brutal reality crashes down, and a wave of revulsion surges through my stomach.

They're tagging people!

It's exactly like what ranchers do to their cattle to keep track of them and make sure they stay in place. The vampires are tagging human beings, treating them as property, as livestock marked for death. Each one—a person, someone's friend, someone's family—reduced to a meal.

I double over, a loud gag tearing from my throat, yet the sound falls on deaf ears. No one even glances up at me. The prisoners are either asleep or too lost in their own despair, lying on the dirt floor that's become their bed, their graveyard.

The ones that are awake have big blank eyes devoid of caring. Listless and hopeless. There's no more crying or moaning like the early days, like the last time I was at the slaughterhouse weeks ago looking in from the window outside. The prisoners must now be desensitized to everything and everyone.

Inside the pens are people of all colors, shapes, and sizes —white, Black, brown, skinny, heavy, tall, short. One thing about these vamps, they don't discriminate. The only thing I notice missing are children and babies. There doesn't appear to be anyone younger than a teenager in here.

It's so odd. I wonder why? What happened to them?

This town must have had its share of young kids before the vampires took over, so where did they go? They didn't just disappear.

And then I think of veal.

A sense of overwhelming horror washes over me. It's a raw, primal fear that clenches at my heart. My chest tightens with dread at my suspicion. For a moment, my world spins out of control.

Veal—the baby male cows—have the most tender meat since they're so young. They're slaughtered early, while still adolescents, because people find their meat extra delicious.

What if it's the same with vampires and little kids? What if that's why they aren't in here with us?

The revulsion threatens to overcome me, but I force myself to swallow back my nausea and harden myself against any emotion. I can't go there. I can't allow myself to break down yet—not before I've done what I came here to do. I have to focus on my plan. Saving my friends. That's all I have the mental and emotional bandwidth for right now.

I work my way over to the back of my pen and sit down on the ground, feeling around. The dirt is moveable, pliable beneath my fingers.

Good. That's exactly what I was hoping for.

I glance around to make sure no one is watching me. The vampire from earlier, Johnny, has left and gone back to wherever he was lurking before I showed up, probably to one of the offices. Above, I see a few cameras attached to the ceiling, pointing down on the pens. I doubt they're working with the Wi-Fi and cell service still out, but, even if they were, I don't think they can see what I'm doing this far down on the ground.

I need to work fast. The orange tags on the other prisoners lets me know there is some kind of intake process here, though I'm not sure what it entails. At some point, probably soon, someone is going to come for me. I can't risk them finding my weapons and tools and figuring out what I'm up to.

Down on my hands and knees, I start to dig. None of the other human prisoners ask me what I'm doing; they don't seem to notice or care. Dirt gets in my nails, but it doesn't matter anymore. My perfect manicure has long since been destroyed. It's almost funny how something like a broken nail would've made me so mad before, and now it's the last thing on my mind. It seems like years ago, not weeks, since I cared about my appearance.

Soon, I've got a hole big enough to hide my knives and tools inside. The idea of being defenseless in here terrifies me so much I allow myself to keep just the oil and lighter tucked way down inside my sports bra. They're so small and hidden away, no one will notice them. Everything else goes in the ground, buried deep. After, I cover it all back up with dirt, so there's no sign of what I've done.

I finish just in time. They come for me moments later.

CHAPTER 25
1:00 P.M.

The Cattle Farm Slaughterhouse

Vampire Johnny returns for me in my slaughterhouse pen. This time he's accompanied by a female. She's almost as big as he is and just as mean, though nowhere near as good-looking.

For some reason, I thought all vampires were supposed to be beautiful. It must be all the movies and TV I watched with impossibly gorgeous actors. This woman, though, is most definitely not attractive. Not at all. She's got a huge hook nose, a broad cleft chin, and a variety of moles and pimples covering her face.

She grabs me by the arm and yanks me out of the pen. She's so strong, she practically rips my arm from the socket, sending a surge of shock through my body. I let out a loud yelp, but she doesn't even blink, just drags me along faster. I get the feeling I'm just one of hundreds she's seen since they set up shop here.

They take me to an empty office at the front of the factory and escort me inside. The room is small. White walls. White floor. White ceiling. There's an old desk and computer in the corner that appears to be unused. This must have been a back office in days before, back when the place was operational for cattle farming and before it was turned into a room for human intakes.

They don't frisk me. They don't pat me down. I'm a nobody to them. Just another pretty blonde. A body to feed on. Certainly nothing to worry about.

I shouldn't have bothered hiding my tools and weapons. Their hubris, the fact they can't even imagine I might be a threat to them, will hopefully work in my favor later.

On one side of the room is a large scale where the woman takes my measurements first, height and weight, and jots them down on a pad. After, she guides me to the center of the room where there's a long white table. She picks me up and places me on it all by herself, without any help from Johnny. The beauty myths may not be true, but it looks like the ones about vampires having supernatural strength are.

Up on the exam table, the woman pokes and prods at me. She takes my temperature and blood pressure and makes notes on the yellow legal pad in front of her. Then she makes me open my mouth and checks my eyes and ears and takes more notes. It feels like a physical at the doctor's office. My best guess is this is their way of making sure their food is healthy and won't give them some kind of illness.

She finishes by pushing uncomfortably on my abdomen and the sides of my neck where my lymph nodes are. After making a few final notes on her papers, she puts the notepad back down onto the desk. Thankfully, it seems I check out fine. I don't even want to know what they do to the poor people that have a fever or cold. They probably put them down, same as sick livestock.

The whole time she conducts her examination, Johnny stares at me and scowls. I wonder what the male vampire is even doing here. The woman is clearly strong enough that she doesn't need his help escorting me or dragging me around anywhere. She's also the only one taking all my measurements and stats. And it's not like I have any hope of escaping or causing her trouble. Unarmed, I'm no match for her. He seems to be totally worthless.

Maybe he just likes to watch?

God, I hope he does have a job because somehow that idea seems far worse than anything he could do to me...

A moment later, I regret that thought.

He walks over to the cabinets and pulls out a large black tagging gun. His eyes shine like a kid on Christmas morning as he heads toward me. That's when I understand why he's here.

It's time for the tagging.

The woman turns away as he approaches. She actually looks a little queasy. Maybe she still has some emotions left, after all.

The asshole doesn't even warn me or count to five. He just grabs my dangly pearl drop earring in my left ear and rips it out. Then he stabs me with the tagging gun right above the bloody gash he's made in my earlobe.

I scream as white-hot searing pain shoots straight into my skull. It's so bad, I almost pass out. My vision blurs. I get hot and cold and nauseous all at the same time.

After the pain passes and I can see straight again, I catch my reflection in a mirror hanging on the wall. My mom's treasured pearl earring is now gone from one ear. In its place hangs a bright orange tag. Number 321.

My mind flashes back to our drive to Allium Valley weeks ago. I can still see the tiny blue sign that read population 3,000. What the hell happened to the other 2,679 people? Surely the vampires couldn't have killed them all in such a short time?

I don't want to believe that's even a possibility, but what other logical explanation can there be? Maybe a handful of townsfolk might be hiding around Allium Valley like Kade and I were, but I have a hard time believing hundreds are. And there's no way they all escaped into the next town over or the Army or Navy—someone—would be here by now.

That means they must be dead.

If all those people are dead, how likely is it that my friends are still alive at this cattle farm somewhere? What are the chances they were spared?

Not good, even I know that.

It's looking even worse than I feared. I didn't think these creatures would go through people so fast. I was hoping for more time, but now I realize Kade was right all along.

I was a fool to come here.

I should've listened to him. I see now that there's no hope my friends have survived. All I've done is come to the slaughter myself, like a stupid sacrificial lamb. I've almost certainly wasted my own life for no good reason at all.

Even worse, I could be on the road right now with Kade, trying to warn other people. There's still the rest of the world that has no idea what's happening here. I could've helped them all. Maybe I could've saved my dad.

But now, I'm not sure if I can even save myself.

Intense regret and a looming sense of dread both consume me as the female vampire leads me back to the pens. Her touch is a little gentler now as she guides me down the halls, as if she almost feels sorry for me.

Well, that makes two of us, sister.

My heart drops even further as we go past the pen where Johnny first put me, and she keeps on walking. We get about a hundred feet away, to an entirely new pen, and then she opens the door and pushes me inside.

Wetness starts to form in my eyes. Not only am I trapped in a fenced-in pen with no hope left to find my friends alive, but I'm not even near my weapons and tools anymore. There's no way I can get out of here without access to them.

Sorrow threatens to overcome me.

This is it.

This is the end of the road for me.

I'm going to die in here, all alone, and all for nothing.

Soundlessly, I shuffle my way through the pen. I shove past the silent, lifeless people clumped together in the center and those drinking numbly at the big metal water troughs, until I reach a spot in the far back corner where I can be alone. Then I drop down to the floor and bury my head in my hands, allowing the tears to fall.

They drip down my cheeks and onto the dirt floor at my feet, turning it muddy. Now I see why everyone here is walking around half-asleep. There's nothing else to do among all this despair, except lay here and wait for death. Might as well be unconscious...

"Alix?"

No. It can't be...

I must be hallucinating or dreaming. The voice is so familiar to me, but there's no way—

"Al? Is it really you?"

I jerk up and whip my head around, gasping as Zoe comes into view.

Logan is at her side, with Jenny right behind him, clinging to his arm. They all wear the same outfits I last saw them in back at the woods, though their clothes are now dirty and torn. They look pale and weak. They've lost a lot of weight. Logan seems to have gotten the worst of it. He has a big bruise on his face, a nasty purple mark that takes up the entire bottom part of his chin.

It takes a moment for the shock to wear off and for understanding to dawn on me.

They're real.

This isn't my imagination.

My friends are alive!

It finally seems like things are looking up. And it's not just that they're okay, which is a miracle in and of itself, but it's also that I've found them so fast. I can't believe it. Of all the pens in this entire godforsaken place, the vampires chose to put me in theirs.

CHAPTER 26
4:30 P.M.

The Cattle Farm Slaughterhouse

Zoe and I cling to each other, hugging, our sobs and laughter mingling in a bittersweet reunion. Even after we finally pull away, I keep squeezing her hands, needing the reassurance of her presence. I wish this moment between us—this fragile bubble of joy amidst chaos—could last forever.

"Thank God you're all right," Logan says, his voice rough with emotion, eyes glistening.

"Logan!" I breathe out his name in a mix of happiness and tears.

Our eyes lock and a warm glow, like the first ray of sunshine after a stormy night, flows through me. My body fills with relief and joy at seeing him standing in front of me.

Alive.

"Worried about me?" he teases.

"You have no idea." My voice cracks as I throw my arms

around him, the rush of emotions overwhelming me for a moment.

He tries to smile at me as we step apart, but pain crumples his expression, a wince slicing through his attempt at bravery. My heart clenches with sorrow as my eyes drift back to the massive bruise, spreading like a shadow across his jaw. It's clear by their appearances how much my friends have already suffered in this terrible place. I can't imagine all they've been through since I last saw them in the forest.

I pivot, my gaze drifting over to Jenny next. "And Jenny —wow! I'm so glad to see you," I say, genuinely meaning it as I pull her into a warm embrace. "How—how are you here?"

"It's a long story." Jenny hesitates, a shadow passing over her features before she blinks it away with a shaky smile. "After we got separated at the festival, I tried to make it back to my aunt and uncle's place to find you guys. But when I got to the camping grounds, I... I got attacked." Her eyes dart away for a moment, and she takes in a long, trembling breath before continuing. "They brought me to the cattle farm, where they've been holding me ever since. I was all alone until Zoe and Logan showed up. It's been so awful..."

"It's okay, Jen. We're all here now," Zoe says, resting her hand on Jenny's shoulder, offering solace.

"God, Jenny, that must've been so terrifying," I say.

"Yeah, it was... But, you know, I managed." Jenny shrugs, almost a little too nonchalantly.

I step back, studying her face. There's a strange undertone in her voice, a hint of something that doesn't quite fit.

Her story isn't the problem—it's her eyes. They don't hold the amount of fear or desperation I'd expect from someone who's been trapped in a vampire slaughterhouse for weeks now, waiting to die. Something feels... off.

Detached. Like she's holding back a crucial piece of the puzzle.

But then I decide I'm being unfair. I remember how it was after Mom died and how the therapists all told my dad that trauma effects everyone in different ways. It's not reasonable to expect Jenny to look or act any one way after what we've all been through. Besides, she's always been a little strange, even before all of this.

"I was so worried about you all alone out there," Logan says, his eyes still trained on me. "I should've known you could take care of yourself."

"Yeah, what happened?" Zoe stares at me in wonderment. "Where did you go after the woods?"

"Kade helped me," I explain. "I got shot, too, and was really sick from the darts. I should've died, but he took me to his house and gave me medicine."

"Good, I'm glad he was there for you," Logan says, his glance soft and earnest. In the depths of his big blue eyes, there's a sincere concern that overshadows any sort of rivalry he may have had with Kade.

Zoe cocks her head. "But what happened then? How'd they catch you?" She peers behind me. "And where's Kade?"

"They never found us. I came for you."

"I don't understand." She takes a step back, her brown eyes narrowing into small slits as she studies my face. "You came here by yourself? *Voluntarily?*"

I nod.

"You idiot!" Zoe's voice erupts, a mixture of fury and frustration. She lashes out, both hands pushing against my chest. If she wasn't so weak, it probably would've hurt. "Why the hell would you do that?"

"I had to." I shrug. "I couldn't let you die in here."

"You're so stupid, Alix!" she hisses, looking like she wants to shove me around some more. "So damn stupid..."

"Well, gee, not exactly the warm welcome I was hoping for," I mutter sarcastically. "How about—thanks for saving the day, Alix? We're so happy you're here, Alix?"

"You shouldn't have done this!" Logan's eyes flash with anger like I've never seen from him before. "You don't know what we're up against. It's *hell* in here!"

I glance around the pen, worried our arguing is drawing too much attention to us. I don't want anyone but my friends to hear what I have to say next.

Luckily, no one is watching us. It's truly a miracle my friends are all still alive, but that could change at any moment. We need to act fast. There's no telling how much time we have left.

I lean in and whisper, "Then I guess it's a good thing I'm going to get you out."

"That's impossible!" Logan huffs. "Believe me, I've already tried everything," he says and absentmindedly rubs at the huge bruise on his face.

"Well, I've got a plan." I purse my lips, hands on my hips. "A good one."

At least it was a good one before I got put into the wrong pen...

Still, as long as I can get to my tools and weapons, I'm pretty sure I can get my friends out of here.

"You'll need a lot more than just a plan to escape this place," Logan says. "You'll need weapons. Soldiers. Tanks and warships would be good. It's like Fort Knox in here."

"Trust me, this will work," I say.

"You haven't seen what we've seen, Alix." Jenny inches in closer to Logan, wrapping an arm around him, almost possessively. "Last time Logan tried to get us out, they beat him so badly he almost died," she says. "And no offense, but

Logan is a lot bigger and stronger than you, and smarter too—"

I snort. "Oh, no offense taken."

"I mean about this kind of stuff—military stuff," she clarifies.

"Right, of course." I roll my eyes.

"And all it got him was a bunch of fresh bruises and pain for his efforts, so forgive us if we have our doubts that you'll have better luck," she continues. "I mean, this is a war, not a fashion show."

I stare at her, baffled. I'm certain that last part was an intentional dig, even if Jenny's face looks all clear and innocent. And she doesn't even seem worried about saying it, or scared of me anymore. Not like she used to be.

Still, I decide to let it go; I've got bigger fish to fry at the moment.

"It really is hopeless." Zoe sighs. "I'm sorry you did all this for nothing, Al."

"Yeah, well, I'm not." I stiffen my shoulders.

Their lack of faith in me is annoying, but I can't blame them. They have no idea what I've been up to and how much I've changed since they last saw me. They don't know that while they've been withering away here, readying to die, I've been plotting. Preparing. Training.

I give them a sly look and proceed to tell them all about the supplies I've smuggled inside. Lock-picking tools perfect for opening the padlocks on our pens. Knives we can use for stabbing a few vamps in the heart, if necessary. Even the explosive garlic oil and Kade's lighter to blow shit up if worse comes to worst.

But first, before I can execute what I have in mind, I need a little more intel.

So far, I've only seen two vampires since I've been taken inside the slaughterhouse. Johnny and the mean lady who examined me. The gorgeous woman from the woods and at least one—if not both—of the male vampires with her that day are likely in here, too. That makes four or five vampires, at minimum, but Frog seemed to think there were a lot more now. I'm hopeful he was exaggerating to keep me away and that there isn't a whole slew of them I just haven't seen yet.

"How many vampires are in here?" I ask Logan, figuring he's been keeping track. That's what I'd be doing if I were him.

"Not as many as you'd think necessary to be capable of all of this." He gestures around to all the miserable human captives in pens alongside us. "I haven't counted more than ten."

"Ten?" I sigh with relief. "That's not bad."

"It's not just the number," Logan says. "They're strong, Alix. Too damn strong. It might as well be ten thousand."

I don't let his negativity get to me. No matter the spin he puts on it, I'm still elated to hear this news. Ten vampires isn't nothing. It's more than I could take on my own, even if I had all my guns, but it's far better than what Frog led us to believe. Certainly, better than a dozen vampires. Better than fifty. Better than a hundred.

Next, I ask about the schedule here to get an idea of how to proceed with my plan. Logan tells me there are usually two vampires on patrol during the day and two at night. Sometimes more, but never less than two. About half of the security detail are women and half are men. They're all cold and uncaring, though some are worse than others. Some—like Johnny—take actual pleasure in torturing the people trapped inside. The rest just do what needs to be done to keep their meals coming.

In addition to checking pens and making sure nothing is out of place and everyone is relatively healthy and subdued, the vampire patrol also feeds the humans twice a day. Once in the morning and once at night. The food is surprisingly healthy, according to Zoe who has always been a picky eater. Organic fruits and veggies. No sugars or sweets. It sounds similar to how expensive Kobe steak is well taken care of. It's gross to think about, but I suppose human blood also tastes better when properly tended to.

The only other interaction between the vampires and humans is when they come by to refill the water troughs— every few days according to Logan—or when someone is sick and needs to be removed from the pens. Or when the vampires come to collect their dinner, of course.

Every evening, they take at least a handful of people away to be bled out. There's a kill floor somewhere in the factory farm, though Logan himself hasn't seen it and doesn't know where it is. All he knows is that it's where they bring the humans they plan to eat.

Logan also confirms my terrifying thoughts about the kids and the babies. I was right; they were the first to be killed.

That isn't even the worst of it, though. Apparently, the vampires are also running experiments on some people being held captive. They use the elderly because they're the easiest to control and least likely to fight back.

He doesn't know the full extent, just snippets of whispered rumors the other captives have shared. Something about tests involving exposure to diseases and genetic experiments—acts aimed to serve the vampires' goals of increasing their food supply while also ensuring the blood stays clean and healthy.

It seems the vampires are burning through this town. They're going to run out of people to eat soon, but whether they're coming up with new ways to make the food last longer or if they've started to test the waters in neighboring towns, my friends don't know.

Once I get all the facts together, Logan helps me solidify a new plan. Obviously, the strategy Kade and I came up with before won't work anymore, so we have to start from scratch.

We agree a daytime jailbreak is the smartest option. There are less vampires wandering around the slaughterhouse then. Since all the pens are secured with padlocks that lock from the outside, the only option to get to my weapons and tools in the other pen is to somehow steal a key or sneak out of the gate unnoticed when the vampires already have it open.

We immediately dismiss the idea of key stealing. Without any weapons, there's no way to get close enough to the vampires for that.

That leaves option two.

The best chance is for me to escape when the vampires are coming in for one of the reasons Logan mentioned before—food, water, tending to the sick, or getting their dinner. But how to sneak out without being noticed?

Logan suggests a distraction.

If he can avert the vampires' attention long enough, I can hopefully slip out of the opened gate unnoticed. The hardest part will be getting into the other pen where my tools and weapons are buried. I'll have to hide somewhere until the vampires open that pen and then figure out how to sneak in behind them, without being caught. But if I can do this, If I can get my supplies and get back to my friends with everything, we can all escape together.

One thing working in our favor is how much the vampires underestimate us. By now, most of the people in here are weak and have already given up. They've had the fight beaten out of them. The vampires won't be expecting anything like this, not as long as we time it right. It's not the best plan in the world, but it's not the worst, either.

Besides, we don't have a ton of options, so it's going to have to do.

That night, Logan and I study the feeding situation as the vampires come in with our dinner. It's not complicated. One vamp uses a key to open the pen gates and the other walks inside with the food. Everyone is so docile, they don't even carry weapons like batons or—God forbid—a cattle prod.

The four of us sit next to each other, biting into our apples and cheese sandwiches. I have to admit, the food tastes delicious, especially after spending weeks eating game meat and wizened foraged produce.

I wonder where the vampires got fresh bread and cheese from?

It makes me worry that they could already be passing into nearby towns for supplies. It won't be much longer before they start invading there too, if they haven't already begun.

The next morning comes fast.

I'm not sure if I'm ready for this. If I could, I'd take more time to survey things first and make sure I understand patterns and behaviors around here, but there isn't more time, so it's now or never.

The vampires come by at first light, right on schedule, as Logan said they would. There are two of them, also like Logan predicted. It's Johnny again, the masochist. I'm not thrilled to see him, given his penchant for enjoying torture, but his presence doesn't worry me as much as *hers*.

The woman from the woods—the vampire from the factory farm window—is with him this morning. The chillingly beautiful one with the long dark hair and eyes like a snake.

She heads toward the pen. Key in hand. Gait smooth as

a panther. Strolling around the place like she doesn't have a care in the world.

Who knows? She probably doesn't.

Her presence fills me with dread. It's not just the atrocities I've seen her commit but what I'm certain she's further capable of if given the chance. Her slow, precise, confident mannerisms scream apex predator. She instills the same sense of panic in me as I imagine I'd feel being nose-to-nose with a great white shark or a killer crocodile.

My knees shake, but I grit my teeth and force my mind to quiet. I can't focus on her. We have a good plan. I won't let my fear get in the way.

The four of us push to the front of the pen as soon as the vampires get to the gate. The male carries a giant box of food. Just as we practiced, Zoe lets out a scream the instant he drops the box down into the pen.

"He's trying to steal the food!" she yells to the vampires, pointing at Logan.

"No, I wasn't—"

She slaps Logan across the face. *"Liar!"*

Logan acts stunned. He steps backward, tripping into the box. Food flies everywhere, creating a mess. This, too, is part of our plan.

Johnny stalks forward into the pen. He shakes his fist and grins, looking thrilled to start the morning with violence. The female follows behind, but her demeanor is the polar opposite of his. She's calm and collected. Her nostrils flare but only slightly, just moderately annoyed, like this might make her a few minutes late for her morning massage.

Both vamps are in the pen now, focused on Logan. Behind them, the gate is left wide open. Phase I is complete.

Now for Phase II.

Zoe and Logan pretend to fight, shoving each other back

and forth. They fall into the other people around them. Yelps and squeals. Bodies crash to the ground. This is the part where Jenny is supposed to get into the mix, creating even more mayhem and confusion by joining Zoe and Logan in pushing the other captives around the pen, so I can escape through the gate undetected. Instead, she only stares, frozen, with that strange, detached expression on her face again.

What a complete idiot.

Leave it to Jenny to choke, just when we need her the most.

Luckily, her inaction doesn't derail anything. Just as we hoped, the vampires move deeper into the pen to stop the ruckus. This creates even more chaos.

Now everyone is panicking.

Jostling. Yelling.

They're all trying to get away from the vampires at all costs. The crowd surges in one direction and then another. Screams echo in the slaughterhouse as people are mercilessly pinned against the fence in the ensuing stampede.

"Get back!" Johnny yells at the panicked crowd. "Get away!"

Now it's time for Phase III.

I'm so nervous, sweat pours into my eyes. I wipe it away with one hand and grab Zoe's shoulders, like we practiced, and then launch her straight into the female vampire. She falls right on target, screaming in pain. That part isn't acting.

Shit.

I'd forgotten about all the training I've been doing and hurled her way too hard. She and the female vampire both go crashing to the ground.

I wince, feeling terrible. I want to rush over and help her up. Apologize. But there's no time. Before the vampire can recover, I'm at the gate. I slip through the crack without anyone noticing. It's almost too easy.

I can't believe it! Our plan worked!

I've already got one foot in the hallway and am well on my way to the pen with all my hidden tools and weapons when I hear a woman screaming behind me. Her voice sends fear spiking down my spine—

"Stop her! She's escaping!"

But it isn't the female vampire yelling after me or even some crazed Benedict Arnold stranger from the pen.

It's Jenny.

CHAPTER 27
DAY 30: 8:55 A.M.

The Cattle Farm Slaughterhouse

T he vampires are after me.

I race toward the pen that has my weapons, even though I know it's hopeless. Even if I can get there before the vampires catch me—unlikely—I'd still have to figure out how to get inside without a key.

Still, I'm close.

The pen isn't far, only a few feet away. I'm almost there, but the vampires move so fast, even faster than I ever thought possible. Within seconds, they're on me. I never had a chance at all.

It's an important lesson to note for future, if I somehow survive. Never try to outrun a vampire: It's a losing proposition.

Johnny gets to me first. He launches me against the pen's steel gate, so hard I bounce off it like a rubber band and go crashing to the ground. Black starbursts dance across my vision. My body screams in agony. The pain is unbelievable. I imagine it's what it feels like to be hit by a semi-truck.

Oh God.

I think I may have broken my back.

I'm stunned by the impact, defenseless and unable to move anything, not even a finger, as I steal a glance back toward the pen I'd fled. There's Jenny, clinging to the gate, her eyes locked on mine. A twisted smile curls her lips, a silent gloating look that chills me to the bone.

Zoe and Logan scramble to their feet, no longer carrying on the staged scuffle meant to cover my escape. Their faces hold a mix of disbelief and rage as they close in on Jenny, yelling. Their fury is palpable even from this distance.

I try to get up, but my legs won't move. For an instant, I worry I may be paralyzed, but then Johnny grabs me, yanking me to my feet. He holds me, my arms pinned painfully behind my body, as the female vampire approaches. She's clearly the one in charge.

"And where do you think you're going?" she asks. Her face is so close I can see the sharp tips of her canines. The sight sets my pulse skittering at an erratic rate. Panic threatens to overcome me as I remember the last time I saw those fangs and what they did to human flesh.

I blink and look away, trying to swallow down my fear. I need to stay calm. My wits are the only thing that might keep me alive for another try at escaping.

Besides, it's not as if the vampires have any reason to kill me right this second. I can still make a tasty meal for them days down the road. They don't know about my crazy plan. For all they know, I was just trying to make a jailbreak. They have no idea what I have hidden away in—

"A knife!" Jenny cries out gleefully. "She's got knives buried in that pen! And lock-picking tools!"

Horrified, I turn back to Jenny. She points right toward the pen in front of me where my supplies are. Her face is rigid, her eyes colder than I've ever seen. It doesn't even look like Jenny.

"Jen—*what the fuck?*" Logan's jaw clenches, fists shaking at his sides like he'd like to strike her even though he'd never hit a woman—not even one who deserves it as much as Jenny does.

Zoe, however, has no such qualms.

"You bitch!" Zoe slaps Jenny right across the face, so hard her hand leaves an imprint on Jenny's cheek.

Jenny's smile falters for a moment under their withering glares, her moment of triumph souring.

"Show me," the female vampire demands in a deadly tone. She picks me up by my neck. Her talon-like claws dig into my skin as she drags me toward the pen where my weapons are hidden. I have no choice but to do as she says.

With sinking despair, I'm forced to show her the knives and tools I buried beneath the ground the first day I arrived. She grabs it all, so there's nothing left in the hole, and then escorts me back to the pen where my friends are. She shoves me to my knees and holds my knives up to the rest of the slaughterhouse so everyone can see.

"Anyone else who wants to try and be a hero should know the penalty for attempting escape is death—and not just feeding on you, but long, torturous death, where we rip you apart slowly, limb by limb." She stares at me, those canines growing so long they push down into her lower lip. "But it won't be right away. That would be too easy. First, you'll spend hours, maybe days, thinking about how excruciatingly painful your end is going to be."

I'm so broken, both in body and spirit. I don't even bother to get up from the floor. Not even sure I could right now, even if I wanted to.

We were so close, I almost had it! But now we're all going to die. All because of Jenny...

I don't understand. How she could do this? Her betrayal has cost us *everything*.

"Why?" I ask, turning to her with dull disbelief.

Jenny doesn't even look at me as she answers, her gaze fixated on the female vampire alone. "I want to be one of you," she says, her voice breathy and rapturous.

I hear Logan's quick intake of air beside me. "You *what*?"

Jenny shuffles her feet in the dirt, eyes gleaming. "My aunt and uncle told me about the changings," she starts, her voice betraying a fervent eagerness as she leans toward the vampires. "Back in the old days, vampires would turn humans. Not just any humans, but the special ones, chosen to be rewarded." She pauses, biting her lip in anticipation, her body coiled tight as a spring. "I know it can be done. Please—make me one of you. I want to join you!"

"Oh, do you now?" The female vampire tilts her head, almost curiously.

"Yes! Please!" Jenny nods, her face lighting up. "Please change me."

"And why in the world would I want to do that?"

"Because I can help you—like I helped you today," Jenny says. "Today was a token of my loyalty. I've been waiting around for the perfect time to show you what I can do for you. That I'm worthy. That I deserve this chance."

"God, Jenny. Do you even understand what you're asking?" Zoe's face pales, jaw rigid. She looks like she's about two seconds away from slapping Jenny again. "You can't want to be a fucking *vampire*!"

"Yes, I do." Jenny scowls at Zoe. "I want to be special, like you are. It's all I've ever wanted. To stand out, to be important—like you and Alix. Everything has always come so easy to you. You're both so fucking beautiful and liked and admired." She practically spits the words. "You have no idea what it's like to be like me!"

"Cry me a fucking river, Jenny!" I yell, my fury bubbling up like lava, about to explode. "If you want to change your life, you get new makeup or a haircut or even a nose job like everyone else. You don't betray your friends to become a blood-sucking killer!"

I can't believe this stupid bitch. She's willing to kill all of us because... what? She isn't *cool* enough?

She arches a mocking brow at me. "Oh, cut the shit, Alix. You were never really my friend," she says and shrugs. "Besides, this way is so much easier, isn't it?"

"You're insane! You've just signed all our death sentences!"

"Yours maybe," she says to me, tucking a piece of hair behind one ear with a sly grin. "Not mine. I'm going to live forever."

Suddenly, it clicks for me, and all I can see is red.

"You knew! You knew this was going to happen!"

How could we have been so stupid not to see this? Jenny had told us her family had been around this town for ages. She must have known about the vampires this entire time. Maybe this was her plan all along? Trick us, turn us in, and claim her prize.

"Jen, how could you?" Logan asks, his voice trembling with horror. He stares at Jenny like he can't believe what he's hearing. "We trusted you—*I* trusted you. You're just going to trade your life for ours?"

"Oh no. Not yours, Logan." She shakes her head and grabs his hand. "I want you to become a vampire. I want you with me." She turns back to the vampires. "You'll change him, too, won't you?"

The vampires exchange amused grins but say nothing,

like they're waiting to see how this plays out before making any final decisions.

"I don't want to change, Jen!" Logan snaps and yanks his hand away.

"But you have to," she says, a little whine entering her voice. "If you don't change with me, then you'll die. Like them." She points a finger at Zoe and me. "Don't you want to live? Don't you want to be with me?"

"No." Logan glares at her with angry, reproachful eyes. "I don't want to kill innocent people or betray our friends."

He moves with purpose, his crouch low as he reaches out to me, an anchor amidst the chaos. His arms, strong and sure, wrap around my shoulders and he pulls me upright, steadying me.

Jenny's reaction is a physical jolt, her body rigid as if struck. Color floods her cheeks, a crimson tide of indignation and scorn.

"Oh, I see." A bitter laugh escapes her. "You'd rather choose death with her over an eternal life with me, is that it?" Her words come out razor-sharp, each one etched with venom. "I should've known. All you've ever cared about is Alix, the fucking Ice Queen. Even though she never treated you right," she hisses. "Not like I would have."

"Jen, you can't really want this," Zoe says. "You'll have to become a murderer. You'll have to drink blood!"

"Oh, I don't care about that." Jenny waves her hand in the air, dismissively. "Animals kill each other all the time in the wild. Big animals eat the small animals. It's just nature."

I shudder at how casually she talks about murder. She isn't even looking at us anymore, not even Logan. It seems she's already forgotten about him now, too. Her eyes are only on the vampires.

"Please," she says to the female, a reverent look on her face. "Make me one of you."

"Are you sure? That's really what you want?" The vampire moves closer to Jenny with slow, deliberate steps. "To become one of us?"

"Yes!" Jenny's voice is breathless with anticipation. "More than anything!"

The vampire reaches out a hand to stroke the side of Jenny's face.

"So how do we do this? Do you drink my blood?" Jenny tips her head, offering her neck to the vampire. "Do I drink yours?"

"That's one way," the vampire says, a light smile on her lips. "Are you ready right now?"

"Yes!" Jenny cries. "I am!"

"Okay then," the vampire says softly. "You asked for it."

The vampire's movements are a study in chilling precision. With a predator's grace, she clasps Jenny's head between her hands. And then there's a sickening crunch of bone, a visceral sound that tears through the silence, as she twists sharply. A loud crack echoes inside the pen, like a gunshot, and Jenny's body goes limp. A ragdoll severed from its strings. She crumples to the ground, a lifeless heap at the vampire's feet.

"Sorry, sweetie," the woman says to Jenny's dead body. "We may be vampires, but we don't like traitors, either."

CHAPTER 28
DAY 31: 8:30 A.M.

The Cattle Farm Slaughterhouse

S he comes for me the next morning.

The female vampire opens the padlock and strolls toward me, her unusual purple eyes bright with excitement as if she's enjoying this. It almost feels personal, but I don't know how that can be. She probably just doesn't like that I tried to escape when she was in charge. Or maybe she doesn't like that I already evaded her one time before, in the woods. And I guess also back at the slaughterhouse weeks ago as well.

Now that I think about it, I can see why she might have it in for me, after all.

Zoe cries out and tries to hold on to me, while Logan steps in front of us and attempts to take the vampire down all on his own. Poor Logan gets himself knocked unconscious in the process. I appreciate him trying but wish he hadn't bothered. There's no hope for me. No way I'm getting out of this one. The vampires have all my tools and weapons now. I've got no more tricks up my sleeve.

I've made my peace with it, though. I tried my best and that's all anyone can ever hope to do. I just hope Kade has found help and can save the rest of the world and my dad. Maybe he can even come back and save my friends, too, before it's too late.

I've lost hope for myself, yes, but I still have hope left for the people I love.

The vampire brings me to a large utilitarian room on the other side of the slaughterhouse. It's filled with a handful of holding areas for cattle, dozens of individual enclosures like large stalls. Each one has chain cross-ties inside, attached to the walls, meant to keep the cattle in place so they can't get away. On the ground are metal pans for catching bodily fluids that pour out during the last few seconds of an animal's life. Piss. Shit. Blood. The walls are splattered with all of it.

She tells me I'm in the kill room of the old slaughterhouse. This is the place where they used to execute cattle back when the factory farm was up and running. Now, it's the room where they tie up people and feed on them. I know she's trying to scare me.

It works.

I'm terrified.

And yet, if I'm going to go out, I want to go out like a badass.

"You can kill me"—I give her my best shit-eating grin— "but eventually, someone is going to stop you. You won't win."

She shoves me into one of the holding areas and secures me using the cross-ties. "No, I don't think so," she says, pulling the chains around my wrists tighter than seems necessary. "We'll win, and you want to know why?"

"Delusion?"

"You're funny." She smirks. "No, we'll win because we aren't afraid to hide our true nature. We embrace it. Being human is being weak. It's burying your real thoughts, your instincts, trying to fit into the molds of society. At least we're honest about who we are; we embrace our animal nature. We don't fight it. That's what makes us stronger."

"You're monsters is what you are."

"And what makes you think you're any better?" Her face darkens. "Do you regret it when you eat a juicy steak? Feel sorry for your food? That leather on your shoes—where do you think it came from?" She gestures around the kill room with her hands. "Look at this place. Understand where you are right now. How many thousands of animals died here before we took it over? Do you really think they were treated any better than I'm treating you?"

I open my mouth to defend myself, to defend humankind, but the truth is, she's right. We are all the things she says we are.

Still, that doesn't mean I want to die.

In a desperate lunge, I aim a kick at her, but she deflects it effortlessly, sending me crashing into an empty row of shelves directly behind me. Pain explodes in my skull. I taste blood in the back of my mouth as my body collapses in a heap on the floor. Wooden shards pierce my skin, and I struggle to stand, clutching a broken piece of wood in my trembling hand. Maybe I can use this as a weapon? Like a stake in the movies?

But before I can even attempt to stab her, she's already behind me. Her movements unfold with a swiftness that defies sight as she grips my wrist and wrenches my pathetic weapon away. Blood drips down my arm and forehead. The room spins, darkness edging in as I brace for what seems inevitable. I can tell I don't have much longer to live.

And then someone comes charging in, barreling toward me. Paler than I remember, but just as handsome. His dark eyes flash as his gaze locks on me. There's a flicker of anger and his jaw clenches ever so slightly. Someone who doesn't know him well might not even notice it, but I do.

I can't believe he's here, in front of me.

Kade!

I never thought I'd see him again. Not in this horrible place. Not when he's supposed to be miles away, in another town, saving mankind.

My throat locks up with emotion.

What happened? Why did he change his mind?

I'm stunned. I can't believe I mean that much to him that he'd throw away everything for me, even when he said he wouldn't. That he'd sacrifice his life for mine.

But then, to my complete and utter confusion, the female vampire smiles at him, her mouth curving into a grin that spans her entire face. "Kaden!" she cries out.

And wait a second... I realize he's not running to save me at all.

He's running to *her*.

She throws her arms around him, burying her head in his shoulder. "I knew it! I knew you'd come back to me!" she says and then pulls away, gesturing toward me. "I was just about to drain this one. You hungry?"

"Not now," he says, not even bothering to look my way again. It's as if I don't even exist to him. "We need to talk, Lillith."

He reaches out and she lets him lead her away from my cage. I watch them walk hand in hand toward the door, eyes only for each other, while they leave me tied up like cattle at the slaughter. I blink, aghast, unable to believe what I'm seeing.

Kade is a vampire.

How can the guy I spent so many days and nights with be a vampire?

The person that nursed me back to health. Fed me. Trained me. Took care of me. This is the guy who kissed me and slept in my bed. He saved my life.

Why would a vampire save my life?

My body roils with waves of shock and then fury. I don't understand how this is possible…

Everything I thought I knew about him, about this world, it goes right up in smoke. I realize I don't know anything at all. Nothing makes sense anymore.

Was it all an act?

How did I miss this? How did I not see the truth?

Were there signs?

I try to think back but can't recall anything particularly alarming. Okay, sure, he was a little secretive. And he talked to himself and sleepwalked. But so what? Lots of people do that. They aren't vampires!

The room starts to spin. I'm seconds away from passing out from the pain and shock. I bite my cheek as hard as I can and try to keep myself conscious. If I pass out, I don't know if I'll ever wake up again.

"I'm so glad you're here," she says happily to him as they get to the door. "I knew you'd never leave me. I knew you still loved me."

When she kisses him, the darkness opens up and swallows me whole.

CHAPTER 29
AFTERNOON

The Cattle Farm Kill Room

When Kade returns, I'm lying on the cold, hard ground in the kill room, curled into a fetal position. Somehow, I've fallen asleep. I should be too amped up from adrenaline and anger, but you can only sit tied up for so long before passing out from the pain and boredom.

My arms are still in the cross-ties, not a comfortable situation, but at least the chains are long enough to allow me plenty of movement. An unpleasant coppery taste coats my mouth—blood. A souvenir from my fight earlier with the female vampire. My face feels puffy, tight cheeks and a swollen jaw. I may have lost a tooth somewhere. Bruises run all along my arms and neck where she held me, and my injured leg is throbbing again.

Kade reaches out to pull me up from the floor, putting me in a vertical position and unlocking my chains. Blood rushes to my head so fast, it makes me dizzy. I wince, attempting to open my eyes, but the swelling makes it difficult.

"Don't touch me!" I recoil from him, slinking away to the other side of the enclosure.

A look of confusion flickers across his face. "Alix, it's me."

"I don't know who you are anymore!"

"Come on. Please don't say that." His jaw tightens. "I'm here to help you."

Gingerly, he reaches for my face.

"No... stop."

I want to hit him, but I don't have the energy. Instead, I close my eyes and look away, my only ability to resist his touch.

"I'm so sorry," he whispers. His fingers graze my cheek and jaw, flakes of blood visible on the tips of his nails.

I try not to cry. I ache everywhere—like a throbbing mess of agony, worse pain than anything I've ever endured. Something feels broken deep inside me, but maybe that's just my heart.

I'm such an idiot.

How could I have fallen for someone like him? A liar? A monster? Someone who was keeping such a terrible secret from me all this time? Even if it was the end of the world and I was sad and scared, that was no excuse for letting him fool me like this.

And the vampire? The woman? What did he call her again?

Lillith!

As soon as I heard him say her name, I knew. She's the ex-girlfriend he talked about. The high school sweetheart. The girl from New York City. And she isn't dead or being held captive somewhere like he'd led me to believe. No, not at all. She's very much alive.

Well, as alive as a vampire can be.

It's clear he's been playing me from the beginning, from the first day we met probably, but what I don't understand is why? I can't make heads or tails of it.

Why keep all of this from me? Why go to such trouble to take care of me for so long, to heal me and feed me? Why all the make-believe shit back at his house? Reading me stories in bed and pretending like he cared? When he held me in his arms, I felt safe. When he kissed me, I was lost in him. It felt like he had real feelings for me, too.

Was it all just an act?

It's like there are two Kades. The Kade I know—my human-passing rescuer and savior—and Kade the vampire, the guy that showed up to the slaughterhouse to return to his murderous ex-girlfriend.

The question is, which one is the real Kade?

I feel a sudden burst of energy. My eyes fly open, and I fling his hands away. I push at his chest, banging against him, furious I let him touch me for even an instant. That I ever let him touch me.

"Alix, stop! Calm down!" He grabs at my flailing fists, his voice strained with frustration. "I'm not going to hurt you."

I almost lose it.

"Not going to *hurt* me? Are you fucking kidding?"

Does he not understand how much his betrayal has already hurt me? Does he not know that seeing him here, knowing what he is, watching him kiss Lillith—the vampire intent on killing all my friends and me—felt like having my heart literally ripped from my chest?

He drops my hands, hurt and confused. "Sniper, please—"

"Let go!" My throat burns with fury at hearing him use that nickname, like we're still friends and not mortal enemies. "Get the hell away from me!"

I look away again, I can't bear to see his face anymore. The face of a damn traitor.

I get up without his help. My pride won't allow him to touch me. My body is so broken and bruised that I'm surprised I can even stand on my own two feet, but somehow, I do. My injured leg works, though it won't stop throbbing. I touch the back of my calf. When I bring my hand away, it's wet to the touch, slick with blood.

His eyes widen with alarm as he reaches for me. "Let me see."

"Go away." I struggle to keep my eyes open. "Just let me rot here in peace."

He repositions my body in the dim light of the cage so he can see my leg better. The movement hurts so badly, I have to bite my lip to keep from crying out. He examines the wound, and a growl rips from his throat.

"She hurt you!"

"What did you expect, Kade? She's a fucking monster!" I yell. "Of course, she hurt me!"

"Are you okay? Can you walk on it?"

"It's fine. I'll live." I blink hard, forcing my gaze to stay open and make eye contact with him. I put as much fury as I can into my eyes. I want him to *see* it. I need my outrage, my hurt and my betrayal, to burn holes into those pretty, little back-stabbing retinas of his. "Unless, of course, you're here to kill me now?"

He sighs, long and suffering. "Alix, come on. You know I'm not."

"Oh no?" I ask, sarcastically. "You are a vampire, aren't you? A lying, traitorous vampire, I might add."

I hold my breath and wait for his response. I'm not sure what he can say in his defense. We both know the truth now. His lie is out in the open. There's no hiding anymore.

He hesitates.

"A vampire, yes," he agrees, and I can see the pain in his eyes. "Though I'm not sure about the rest of your assessment."

"Good at least you admit it." I grit from clenched teeth. "How could you hide all of this from me, Kade?"

"I didn't want to."

"Want to what?" I ask. "Become some awful monster? Or just pretend you weren't one?"

"All of it." He grabs my hands roughly. Desperately.

It surprises me to feel warm skin, blood beating through his body and inside his veins. Now that I know the truth about him, I expect him to be cold as ice somehow—cold like death—even though I've felt his touch before and know it's not.

"I'm still who you think I am."

"No, you're not! You're a killer!"

He cocks his head. "You kill people. You killed that guy guarding the fence."

"I killed *a vampire*! It's not the same thing!"

He leans back against the dirty wall of the kill room, taking in a deep breath.

"It isn't that black and white. Not like you think," he murmurs. "Vampires are humans. Humans are vampires. I was just like you and then, one day, things changed. It happened when I came home from business school to take care of my dad. I was one of the first—maybe because we're a founding family of Allium Valley.

"I think it might have started with our line," he continues. His hand brushes the dusty floor of the enclosure—a grounding gesture. "Mom and Dad were too old, and Jolie too young. I'm the only one it affected. It was small things at first. I was stronger. Faster. And the hunger... it was hunger like you could never imagine. Blood was the only thing that stopped it." A shiver of revulsion runs through him. "Eventually, I heard about the others. Like Lillith—"

"Right. Lillith—your murderous girlfriend!" I cut him off. "I was wondering when you'd get to that part."

"*Ex*-girlfriend," he corrects.

The status of their relationship is the last thing I should care about, and yet, I find some small measure of comfort that despite the kiss I saw them share, he's not dating that bloodthirsty psychopath again. I'm gladder of that one tiny little fact than I should be, even if, maybe, he's a bloodthirsty psychopath himself.

"Go on," I say.

"It was just a bit at a time. When my mom realized what was happening, she gave me her own blood using a needle. Dad, too," he says. "I alternated with animal blood, though it's not as good."

"Of course, it isn't." I chuckle darkly.

"The thing about human blood," he says, ignoring me, "is that a little is never enough. It's like being an alcoholic. You want more and more. And the more blood you have, the more you change. The more your human feelings shut off and you become like a wild animal. A predator." He pauses, sorrow flickering in his gaze. "Lillith wasn't always a monster, but once she lost control and drained her parents... there was no going back after that. Once you kill a human for blood, you become something else." He lowers his gaze, the weight of his words pressing down on him, on us. "You lose all your humanity."

"So you've never...?"

He shakes his head adamantly. *"Never."*

I pause, taking a moment to digest his confession. I'm so confused and don't yet know what to think. My mind spins with swirling emotions and competing thoughts.

"Okay, so what are you saying?" I blink, bewildered. "You're, what, a good vegetarian vampire?"

"Honestly, I have no idea if there is such a thing, but I'm not going to hurt you or your friends, if that's what you're asking." He loses a shaky breath. "I don't want to kill you, Alix; I want to *save* you."

I scan my horrific surroundings, legs shaking as I try to maintain my balance.

"It's a little late for that, don't you think?"

Regret flickers across the planes of his face. "This was never supposed to happen to you. I'm so sorry," he says with a pained swallow. "So damn sorry."

This time when he tries to hold me again, I let him. His arms wrap around me, pulling me so close I can hear his heart beating.

He still feels human. Looks like a human and talks like a human. Everything in my body wants to burrow in closer, to believe his words and his touch are real. That this isn't the embrace of a monster. That he's someone I can trust.

I don't know what to do.

Am I being an idiot? I could be letting him trick me again, but I can't help how I feel about him. I don't want to believe he's evil. If all is lost and I'm going to die here anyway, I'd rather die in his arms, pretending.

Besides, what he's saying… it makes sense.

Unless he's got some insane, diabolical plan going where he's playing the long game to convince me he's "good" when he really isn't—and I can't think of any logical reason why he'd do that—I have to believe at least some of what he says is true. It certainly explains why I'm still standing here, alive, instead of dead weeks ago in the woods.

I lean against the wall, sweating. The ceiling starts to sway. I've used up too much energy.

"Why didn't you tell me the truth?"

He raises a brow. "If I'd told you the truth about me, what would you have done?"

"I would've left."

"Exactly." He sighs, the sound more a surrender than an affirmation. "And leaving me meant you would die. I couldn't allow that." His eyes meet mine, a storm of emotion swirling within them.

"You still should've told me," I say. "I can't trust someone who lies to me." I slump back down to the ground and curl into myself, hugging my knees to my chest. "It was Lillith in your room, wasn't it? That night you said you were sleepwalking?"

It had to be a vampire. There's no way a human could've gotten all the way up to the second floor of his house without entering through one of the doors downstairs.

"She was trying to convince me to come here to the cattle farm—to be with her," he says, confirming my suspicions.

"You allowed her inside the house?"

I can't believe he let her in his bedroom, right down the hall from me, while I'd been helpless, defenseless, sleeping in my bed.

"She was growing suspicious. If I'd kept her out, she would've known something was going on." His expression darkens. "I was terrified she was going to find out about you."

I want to punch him in the face and burst into tears all at the same time, because it's all so clear to me now. Despite all the deception and lies, he obviously cares about me. Regardless of motives or methods, Kade is the only thing keeping me alive right now. He's been the only thing keeping me alive for a long time.

"What a mess I've made of things." His laugh is sad as

he hangs his head and closes his eyes. "I'm so sorry I didn't tell you everything. I should have. But Alix, listen, I know you have no reason to believe me anymore, but I need you to," he says, pinching the bridge of his nose as desperation seeps into his voice. "You have to trust me, or you won't make it out of here."

The pain in my head threatens to overcome me again. I see bright flashes of light and then darkness begins to descend.

"Come on, Kade. We both know I'm never leaving," I mutter. "Not alive, at least..."

My mouth is like sandpaper. It's becoming hard to form words.

Sleep... I need sleep...

He bends down and presses his hand against my face, pulling me close. Lightly, so lightly, he runs a finger over my lips and down my neck, as if memorizing the feel of me.

"Oh yes, you are." He smiles tenderly. "Whatever I have to do, whatever it costs me, I promise—I *will* save you."

CHAPTER 30
LATE AFTERNOON

The Cattle Farm Kill Room

W hen I wake again, I'm still in the kill room, but this time I'm not alone. Kade is here with me. My head is cradled in his lap as he strokes my hair, watching over me.

Anger tightens in my chest. I kick with my heels, twisting my body back and forth to break free of his embrace. Maybe he's not an evil vampire hellbent on drinking my blood like the rest of his friends, but he's still a liar. I don't know if I can trust him, and he definitely hasn't earned the right to hold me in such an intimate way. Not anymore.

"Alix. Don't…" he says, grabbing me by the wrists and pulling me back in. "Relax, okay?"

"Let me go!"

I beat at him with my fists until he reluctantly drops his arms. "Why are you here, anyway?" I ask, pushing him away as I scuttle over to the other side of my enclosure.

"You refused to come with me. You said you were going to warn people in other towns—"

"I was."

"So what happened?"

"I tried, I really did." His gaze falters, eyes dropping to the floor. "I got all the way to the town's edge, but I couldn't do it. I couldn't leave."

I lean forward. "Why not?"

"Because I couldn't let you die. I care too much about you," he confesses, the words thick with emotion. His hands clench involuntarily, knuckles whitening. Then his eyes lift to meet mine, raw and unguarded. He hesitates for a half breath. "I… I think I'm falling in love with you, Alix."

My first thought is suspicion—that this is just more of his lies—but when I look at his face, I know he's telling the truth. His feelings are laid bare in his eyes.

I feel my heart skip, my throat tightening at his declaration, but I shake the emotions away. I can't let him see how much his words affect me. He can't know that I've got strong feelings for him, too. I'm still not sure he's someone I should be having any feelings for and definitely not love.

"Well, isn't that tragic?" I ask with a mocking lilt to my voice. "A vampire in love with a human about to die."

I reach up, holding my head with a moan. My skull aches with pain like I've never felt before. I'm certain I have a concussion, but I hope that's all it is. For all I know, Lillith shoved me so hard my brain is turning into mush.

God, I'm so tired.

The walls close in on me. I fight to stay awake, but I don't know any more why I'm fighting so hard. It all seems so damn hopeless.

I think of my tag number then and how many hundreds of townspeople the vampires must have already gone through in Allium Valley. Their feeding pace isn't sustainable. To survive, the vampires will have to spread past the town's borders. The way they've drained this place so fast is an incomprehensible tragedy; but what they have yet to do to the rest of the towns, states, countries, even. It will be an abomination on a scale this world has never seen. Not just hundreds—billions of lives hang in the balance.

I lock eyes with him. "You have to save them all, Kade," I say, my voice a hushed, urgent whisper. "It's up to you now."

Slowly, he shakes his head, the gesture one of grim resignation. "It'll be hard enough just to save you. Do you understand how tough it's going to be to get you out of here?" he asks, reaching out to grip my shoulders with an intensity meant to ground me, to tether me to the harsh reality of our situation. "Do you have any idea what Lillith is going to do if she finds out I've betrayed her?"

"But we can't let them just kill everyone."

"They won't." He sighs. "They'll kill some, yes, but many will be changed to make more vampires, and some they'll just leave alone. Those that live in places that are hard to get to, those that hide, those that don't fight back or pose a threat—they won't go after them. They just want to be in control, and they want to eat. They aren't going to annihilate the entire planet, if that's what you're worried about."

"That doesn't make me feel any better," I huff.

He hands me water, and when I balk, he forces me to drink it, insisting that I need to keep up my strength to escape. There will be a lot of running, and I may have to fight back. I can't do either if I'm dehydrated and sluggish.

"We didn't all want it this way," he explains. "Some of us wanted to live in harmony, drinking off donors or blood banks or even animals. We wanted to coexist peacefully, but we lost the argument."

"No shit," I say blackly, gesturing toward the walls of the kill room covered in blood and remnants of human excretions. "But why? Why do they hate us so much, if they once were us?"

"They don't hate you," he says. "Most of them don't think about you at all. They just believe humans are inferior. Subservient animals here only to fulfill their needs and pleasure." He grabs the cross-tie shackles now discarded at my feet and shakes them lightly, his expression somber. "Basically, they see you as cattle."

"Yeah, well, if you really do get me out of here, *this* cow is going to fight back."

"Don't you dare!" He snarls. "When I get you out, you run. Do not try to save your friends or anyone else. You go hide and you don't ever come back, got it? You're up against something far beyond your capacity to fight."

"Watch me."

"I'm serious, Alix. Don't be stupid and try to be a hero."

I peer up at him warily. I can't help but notice he only said I should go hide—me.

Alone.

"What about you? You aren't coming with me?"

"I'll help you escape, but after that you're on your own," he says. "I'll need to stay here and distract Lillith and the others to buy you time, or you won't get far."

I gulp.

"She won't... she won't hurt you, will she?"

Just like that, the switch inside my heart flips. As angry and upset as I am by his betrayal, I'm afraid for him, too.

"No," he says. "I'll be okay as long as she doesn't know I helped you."

"Okay, good." I nod. "Tell me then, what's this grand plan of yours anyway?"

A tiny smile cracks across his otherwise serious-looking face.

"It's simple," he says. "You're going to sneak out of here like cow shit."

I blink, sure I've heard him wrong.

"Excuse me—*what?*"

"When this farm was built, it was designed to house thousands of cattle," he explains. "All that cattle made a lot of crap. The original owners designed a waste removal system underground. They ran pipes along the bottom of the pens so the waste and runoff would flow out to a treatment area near the other side of the river." He taps a hand down on the dirt floor of the cage, pounding lightly. "It's all there, right below us. I'm sure you've noticed the smell?"

I wrinkle my nose. "Well, yeah. I just didn't realize it was sewage."

"Lillith told me they've been trying to use the pipes again for the, uh, human waste." Kade shifts uneasily beside me, the grimace on his face betraying his obvious discomfort with the treatment of people here. "Once I get you back in your pen, all you have to do is dig until you find the pipes. You'll follow them down and out of the factory, all the way to the river and to safety. You remember the rule about running water and vampires, right?"

"Yeah—the vamps don't like to get too close," I say, reciting what Frog taught us. It's only been weeks since we hid out by the river, but it seems like ages ago. I feel like I've aged a hundred years since then.

A flash of memory comes back to me in that moment. I remember Kade at the Devil's River, sitting apart from the group. He'd said he wanted to watch the forest for any incoming threats, but now I realize exactly why he'd picked that precise spot, so far away from the running river.

"If you can find the pipes," he continues, "you should be able to use them to get to the Devil's River."

My mouth drops open. "You want me to crawl *inside* crap tunnels to get out of here? Are you serious? That's the best idea you've got?"

I can't believe we're even contemplating this. Never in a million years would I think a pipe system of human and cow excrement would be the secret to my survival. Except, well, I guess it is sort of brilliant.

Escaping underground is far less obvious than trying to pick locks on gates and doors. If we leave in the sewage pipes beneath the factory, the vampires might never realize we're even missing. Not until it's too late.

Even if the vampires somehow do notice we've escaped, I can't imagine any of them are going to crawl into shit pipes and come after us. I'm not sure if sewage counts as running water, but even without the whole vampires-hating-running-water-thing, it's still plenty off-putting. It's hard to picture gorgeous Lillith getting her hands dirty like that.

"I know it's not ideal," he says, lips twitching with dark humor, "but it's going to work. I may not be able to save the world, but I will save you."

I notice again his use of the word "you" instead of "us."

One thing is clear. This escape plan is for me and me alone. He won't be joining me. Not now. Maybe never.

By helping me, Kade is crossing into dangerous territory. A dividing line between humans and monsters. Even if he is a vampire, even if he has kept a terrible secret from me, I can't stifle the surge of concern for him swelling in my heart.

I have a very bad feeling that if he gets caught crossing this line, he won't be able to come back.

CHAPTER 31
EVENING

The Cattle Farm Slaughterhouse

At sunset, Kade is allowed to return me to the pen with my friends. He's somehow convinced Lillith to give me time to say goodbye and to spend one last day of life with them.

I'm not sure what he had to do to convince her. I don't want to know, either.

The plan is for me to explore the pen, digging around all night if need be, until I find the excrement pipes. After that, we both agree the best time to escape down through the pipes will be in the morning, right after feeding time. Since the vampire patrol doesn't come back until dinner, that should give me hours to get to the river before they ever discover I'm missing.

According to Kade, the plan is only supposed to involve me. Me digging. Me in the pipes. Me getting to safety.

Except there's no way in hell I'm leaving my friends

behind. I keep that part of the plan to myself, though. No point in telling Kade in advance so he'll argue with me about it or—worse—do something to mess it up. I decide it's best to spring it on him only if I need to. At that point, it'll be too late to do anything but go along with it.

When I later explain the plan to Zoe and Logan, they're rightly distrustful. Zoe doesn't want to work with a vampire at all—not even Kade—though she doesn't think he's necessarily setting us up for anything bad. Logan, on the other hand, is convinced this is a trap. He doesn't know why or to what end, but he's certain the outcome for us is not a good one.

I'm not sure I disagree.

I was fooled by Kade once before. I have no way of telling that I won't be fooled again.

For all I know, he's off right now drinking some poor human's blood or reuniting for more make-out sessions with Lillith. Maybe he's holding her in his arms this very second and kissing her like he once kissed me.

Yes, it's possible this "plan" of his is more subterfuge and lies. And yet, if that is the case, it seems like a colossal waste of his time and energy.

What does Kade need to trap us underground for?

We're already captive here in the slaughterhouse pen. If he wants to hurt us, kill us, he can do so anytime he wants. No need to play games.

Not to mention the fact that Kade has saved my ass more times than I can remember. And that he could have killed me a hundred times over when he had the chance. And that there's something about him, something tormented and sad and terribly, terribly lonely—like he's the one who needs saving and not me, the human captive, trapped in the slaughterhouse.

Ultimately, I decide there isn't enough time to untangle

what his real intentions are. I can't be certain whether they're good or bad—not when my life and my friends' lives depend on such a determination. Kade may not mean me harm, he may even want to help me, but I can't trust him.

The good news is—I don't have to.

It's all irrelevant, anyway. We're going to use Kade's escape plan because we have no other options on the table. Since I don't have my tools and weapons anymore, the only way for us to get out of here is if Kade's underground digging idea works.

But I make no mistake about it this time. I have no silly notions anymore that Kade is my ally or here to save me. My friends and I are on our own. If at any point Kade or his plans no longer serve our purpose, I'll have no qualms about taking him down, just like I'd take down any other vampire that's a threat.

As soon as the vampires deliver our dinner and leave, Logan, Zoe, and I begin digging in unison, using our hands to try and find the excrement pipes. When our hands grow sore and tired, we take off our shoes and dig with those instead. I really wish I had my tools with me for this. The flashlight, especially, and the Swiss Army knife would've been helpful. But it's no use crying over spilled milk. We just have to do the best we can with what we have.

We work and work and work. Part of the job is digging beneath the earth, searching for the pipes; the other part is patching the holes back up when we find nothing. We don't want there to be any evidence of what we've done when the vampires come back in the morning.

We search all corners of the pen for the pipes, pushing people out of the way when necessary. There are fewer people in here now than when I was taken to the kill room —only a handful at best. Most are asleep. The few that are awake don't fight back; they don't even seem to notice.

They're all so far gone, no one even asks what we're doing. I'm pretty sure they assume we've gone as crazy as they have.

While we dig, we also take turns keeping a lookout around the pen's perimeter to make sure the vampires on guard don't see us. It's only one vamp tonight. I'm not sure where the others are—probably out hunting. Unfortunately, the one who is left is the big masochist, Johnny. He seems distracted tonight, though. He only walks by once every few hours, and he isn't even watching us when he does.

Logan is the first to find the pipes.

It must be almost the middle of the night when he lets out a little yelp of excitement that sends Zoe and me running to his side. Sure enough, just like Kade said, there's a long round pipe buried a few feet below the pen's flooring. As we clear more dirt away from the grimy surface, an aged, hardened plaster structure emerges from the layers of crusty sediment.

Logan unscrews a nail at the top, using the nubs of his fingernails to crack it open. A pungent, putrid smell seeps out, so awful we all gag. The interior of the pipe looks smaller than I'd hoped but still more than big enough to fit us all—even Logan—if we hunch inside.

We glance at each other, sharing a triumphant grin. What was once just a channel for cattle waste, has now become our shot at freedom. I still don't trust Kade, but at least the pipes weren't a lie.

With just a few hours left until morning, we cover the pipes back up. We make sure to pack the dirt loose so we can get through fast when it's time. Then we curl up next to the hole and try to sleep to regain our strength and be ready for the day ahead.

We rotate turns, making sure we don't all sleep at the same time. There's too much at stake here. We can't afford to oversleep and miss our narrow window of escape after the vampires come to feed us breakfast.

What seems like minutes later, Logan shakes me awake. It feels like I just fell asleep. I'm groggy and disoriented, and it takes a few moments to get my eyes fully open. My face is still swollen, my head and knee still aching from Lillith's beating, but I'm grateful to get to my feet on my own.

I stand, stretching my arms above my head. Logan stares down at me, seeming concerned, but then he doesn't look so great himself. His eyes are red and bloodshot, his entire face now covered with bruises from all his vampire scuffles.

The morning feeding goes pretty much as planned. Two vampires. Neither Johnny nor Lillith are on patrol this morning, which I think is a good sign. They must be busy somewhere else. Hopefully, whatever they're doing will keep them occupied until we're long gone.

Once we've eaten the harvest oatmeal barley they give us for breakfast, we wait a few minutes until they've disappeared from sight. Then it's go time.

We scoop away the dirt and Logan cracks the pipe all the way open this time. I go in first, Logan helping me down into the cylinder. Zoe follows and Logan is last, doing what he can to cover up our exit behind us. He pushes dirt over the pipe as best as he's able to, but it's hard to fully disguise it from our location now inside. We knew that would be a problem, though. That's why we made sure to leave right after the vampires did their morning check. If we're lucky, it will be hours until they return at dinner time and notice anything amiss.

The pipe is narrow and tight inside. The only way to move through it is to scuttle forward on our bellies. Feces and dirty warm slush cover our bodies as we begin our crawl away from the pen and to freedom. I stretch my neck out and try to keep the muck off my mouth and face, but other than that, it seems to go almost everywhere else.

The smell is horrific. I gag, almost puking. At first, all I can do is hold my breath and focus on anything else but the stench, but then a crazy thing happens. After a short while, my olfactory senses seem to adjust to the terrible odor. Soon, it barely even bothers me. It's as if my sense of smell is so traumatized, it goes totally numb.

The endless darkness, however, is another issue.

It's hard to see more than an inch or two in front of us as we move soundlessly through the pipes. None of us were prepared for it to be this dark, though we probably should've been. We're in an underground pipe, buried feet away from the surface, after all. Good thing I'm not claustrophobic.

On the bright side, we don't need our sense of sight to know we're going the right way. We just have to follow the sound of running mush and waste runoff as it trickles through the pipes. Thanks to the design of the waste disposal system, there's only one way it flows. Outside and to the river.

I do my best to forge ahead, scooting along the shaft as fast as I dare in the darkness. Something keeps poking me in the chest, perhaps a loose piece of tubing? I ignore it, pushing forward. No time to investigate.

I move fast, balancing the urgency of knowing my friends are counting on me to get us out of here quickly, but not so quickly that I accidentally lead them somewhere dangerous like into a broken pipe. We don't dare to speak as we scuttle onward. We're too worried we might be heard by someone, even if we are far underground.

On occasion, I pause to listen and make sure we aren't being followed. Thankfully, all I hear is my own heavy breathing and the movement of my friends behind me. No signs of vamps or anything else alarming.

Though it takes a considerable amount of energy to inch along in such a tight space, it's the first time in weeks I'm not sweating up a storm. The air is cool in the pipes, brought in from outside and kept safely underground, away from the sun and heat. It's one thing to be thankful for.

The other thing I'm thankful for is that we appear to be the only ones down here. Other than the human feces and piss and wastewater occasionally floating by, it doesn't seem like there's anything else disgusting. No rats. No roaches. Gotta stay grateful for the small things.

Finally, I spot a light bluish-green glow in the distance and hear the telltale signs of running water. My pulse skitters with excitement.

We've done it! The river must be just up ahead!

We crawl a little bit further, and I notice one end of the tube tunnel seems to dead end. That must be where it connects to the water treatment center, perhaps? Above my head, where the daylight flickers in, is a metal grate that appears to be another exit of the pipe system.

I scuttle toward it, peering upward to examine. My fingers twine around the latch. I think—

Yes!

It's unlocked!

All I have to do is turn the latch, lift the grate up, and exit. We'll be at the river in no time. I can't believe that after everything we've been through, after everything that's happened to us, we're finally free.

And then, I hear voices that stop me cold in my tracks…

CHAPTER 32
DAY 32: MORNING

Devil's River

I hold my breath, not daring to make a sound, as I peer through the grate and scan our surroundings. Ahead, the Devil's River looms before us less than a hundred yards away. This part of the riverbank is nowhere near as picturesque as where we camped weeks ago. We must be on the commercial side, the lifeblood of the small farm town.

Aqueducts from several farms in the area, weathered but sturdy, snake their way toward the river. To the left of me appears to be the old waste management plant Kade mentioned. It's a large structure with peeling paint and patches of rust forming along the metal surface. Pipes criss-cross the walls like veins, towering smokestacks standing silent against the horizon.

"How did they escape?" Lillith shouts, sounding close.

My gaze shifts right, and I spot her. She's just a few

dozen yards away, coming up the hills adjacent to the river. Johnny walks beside her.

Horror washes over me, and I duck back down into the pipes before they can see me.

Shit!

They're here! But how?

Zoe meets my terrified gaze in the darkness, fear glittering in her eyes as she reaches for me. Our hands shake while we listen to their heated argument from beneath the ground.

"We don't know," Johnny says, his booming voice carrying in the wide-open space.

"You had one job!" Lillith barks. "All you had to do was keep everyone in the pens. How could you screw that up?"

"It's not like they walked out the front door," he says weakly. "They dug through the ground. How were we supposed to stop that?"

"Well, perhaps if you hadn't been gorging yourself like a mindless goblin on that boy, you might've noticed a big fat hole in the floor!"

"Come on, Lillith. Don't be a bitch." He groans. "How many times do you want me to say I'm sorr—"

There's a loud smacking sound, and I hear Johnny cry out and stumble backward. She must have hit him.

"Shut up! Just stop talking and let me think." Lillith starts to pace back and forth, each step echoing with dull resonance against the ground. "The pipes from the pens must end somewhere around here…"

"Yeah, okay, but where?" Johnny asks. "There's farmland everywhere. Everyone's got waste pipes and aqueduct systems coming through this part of the river. How do we know which one they're in?"

"We don't!" she snaps. "But they'll have to pop up here eventually. We'll just have to wait them out."

He coughs loudly.

"Yeah, but for how long?"

"However long it takes, moron!"

There's a loud shuffling noise. They've taken a seat somewhere nearby in the grass, though I'm not sure how close they are to us. Could be yards or feet. It's hard to tell based on their voices alone, and I don't dare another peek outside.

I sink down deeper into the pipe, panic rioting within me.

"Kade!" Logan says in a furious, hushed whisper. "I knew we couldn't trust him."

Zoe shakes her head. "He didn't... he wouldn't."

Though I'm not as certain of Kade's innocence as Zoe is, it doesn't matter at this point. All that matters is finding a way out of this.

"What do we do?" I whisper, terror edging my voice.

"You heard them. They're not going to leave," Logan says. "We'll have to make a break for it."

"Are you insane?" I hiss. "Haven't you learned by now? We can't outrun them."

I've made that mistake one too many times already. I'm not eager to make it again.

"We don't have any other options." Logan's jaw clenches, a steely resolve hardening his expression. "We can't go back. The only way out is forward."

"But that's suicide!" Zoe's eyes widen with fear. "Logan, we can't!"

"Don't worry. I'll distract them first," he says.

"How?" I ask.

"I don't know, but I'll come up with something."

I try to visualize the path to the river again. It's close... so damn close. Logan is right. We can't turn around, and we can't stay here, trapped in these pipes forever. I don't want to run, but what other choice do we have?

Inside the narrow pipe, I curl into myself and stretch, warming up my muscles to move. As I ready my body, something sharp pokes me in the sternum again. I let out an angry little hiss of air.

What the hell?

I clutch at my chest anxiously. For an instant, I worry that a rib or something internal has somehow become dislodged during our crawl through the tunnels. Maybe I scraped myself on a broken pipe, after all?

And then I remember.

Of course! The garlic!

I fish out the tiny vial of Kade's garlic oil and his lighter from within my sports bra and hold them up to show my friends. Laughter bubbles in my throat.

"Is that what I think it is?" Logan asks, his eyes lighting with a flicker of hope.

"I totally forgot I had it!" My words tumble out in a rush of disbelief.

"Give it to me!" There's a sense of urgency in his command. He doesn't wait for my response as he snatches the oil and lighter from my hands. "You and Zoe make a break for it. I'll hold them off."

A moment of hesitation anchors me to the spot as the weight of his words and what he plans to do fully sinks in.

"Logan—are you sure?"

"Don't worry about me," he says. "Get ready to run."

In the scant light inside the pipes, his smile reaches me— a small, brave curve of his lips that speaks volumes. It's a silent vow to protect Zoe and me, at all costs necessary.

"Thank you," I whisper.

Zoe's lip trembles. "You guys, I really don't think I can do this."

"You can," I insist. "I won't let anything happen to you. I promise."

I grab her hand and squeeze her thumb twice. *I've got you. We'll be okay.*

She blinks rapidly, fighting back the panic that threatens to surface, then nods.

"All right, on three," I say. "One… two…"

On three, I slam the heel of my boot into the grate and leap out, pulling Zoe along with me. We sprint toward the river, our only focus now.

Shouts echo behind us, the vampires in hot pursuit. I can't help but think about how fast and strong they are or what they're going to do if they get to us before we get to the water.

Zoe struggles to keep up. I adjust my pace to hers, determined not to leave her behind. My heart thunders in my ears, my pulse racing with terror.

Suddenly, there's a loud explosion behind us.

I glance back just in time to see a burst of flames where Logan is. He's used the garlic oil and lighter, creating a fiery barrier. The vampires recoil from the flames, hissing in anger and confusion.

In the chaos, I see Logan grappling with Johnny. Logan fights with everything he's got. With a swift move, he douses Johnny in more oil and sets him ablaze. The vampire screams, a sound that makes my blood run cold. I think— hope—he's dying. To the side of his black, charred body is Lillith, distracted by her own injuries, tending to what looks to be a burned arm.

Elation bubbles inside me.

He's done it! Sweet, wonderful, amazing Logan has done it! He's given us the precious seconds we need to get away.

"Keep moving!" I yell to Zoe.

We're almost there, just a few feet from the river. The sound of running water is like a symphony of hope. We're almost free!

Without warning, Zoe cries out and stumbles over a root sticking up from the earth. She goes crashing to the ground, but somehow, I keep my balance. I crouch down and reach for her hand.

"No!" She pushes me away, clutching at her ankle. Tears of pain stream down her face. "Alix, go!"

But I can't.

I won't leave Zoe.

I grunt and bend lower, grabbing her around the waist and lifting her up.

"Alix, stop!" She swats at me. *What are you doing?"*

"Saving your ass!" I hiss, putting her arm around me and using all the energy I have left to get her moving. I push us as fast as I can toward the riverbanks.

Soon, we're only twenty feet from the river.

Then fifteen feet.

I can't believe it—we're going to make it!

Logan is in front of me now. Huffing from exertion and too tired to even speak, I simply push Zoe into his arms without saying a word. He knows what to do. He takes her from me, and they dive for the water. A moment later, Logan and Zoe are in the river. My heart fills with joy.

They're free!

I'm right behind them. Just a few more feet to go. I can almost feel the water on my boots as tears of joy fall down my face.

And then I go airborne.

Arms like a vise wrap around my waist, ripping me away from the riverbanks. Zoe screams and I know, without having to look back, what's happened. Lillith throws me to the ground with such force, I worry my neck is broken.

Not that it matters. Dead people don't need a neck. Because as Lillith stands over me, I know without any doubt in my mind, that I am just that—dead.

At least, I will be shortly.

"Gotcha," she singsongs.

I lie on the ground speechless. The impact has knocked all the air from my lungs.

Even if I could breathe, I have nothing to say. All I can do is stare right into Lillith's cold eyes and wait for the inevitable, for this monster to tear me limb from limb.

Water splashes furiously nearby and my eyes fly toward the river. To my horror, instead of swimming away like any normal, sane person would do, I see Logan swimming to the shoreline of the river and then stepping onto land. He heads straight for me.

"Logan! No!" I cry, desperately. "Don't!"

He's just going to get himself killed, too, and it'll all be for nothing because I can already feel the vampire's breath on my neck. It feels like death. I know I only have seconds of life left now…

Lillith grabs my shoulders, digging her talons into my skin. Her two front canine teeth sharpen and elongate at the ends. I shudder as her lips peel back and her cold fingers graze my throat.

My body shakes. All I can see are those teeth.

I want to be brave, but I don't know if I can be. I'm scared.

So damn scared…

Off in the distance, I hear Zoe scream my name from inside the river, but the sound blurs into the background.

With my last prayer, I pray Zoe will get somewhere safe —to the next town, the next state. Logan will help her. She's going to need him after I'm gone. I pray they find my dad and help him, and that they help protect others, too.

And I pray for Kade. Even if he is a vampire, even if he did turn on me at the end, I still want him to be okay...

Then, as if my thoughts alone conjure him up, Kade is there.

My heart fills at the sight of him. He rips me from Lillith's grasp and growls at her, teeth sharp and pointed. Deadly. For the first time, I see him in all his vampire glory. It should be terrifying, but I'm not scared. Not of him.

He looks like a beautiful dark avenging angel.

"What are you doing, Kaden?" Lillith's eyes narrow.

In one swift move, Kade shoves me toward Logan's waiting arms. "Get her to the river!" he orders, blocking us with his body, protecting us from Lillith. In that instant, I'm ashamed for ever doubting him. I know, with absolute certainty, that he never betrayed me.

Seconds later, I'm submerged in the river, cool water cascading around me while Logan holds me. Zoe hurries to us, embracing me and crying against my neck.

Safe.

We're all safe.

All of us except...

I turn back to the riverbank where Kade remains.

"It's over," he says to Lillith.

"You're really going to throw away everything we have?" Her jaw drops with shock and anger. "For *her?*"

"We don't have anything anymore," Kade says. "We haven't had anything for a long time."

"Don't do this," she begs. "Please, Kaden."

"I have to," he says. "I love her."

For a moment, the coldness lifts from her face as hurt flickers across her lovely features. I can almost envision what she once was before she turned. I can see the woman Kade must have loved. Beautiful. Vulnerable. Human.

But then, just as fast, the stone mask slams back down again. "Fine then. Have it your way," she says.

She lunges for him, her movements a blur of deadly precision. She's swift—startlingly so, a striking viper. But Kade is even faster. He sidesteps her onslaught with an effortless defensive pivot to the left, making it almost look easy.

I watch from the river, my body wrought, sick with tension, as they circle each other like partners in a deadly dance. I don't know much about vampire powers. Based on what I've learned so far, I'd guess she's stronger since she's fed on human blood and killed people.

But I've also seen Kade during all our training. He's sharp. Fast. Skilled. That must mean something, too, right?

Plus, I sort of remember Frog saying the time of the changing was important. If Kade had changed first, like he told me, that might also give him even more strength, wouldn't it?

God, I really hope so...

They continue to spar, each taking vicious shots at the other. Teeth snap. Blood goes flying. Then I see the knife—my hunting knife, the one I'd buried in the pen along with my tools—flash in his hand. He aims for her heart, putting all his strength into the movement. My breath catches as it almost goes in, but at the last minute she moves to the side. It lodges in her stomach instead.

She lurches to the ground, screaming. Rage and hurt echoing in the sound as she struggles with the knife, attempting to yank it from her abdomen.

Footsteps pound in the distance. Over the hill, two male vampires—the ones from the woods weeks ago—appear and race toward us. My stomach churns with fear at the sight.

Kade turns to me, now weaponless.

"Go!" he yells.

I know I should listen to him, but I can't seem to get my body to cooperate. My limbs are leaden, frozen in the water as the cold current laps against my skin. The thought of leaving Kade, just when fate has woven our paths back together once more, is unbearable.

He spins toward Logan. "Get her out of here!" he commands, his voice slicing through the tumult.

"Kade!" The scream wrenches from my throat, a plea, a prayer. Logan's grip tightens as I struggle in his arms, desperate to break free and bridge the distance between Kade and me. "Please! Come with us!"

Kade's gaze is torn, flicking first to Lillith who rises like a phoenix, bloody knife from her stomach now in her hand, a murderous expression on her face. Then, to the other approaching vampires. Finally, he glances at the water with heavy, sad eyes. The water that protects and shields me but harms vampires—vampires like him.

"I'm sorry, Sniper... I can't."

With a powerful surge, Logan propels us both into the current's mercy, pulling us away from Lillith's wrath. Away from the deadly incoming vampires.

Away from Kade...

Kade's voice cuts through the river's roar. "Take care of her," he tells Logan, his words etched with finality.

Then, his eyes lock with mine, one last time. A silent exchange passes between us—a goodbye, but also so much more.

"I was wrong," he says, a wistful smile touching his lips, bittersweet and fleeting, as the current takes me from him. "Some things are worth fighting for. Fight like hell, Alix. Fight and don't ever stop."

EPILOGUE

By the time night falls, we're miles away from the factory farm and hopefully the vampires, too. We've followed the river as far as we can go for the day and are ready to camp for the long night ahead. Logan thinks we'll reach the next town by morning. As far as we can tell, the vampires have let us go—for now.

Perhaps they don't think we're worth the headache to track down, or perhaps they've already infiltrated the next town over and don't see us as a threat to their invasion. If that's true, if the closest neighboring town is already too far gone, then we'll go on to the next.

And the next.

And the next.

We'll keep going until we find a place where the battle can be fought. We won't give up.

We lie down by the water, settling in for a short rest to regain our strength for whatever is next. I curl into a ball at the foot of the riverbank, sobbing silently, my entire body wracked with agony.

"Is your leg hurting again?" Logan asks. He brushes his knuckles across my cheek, wiping my tears away.

I nod, even though it's not my knee that's to blame at all. It's my heart that's broken.

"You're going to be okay, Alix," he says and places something cold and solid in my hand.

Kade's lighter.

"He'd want you to have this back, I think." He touches my shoulder gently and goes to stand guard so Zoe and I can take the first sleeping shift.

Zoe lies down next to me in the dirt and muddy grass. She puts my head in her lap and strokes my damp, knotted hair.

"He was very brave," she whispers low in my ear so Logan can't hear. "He saved us."

Of course, she understands why I'm crying.

Zoe gets it. Gets me. She always has.

"He could still be alive... maybe they spared him?" she asks, her voice hopeful.

I choke down a sob, shaking my head. "No, I saw the knife in her hand..."

Except...

Suddenly, I'm not so sure.

I remember Logan swimming us down the river, and watching helplessly as Lillith got her knife loose. I saw her stalk toward Kade, holding the knife over her head and circling around him, coiling up for a strike. I'd screamed for him to run, to do anything but sit there and wait for her attack.

I remember the other vampires closing in. And then...

Nothing.

We were too far down the river to hear or see anything anymore.

Maybe…

Maybe he is still alive.

Maybe Kade is staring up at the same dusky sky full of stars and big, beautiful moon that I'm looking at right now. In the end, maybe he was stronger, faster, and more powerful than Lillith and all the other vampires.

I think back to all I've learned about him. His family *was* one of the original settlers, after all. And he was one of the first vampires in Allium Valley to turn. Possibly *the* first.

What if Kade is a Stage III?

Frog had said those were the strongest vampires of them all.

I never did get a chance to ask Kade about any of that. We never had enough time for the details, even the important ones.

We never had enough time for anything…

"Thank you, Al," Zoe says and plants a gentle kiss on my forehead, her eyes brimming with love.

"For what?"

"For saving my life."

A smile tugs at the corner of my mouth, my heart swelling with warmth for my best friend. "You've saved me, too, in so many ways. Over and over again." Our hands entwine, fingers lacing and locking with a newfound strength. I give her a reassuring squeeze, a silent promise that speaks louder than words. "Consider us even."

We close our eyes and drift off to sleep while Logan watches over us. The world descends into darkness, but I know the light will return again soon.

It always does.

And when it does, we're going to fight.

In the next town. And the town after that. We'll find people like us, people who want to fight back. Maybe even vampires like Kade—the good vampires, the ones who want to help.

Together, we'll keep on fighting as long and as hard as we need to get our world back. We'll do whatever it takes, and we will never ever give up.

Like Kade said, some things are worth fighting for.

GARLIC GROOVE FESTIVAL PLAYLIST

"I Knew You Were Trouble" (Taylor's Version) —Taylor Swift

"People Are Strange" —The Doors

"Till The World Ends" —Britney Spears

"Reclaim the Rain" —EcoEcho

"Tough Girl Like You" —The Blue Moon Outlaws

"Murder on the Dancefloor" —Sophie Ellis-Bextor

"Bad Moon Rising" —Creedence Clearwater Revival

"The Kids Don't Stand a Chance" —Vampire Weekend

"It's the End of the World as We Know it" —R.E.M.

"Vampire" —Olivia Rodrigo

"A Forest" —The Cure

"Finally // Beautiful Stranger" —Halsey

"(Don't Fear) The Reaper" —Blue Öyster Cult

"Sympathy for the Devil" —The Rolling Stones

"Standing on the Shore" —Empire of the Sun

"My Hero" —Foo Fighters

"Wonderwall" — Oasis

"Love Lost" —The Temper Trap

"A Sky Full of Stars" —Coldplay

Listen on:

Spotify | YouTube

CONNECT MORE WITH REKTOK

I hope you enjoyed this book, and if so, I'd be very grateful if you could write a review. I'd love to hear what you think, and reviews make a big difference in helping readers discover my books.

If you'd like to be the first to know about my new releases and giveaways, please sign up at the link below. I'll never share your email address, and you can unsubscribe anytime.

Sign up here >>> www.RektokRoss.com

I adore hearing from readers. You can contact me at RektokRoss@gmail.com or through my social media (@RektokRoss, everywhere). You can also follow me on Amazon and BookBub, and if you like readalongs, you can join my Facebook group The Book Nook by Rektok Ross or check out my website at www.RektokRoss.com. Thanks for your support, and I hope to hear from you soon!

AUTHOR'S NOTE TO READER

Dear Reader,

As always, thank you for your support. I am so grateful you picked up this book and hope you'll consider reading more of my work!

If you're familiar with my books, you may know that I love writing thrilling stories, but I also enjoy exploring social themes I am passionate about. In my debut thriller, *Ski Weekend*, I examined harmful stereotypes and judgments; in *Summer Rental*, the focus was on bullying and toxic female friendships. For *Spring Harvest*, I wanted to delve into animal cruelty, specifically factory farming and trophy hunting.

I've always been an animal lover and supporter of animal rights, ever since I was a kid, volunteering at the Humane Society in high school in my home state of Florida. Then, as an attorney, I dedicated countless hours working pro bono for animal rights organizations, helped fundraise for animal charities, and even lobbied for stronger laws to protect animals when I lived in Texas.

My hope is that this book might serve as a positive discussion point for others to examine and, perhaps, explore how they feel about the treatment of animals that are part of the food chain. It's certainly not my place to tell anyone what to eat; however, I think from a humane, moral, and ethical perspective, it's beneficial to (at least occasionally) examine our stewardship with respect to how we care for the

Earth's creatures and resources. Even small changes can make a difference. It doesn't have to be as dramatic as going vegan or vegetarian—though I respect those who do—but something as simple as eating a little less meat or buying free-range eggs and chicken can make a big impact. Anyway, it's something to think about, at least, I hope.

As for the plot, the idea for *Spring Harvest* first came to me years ago when I was driving from San Francisco to Los Angeles one weekend with my dog Falkor and drove by Gilroy. If you've never been, it's a small town that feels almost in the middle of nowhere (especially after a long drive), with signs proclaiming it the "Garlic Capital" of the world. My mind wandered, as it often does, to why a town would want to become the garlic capital (to stop vampires, of course!), and what would happen to the town if garlic suddenly stopped growing there. It was an interesting idea, but nothing came of it for a while. (More on that later.)

When I was deciding what to write for my third book in the "Seasons" thriller series, I started first with subgenres. You may have noticed that the books in this series explore different popular thriller/horror subgenres: *Ski Weekend* is a man-vs-nature survival thriller; *Summer Rental* a slasher/murder mystery. I got the idea to write an action thriller after convincing a group of reluctant friends—who are not horror fans—to watch *Halloween H20* (possibly my favorite *Halloween* ever). Surprisingly enough, everyone loved the movie. I sat around for a bit wondering why, and then it hit me—they loved it because of how exciting and fast-paced the action was, despite the horror elements they were nervous about watching. It's just like how people who don't normally watch scary movies still love films like *Aliens, Predator,* and *The Terminator*. Action is universal!

Once the subgenre was decided, I landed on a trope. That part was easy. I'm a sucker for anything vampire. (I can't get enough *Buffy, The Lost Boys, Twilight, 30 Days of Night, The Vampire Diaries, Vampire Academy,* etc.) I always knew I'd write a vampire book one day. Flash back to my idea all those years ago about a garlic town running out of garlic and BAM — *Spring Harvest* was born!

I truly hope you enjoyed reading this book as much as I enjoyed writing it. And if you take away nothing else, I hope you'll take away the importance of showing bravery in the shadow of fear and standing up for what you believe in. Remember—courage is the new black! :)

All my best,

Rektok Ross

Don't miss **SUMMER RENTAL,** the bestselling thriller from Rektok Ross! **Available now!**

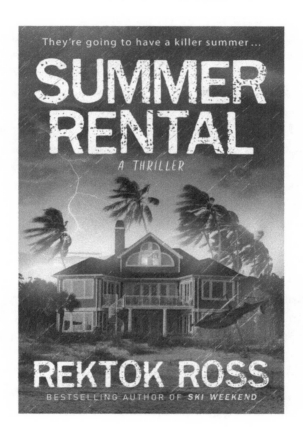

EXCERPT FROM *SUMMER RENTAL*

CHAPTER 1
DAY 1: Thursday—Three days before July Fourth

It isn't supposed to rain in paradise.

At least, that's what the sign said when we turned off the highway and onto the rickety, two-lane bridge moments ago. It was painted a bright tropical yellow and read, *"Palm Key Island: it's always sunny here!"* Naturally, the "i" was dotted with an orange.

As I watch the rain fall from my cramped middle seat in the back of the SUV—the absolute worst spot in the car, of course—I tell myself it's just one of those quick summer showers we get in Florida. It won't last long. They never do. But when we pull up to the driveway of our rental home for the weekend and the rain still hasn't stopped, I start to worry.

We all hop out of the car and I eye the dark, ominous clouds with growing concern. The five of us hold jackets and sweatshirts over our heads and rush to grab luggage from the cargo area of Cam and Val's brand-new Range Rover. It's just one of the lavish gifts the twins received from their parents at graduation a few weeks ago.

"Just a little rain, everybody," Cam says next to me, overly cheery as usual. She runs a hand through her dark sleek bob, pushing glossy hair off her face and behind pearl-studded ears. "It'll clear up any minute."

"You sure?" I ask, dodging raindrops.

"Yes, Riley. I'm sure," she says, laughing as she elbows me lightly in the ribs. She surveys the rental house with a pleased expression on her pretty face. "Look! It's perfect—just like I said it'd be!"

Other than the pesky drizzle, I have to admit she's right. It looks way better than I expected. For starters, the two-story house is much larger in person than it was in the photos. Elegant and charming, it even has a big wraparound veranda and two dreamy, towering columns that make it seem like something off the cover of a romance novel. A row of palm trees on either side of us catches the late afternoon breeze, green leafy fronds gently blowing back and forth. The unmistakable salty scent of the ocean wafts in my direction.

When Cam first told me about the summer rental, I'd been suspicious. We were still dressed in our orange and blue Bishop Lake Preparatory High School graduation gowns when she pulled out the rental agreement from her shiny white Gucci tote. Another graduation gift. Val got one too, although hers was fire-engine red, her "signature" color.

Right away, I thought the posting was fishy. No way a house directly on the sand in ritzy Palm Key Island was only a few hundred bucks during the busy July Fourth holiday weekend. Something had to be wrong. My money was on a broken air conditioner, or maybe a gross, putrid smell like rotten eggs the owners couldn't get rid of. Not that I could be picky. The only reason we were getting a rental in the first place was because I couldn't afford a room at the fancy hotel where everyone else from school was staying. Somehow, Cam convinced her snobby twin sister Val and our other two best friends, Blake and Nia, to join us.

"I can't wait to see the inside!" Cam races toward the house, rolling her designer luggage behind her. Her initials "CGR"—for Camila Gisele Ramirez—are custom-painted in pale pink along the trim.

Her twin sister sprints after her. Val's colorful, vibrant dress billows behind her and catches the wind. Full and plush lips, painted her usual bold shade of red, are set in a pout as her stiletto Louboutins click along the pavement. Val bought the shoes yesterday even though she already has dozens, just like them, in her closet back home. What Valentina Lorraine Ramirez wants, she gets.

"I get first dibs!" Val yells as Cam opens the lockbox hanging on the front doorknob.

The rest of us watch from a safe distance by the car as the twins fight over the key. Val attempts to claim the biggest room in the house, even though she did none of the work to book our trip.

"What a brat," Nia mutters next to me, rolling her eyes. Nia has the most gorgeous eyes. Fox-shaped and the color of liquid onyx with lashes so long and thick you'd think they were extensions like Val has, but Nia's just lucky to be naturally stunning.

"Typical Val," Blake says. "Fifty bucks says Cam caves and gives her the master. She's such a pushover."

"Cam's just a people pleaser," I say, defensive of my best friend, even if I sort of agree. We all know Cam lets her twin get away with murder. "Besides, I'm sure all the rooms are nice."

"Whatever." Blake grabs her surfboard and throws it over one tan, muscular shoulder. Beautiful, beachy blonde hair bounces down her shapely backside. "Let's just unpack and change. I wanna hit the beach."

Nia gives me her suitcase to bring inside and pulls her iPhone out of her pocket to film her arrival for her social media followers. She smiles and waves at her "Nia-mani-acs," as she likes to call them, her toothy grin even brighter than usual against her flawless dark skin. Nia just landed a brand deal with a toothpaste whitener, and they gave her a year's supply of product.

Just like Cam predicted, the rain stops, and the sun appears as Blake helps me unload the car. We go fast, hoping to have time to lay out before the sun goes down. The six-hour drive from Bishop Lake took far longer than expected.

First, Val made us late by insisting on bringing two enormous suitcases, even though we didn't have room. Cam's begging didn't work; it wasn't until Blake threatened to throw Val's suitcases into the lake in front of the twins' house that Val recanted. Blake could do it, too. She was our state champion in both shot put and discus throw and has a full ride to Stanford in the fall.

Then, after waiting for Val to repack—and listening to her complain the whole time—we missed not one, but two, of the highway turnoffs. Combining that with Nia's demands we make multiple bathroom stops on account of the new flat-tummy tea she was drinking for an Instagram collab, it's a miracle we made it before nightfall.

"Jesus, Cam. What'd you put in here—bricks?" I ask, entering the foyer like a pack mule with Cam's massive nylon duffle slung over my shoulder and dragging Nia's bulging suitcase and my roller bag behind me. I drop Cam's bag down and wince, rubbing at my aching muscles.

"Sorry." She grins. "I didn't know what we'd need, so I packed everything. Beach towels. Sunscreen. Paddle ball," she says and then gestures around the place. "So what do you think? Cute, right?"

"Totally." I suppress a groan. Only my friends would call this place "cute."

The rental is huge. The apartment my mom and I share back home could fit in the foyer alone. The dark wooden floors are freshly mopped, and the rich cream walls, though bare, are crisp and bright, as if newly painted. Cool air blows from the vents above my head, so I know my fears of a broken air conditioner were unfounded. Best of all, no bad smells. If anything, it smells strongly of bleach, as if recently cleaned and scrubbed from top to bottom.

I take a few steps down the hall to find a formal dining room. Past that, the hallway opens up to reveal a gorgeous spiral staircase and spacious living room amply furnished with two overstuffed leather couches and matching recliners. On the other end of the house is a kitchen that butts up against floor-to-ceiling glass patio doors. A big deck and screened-in pool is out back. I can even see the beach from here.

Blake rushes into the living room and stands in front of the enormous fifty-five-inch flat screen TV. She grabs an iPad off one of the couches and starts pushing buttons until Lady Gaga comes on, and upbeat dance music plays from the wireless speakers overhead. Blake grins over at us and turns the volume up super high, singing along and shaking her booty to the beat.

Val inches toward the stairs. "So, I'm just gonna head up and unpack and—"

"I already told you," Cam says. "You can't take the master bedroom, Val. We're drawing numbers."

A strangled whine erupts from Val. "And I told you, *Camila*. I need the biggest room for all my clothes and makeup."

"It's fine with me," I say to make things easy for Cam. She's always caught in the middle, trying to appease Val's over-inflated sense of entitlement while not pissing off the rest of our friends.

"Me too. I don't even wear makeup," Nia says, coming up behind me. If I didn't know better, I might believe she's being sincere. She really doesn't need makeup. "Besides," she adds with a mean little smirk, "you're gonna need all the help you can get with that nasty little breakout on your chin."

Val pulls down her oversized designer sunglasses. "Very funny," she says, curling her freshly painted nails into a fist. "Keep it up and you're gonna need help for a black eye."

Val and Nia don't exactly get along. Cam told me they used to be tight, but that all changed last year. Before then, the wide consensus was that Valentina Ramirez was by far the most beautiful girl at school. That all changed, seemingly overnight, after Nia's braces came off and her boobs grew in. Now they're rivals. I guess it also doesn't help that Nia just started dating Val's latest ex-boyfriend, Tyler Singh.

"Great, so we all agree Val can have the master," I say in my peppiest voice, trying to diffuse the tension. "Put me anywhere. I'm just happy to be here."

Blake frowns at me and I know what she's thinking—that I'm a pushover, too, just like Cam.

She's not wrong.

"I still can't believe your mom wouldn't give you enough money for the hotel," Val says. "The Seasider looked so lux, and the spa has those special hydro-facials from Sweden, and—"

"Val," Cam warns.

Val shrugs. "I mean, I guess this is fine, too."

"I'm really sorry. She's the worst," I say, shoving my hands into the pockets of my cut-off jean shorts and doing my best to ignore the winces of guilt. I don't like lying, but it's necessary. I've worked too hard building up a certain image for myself, and I'm not going to jeopardize that now. I know people say real friends should like you for the "real you," but those people don't hang out in the same circles I do.

My friends would never understand the truth. Their families are all *rich* rich. Nia's dad is a former professional basketball player, and Blake's parents own a real estate business, building homes all around the state. And the Ramirez family, well, they're one of the wealthiest families in the South. The twins' grandparents started the largest American-Spanish language television network in the country.

I used to be like them. My dad was a well-respected financial adviser in Miami. We had it all. The six-thousand square foot house. Luxury cars. Ski trips to Aspen in the winter and beach trips to Saint-Tropez in summer. Everything was perfect until Dad's firm got caught embezzling client funds. He went to prison, Mom filed for divorce, and we changed our last names and moved to central Florida. The only thing we had left was Dad's old 'Benz and enough money for a shitty, low-income housing apartment to start over.

I was lucky to get into Bishop Prep for senior year. My academic scholarship paid for school, but I had to get an afterschool job for everything else. Working at the Mouse Trap, a cheesy restaurant near Disney, gave me money to help Mom with bills and just enough left over to afford the right clothes and makeup so I could fit in. If it wasn't for Mr. Ramirez's black Am Ex helping with my share of the already cheap rental, there's no way I'd even be on this trip.

"I'll take this room," Blake says and plops her surfboard in front of the downstairs bedroom closest to the pool. I know from the pictures it has an insane ocean view. Blake might not go head-to-head with the twins, but she's not going to take scraps, either.

"I'll take whatever's left. I don't plan on sleeping here, anyway." Nia digs into her suitcase and pulls out a skimpy neon green bikini. "I'm gonna freshen up and meet the guys."

"Guys?" Val asks, her voice tight. "What guys?"

Nia struts toward the guest bathroom and closes the door without answering.

"That little *puta*!" Val turns to the rest of us, angry red blotches forming on her tanned, over-contoured cheeks.

"She's talking about Ty, isn't she?"

"Relax," Cam says. "It'll be fine."

"But I told you. I don't want to see that asshole!" Val hisses.

"What's the big deal?" Blake asks. "I thought you dumped Ty. And Nia likes him."

"Nia likes to piss me off—that's what Nia likes," Val grumbles.

"She's been like this ever since second grade. Remember when I won the Miss Orange Blossom Pageant instead of her? She always wants what I have. It's pathetic." A flash of panic flickers across her face and she turns, grabbing me by the elbow. "You don't think Ty really likes her, do you? I mean, she's not even that pretty."

"Oh no." I hold my hands up and back away. "I'm not getting in the middle of this."

"Ugh, you're so spineless, Riley," Val says and turns hopefully to Blake.

"You're joking, right?" Blake asks. "Nia's smoking hot."

She starts changing out of her tracksuit right there in the hallway and puts on a sexy one-piece that runs so high up her backside it might as well be a thong. Blake has an amazing body from sports. She's not afraid to show it off, either. To boys. To girls. She doesn't discriminate.

"Oh, never mind." Val makes a dismissive face at her. "You'd screw anyone."

"Forget Ty, would I?" Blake proceeds to throw sunscreen, towels, and a football into her beach bag. "This place is gonna be crawling with hotties. You don't bring sand to the beach."

Val seems to consider this for a moment, licking at her bottom lip thoughtfully.

"You know what? You're absolutely right," she says. "And at least if that dirtball is here, that means Seb's coming." She lets out a dreamy moan. "He's soooooo sexy."

My chest flutters at his name. Sebastian Ramos is easily the best-looking guy in school: dark green eyes that turn colors with his mood, six-one inches of muscled, ripped body that just won't quit, and a Colombian accent so hot he could melt ice. The boy is charisma incarnate.

Unfortunately, he's off limits. Val's been in love with him for years.

"Hate to break it to you, babe, but that's never gonna happen," Blake says.

Val crosses her arms over her chest. "You don't know that."

"Yeah, I do. You've been trying to get back with Seb ever since he dumped your ass in ninth grade," Blake says. "If it was gonna happen, it would've happened by now."

"That's not—"

"It's okay," Blake says, cutting Val off with a knowing grin. "He doesn't like me either, and trust me, I've tried many, many times. Such a shame. I bet he's a great kisser. And other things." Cam and I giggle as Blake pretends to hump her surfboard. "Sadly, Seb's a sucker for those nice, quiet, do-gooder types. Like our little Ri Ri over here…"

"Oh no. Seb and I are just friends," I say, my cheeks heating. Sebastian doesn't like me like that. He's made that painfully obvious, which is probably a good thing. Val would lose her mind if Sebastian and I ever got together.

We'd been close all year, it's true. Sitting next to each other in class and studying in the library. I went to as many of his soccer games as I could. Sebastian was the star of our school's team with a full ride to Princeton. Of course, I had a huge crush on him—like everyone else in school.

There was a time I thought he might have feelings for

me too, right after he kissed me at Nia's graduation party, but the next day he acted like nothing happened. He's avoided me ever since. I had no idea he was coming this weekend. I wonder if—

"Forget Sebastian Ramos." Cam gives me a sympathetic look. She's the only one I told about the kiss. "I've got someone way better and—good news—he just texted he's here."

"Who?" I ask, my chest tightening. I'm pretty sure I know the answer, and I'm not nearly as excited as she is.

"Jonathan?"

"Yes!" she shrieks.

Cam has been trying to set me up with Jonathan Chang all year, always trying to get us together every time he's home from college on break. He's a year older than us and cute enough, but… I don't know. He's so awkward. Always getting too close and trying to touch me. Always staring at me for too long or when he thinks I don't see. He's never crossed the line or anything, it's just… Something about him creeps me out a bit. The girls used to be tight with his younger sister, Jordyn.

She died last summer. I never met her, though, of course, I knew of her. Everyone knew the 10-Squad. They were the most beautiful girls in town—the rich bitches that ruled Bishop Prep. The Ramirez twins, Blake Sampson, Nia Williams, and Jordyn Chang. People called them the 10-Squad because they were all tens. Tens in looks. Tens in wealth. Tens in status. After Jordyn died, the nickname fell away, but there's never been any doubt who ran the halls at school.

"Lucky you, Ri Ri." Val sneers. "Jonny boy's a real catch —if you like your boyfriends slightly unhinged."

"Don't be a jerk," Blake says. "Jon's a great guy. I'm glad he's here. It'll be good for him to get away—you know, with it being July 4th." An uncharacteristically sad look passes over her face, and I remember hearing that Jordyn died over the holiday weekend last year.

"I'm just being honest." Val gets to the top of the stairs and hangs over the railing, looking down on us. "We all know Jon's got a few screws loose. He did go to the loony bin."

"It was a mental health clinic," Blake corrects.

"Besides, he's fine now," Cam says. "That was months ago."

"Just to be safe, we should probably find the nearest nut house and make sure they've got an opening." Val giggles and disappears inside the master bedroom.

"Don't listen to her." Cam gives me an encouraging smile. "You two will hit it off."

"Can't we have fun this weekend—just us girls?" I ask.

"Hell no," Blake says. "I didn't drive all this way to sit around braiding each other's hair and have pillow fights. I'm getting laid." She looks me up and down with a slow, measuring glance. "And you should, too. You're way too cute to be single, Ri Ri."

It's not that I'm anti-dating. I've just got other things on my mind. Like for one, I still have no idea how I'm going to pay for college in the fall. I'd been holding out hope until a few weeks ago when I'd gotten the bad news no scholarship was coming. Soon everyone will head off to their fancy universities and, despite having one of the highest GPAs in school, I'll probably be at the community college down the street.

"The bed in here is huge!" Val pops out of the master, her lipstick and blush already touched up. "Hey Ri Ri, wanna room with me?"

"She's taken," Cam says, throwing an arm around my shoulder.

I smile back gratefully. From personal experience, I know Val is a terrible roommate. She's a total slob who leaves mounds of clothes everywhere and expects me to pick up after her like her housekeeper does back home.

Cam grabs her bags, and I follow her to the wraparound staircase. As we get to the base of the stairs, there's a loud clicking noise and the floor shudders below us like the sound of something turning on. I take another step closer and notice, with a little shock, that the staircase continues down to another level.

"Looks like a basement," Blake says, coming up behind me and gazing over my shoulder.

"In Florida?" I ask.

"It's expensive, but my parents have them in some spec homes. You can reinforce them with concrete," Blake says and heads down to check it out. She gets to the door and reaches for the knob, twisting it. "That's weird. It's locked."

The sounds below us deepen and then vibrate.

It's just a coincidence, I tell myself, my mind going instantly to the bad dreams I've been having recently. They started right after graduation. Crazy, vivid nightmares of someone with an axe chasing me down into a basement filled with the bodies of all my dead friends. It freaked me out so bad, I'd Googled it. Apparently, dreams about being chased are super common. It means you're stressed out and avoiding something important, which I guess I am.

A loud knock sounds at the front door, and Nia bursts out of the bathroom. She races across the hall, her dark box braids piled on top of her head. She looks amazing, like she just stepped off the cover of the *Sports Illustrated Swimsuit* edition.

At the same time, Val prances out of the master bedroom in the hottest scarlet red bikini she owns. Her jaw locks on the back of Nia's head, eyes sparking. I know it's about to go down. Valentina doesn't give up anything, especially a guy, without a fight.

A war is coming.

I just hope we all make it out of this weekend alive. . .

Mean Girls meets **Scream** in this heart-pounding psychological thriller filled with danger, twists, and shocking betrayals where nothing is as it seems. Perfect for fans of '90s horror movies and books by Holly Jackson, Frieda McFadden, and Natasha Preston!

GET SUMMER RENTAL NOW!

ACKNOWLEDGEMENTS

I'll try my best to keep this short(ish) since I'm now a few books into this and at this point most of you already know how much I love and appreciate you!

As always, thank you first and foremost to my readers. You are everything, and I truly appreciate every single review, post, share, DM, and email from you. Connecting with you and building my reader community is the greatest joy. Special thanks to my Street Team—you guys are the best!—and also to all the "Book Nookers" in my Facebook book club and reader group "The Book Nook by Rektok Ross." (We're always looking for new members, so just holler if you want to join us!)

Huge thanks to my publishing team: my fabulous editors Amy Tipton, Stephanie Elliot, Crystal Blanton, and Tandy Boese and my wonderful publicist Paul Christensen. Couldn't do this without you.

Continued thanks goes out to all my friends in the publishing and entertainment industries for your support of my work. Thank you always to the incredible booksellers, librarians, educators, and media who continue to champion my books. I see you and appreciate you!

Special thank you to all the dear friends that are always supportive of me and this journey. Most especially, thanks to those that didn't ignore my constant texting for *Spring Harvest* asking which cover you liked best, which tagline was the catchiest, and any other number of questions I hounded you about. This includes, but is not limited to (lawyer language in case I forget anyone — sorry!): Fab 5, Kate, Ashlee, Ryka, Joannie, Jen, Cynthia, Mila, Sorboni, Kathy, Filly, Aurora, Gena, Ye-hui, Pris, Nicole, Jill, Lynn, Tanya, and Sherie.

Finally, a huge thanks goes to my family. To my mom, the one who first instilled a love of reading in me. Dad and Lance for all the amazing pep talks and love, and L and Scarlett, and all the DeCesares—thank you for always cheering me on. Derek, Dani, and Ro for everything you do —I love you guys so much! To Michael, the one who makes this all possible and is shockingly good at publishing advice for a tech guy. You're always my first and my favorite reader. And to the best furry writing buddies—Falkor and Blair.

Falkor, most especially, my heart dog—you were truly the best "good boy," always living up to your luck dragon name, a dog who loved every single creature he ever met. This one is for you, baby boy.

ABOUT THE AUTHOR

Author photo © Agency Moanalani Jeffrey

Liani Kotcher (writing as Rektok Ross) is a trial attorney turned award-winning and bestselling author, screenwriter, and producer. An avid reader since childhood, Liani writes exactly the kind of books she loves to escape into herself: exciting thrillers with strong female leads, swoonworthy love interests, and life-changing moments. She graduated from the University of Florida School of Journalism and obtained her juris doctorate at the University of Miami School of Law. Originally from South Florida, she currently splits her time between San Francisco, Los Angeles, and Las Vegas with her husband, step kids, and her dogs. She is the recipient of several awards, including the American Fiction Awards, IAN Book of the Year Awards, Readers' Favorite

Book Awards, the Chanticleer Dante Rossetti Book Awards, and Women Writing the West. You can find her online just about anywhere at @RektokRoss, as well as on her website, www.RektokRoss.com, where she blogs about books and writing. Sign up for her newsletter and stay up on all the latest Rektok Ross book news here: www.RektokRoss.com

Facebook: @RektokRoss
Instagram: @RektokRoss
TikTok: @RektokRoss
BookBub: @RektokRoss
Twitter: @RektokRoss
Readers Group:
www.facebook.com/groups/thebooknookbyrektokross/

"And don't say that worthless piece of amber is more valuable, because it's not."

"To me it is," I say.

"Well, now you have some things from me that are indisputably more valuable, and there's plenty more where those came from."

The next twenty-four hours pass in a bit of a blur, the most notable moments being our practice ride—I'd forgotten what a joy it is to ride Obsidian—and the way he completely soothed John's and my dad's concerns about his absence and Obsidian Devil's last minute substitution.

"You never handled my dad that well before," I say. "And I don't think you ever even tried to get along with John."

"First of all," he says, "I had no idea what to do or say when you first turned me human again. And secondly, I wasn't trying yet." He winks. "But now I'll do whatever it takes to make anyone you care about listen to me."

"Just listen?" I arch one eyebrow.

He casts his eyes heavenward. "And like me, if that matters to you."

The day of the race, I'm in Obsidian's stall, running my hand down his sleek, shiny neck when John bangs on the wall of the stall. "Kristiana Liepa, you'd better be dressed. You're due for a weigh out in ten minutes."

Although I told them that Aleksandr's also back—they weren't delighted—John's still listed as the official trainer for Obsidian Devil on our paperwork. He's taking his role seriously, it seems. "I'm so sorry. I wasn't paying attention. I'll head over right now."

"I'll saddle his royal highness while you're gone." John walks into the stall while I walk out.

I get changed and jog over to the weigh out. It only takes a moment, and then I walk across to the handicap center with my ticket. John meets me there with Obsidian. We take his weights and get the designated amounts slid into the compartments on the saddle that were made for this. It feels even heavier than usual, but that's probably just because of my nerves.

"You ready?" John asks me.

"Well, let's see. My hands are shaking, my stomach's churning, and I feel like running into the smallest corner I can find and curling into a ball."

"That's all fine as long as you don't puke. You've got to be within four ounces of your current weight for the weigh in after the race."

"Very reassuring. Thanks, John."

He chucks me on the shoulder. "You've got this."

Obsidian bumps my hip, and I absently rub his forehead.

I see Finn a moment before I hear him. "Even with the Backstreet Boy in weight you're carrying over your saddle, you're going to be fine." Finn leads his horse, Some Like It Hot, next to me. He's a nine-year-old two-time veteran of the Grand National, and he looks as calm as Finn.

"Of course you're not worried. You've ridden in this melee a dozen times, and only been unseated once."

"Becher's Brook is a sadistic beast." He grins. "But I reiterate: you will be fine. You're the second best jockey I know."

I grin. "Narcissist."

Obsidian snaps at him, but it's half-hearted and Finn smiles this time.

"Your horse is a real pain, you know. I told my mum to bet on me, but she liked Obsidian Devil at King George, and she insisted on putting fifty quid on you again. You better not let her down a second time."

"Or I won't get ice cream after this?"

"I'd love to take you for ice cream." Finn's look is a little too intense, but my hands aren't shaking anymore, and my stomach isn't so queasy. Finn's a good friend.

"I heard about you and Sean," he says. "I meant to say something, but at first it seemed too soon, and then it just seemed too late, so ya know. I'm sorry."

Obsidian's ears perk up and he turns to me. He bumps my arm.

"Two minutes until the parade, then the girth check, and then we're off. We better mount." Finn repositions his reins.

"Good luck," I say. "If we don't win, I'd rather it be you who beats us."

"This is weird timing, I know, but can we talk after the race?" Finn looks. . .nervous, almost.

"It might be sort of crazy after the race," I say, "but maybe we can grab drinks once things settle down, before I head back home."

"Yeah, I'd like that." Finn's holding my gaze a little too long.

Obsidian whinnies and tugs.

I pat his neck. "It's alright, boy. We have time."

Finn shakes his head and swings up onto Some Like It Hot. He circles around to line up for the parade, and I swing up, too. Obsidian keeps turning back to look at me, for all the world like he's angry about something.

"We're about to race. We can talk about whatever is wrong later."

Obsidian keeps laying his ears flat against his head during the parade. The onlookers are pointing, and I can hear the announcer jabbering about how the devil and I don't look good, like we're having another off day.

I'll show them an off day.

The other jockeys dismount for the final regirth, but I don't want to deal with Obsidian trying to send me messages in the sand or whatever. When I'm standing, it's easier for me to pretend he's a normal horse.

Plus, unlike most horses, I know his girth's plenty tight

already. Even so, with so many horses in an enclosed area, there's some shifting and general unrest. Earl Grey jostles me on the left, and Obsidian almost bumps into Brigadier General on the right. His jockey, Rex McComb, turns around and leans right up against me, grabbing my leg with one hand. "Watch out, tramp."

"Get your hand off her," Finn says. He brings Some Like It Hot around, angling to press in between Rex and me. Brigadier General shies away and slams into me pretty hard. Finally, Rex steps back and remounts, and I have to pull Obsidian back before he has time to retaliate.

I can't have him doing anything stupid, not today, even if Rex is a tosser.

Finn and the other jockeys all remount, finally, muttering and glaring at me and Rex. The horses are quite wound up, having passed the crowds in the stands and circled around almost to the first jump. The last thing they needed was an altercation between jockeys.

"Here we are," the announcer yells through the loud-speaker. "John Smith's Grand National." Then the tape drops, and we all surge forward. I give Obsidian his head, because I want us to push past some of the chaos. We hurtle toward the first fence, pounding across Melling Road, just a length behind Brigadier General and Some Like it Hot. This course has a longer approach to that first fence than any other race on the steeplechase circuit. My biggest concern with that first obstacle is that we may over-jump it. It's not a huge fence, but there's a big drop on the back end. Over-jumping it would put us at risk of bowling over or stumbling through that drop, and we're both keyed up and overexcited. Obsidian leans back into his hocks slightly and then he sails over, not even brushing the spruce branches. I brace myself for the drop at the back end, but Obsidian lands so lightly I can hardly believe it.

Once we're past, I urge him around the inside and we

pass a bay, a chestnut, and a dapple, just before closing in on the second fence. Usually I know all the other riders, and in theory I've studied them all for today, but forty-four pairs is too many for me to remember them all by name.

This next hurdle's larger than the first, and there's a big ditch in front. This one requires a little more momentum, because it needs a big horizontal launch. He picks up speed just a bit, and then launches, landing lightly yet again. He recovers beautifully as well.

I pull back on the reins a little as we race through, so Obsidian knows we should hold our position in the line-up until the ditch on four, just like I told him I would. I plan to pull ahead some on five, since it's an easy fence, but we end up shifting sharply left after a grey and a roan go down in a heap, and my heart rate spikes. Obsidian springs quickly, and we move clear of another horse sprawling out from the cluster just in time.

We pass two horses while going over fence five, but I notice Obsidian's hooves graze the spruce on this one. He can clearly feel the extra weight, and I worry. Obsidian and I practiced plenty, but the King George wasn't a weighted event, and we haven't trained in months.

Is he too out of shape to hang in there?

I make out the flash of Finn's colors just ahead as we approach the worst jump of the course, Becher's Brook. It's one of the biggest fences, and it has a massive, nearly seven-foot drop on the back end. Clearing it for the first time in a massive bunch of horses at racing-speed, I get why people compare it to jumping off the edge of the world.

Obsidian sails over the front end easily, but with the drop behind, his head goes down hard. As he and I slam into the turf, chunks of the track fly every direction. Obsidian rights himself quickly and springs forward, correcting the speed of his gallop and rebalancing my weight.

Before I've had time to even go over adjustments I'll make our next time around, we're up and over Foinaven, which is a small fence. It has, however, claimed its share of horses, coming as it does right between Becher's and the Canal. We swing toward the Canal Turn with a little more speed than I'd have chosen, but I'm not entirely in control when I'm riding Obsidian. It's one of the blessings, and it's a drawback in some ways. The Canal's a huge fence in its own right, but it comes just before a sharp left turn, and it rivals Becher's for the sheer number of jockeys it's unseated over the years.

Including my mother.

There's a horse on either side of us as we bound toward it. I can barely breathe as we're forced into the Canal Turn straight on, which will force Obsidian to pivot ninety degrees upon landing.

It's exactly how my mom hit it.

My hands tremble.

The neurons in my brain all fire at the same time. Danger, danger, danger!

But when I freeze, Obsidian takes over, pulling ahead of the other two horses beside us far enough to pivot without colliding with either of them. I'm not piloting him at all, but I manage to stay in the saddle as Obsidian rights our path. Finn swings wide to avoid losing his balance and falling off up ahead, and we pass him quickly thereafter. As if he can sense how much I want to be away from the Canal, Obsidian puts on a burst of speed, passing Brigadier on the gap leading up to Valentine.

He eases up a bit once we're past, and we clear the large fence beautifully, pulling ahead of a dark grey in the process. A smile creeps back onto my face, the tension and anxiety that had built up leading up to the Canal finally dissipating.

We may have been seated near the bottom, but now we're out in front.

The crowd goes wild as we clear the smallish ditch and cross Melling Road, swinging past the completely packed stands. People are wildly waving signs. I tune it all out, and prepare for the Chair, the biggest and narrowest jump, with another massive ditch on the back. We clear it, but Obsidian's tiring and birch branches fly on all sides as we land. One of the branches gets lodged between my leg and the stirrup, scratching my leg through my pants with every stride. I ignore it as best I can as we breeze past the water on sixteen. We must've gotten lazy at the front, because as we circle the winning post, I notice the horses trailing us out of the corner of my eye. They're closer than I thought.

I urge Obsidian ahead, but I can tell he's flagging a bit on the nineteenth fence, yet another ditch. He knocks a whole flurry of branches down, which is normal for most horses, but it's anything but for Obsidian. That birch from the last jump's still digging into my leg. "Let's ease up a little. We're out in front—don't worry so much."

We take the next few fences slow and steady, and I focus on keeping calm, balancing perfectly, and ignoring the infernal branch that seems to be digging its way into my body, one bounding leap at a time. By the second fence of round two, I can't take it anymore. I push up harder on my right leg, to relieve some pressure on my left, and I reach one hand down to grab the branch. I've just touched it when my girth strap snaps and the entire saddle cants to the right. I'm almost flung onto the ground as the saddle slides sharply. I reposition my legs, pushing hard on the stirrups on the left to adjust the position. The only thing connected to my saddle at all now is the breastplate that circles Obsidian's neck, but that won't hold it steady.

How could my girth break? It was almost brand new.

My panicked mind reviews the past fifteen minutes frantically. John saddled Obsidian, and obviously he checked and double-checked everything. I'm distracted from my rehash by a fence approaching. It'll be our first fence since the saddle strap gave out. The cinch is still dangling on the left side, slapping against Obsidian's legs and occasionally his belly.

I consider giving up and going around it. Equipment malfunctions suck, but bowing out is the safe move.

But Obsidian shows no fear, surging ahead, trusting me to stay on. The least I can do is follow his lead. He leaps as smoothly as he can, but even so, the saddle shifts. I slide right and my heart flies up to my throat. This jump was a simple one, and it almost unseated me. I'll never make it when we hit Becher's, much less the dreaded Canal Turn. I consider unlatching the breastplate connections and just tossing the saddle. I could probably do it without losing my seat. I've ridden bareback since I was a child, and I regularly take jumps bareback as well. The saddle's more of a liability than anything else at this point.

But losing the weights would disqualify us.

We manage to clear the next fence too, and now we're bearing down on Becher's Brook fast. Riding on an unsteady saddle feels like trying to stay on a bucking bronco. The thought of hitting that ditch without a solid connection to the horse makes me want to hurl.

I do reach down and snag the unruly girth when it swings up high and flip it over the top of the saddle, clutching it as tightly as I can while still managing my reins.

As we approach Becher's for the second time, Brigadier General pulls up behind us on the right, and Some Like It Hot races toward us on the left. Obsidian has slowed dramatically to keep me safe, which I appreciate, but we're not going to keep our lead, not if we keep hanging back. I wish I could drop my feet from the stirrups and cling with my thighs, but the saddle will swing loose for sure without my legs in the stirrups to keep it centered.

With the other horses approaching, I urge Obsidian to greater speed. His ears lay flat. He doesn't want me injured. We clear Becher's Brook, and I manage to keep the saddle steady. I'm getting better at it, but it's not enough. Brigadier passes us on the outside as we pound toward Foinaven.

I made it over before, but I can't stop thinking about my mom's fall. The closer we get, the harder it is to put that image out of my mind—her small body, crumpled on the sod. All it'll take is one misstep or one out-of-control horse to slam into us and we're goners.

A commotion behind me pulls my attention, and I glance back to see that Finn's horse clipped the fence at Becher's.

Finn loses his seat, rolling over himself into a heap at the corner of the jump. Two more horses are close behind him. I don't even look forward as Obsidian clears Foinaven, because I'm too worried about Finn. Surprisingly, even with the slight curve and my inattention, my saddle stays upright. I must be learning to compensate for it better.

When Finn stands up, I breathe a hearty sigh of relief. Some Like It Hot, now riderless, thunders along next to us going into the Canal Turn, with Brigadier General now a full length ahead. We apex the turn, just like we're supposed to, but Some Like It Hot bumps into Obsidian and sends me and my cursed saddle slamming into the side rail, effectively crushing my left leg.

An inferno burns its way through my thigh, and I drop down into the saddle, unable to post. The pommel slides back and forth, and I know I should just swing off.

It's too many problems.

I need to quit.

Another horse passes us on the left. Earl Grey. And yet another edges past us on the right, a white horse, The Masochist, I think. I can't help thinking about my mom and the pileup she caused when she fell. The horses careening over her. One of them clipped the back of her head as she was sitting up, and that's the blow that killed her. It's too dangerous, what I'm doing, and we clearly aren't going to win.

If we can't win, what's the point?

I pull back on the reins. Obsidian glances back, one ear cocked. He whinnies. He's clearly asking whether I'm alright.

My leg howls at me while my saddle slides back and forth like a stumbly drunkard on ice, and we've fallen back from first into fourth. Soon to be fifth.

No, I'm not okay.

I want to scream and cry and shoot something. My mom's face swims in front of my eyes, and I want to explain to her that it's not my fault. I made it here, and I did everything right. Someone must have sliced my girth strap. No one could win under these circumstances. Tears well up, and when I turn my head to shake them off, I glance at the stands. An elementary girl with blonde hair and a cute little navy coat holds a sign that reads, "Kris and Devil. For Your Mom. For girls everywhere. Girl jockeys are here to stay."

I can't quit now.

Women have always had the odds stacked against us. Nothing's ever fair, and even though one of us won, once, that doesn't mean it's enough. A hundred plus wins by men aren't leveled with one girl winning. We can't ever give up. We have to try harder, because for us, things *are* harder. I lean forward into a post and my leg screams so loudly that I almost black out, but I tell my body to shut up.

My mom wouldn't quit now, and I won't either. I pat Obsidian's neck. "Let's do this. Catch them."

We clear Valentine with Some Like It Hot still rocketing alongside us like a bumper car. My leg's throbbing, and every time I use it to keep from sliding off, it practically buckles, but we manage to pass The Masochist anyway, which feels fitting, with the pain this race is inflicting on me.

We only have three jumps left, and I try to think about anything but my leg. I pretend it's not really my leg, that it's someone else's. I pretend I've been shot in the middle of a war, and I have to keep riding or the entire army will die.

Obsidian leaps ahead, putting on speed I didn't think he had as we close on the ditch. We come up fast on Earl Grey as Obsidian leaps, and the pressure from the landing shoots pulses of heat up my leg and into my hip. I bite down on my lip until I feel blood in my mouth. I don't know where his last minute energy's coming from, but Obsidian's powerful flanks push even faster in a massive burst of speed, and we clear the second to last fence with just a half a length separating us from Brigadier General.

By some miracle, I've kept the cursed saddle on his back. By an insane amount of luck, we're closing on the frontrunner.

My mouth's full of blood, and I turn and spit to clear it. I grit my teeth and hold the post position, urging Obsidian onward. When we fly over the last fence and we're coming up on the elbow, we're neck and neck with Brigadier. Rex McComb pulls him sharply toward us and I know if he bumps me, we're done for. I need to prevent the impact, so I wrench Obsidian to the left, and luckily the course curves around the elbow, so I don't slam into the rail again. We have room to pull a tight curve, but the saddle cants sideways, and my leg gives out. I collapse against it, both to save my leg, and to try not to fly off.

Brigadier pulls ahead.

I can't tell whether he pulled ahead before or after we

crossed the finish line. As Obsidian continues to slow, he glances back at me and I realize that neither of us knows whether we won or lost. We both turn to look at the announcer.

"We have a photo finish folks, a photo finish!" The audience murmurs. Obsidian Devil whinnies.

I grab his mane just to keep the saddle upright. Now that we're still, it feels almost harder to stay on, not to mention the difficulty of ignoring my throbbing leg.

But finally an image flashes up on the large screen and the announcer bleats, "It's Obsidian Devil by a nose, with Brigadier General just behind. That makes Kristiana Liepa the second woman to ever win Aintree's Grand National Chase!"

I lean over and hug Obsidian's big, sweaty black neck, patting my martingale with appreciation for its role in keeping me in my seat. "We did it, Aleks. We won!"

The crowd's going wild, but I turn to look for one little girl. She's running toward the finish line, and her blonde hair shines in the sunlight as she moves toward us. I raise my hand and wave at her, and she beams.

We didn't just win for me. We won for all of the little girls everywhere who needed to know that it wasn't just a token win last time. It wasn't a fluke. Life hurts sometimes, but if we don't quit, we really can do anything.

Things get really crazy after we win. I think about what must've happened and I'm absolutely convinced that Rex cut my girth strap at the re-cinch. I register a formal complaint, and the officials disappear with my saddle for testing on the strap. They seem to agree with me that it was cut. They'll review the video feed, check Rex's person for anything he might have used, and search the strap for DNA. All in all, it's more than I expected them to do. I'd love it if that cheater had to pay.

I stay upright for my official weigh-in, gritting my teeth the entire time against the almost constant pain in my leg. They draw blood from me and Obsidian again, just to verify we weren't on any performance-enhancing drugs. I secretly worry that his blood test might show something funny, but I'm not sure what we can do about it if it does.

It takes a boost from an official for me to remount Obsidian, now blessedly bareback since the saddle's evidence. With my leg hollering at me, riding is feasible, but walking is completely out of the question. Obsidian trots over to the winner's circle, where a million bulbs flash in our eyes from the moment we arrive. I try to smile in between blinks, but my leg hurts so badly now that I worry my smile's more of a grimace.

They're all hurling questions at me that I'd rather not answer. "Do you plan to bring any actions against the person who tampered with your saddle?"

"How did you manage to win, without a saddle that was properly functioning?"

"Do you think you were targeted because you're Latvian?"

"Rumor has it you sold Obsidian Devil. Why are you riding him here, today? Did you lose faith in your other pony, Five Times Fast?"

"There are rumors you're set to marry Lord McDermott's son, Sean. Is that true?"

Ignoring them is simpler when I focus on my leg, but there are so many of them, and there's no clear path through which to escape. After a few moments, a familiar voice shouts at the gathered reporters. "You've all gotten your photos. I'm sure these two are tired. Why don't you let them go?"

I follow the sound of the voice to his face. Sean McDermott's yelling at reporters on my behalf. The funny part is, they actually move. He's always had a commanding presence for things like this. I slide down from Obsidian's back, and Sean walks toward me, arriving just in time to grab me when my leg hits the ground.

If he hadn't been here, I might have crumpled. Obsidian neighs loudly. The cameras flash.

"Are you injured? What's wrong?" a reporter asks.

I wave them off. "Just sore from that ride."

They all smile and make dumb jokes that I ignore.

Sean puts his arm under mine and gestures to John. I notice my dad's standing behind John, so I'm guessing they walked over together.

Obsidian bumps me with his nose gently. He's staring at

me intently, and then his eyes dart down to my leg. Then he bumps my arm again.

I whisper, for both Sean and Obsidian's benefit. "I can't put weight on my leg right now. I hurt something when I slammed into that rail at the Canal Turn. I'm not sure what I did exactly."

John appears and takes the reins from me. "Let me cool him down. You go with Sean."

Obsidian neighs loudly, but there's nothing he can do for me, not here, not right now. I shouldn't have dismounted yet, I guess. "It's okay. Once I can move again I'll come see you in your stall." I rub his nose and he calms down enough for John to lead him away.

"Where did you want to go?"

"Let's head to the stalls." I can't exactly tell him that I think Obsidian may be able to heal me, once he's human again.

Sean frowns. "Is Aleks there?"

I almost choke, but I recover quickly. "Maybe."

"Once I saw you on Obsidian Devil, I figured he had to be back."

I want to tell him that it's not like that, but it kind of is. Lying to him won't help anything.

"I wasn't going to come, you know." Sean angles us toward the stables and moves slowly, one hop at a time. "But as it grew closer, I couldn't *not* come. We didn't work out romantically, but we're friends too. What kind of jerk would I be if I didn't come to support you in your biggest, and possibly scariest, moment?"

"Thank you."

"And it turned out to be way scarier than I could have imagined." He shakes his head. "What were you thinking out there, you lunatic?" Sean sounds genuine and sincere, and it makes me happy. The idea of us coexisting with nothing but positive thoughts about one another going forward is a good one.

"I wasn't thinking," I say.

"You shouldn't have done all that, just to earn the money to buy your land back." He shakes his head. "I'm still happy to secure you a loan, you know. The offer wasn't ever predicated on us dating."

"Actually, I already got my land back," I say.

"You did?" He beams. "That's great. How?"

"Aleksandr was the buyer, it turns out."

Sean swears under his breath. "I knew I should've bought it, but you were so firm when you said not to."

I shrug. "You listened to me, and I'll never fault you for that."

"But I didn't get the girl." He sighs. "Note to self. Next time, less listening and more grand gestures."

I laugh.

Sean looks around as if he's just registering where he's helping me hobble. He frowns. "Why's Obsidian Devil in the farthest barn from the rest of the complex? I went by and saw Five—he's in the main barn. If you were in the main barn, we'd have been there a long time ago."

I could probably explain that Aleks showed up last minute, and that there wasn't any space in the main barn. But we could have switched Five and Obsidian easily enough. The real reason why we took a space out here is that it's essentially empty. And I need very few people to be watching Obsidian's stall, or there will be no way for him to switch back to Aleksandr.

We're still two dozen yards from the overflow stable when I hear John shouting behind us. "No, stop, you stupid, demonic beast. We just cooled you down. You can't drag me all the way to the stalls—"

When I spin around, that's exactly what's happening.

Obsidian, exhibiting the worst ground manners in existence, is pulling John along behind him at a trot.

They stop when they reach my side, Obsidian Devil snorting and pawing the ground. When Sean and I just stare at him, he tosses his head, dislodging the lead rope.

"This horse is still just as much of a lunatic as he ever was," John says. "Tell that moron Aleks to take him back."

I laugh. "I'll take him from here. Aleks will be here to collect him any moment."

"But you can't even get to the barn without help," Sean says.

"Boost me." I look at Obsidian's sweaty back and suppress a cringe. I was up there a few moments ago. It's not like I'm not just as gross.

"You can't go riding around with him in a halter, bareback, with an injured leg." Sean's looking at me like I've lost my mind. The same way he looked at me the day Obsidian Devil crashed our date.

"It's fine," I say. "I swear, he'll be very careful with me."

"What if he spooks?" John asks. "We can't have our star rider, who's already injured, falling off and breaking her neck after the big race."

"Nonsense," I say. "Obsidian doesn't spook. It's one of his best traits."

Obsidian Devil looks positively delighted right now, and it's annoying me.

"The thing is," Sean says, "I can't really leave without—"

"Sean," I say. "I'm so flattered that you're here, and that you still care about me, but—"

He clears his throat. "It's not what you think." He looks down at his shoes. "But see, my dad said, if I bumped into you, that I might check and see whether you still wanted to keep that heart-shaped diamond."

Well, that's embarrassing.

"It's just that, he thought we were getting married, or

he'd never have suggested I give it to you, I guess." His head snaps up, and his eyes look pained when they meet mine. "I know this is the height of rudeness."

I laugh.

Laughing at a man in pain is also rude, and I know it is, but I can't help it. "Oh, Sean, it's hilarious when you think about it. I'm sitting here feeling sorry for you. I've started dating Aleks, and I thought your feelings would be hurt, and I was trying to be kind, but really, you're only back to collect the hundred thousand euro diamond you gave me."

"Two hundred," he says. "Actually."

That just makes me laugh harder.

"So, is that a no?"

I finally manage to stop. "Not at all." I wipe the tears from my eyes. "It's not here with me, but as soon as I get home, I'll make sure it's available for you or your men to pick up."

"Thank you," Sean says. "And I appreciate you being so understanding." He turns to John. "I'll leave her in your care. I think that perhaps my presence isn't needed any longer."

John's smiling when Sean darts off. "If you think I'm letting you boost up on this horse, you've lost your mind." He insists on sliding his shoulder underneath mine instead, which is hard because of how short I am.

If either of them would just let me touch Obsidian, he could probably start to heal me now. Assuming the injury's something that will heal on its own, I suppose, and maybe it's not.

"Your dad's going to flip when he hears you're dating that crazy trainer."

"Are you upset?" I ask. "About Aleksandr, I mean?"

Obsidian Devil's trailing us, behaving as meekly as a lamb now that I'm standing with John instead of Sean. In fact, John's barely holding the lead rope. His deep black ears are turning slightly left and right, listening intently to this whole conversation.

"You probably think I'm a huge fan of Sean's, given that we're both British." John stops, and then he sighs. "But he hurt you years ago, and I never really forgave him for that."

"Oh." That's a surprise. He never said a word against him. We're nearly to the barn, just ducking under the covered patio out in front of it.

"And what kind of guy, whether at his father's prompting or not, asks to get a gift back?" He shakes his head. "Rich people are the biggest cheapskates of all."

I can't help chuckling at that.

Actually, both of us are laughing when the support beam holding up the metal cover over the courtyard creaks, moans, and collapses sideways.

It's so unexpected, so shocking, that none of us are prepared in the slightest, including Obsidian. The ceiling crossbeam strikes John on its way down, and I'm terrified, as I'm knocked to my stomach, that he's dead. I think I'm uninjured, except my leg, which feels worse, and a sharp pain in my shoulder where the impact of the fall wrenched it. I crawl toward John and press two fingers against his neck. I feel a pulse.

Thank goodness he's just unconscious.

I look around desperately for Obsidian, worried that since he's much larger, he could be more badly injured. I finally locate him. Perhaps as a defense mechanism, he shifted to his human form. It's definitely for the best. The ceiling was made of a simple tin, but it's vast and heavy, and there's only about twenty inches or so between the ground and the new resting place of the tin above us. Aleks army crawls toward me, and once he's close enough, his hand reaches for mine across the rubble.

When I take it, a warm and buzzy kind of energy passes through me. My leg, blessedly, stops throbbing. The acute pain in my shoulder also lessens, and it finally occurs to my groggy brain that he might be able to help John, too.

"He's unconscious." I gesture past myself toward John.

"That wasn't an accident," Aleks says. "They're here."

"Who's here?" My heart rate, which had finally started to come down, spikes again.

"I couldn't figure it out, before. It's why I finally gave up on the idea. How could Mikhail and Boris possibly still be alive, unless they were using the three of us to boost our powers for a preservation spell?" He closes his eyes. "Since I couldn't find any evidence that Alexei and Grigoriy are alive, I thought maybe I was the only one left." He opens his eyes. "But now? They must be here to kill me."

"What?"

"I know you said no destroying," he says. "But Kris?"

His face is beautiful, even covered with grime, even lying sideways on the ground, even with desperately grim eyes.

"I'm not going to let them kill me today, which means I'm going to have to do a little destroying myself."

❧ 26 ❧

"**Y**es," I practically shout. "Kill them. Fast."

Aleksandr chuckles.

John's unconscious. We're both stuck under a collapsed building. Villains are here trying to murder us, and he's *laughing*.

"You're deranged," I say.

"I'm just proud of how far we've come." He's also naked, and it's freezing, and he's pontificating on *this*? "You want me to do whatever it takes to keep you safe, and I'm the one wondering if there's another way."

"If it's the same guys you thought you saw before, they froze you as a horse for a hundred years, and they're still alive, somehow, and now they're trying to kill you. So, yeah. I'd say eliminating them is an appropriate action."

"When you're mad about how this goes down, just remember you told me to do it."

There's a huge rumbling underneath me, and then the ground opens up and swallows me.

Which, really, frankly, is not at all what I had in mind.

I try to scream, and my mouth predictably fills with dirt. It's really hard to cough when you're underground. All

:inds of thoughts zoom through my head in this moment, some of them pretty morose.

Presumably Aleks tossed me under here to keep me safe. But what if he dies? I mean, I hate to think it, but what if he isn't stronger than the two mega-villains who have somehow lived a hundred years, and they kill him?

Would he just leave me stuck down here?

That makes me flail around, and I realize that I'm not really buried underground. He *moved* me, using the earth to keep me from being seen, probably. I'm inches from the surface, which is probably why, when I'm no longer trying to scream and I expel the dirt I choked on earlier, I'm able to breathe.

I push my way upward slowly and notice a lump next to me. I pull myself out far enough that I can scootch toward it—is it Aleks? I tug and claw and yank until John's craggy face is exposed.

So at least he's also hidden.

Then I hear the *boom*. I leap from the ground and pelt toward the sound, realizing that Aleks did entirely heal my leg at least, before burying me away from the action. Why did Aleks move me so far away? I'm running as fast as I can, but I can barely make out three figures, standing just in front of the collapsed cover from the barn courtyard.

Aleksandr's facing two other men—both of them large, both of them imposing. One of them's hurling fireballs at him. The other. . . *Sūds! Svētais sūds!* Is that a lightning bolt?

By throwing up huge walls of earth, Aleks manages to deflect most of the damage, but one of his arms is smoking, and the other is blackened.

Can he really kill them? It's two on one, and he has a bunch of dirt, while they have *flame* and *lightning*. Plus, he just healed me, and moved me and John, and he said that has a cost.

What is the cost? How tired is he?

If he was sure he could win, why did he send me away? I can't think this through, not now, not watching this. So I race, as fast as I can, as bravely as I can, toward the danger. I may not be able to do much, but somehow I got Aleks to access his powers. Somehow, I was able to help him do things he couldn't before. He might need me again.

And I can't just watch. Now that I love him, I can't stand and watch while he tries—and possibly fails—to kill the men who locked him in a horse's body and stole his ability to use his magic.

They're all so intent on hurling things at one another that they don't even seem to notice me. Actually, that makes me wonder. Why isn't every person within a hundred yards running over here? Where are the paramedics, the police, and *everyone*? I slow down for a moment and look around. There *are* people milling around over by the main racetrack, and beyond that, there are loads of people near the main barn.

None of them are even looking our way.

One of them must have cast some kind of, I don't know, cloaking spell or something.

But if they did, why can I see them?

It only makes me more determined to force my way to where they are and even up the odds a bit, even if my only aid comes from distracting the bad guys. I'm a dozen feet away, when I decide it's time to alert them to my presence.

"Hey, losers," I say in Russian. "If you think Aleks is scary, wait until you see what I can do."

All three of the men swivel toward me. Aleks' eyes widen and his mouth dangles open. The other two men, who look almost same age—early thirties?—grin maniacally. And then they fling their fireballs and lightning bolts right at me.

So much for distracting them.

I clench my hands and close my eyes, expecting to be

fried and fricasseed. *I am a complete moron, and if I weren't about to die anyway, Aleks might kill me.*

That's my last thought.

Or it should have been my last thought. Except, when the fire and lightning hit me, nothing happens.

The two guys look as confused as I feel. They shake their hands and then fling *more* fireballs and lightning bolts at me. This time, I watch intently as they simply *disappear* when they get near me.

They start to swear, loudly, in Russian.

And then they turn tail and run.

Aleksandr glances over at me in distress, and then his eyes follow the men.

"Go after them," I say.

I regret my reassuring command almost as soon as I make it. He didn't seem to be doing that well against them by himself. Why did I send him after them?

"Wait," I shout. "What about John?"

That distracts him, and they duck around a corner. It only takes me a few moments from there to convince him to let them go.

"They could return anytime," he says.

"You better keep me with you, then," I say. "Apparently I'm like a magical vacuum."

I expect him to laugh, but he just frowns.

"I'm kidding," I say.

"I'm not sure what you did, zaychonuk," he says, "but that was clearly some kind of magic."

I swallow.

"You're connected to this somehow," he says. "And I think it's time we do whatever it takes to figure out *how*."

Whatever it takes sounds ominous.

I'm not someone who ever wanted to be magical. I never wanted to fly, or to own a unicorn, or to perform spells with my magical wand. Mirdza's the one who liked

302

that stuff. I'm the kind of person who wants both feet solidly on the ground. I want a nice home, some cute kids, and a husband who makes my friends jealous.

I'd be fine with a huge castle, or whatever, but I really want nothing to do with the lightning bolts and the fireballs.

"Maybe you put some kind of ward on me and you didn't even know it," I say. "Or maybe it's like that wizard movie where the parents kept the kid safe. Maybe it's the power of love."

Aleks chuckles again. "I mean, that would be nice, but in my experience, love is nothing but a liability."

I wince at that, and he wraps a muscular arm around me and drags me up next to him. I realize for the first time that somehow, he's not naked. "You have clothes on."

He grins. "My powers are back."

"You're saying that all this time, you could have—"

"Only if you were touching me, and you never wanted to get close to me when I was naked."

"You're saying it's *my fault* I kept seeing. . .all the things?"

His grin is now a full-blown, self-satisfied smirk. "All the things? And how do you like those things, now?"

I roll my eyes.

"Let's see if we can get all evidence of our involvement in this erased and get out of here, because I doubt any one of the humans who runs this facility is going to be delighted to find that the base of four support beams was somehow incinerated at several thousand degrees, causing them to simultaneously collapse. I'd like to be nowhere near all this when they start investigating."

"Ditto," I say.

John's fine, thankfully. He just happened to be knocked out at the perfect time—he had no idea what happened. And if I lied and told him that he tripped on a rock and hit his head?

Well, I stand by that decision.

It's not going to do any good for me to start telling Dad and John that Aleks is a horse-shifter and a magician who can manipulate the power of the earth. They're mad enough that he decided to leave early with Obsidian Devil, and they're furious that I decided to go with him.

Judging by the tone of Dad's voice on the phone, John has told him that Aleks and I are dating.

"You're both to head straight home," he says.

"I will."

"And you'll get separate bedrooms at any hotels where you stop."

"Sure, Dad." I don't bother telling him that my horse turned into a human, and now, while they're painstakingly taking a ferry and driving from Liverpool to Latvia with Five Times Fast, I'm flying home. . .by way of Russia.

"Kristiana Liepa, mīlu, promise me."

I inhale slowly and then exhale. "Yes, Papa. I will."

When I hang up, Aleks says, "Really? Separate rooms?" His eyes roam just a little bit.

I laugh. "You men are all so predictable."

But there's nothing predictable about my first time flying first class. "Whoa," I say. "How much did these tickets cost? Shouldn't we have gotten economy tickets?"

Aleks rolls his eyes and wiggles his fingers. "Did I mention that my province at home is absolutely full of two things that I can easily find and call to the surface any time I'd like?"

"You might have mentioned it."

"The world has changed a lot in the past hundred years, zaychonuk, but one thing hasn't changed much. People still value gems."

"And now they're hungry for oil, too." I ask him something I've been wondering. "When the communist government collapsed, they just gave it back to your cousin's grandson? Why?"

"My cousin was smart. He was illegitimate, so he knew how to hoard wealth, and how to use it effectively. After the revolution, he bided his time in Europe, investing wisely. He taught his son to do the same. The grandson wasn't quite as skilled, but he still managed to worm his way back to Russia, bribe the right people, and buy our ancestral land for a song once his friends needed a favor he could provide. And I've been able to pick up where that grandchild helpfully left off."

"I guess I'll take your word for it." But the second I sink down into the plush leather of the first class seat, which should really be called a bed, I resolve never to question him again. "This is amazing."

"Think your father would object?" Aleks reaches over slowly and covers my hand with his. "I mean, we're awfully close here, and we're reclining." He lifts his eyebrows. "There's no telling what I might do to you."

"Aleks," I hiss. Then I cut my eyes toward the flight attendant walking past.

He yanks the curtain next to his seat sideways and suddenly we're in our own little private area.

I giggle. "My father most certainly would not approve."

"Is this a bad time for me to ask you about that heart diamond?" He frowns. "The one that Sean's father wants you to return?"

I blink. "Um, a bad time?"

"I heard what he said—he came over to congratulate you, but also to ask you to return a gift." He shakes his head. "Horribly tacky."

"Why?" I ask. "When you dumped your many girlfriends, you never asked any of them to return a particularly lovely gemstone?"

His fingers gently stroke the top of my hand. "I never liked any of the women I knew well enough to call them my girlfriend."

"Oh?" Something about that makes me uneasy. "And you still don't?"

He twists my hand over then, intertwining our fingers. "I don't like you well enough, no." His voice drops even lower then. "Because I love you, Kristiana Liepa."

My heart skips more than just a beat. It skips all the way around the corner. "You do?"

"I love your laugh. I love your smile. I love your lower lip. I love the way your hair always gets a little fuzzy when you're riding and the way you brush it back from your face. I love the way you hum to yourself when you're preoccupied, and it's never on key, but you don't seem to notice."

I swat at him with my free hand. "Stop."

"You are everything I didn't know I wanted, and now that I've found you, I would never, ever ask you to return anything. If you dumped me, I'd follow you around pathetically, begging. I'd bury you in heart-shaped diamonds."

I'm laughing now. "Would you?"

"In fact." He releases my hand, pivots a bit, and drops to one knee. "I did some research, and I know your mother's American. It's a little unclear what they do in Latvia, but in America, the men get on one knee to do this for some reason."

Maybe the plane's circulation system is malfunctioning, because I suddenly can't breathe.

"Zaychonuk, I know your dad won't be pleased. I know Sean will probably cry all night when he hears, and I realized recently that even your stupid jockey friend who rode me the day we met likes you. Every guy around you falls prey to your honest charms, and I'm no different. But please, pick me anyway. Be mine forever."

I swallow.

He pulls something out of his pocket. It's not a box. It's not a bag. It's a tiny, platinum band, with a huge, pale blue stone set on top of it. It sparkles like a clear lake on a sunny day.

"I need to explain something before you answer me," he says. "You mentioned past girlfriends, and I think I've failed to make something clear."

"Okay."

He's still kneeling, as if it doesn't bother him at all, even with the plane's turbulence. "I've been alive for quite some time now, and I've met a lot of women. I've also found quite a lot of stones in my lifetime. Most of them, like the women, were quite beautiful. In fact, each was unique in its own way. The amber I found for you had a butterfly inside of it. Diamonds sparkle in ways that the entire world recognizes as spectacular. I was able to buy your land from you by locating exquisite and rare demantoid garnets on your own property. I also located garnets you had never even noticed were present, they were buried so far beneath the earth."

"But—"

He holds up the ring. "But this stone can't be found anywhere on earth, other than a few select mines in India, South Africa, and Australia. This one, specifically, came from India, because it was the closest to me."

"Wait, you found it?"

"Blue diamonds sell for almost four million US dollars per carat. I did some research and found that this was the single most expensive stone in the world. Of course you needed the largest one that could be found with the most impeccable purity and clarity."

My jaw drops.

"This one is almost four carats, and it's flawless. I almost got shot the day I stole it."

I gasp.

"But don't worry. They didn't catch me, and I'd have been able to heal even if I had, so it was fine."

"Aleksandr Volkon—"

"Just listen. You can chide me later."

I sigh. "Go ahead."

"You're unlike anyone I've ever met. When your entire farm was at risk, you blew the money that could have saved it on buying a horse who needed your help. And when you found out that I wasn't really a horse, and your entire purchase was a total waste, you didn't rail and complain and demand money from me." His eyes soften. "You are both fierce and kind at once, through and through. And even though you're impossibly small, zaychonuk, you never stop fighting for what you want, or for what you think is right."

He slides the ring on my finger. "I know I'm supposed to wait for you to say yes, but I've learned with you not to wait. Not to listen. Not to argue. Just to do something that matters to me, and if you really object, you'll show me with a right cross to the face."

"I would never—"

"Spare me," he says. "You already have."

"My answer *is* yes, you boorish brute."

"I thought so," he says, "because even with as amazing you are, I'm also quite the catch. I mean, how many guys could steal a blue diamond—the most valuable stone in the entire world, for the most valuable woman?"

"How romantic," I say. "You *stole* me the diamond you proposed with."

He snorts. "Those morons would never have found it. It was entirely the opposite direction from where they were mining and a hundred yards down to boot. If we're being honest, I stole it from their great, great, great-grandchildren. Maybe."

"I'd have been happy with a plain metal band."

"But you'll be showered with jewels anyway," he says. "In fact, I propose we send that idiot an entire box of rocks when you send him that necklace. Show him that you don't need him or his diamonds, because you're going to be cared for by someone much better instead."

"You're like a male peacock, fanning his feathers."

He shrugs, stands up, and sits back in his seat. "So what? I got the most brilliant female peacock of all time. I should preen."

"Aren't you worried?" I ask. "Those two guys are still out there. It's not like you've hidden who you are."

"I think I'm safe at home—they waited for me to leave. That gives me the upper hand. I can plan when and where I'll see them."

"I can't stay in Russia," I say. "I have to go back to Latvia."

"And I'll come with you," he says. "For as long as you

want. I can set up the same wards and protocols at your farm that I've laid at home. We'll be safe in either place."

"Protocols?"

"Guards who sweep at intervals, security cameras, perimeter dogs. That sort of thing."

"Whoa," I say. "That sounds intense."

Aleks takes my hand, sliding his fingers between mine and turning my hand so that the back is facing up. "See that rock?" He meets my eyes. "That says you're mine, now. And I always protect what's mine. They won't catch me off guard ever again, I promise."

ACKNOWLEDGMENTS

My readers are epic. I love you all. Thank you for your ongoing support. (Especially my ARC team!)

My husband is so much better than any romance novel hero that he doesn't even need hair. And one day, I'll write a hero who's so perfect, he doesn't need it either. (But this was not that book... sorry. Flowing black hair felt like a must...)

My kids are so supportive, and I love their eager and never-ending support. You help me more than you know.

And my horses bring me so much joy. I hope that this story will help share some of my love for them with the world. They may not find me precious gems, and they may consume both my time and my money, but they also bring me a lot of light and happiness, even when sometimes the world feels dark.

My editor, Carrie, ALWAYS fits me in. I *have* to say thank you to her on every book. She earns it.

MY QUEENDOM FOR A HORSE

BRIDGET E. BAKER

Purple
Puppy
Publishing

I have a history of making rash decisions. You know, the kind of move that saves the day in fairy tales. Only, when I climb the beanstalk, the giant smashes me into jelly. When I ride to a ball in a carriage made of pumpkin, my gown that was sewn by rats splits up the back, and I wind up covered with pumpkin innards.

Big, bold decisions just don't end well in real life. At least, not for me.

I know this.

Which is why I ought to turn around and walk away, but I don't have much choice. It's all or nothing today, thanks to my dad and his idiot rivalry with an old university nemesis.

Well, that and his lifelong gambling problem.

And yes, it's a little hypocritical that I'm planning to fix his mistake. . .by placing a risky bet and hoping it pays out.

But I worked hard and I have faith in myself. Today's race may be a Hail Mary, in American football terms, but there are only seven horses, and Five Times Fast is the best one. I know it. Plus, the only person my gamble might hurt is me.

If this works, I'll save the family farm we've had for ten generations. I can't even think about what happens if I lose today. If I take time to think about it, I'll start crying again. That won't help anyone.

I squeeze the wad of fifty-euro bills in my fist and force myself to take a step forward. Every step feels harder than the last. I've saved for *forever* for the down payment on my own horse hospital, but losing our farm would be even worse than delaying my dream yet again.

Finally, I reach the front of the line, but before I can say anything, someone grabs my arm and spins me around. It's the very last person in the entire world that I ever thought I'd see standing in front of me.

Sean bloody McDermott.

I haven't seen his face in person in more than ten years. It feels surreal to have his hand on my arm. He's wearing an impeccably tailored suit, like he was the day we broke up. His blonde hair looks exactly the same as it did. It's like time hasn't touched Sean. His face is unlined. His eyes are just as bright as ever. And his shoulders might even be broader.

Why am I even surprised? The aristocracy never changes. Eventually he'll gain a few grey hairs that make him look dignified, but everything else is a constant.

I hate that his appearance affects me this much, even after ten years. He dumped me, but that doesn't mean I'm still the pathetic girl I was back then. I'm a confident, capable business owner now. I need to remember that.

I wrench away and back up with so much force that I run into the window. The employee inside clears her throat.

"We have some business to handle first," Sean says smoothly, with a practiced smile on his face. "She'll come back."

He turns and starts to walk, just assuming that I'll follow after him like a good little baby duck.

Too bad, Sean. I'm not a baby duck anymore. I'm in my mid-thirties, and no one tows me around behind them.

I turn back to face the Totes employee. "I'd like to put fifty thousand euros on Five Times Fast. To win."

The Totes employee blinks. "There's a €250,000 winning limit per day in Ireland."

I shrug. "With the odds on Five, that'll be just about right."

"Kristiana." Sean's tone is terse. I wonder how far he went before he realized I wasn't following him and circled back.

"I don't have much time before I need to report for the race," I snap. "Go away and leave me alone." I start to hand the money through the window.

Sean snatches it from my hand.

"This is new," I say. "Is work not going well? You're stealing now?"

He grits his teeth, his gorgeous blue eyes flashing. "I'm trying to help you."

"Kris." My dad's voice floats toward me from several paces away.

Something in my stomach twists. "Dad?" I turn around.

"Miss, if you aren't betting. . ."

I step aside. If my dad's here with Sean, and he's not jumping in to defend me. . . Suddenly my blood runs cold. We *are* in Ireland, which is much closer to where Sean lives than I usually am, but what are the chances we'd run into him by accident?

He's a banker, not a jockey. His family still races, but I imagine his work keeps him from trolling the racetracks every so often.

"Dad." I don't even have to ask.

I can tell he's guilty from the look on his face.

"You're in silks." My dad steps out from behind the

awning that was blocking him from my view. "You fired our jockey and you're planning to ride. Aren't you?"

He's got me there. "I had to let him go. He was drinking again. His carelessness was ruining Five." And also, we couldn't afford to pay him, anyway.

Dad inhales slowly. "I know I'm the one who called him, but like you, I had no choice." He glances sideways at Sean.

"Your dad made the right call. The terms for the balloon note he showed me are just awful, and—"

My head pivots. "Go away. This doesn't concern you. It's between my dad and me."

"Kris," Sean says, "be reasonable. Your farm has been in the family for more than a hundred years, and—"

I snatch the money he just took back. "After the way you dumped me? I wouldn't dump my soda on you if you were on fire." I shake my head. "Go away, Sean. We don't need your help."

He flinches, but he nods and pivots on his heel. One thing rich Brits are excellent at is walking away without a fuss. The only thing worse for them than talking about money in public is making a scene.

"And as for you." I spin around to face my dad again. "You're the reason we're in this mess, so you don't get to question the way that I fix it. How could you call him without even asking me first?"

Dad inhales shakily. "But Kris—"

"But nothing. Go away and let me place my bet."

If he wasn't torn between chasing after Sean and yelling at me, he might have ignored me. But as it is, Dad's already struggling with the fact that his meal ticket is practically jogging away.

The odds against Five Times Fast aren't terrible, but they aren't great either. He's not a favorite, for sure. Which means with a bet of fifty thousand, I'll make enough to pay the first balloon payment that's due next week.

Only, when I try to place the bet a second time, the woman narrows her eyes at me. "You're wearing silks."

It's her job to ask. My bright yellow silks mark me as a jockey, and jockeys can't bet against their own horse. Most jockeys don't bet at all. It's poor form, really. You run the risk of pissing off the boss, or making future employers nervous, or both.

I hand her Five Times Fast's registration papers and my passport. "I am a jockey, but I'm also the owner."

She glances at my paperwork. "You're the crazy rider-owner." She slaps her hand over her mouth.

It's not common to ride a horse you own. Usually you're a terrible rider, or you've got a terrible horse. I'm hoping to disprove that particular stereotype today. "That's me."

Owners can bet on their own horses, as long as it's to win or at least to place, so she accepts my money. "You're optimistic."

Desperate is probably the more accurate word, but saying 'optimistic' is more diplomatic. I extend my hand and she hands the papers back. She runs my money through a counting machine, shakes her head, and hands me my ticket. "Don't lose that, now. It might be worth a lot."

I really, really hope it is.

I push past dozens of people waiting to place bets. The constant noise at the racetrack is comforting in its familiarity. I try to pretend this is like any other race, but my stomach isn't buying it—it's twisting into knots. The fourth race at Down Royal, the Ladbrokes Champion Chase is the first Grade One race of the Irish steeplechase season, and it starts in thirty minutes. Ladies' day is always packed, but the beautiful weather today probably contributed to the mass of bodies.

I navigate briskly through the throng of people, jumping to the side to avoid impalement on a ridiculously long peacock feather. The best-dressed contest this year is

offering a trip to Rio de Janeiro, and the women have stepped up their game accordingly. It's all part of the fun of racing, but I don't have time to look around. I need to do my final check-in and then get Five ready. It always passes in a blur, the final moments before a race. It's been seven years since I rode as a professional jockey, and I'm a little nervous to be doing it again.

At least my tall bay pony is perfect.

Five Times Fast is sleek and shiny and his feet practically float as I lead him toward the racetrack. I think he's the prettiest bay here, and he's easy to recognize with just the one small dollop of white over his front right hoof. His coat gleams and has very faint dapples. His ribs don't show, but they almost do. That's what you want with a racer, really. As fit as he can be without looking half-starved. He isn't sweating at all in spite of the workout we just finished, the warmth of the sunshine, and the anxious energy that always precedes a race in a strange place.

Five loves to race, and it shows. His ears swing right and left, but his eyes are calm. I lean my head against his, and he exhales loudly, as if to tell me he's ready. I hope he really is.

I've always felt like I understood what my horses felt and what they wanted. I don't ask them to do anything they aren't ready for, and I never jump a horse that doesn't love it. Five Times Fast pulls eagerly toward every fence I point him at. I've been riding since before I could walk, thanks to my mom, and I've never been thrown, not once. Even when I was a professional jockey for two years, I never came out of my saddle. It earned me a rather irritating nickname.

I glance around at our competitors. There are only six horses in the race with us, for a total of seven, but they're some of the very best horses in Europe. The excitement is nearly palpable as the race with the biggest purse of the

entire weekend approaches. It's not National Hunt money, but still, 125,000 euros attracts some attention.

Earl Grey, a clever name for the grey gelding next to me, is favored heavily to win. He's larger than Five Times Fast, but he looks nervous. He didn't travel far enough to look that nervous—fifty kilometers to our three thousand. His rider's also a grade A jerk. Jackson Buley doesn't even make eye contact with me. If I lose today, I really really hope it's not to him.

Persnickety, a bay gelding to my right, shifts from one hoof to the other repeatedly and his ribs are a little too prominent. They're working him too hard. I bob my head at his jockey, Natalie Coolie. There aren't many female jockeys, and it makes me smile that there's another in the Ladbrokes Chase. I don't really know her, though. She started a few years after I retired officially to focus on my veterinary practice.

In It To Win It is a nut-brown gelding who was favored to win last year. He's back this year, and his owner, a twenty-year-old IT millionaire from America, has been emailing me. Odds are against him, but that's what makes chasing fun. The odds don't always mean very much. In It To Win It's sweating a little more than I'd like if he was my mount, but sometimes the nervous sweaters win. I don't know his jockey, a young man who looks quite dashing in his red silks. I raise my hand and he salutes back.

"Hey Sticky," a familiar voice behind me says.

I turn to see Finn McGee, resplendent even in his traitorous green and blue silks, walking toward the starting line. He doesn't like Rickets much more than I do, but he can't afford to snub the owner of the wealthiest barn in Europe. Finn's the most successful jockey in Ireland, maybe in the entire UK, but he still has to make a living. I've known him for years now, so he doesn't intimidate me like he used to. I should've properly greeted him—I should pay

attention to my old friend. But he can't possibly blame me. I can barely squeak out any words at all.

"Hey, Finn," I manage to say.

Given the beast he's leading, he'll understand my distraction.

His horse is entirely ebony, a stallion I notice, not the typical steeplechase gelding retired from a career on the flat. His coat and mane shine like a reflection on water. His eyes flash. His hooves strike the ground sharply with cracks, like flint on steel.

I don't think I've ever seen a more beautiful horse.

He's also monstrously tall, a good hand taller than Five Times Fast, and Five's just above sixteen hands. "What the devil are you riding?"

"Aptly worded question." He grins. "His papered name is Obsidian Devil. It'll be our first real ride together. Forrest hates him, and I guess we'll find out why Rickets is willing to defy the best trainer in the country. He picked him up in Russia, of all places."

Forrest Smithers is arguably the best trainer in England. If he hates this black beauty, he must have a reason. But he has managed Rickets' stable for a decade or so, and I know Rickets trusts his opinion—he'd be a fool not to—so it's strange to hear that they don't agree on something.

"I always heard vodka was the only good thing to come out of Russia."

Finn winks at me. "It may still be."

Obsidian paws the ground and snorts heavily. His mane shimmers, and I want to touch it so badly that my hands practically itch. As though he's similarly affected, Finn reaches over to pat his neck, but Obsidian snaps at him.

Finn snatches his hand back and shakes his head at me. "I've never seen a more ill-mannered horse," he says, "and that's saying something. The good news is, I negotiated a

bonus that's actually more like a small fortune in exchange for riding him."

On impulse, I lean forward and place my free hand on Obsidian Devil's magnificent muzzle. Even with my riding gloves on, a zing runs through my entire body. Obsidian calms immediately and presses his face gently into my palm.

"He likes you?" Finn rolls his eyes. "Of course he does. Every horse on the planet loves you. It's so unfair."

Five tosses his head jealously, and I step back from Finn's magnificent creature. As soon as I move my hand, Obsidian snaps at Finn again. I can't help laughing.

"Forrest should be paying you two small fortunes," I say. "I don't envy your ride today." But that's a complete lie. I want to ride him so badly I could cry.

Five tosses his head again, which is unlike him. If horses could scowl, he'd be scowling at Obsidian. As it is, he's stuck flaring his nostrils and stamping.

"It's okay, boy," I whisper. "He may be beautiful, but you're gorgeous too, and you're much better behaved. I still love you the most. Now, make sure you run your heart out today. Mom put all her money on you. I'm utterly *doomed* if we lose, and that Obsidian is making me very nervous."

Obsidian's ears flick my direction while I'm speaking to Five, and I have the most uncomfortable feeling that he's listening to me. I shake it off. Horses are intuitive, yes, and I believe they understand far more than we give them credit for, but there's no way he could even hear me whispering from here, much less understand the words I'm using. I scratch underneath Five's forelock, and he leans his head against me and sighs.

"It's you and me, Five. We can do this. We *have* to do this, or I'll lose the farm." I snort. "No pressure."

I've just mounted when Sean shows up again.

"You aren't supposed to be over here," I hiss. "We're about to be called up."

"A win here is temporary," Sean says. "I can loan you whatever you need and give you real time to repay it."

"Please go," I say. "Now."

But he isn't giving up as easily this time. He sets his jaw, like he's determined to be some kind of superhero, coming boldly to my rescue. He drops his voice even lower. "I know racing still scares you. It's not worth the risk."

"You're a little late to start caring about me." I roll my eyes. "It's been a decade. Or were you stuck in some kind of stasis all this time?"

I swear, at that exact moment, Obsidian Devil snorts. The timing is so perfect, that I almost believe for a moment that he's paying attention to our interchange and that he understands it. He's also dancing around a lot less than he was—and maybe it's because Finn's finally on his back, but it feels like it's because he's listening in.

I'm going crazy.

Sean's brow furrows. "I know I screwed up, but I'm here now."

"I don't need you here," I say. "Not anymore." I urge Five forward.

Sean starts after me, clearly not dropping anything.

Obsidian lunges forward at the same time, nearly running Sean over.

Then they call for us to enter the track. Sean finally grits his teeth and walks away. A moment later, when they call us to approach the tape, Five prances up perfectly, prettily even. Obsidian's chomping at the bit and dancing left and then right like a drunk bumblebee. It's even worse than it was before, on the ground, and I can't help laughing.

"It's not funny, Sticky. Knock it off." Finn's smile belies his gruff words. We circle up and move toward the tape in an inconsistent bunch, the horses shying and head-tossing

as they move forward. As always, my jittery nerves fade away when they finally release us. I know what Five Times Fast is capable of, and I'm ready to help him win.

We pull ahead quickly at the beginning. Five did quite well with flat racing. If he didn't jump quite so beautifully, I might have kept him there, but as we approach the first jump, his timing's perfect.

He's ready to win this.

He sails effortlessly over the first fence and heads into the bend in perfect position, a full length ahead of the other horses. The cool November air streams past my face as we clear the next fence and round the bend to the ditch. From the corner of my eye, Earl Grey's bearing down hard on the inside. When we reach the ditch, he's only half a length behind me, so I push Five toward the inside and Earl Grey falters on the ditch.

We pull ahead again.

Five and I sail over the fourth and fifth fences and into the downhill jump on the sixth, just as I planned. We're rounding the turn toward the stands when a pounding sound has me glancing to the outside, just in time to see Finn's salute as he and his monster fly past me.

I could scream with frustration.

Five can't pick up that much speed, not going into the seventh and eighth fences, which are brutal. I hope maybe, just maybe, Obsidian will botch things, going so fast over the fences, but he doesn't. He clears them with nearly a foot to spare. I've never seen anything like it. The crowd's going wild. Finn's always been an attention monger, but this is shaping up to look very, very bad for me. I try not to think about the fifty thousand pounds I'm about to lose, not to mention the purse money.

I lean down near Five's neck. I don't use a whip on him —never have. "Come on boy, I know you're really flying, but I need a little more. We've gotta beat that big bully or

we lose the farm. You can do it. I know you can. Let's stay as close as we can, and at the end we'll really push, okay?" I pat his neck, and I swear Five bobs his head. Horses understand me, and I understand them. If Five can possibly win this for me today, he will.

We gain on Obsidian on the long stretch between eight and nine, and pull up until we're almost neck and neck.

I look Finn in the eye and he winks. That jerk winks at me. Like he knew Obsidian would eat Five for breakfast. He whips Obsidian once as we approach the ninth fence, and Obsidian's ears flatten. The black stallion clearly hates the crop.

Some horses don't mind a tap now and again—it encourages them, letting them know when to move. I've rarely used it, because my horses understand me. I only race horses that love to run. But for most jockeys, it's an invaluable communication tool.

Finn should already have known that Obsidian hated it, but clearly he didn't. After we clear the ninth fence, he uses it again. Obsidian actually slows down, and we pull even with them. I smile broadly at Finn.

He scowls back at me. He has the faster horse. He should beat me. But he doesn't know his horse like he should.

We both clear the first ditch on the second loop, Five and I on the inside, and Obsidian giving us a wide enough berth that it almost feels like he's being polite.

After the second ditch, with only five fences to go, I lean down and croon in Five's ear. "You can do it, boy. You can pull ahead. I know you can beat that evil, black beast." My sweet pony hunkers down and runs, putting everything he has into it.

He's tired, though.

He clips the fence on fifteen and nearly stumbles. Obsidian pulls ahead.

An entire length ahead.

Five's giving me everything he has. . .but it isn't enough.

I don't want him hurt—I can't stand the thought of that —so I pat Five's neck. "It's okay. You're magnificent, but if he beats you, it's okay."

Nothing's okay.

If we lose, I lose everything. My life savings, my family farm.

Maybe even Five.

Tears stupidly well up in my eyes. As we clear the sixteenth fence on a downhill incline, Obsidian's three full horse lengths ahead. Even if Finn screws up, we can't catch him.

I've lost.

Everything.

Then inexplicably, with one fence to go, Obsidian slows. Finn's whipping him, but it doesn't seem to matter. Five and I race alongside him. Five pulls around on the outside, clears the last jump, and puts on every bit of speed he has. We fly past Obsidian, and I swear he bobs his head at me when we pass him to win by a nose.

Obsidian pulled back and let us win.

I'm sure of it.

A *horse* let me win. A *horse* just granted us a stay of execution.

I can hardly hear myself think for all the cheering, the loudest of which is coming from my father. The world feels crazy and confusing, but when I see his smile, I know everything's okay.

❦ 2 ❦

"That was incredible." Sean's dragging a wreath of roses toward me that's even larger than the winner's wreath already hanging around Five's neck. "I haven't seen a race that flawless in a decade or more." He's beaming from ear to ear.

He looks his best when he's smiling.

"Thanks." I don't try to stop him from setting the wreath around Five's neck, though my pretty boy's eyes roll a bit when yet another huge flower-laden wreath goes around his neck.

"You did it." Dad pats my boot. "That was just amazing."

I'm not so distracted by the congratulations that I don't notice the tongue-lashing my friend Finn's taking a dozen paces away. "—the crop. I told you he hates it."

"All horses hate it at first," Finn says. "It's your job as trainer to—"

Obsidian's dancing around like he's auditioning for *Riverdance*. No one's paying enough attention to his frustration. They're just arguing among themselves, and it worsens with the arrival of Rickets.

"Absolutely unconscionable," he shouts. "There's no reason we shouldn't have won that race. You pulled him back."

"Kris," Sean says. "Earth to Kris."

But I can't seem to pry my eyes away from Obsidian Devil. He looks furious, like he's about to chuck Finn off and trample his owner. Not that I'd care much about Rickets being trampled, but I'm sure that won't result in anything good for the gorgeous stallion, either.

And then he looks up at me and my eyes lock with his.

We both freeze.

It's like I can't hear or see anything else. Just that big, bold stallion, and the furious pounding of my heart. In that moment, I've never wanted anything more than I want that horse.

Only, it's not like he's for sale. And even if he was, I can't afford him. I can barely afford to make the first balloon payment so we can keep the farm. And all that does is delay our troubles. Three more huge payments are looming on the horizon.

"Here." John takes Five's reins and gestures for me to climb down. They're already prepping for the next race of the day, the work crews sweeping through to clean up and shift the jumps.

Nothing slows down around the racetrack for long.

It's one of the things I've always loved about it. But not today. Today, I'm dreading having to talk to Sean. And I'm still furious with my dad for calling him.

"I don't need your help," I practically spit, the second my feet hit the ground. "Besides. I'm sure the perfect Clara would be livid if she knew you were here."

"We divorced," he says. "Almost five years ago, now."

Divorced.

How did I not hear about that? I force myself to

swallow the lump that's taken up residence in my throat. "I'm sorry."

"I'm not. I never should have married her in the first place."

I grit my teeth. I can't listen to this. Not right now. Not ever. "I better go collect my winnings and get changed."

"Kris," Sean says in the voice he always used when we were alone. The voice that turned my knees weak and made my heart accelerate. "Shortcake."

He used my nickname. My special nickname. When other people teased me for being short, it made me mad. But Sean turned it into something sweet—literally. We got strawberry shortcake on our first date, and he called me that from then on.

But shockingly, the more I think about it, the more it ticks me off. When you dump someone and marry someone else, you forfeit the right to use their nickname, especially to manipulate them. "I'll never forgive my dad. This was worse than his gambling."

"We bumped into each other by mistake, and I'm the one who has been calling him ever since."

"I won today." I purse my lips. "Which means I don't need your help. So thanks for coming, but it was a waste of your time."

"Nothing that lets me see your face is a waste," Sean says.

"Stop." I hold up my hand. "No more."

"No more?" Sean's voice sounds nervous. That's not like him.

I want to turn toward him and see his face, but I can't. If I do that, I won't be able to walk away.

And I need to be able to walk away.

"I have to go." I swing down from Five's back, pull the wreath Sean brought off, and chuck it at him before I stomp away. Hopefully that monstrously large pile of

flowers will slow him down enough that he can't chase after me.

Now that I've dismounted and I'm not staring at Sean, the wheels in my brain begin turning again. I keep coming back to how that huge black stallion threw the race so I could win, and my brain rebels against the thought.

It must have been some kind of stress-induced hallucination. I've never had one before, but I've heard of ocular migraines, so there must be similar occurrences for hallucinations. Five was always a strong contender, and that huge black beast must have overextended and not had enough energy to push through the finish line.

Before I can go over it in my head again, my dad's arms fling around me and pull me toward him for a backbreaking hug. I almost drop the reins. He must have finished up the paperwork and run all the way over here to catch me. That's unlike him.

"You did it, Kris," he says. "You're safe, and now you never have to do that again."

I roll my eyes. "Right Dad, never again." Except that another balloon payment is due in three months. . .so. Whatever helps him sleep tonight, I guess. The good news is that Five did awesome, and if we can repeat this a few times, we might not lose the farm at all. In fact, if we can get far enough ahead in the next few months, we might be able to convince a local bank to refinance the horrible loan Dad took out to pay stupid Rickets.

"Hey, I'm excited too," I say. "But I've got to cool Five down, so. . ."

"Yes, you do need to go." Dad finally releases me. "We can't have him coming up lame."

"Exactly."

No matter how many times I go over it in my brain while Five and I walk around the warm-up ring, I keep seeing it play out exactly the same way in my head.

Obsidian Devil's too far ahead for us to catch, pounding his way toward the finish. Then his ear flicks back toward me, his eye meets mine, and he slows.

He slows.

Finn's whipping him and pulling—because ironically, pulling is really the best way to get them moving—and he slows anyway. I can't shake the feeling that he threw the race. I firmly believe that *a horse threw the race for me.*

As if.

I'm going crazy.

I look around for John. The stress from the loan coming due, and from seeing Sean, and from betting all my money and almost losing it must really be getting to me. I whip out my phone and text our trainer. A moment later, our tall, rail-thin trainer's walking toward me.

"That was an amazing run," he says, "but what happened at the end there? It looked like that demon horse just tired out." John's calloused hand brushes mine as he takes the reins, the sweet and pungent smell of his chewing tobacco familiar. John's not quite as old as my dad, but I've known him since birth. He was a groom at our stable for a while, but everyone starts there. He left our stable for almost a decade to prove himself, and when he returned, he was a renowned trainer. Thankfully, he wanted to come back. He's British, but he saw our stable as home.

I've long suspected that my maternal grandpa pays him a little something to stay with us, because I've seen the books. We don't pay him nearly enough for a trainer of his caliber. We would, but we've never been able to afford a raise.

"I guess so." I shove down my discomfort over the fact that John noticed something strange, too. "Finn didn't want to ride him, and maybe that's why. He isn't a winner." Some horses just don't care about the race.

John's dark grey eyes fly wider, and his bushy red

eyebrows bob. "Finn never takes a ride he doesn't want, not anymore."

I shrug. "I heard his niece is sick. I think he may need the money." I can't help my guilty feelings. Winning jockeys get success bonuses, and I kept him from getting one today.

But Finn almost always wins. One loss won't set him back too much.

I've barely passed Five off to John when I hear a commotion around the corner. "What's that?"

John glances back in that direction. "No idea."

"Did you hear it, though?" The sound of screaming pierces my ears again, and I cringe. "It's an animal, right?"

John shrugs this time. "Maybe. I can't tell."

He must be losing his hearing. "I need to get our winnings right to the bank. Are you alright handling Five for now?"

John nods. He never has too much to say, but I love that about him.

In a rush or not, as a vet, I need to check on that horse that's in pain. I move as quickly as I can toward the noise coming from the front of the parking lot. It isn't as loud as it was, but I still intermittently hear it.

Before I can figure out what's going on, I round a corner and bump right into Sean. Why is he still here? He's *everywhere*. My hands fly wide so I don't lose my balance, but he catches me, circling both my wrists with his hands. "Whoa, there."

"Let go," I say.

"I think we need to talk."

I shake my head. "We don't."

"When I bumped into your dad," he says, "I almost couldn't bring myself to ask about you. I was sure you'd be married by now with a handful of beautiful children."

The very future I'd planned for the two of us.

His voice drops to a husky whisper. "When he said you'd never married. . ."

I shake my arms free. "Sean, I can't."

"That's why I came today," he says. "Your dad told me you were still angry. I hated hearing that, but I didn't barge in because he said it wouldn't go well." He inhales sharply. "But then he called me."

I open my mouth to argue.

Sean's brilliant smile stops me cold. "I'll loan you the money. You can pay off that other note in full, and then you can repay my bank whenever you want."

I swallow.

"Even if you make that first note, the huge payments just keep coming."

If I don't get away from him soon, I might not be able to keep saying no. I need him to stop telling me how he got divorced and how happy he was to hear I'm single. I need him to stop offering to save me, or I may forget that I save myself. "I'll figure it out, okay? Still no." I step around the corner, and the horse who's been screaming comes into view.

It's Obsidian Devil. It looks like they've finally calmed him down, though. He's standing utterly still, staring right at me. His ears are pricked up, like he's listening to me.

"One date." Sean followed me around the corner, blast him.

Obsidian Devil paws at the ground, his nostrils flaring, and he lets out a loud neigh.

That's exactly how I feel right now. Angry. Confused. Maybe a little scared. And I need to be just as firm as he looks. "No dates," I say. "You dumped me, remember?" I clench my hands at my sides. "Please, Sean. Please leave me alone."

His eyes are hurt. His body stiffens.

Guilt rolls through me, but I hold the line. What else can I do?

I walk away from Sean and toward Obsidian Devil, trying not to watch as Sean stuffs his hands in his pockets and spins around. I'm not quite as unconcerned with his departure as I wish I was, because if I were paying more attention, I'd never run right into Alfie Rickets, knocking his perfect top hat off his head and into a mud puddle.

A top hat? Really? Some people take the retro look a little too far. Does he think he's Charles Dickens? I ought to choke out an apology and pick up his hat. As a matter of common courtesy, I ought to at least try to brush it off. But when I think about how he's treated my dad, I can't bring myself to do it.

Now that I'm a little closer, I can see that, while Obsidian Devil is standing relatively calmly, he must not have been recently. Four men are holding onto ropes that are wrapped around various parts of him. The one around his face is already strung with a stallion chain, for all the good it's doing them.

Obsidian tosses his head and whinnies loudly, as if he's calling me over.

I really need to get the bank paid so I relax. I need to stop seeing things that can't possibly be real.

"Come on," the man at the front says. "Let's go, you tosser."

But Obsidian Devil isn't going anywhere, apparently. He sets his legs and throws his head, flinging the guy who just yelled at him two feet forward. The man almost drops the rope.

They're clearly having a hard time shoving him into a trailer. One rope's attached to his halter, and the other three are looped around his legs. A fifth man wearing a blue coat's approaching with a tranquilizer gun.

Was he even properly cooled down? He looks sweaty

and winded. Surely Finn would have seen to that much, right?

"What's going on with him?" I turn toward Rickets. "Why would you bring a horse you can't handle?"

He scowls.

"You should have given him Ace long before it got to this point."

"It's none of your business."

Instead of the apology I should really be making for running into him, for butting into his business, and for being absurdly rude, I find myself jabbing Dad's nemesis in the chest. "Mister Rickets."

"You have nothing to do with any of this." Alfred Rickets raises one eyebrow and glances down at his hat, which is still soaking up mud in a puddle on the ground.

The man in the blue jacket's still walking closer, holding the tranquilizer.

"Have you already sedated him?" I ask, playing a hunch.

"Butt out," Rickets says.

But at the same time, the man with the gun says, "Two doses. Bastard's still kicking."

Two doses? His head should be low, almost hanging. Giving him any more than he's had isn't safe. "You can't give him more," I say. "His heart could stop. At a baseline, he won't be able to respond to starts and stops. He could get injured."

"He's not yours," Rickets says. "The last thing I need is the advice of a hack."

"I'm a licensed veterinarian," I say. "At least let me try to load him for you before sedating him again."

Alfred Rickets scowls. "I'll repeat myself because I know your intelligence level is quite low. He's not yours, so toss off."

I take a step back. *Toss off?* "When you resort to name calling, you've already lost the argument."

He finally leans over to pick up his hat.

I can't quite help my smile when muddy water runs over his hand and splashes on the front of his pristine khaki trousers. "I don't believe an argument ever took place, and stating facts isn't the same as calling names." He sighs. "You poor girl. You seem to have taken after your father instead of your mother. A real shame."

I want to punch him. Instead, I simply repeat, "Let me offer you my services one more time. It's clear you can't handle your own horse."

There's a lot of snorting and shuffling behind me. The men are pulling and pushing Obsidian Devil toward the trailer and the tall man with the tranquilizer gun is sidling around the other side of his big, shiny body. If he thinks Obsidian Devil isn't watching him, he's mad.

I don't wait for Mr. Rickets to approve my actions or call his men off. I dart past him and rush toward Obsidian Devil. He's currently kicking and snapping at the men as they yank, but who can blame him for that?

"He's a stallion who just raced." I'm pleading with the men now, not their boss. "Of course he's upset. He needs to be properly cooled down and given a warm blanket. What are you thinking, yanking him over here and shoving him into a trailer? Do you want him to injure himself?"

I place myself between Obsidian Devil and the man with the tranq gun. "Here. Let me try to load him."

"You think you can handle the horse we can't?" The man in the blue jacket waves his free hand in the air. "Fine. Let's see you try."

The second I reach for his lead line, Obsidian calms down. He tosses his head toward me, but not aggressively. "There, boy. I've got you."

The man who was shouting before offers me the lead for his halter.

"Drop the other ropes," I say.

No one listens to me, of course.

"Drop them," I shout. "Now."

Alfie Rickets raises his voice. "We always have to tranq him several times, Miss Liepa. He's the picture of that saying, 'healthy as a horse,' so move aside, and let my men do their job."

The second the men start to pull on the ropes again, Obsidian Devil's nostrils flare, his ears pin against his head, and he screams. I hate the sound of a horse's screams.

The man who just handed him to me snatches his lead rope right back.

Adrenaline floods my body. "Mistreatment of animals is illegal. I'll report you."

Alfie's eyebrows shoot upward. "To whom would you report me, you little miscreant? I have the entire board of the British Horseracing Authority on speed dial. Not to mention, the entire panel for the Grand National just came to a fundraiser I hosted. I hear you've put in an application for Five Times Fast. Would you like me to weigh in on his suitability?"

'Weigh in' is almost certainly double entendre. The Grand National's a handicapped chase, and Five's weight will depend on his handicap. Alfie might not be able to get Five excluded, but he could almost certainly bump up his BHA rating, dramatically increasing the weight he would have to carry and eliminating our chances of winning. My stomach drops at the very real threat.

But then I'm filled with a shaky rage.

Bullies never stop—if no one ever stands up to him, then they just get worse and worse. "You can't mistreat your horses if you want to keep racing, and you can't threaten me, either. I'm a veterinarian, Mr. Rickets, and I took an oath—"

"Let's all take a step back, gentlemen," a deep baritone voice says. The men immediately respond, loosening their

hold on Obsidian. "No one wants to injure themselves, or the Devil either. Miss Liepa, always a pleasure."

I turn to face Mr. Ricket's trainer, Forrest Smithers. He's six and a half feet tall, built like a brick wall and wearing a tweed suit. He has a forcefulness to his face that makes you believe he can handle anything. Combined with over twenty-five years of consistently producing the best chase horses in the UK, he's hard to ignore. I can't help wondering how Rickets convinced him to train Obsidian to begin with if he dislikes him as much as Finn seemed to think.

Mr. Rickets' lips compress into a line. His eyes narrow. "Miss Liepa was just leaving."

"It appears she disapproves of your treatment of the beast." Smithers smiles at me. "As it turns out, I also disapprove, of nearly everything surrounding that demon. Ever since you won him in that card game—"

"It doesn't matter how I came to own him." Rickets pops his hat back on his head. I really hope mud drips down into his collar. "He's mine, and he's going to win the next race for sure."

Smithers shakes his head. "No, he isn't. If Finn can't ride him, no one can. Every jockey on our roster has now refused. He's a waste of space, feed, and resources, and like Miss Liepa here, I happen to believe he's being mistreated by our staff on a regular basis, because we don't have another way to handle him."

"He should've won today. Everyone with eyes in their head saw it. Finn threw the race to his friend here. He's the one we should be reporting."

I gasp. "He did no such thing."

"Poppycock," Smithers says.

Mr. Rickets takes a menacing step toward me. I'm not a fearful person, but I am tiny. I weigh around a hundred pounds, which is small even for a jockey. I'm used to

standing at my full height and still counting nose hairs all day long. A new round of shouting behind me would have drawn my attention if Mr. Rickets didn't look like he was about to strike me with his long, brown cane.

I throw one arm up, but as I do, something enormous looms on my right. Obsidian has broken free from the men holding him and is standing beside me, his nostrils large and puffing, and he's staring at Mr. Rickets. I may be small, but Obsidian's staggeringly large. Mr. Rickets backs away slowly. I reach over and place my gloved hand on Obsidian's nose, rubbing it gently. He leans into my hand again and sighs, and I reach over and gather up his lead rope. He seems to like me, but still.

Better to be in control than to be sorry.

Forrest Smithers' baritone carries over the chaos of the men scrambling toward me. "You wouldn't be interested in buying a horse, would you, Miss Liepa?"

I raise one eyebrow. "I'm not in the market for one, no." I have a loan payment due, which Rickets knows, because his family owns the bank my dad used for the loan. I think about Obsidian, the most stunning horse I've ever seen, drugged at double the allowable amount every time he travels. Whipped and prodded as a matter of course. Our family farm means a lot, but some things are more important.

And poor Obsidian Devil is as much a victim of Rickets as we are—he won him in a hand of cards. Unlike me, he can't do anything about his bad luck. But I could.

"That's a pity," Forrest says. "He seems to like you."

"He does have bad taste," Rickets says.

If it was anyone else, I could probably walk away. But the idea of Rickets gloating while he abuses this horse? In spite of knowing how idiotic this is, I ask, "How much are you asking for him?"

"Why don't you make an opening offer?" Forrest says.

Obsidian bumps my hand almost as if he understands what's going on.

The corner of my mouth goes up. My dad will lose his mind, but I can't let Rickets keep him. We have a little bit saved toward the payment. I can probably use the winnings and still scrape together enough to pay the loan. "I could pay €125,000."

"The winnings you robbed me of today? That's what you're offering?" Rickets scoffs. "I wouldn't even consider a farthing less than a quarter of a million pounds."

The exact amount we owe on the first installment for the farm.

"Be reasonable, Mr. Rickets." I scratch Obsidian under his forelock, and he bumps me again. "I don't have anywhere near that. My offer's a good one."

"He'll win that in his next chase, and you know it."

"And you know that you won't win any chases with him. You don't have a jockey."

"Why do you even want him?" Forrest Smithers asks. His eyes are clear and bright, and he looks genuinely curious.

"It doesn't matter why she wants him," Alfred Rickets says. "What matters is that her pathetically impoverished family can't afford him. They won't even be able to afford a pot to piss in come next week, from what I hear."

I'm usually pretty even-keeled, but I can see why my dad hates this man. I'd like to scratch his eyes out. "You've heard wrong. My dad and I are just fine."

I'm being an idiot. I need to walk away. I have no idea what will happen to this poor horse, but we need every cent I just won and then some.

Besides, I know that rash decisions never work out well for me. They just don't. I wish fairy tales could come true, but in the real world the glass slipper always breaks, and poking the top of a spinning wheel doesn't save me.

My finger gets infected, I wind up with sepsis, and then I die.

Walk away, Kristiana. Walk away and keep your money and the farm.

"My mistake, then. My price is a quarter million because my trainer dislikes him and not a pound less. No matter how well you are or aren't doing, you can't afford that." He gestures to the man with the tranquilizer. "Do what it takes to load him, Freddy."

He thinks my family's trash? He thinks we can't afford him? He's wrong. I have the money right now. I never thought I'd have a chance at winning the Grand National, with its one million pound purse, but I just might be holding the lead line on a horse that could take me there. "Fine. Two fifty."

I glance up at Obsidian Devil's perfectly beautiful face and wonder. Am I happy right now because I've just bought the most beautiful horse I've ever seen? Or am I secretly delighted because it only leaves me one solution to my problem?

If I don't want to lose the farm, I'm going to have to call Sean McDermott.

I can't decide whether that wrecks me or secretly thrills me.

Maybe a little bit of both.

3

Some things in life are easy, like handing over a huge wad of cash for a horse I've wanted to own since the second I set eyes on him.

He walks alongside me toward our trailer calmly. The horse I watched Rickets' men struggle with is gone. But somehow, that makes this harder. Without a horse to wrangle, I'm stuck thinking of what I just did.

"What will I even say?" I ask myself.

Obsidian turns toward me, for all the world like he's really listening. If he could speak, would he have an answer for me?

I stop walking. "I can't do it." I sigh.

Obsidian bumps my arm.

I lean against him. "You wouldn't understand."

He whuffles.

"It's boring human stuff. But I really shouldn't have bought you. See, there's this guy who I was in love with a long time ago, and, well." I sigh. "He married someone else, someone his family approved of, but I never really got over it."

29

I must be losing my mind. I swear, Obsidian's both listening, and he looks sad about it.

"The thing is, he's really, really rich. So wealthy that his family didn't like me. I'm not British, and I'm not snooty, or posh, or whatever. We own a nice big farm, but it's in Latvia and by comparison to them, we're poor. A lot poorer since my dad lost a hand of poker and we had to take out a really lousy loan against the farm."

I force myself to start walking again.

"My ex showed up today, and he offered to give us a loan with great terms—low interest and a long time to pay. But that means I'll have to talk to him, and see him, and be grateful to him, and what I need to do is hate him. So you can see the issue, right?"

Obsidian Devil turns his head sideways, and then he snorts. I'm guessing that's a no.

"Human stuff," I say, "is complicated. But if we can win a few races, I can pay that loan off and be done with all of it." I scratch under his mane—almost all horses love that. Apparently the Devil's no exception. "But look, I hear you're from Russia. We're headed back there, sort of. At least, Latvia's a lot closer to Russia than you are now. So I need you to do me a favor and be easy to load and work with, alright?"

He nods.

It's not a hallucination, not this time. It's not something I imagined, either. He actually bobbed his head.

"Can you understand me? Nod if you can."

He does it again, and I drop the lead rope. I can barely catch my breath.

The horse who was literally able to pull away from five grown men just stands there, calmly, looking at me with faith in his eyes. Is it faith?

It can't be. I'm going nuts. It's a strange coincidence, but there's no way he can understand me. Horses get me,

and I get them, but thinking that he communicates like a human? He can understand Latvian?

It's too much.

Once we reach the trailer, John waves me over. "What's going on?"

I scrunch my nose. "So, remember that screaming?" I bite my lip. "I did something."

John's eyes widen. "Why do you have that monstrous horse?"

I can barely meet his eyes. "I might have bought him."

John groans. "Forrest thinks he's possessed. That's why they named him Devil. Kris, what on earth were you thinking? Did they pay you to take him?"

Dad's definitely going to kill me. "Not exactly."

The string of expletives exploding from John's mouth is fairly impressive, really. I didn't know he knew so many Latvian swear words, but he even throws out some British ones I haven't heard in years. Eventually, though, even John quiets down.

It helps that Obsidian's standing as calm as a baby deer, staring at him with wide, innocent-looking eyes.

"How bad can he be?" I ask. "Look what a sweet guy he is!" I rub his nose again, and he leans into it.

"What's that thing doing here?" Dad sounds even more shocked than John.

I wince. "I might have fallen in love with him."

"But that's Rickets' horse," Dad says.

"About that," I say. "I'm going to need to call Gustav."

Dad's entire face drains of blood. "No. I forbid it."

"I didn't say I was calling Grandpa," I say. "I said *Gustav*." My brother left us years and years ago, ostensibly to study in the United States with my grandparents and a few cousins. He never came back, not even for a visit. We don't talk much.

"Just call Sean," he says. "He already said—"

"If you don't want me to call Grandpa, then you understand why I can't call Sean." Pride's a very strange thing. "Let me just see what he says."

Before Dad can stop me, I toss the lead rope for Obsidian Devil to John and race away, whipping my phone out of my pocket. What are the odds my brother will even answer? I hit talk and wait.

It only occurs to me then that I should think about the time in the United States. I do the math quickly—I'm fine. Middle of the day. Phew.

"Hello?" Gustav's deep voice doesn't sound Latvian at all.

"Hey," I say. "It's Kristiana."

Silence.

"Your sister."

"I know who you are," he says. "I'm just surprised. It's not my birthday, and yet you're calling. I take it you need something."

Wow, it almost sounds like he's as hurt as we are. "Actually." I hate that he's right. "Dad lost a big card game, and we're about to lose the farm."

"That's great news," he says.

His sense of humor is warped. "It's very bad news," I say. "I'm not asking for anything for free, but if you could get Grandpa to loan us the money, or if you could—"

"I'm not even going to ask how much," he says. "I can guess that it's not small, or you'd never have called me."

"The thing is—"

"I don't want you to think I don't love you," he says. "It's actually because I *do* love you that I'm saying this. Let that stupid farm go. Move to America. Bring a horse or two if you want, whatever. Grandma and Grandpa like horses too. They'll let you play with theirs as much as you'd like."

"But Gust—"

"Dad's a broken mess, and I don't know whether it was

32

Mom's death that did it, or whether he was always like that. I can't tell, but it doesn't matter. If you walk away, you'll finally be free. Don't you see that?"

"So you won't help us?"

"I am helping you," he says. "Come to America, and you'll see what I mean. I'm doing the very best thing a brother could ever do. I'm helping you to finally move on with your life—to live a much better way in a better place."

I wonder if Grandpa would say the same thing. Probably.

"Thanks," I say. And then I hang up.

When I walk back to the truck, Obsidian's already loaded, his head hanging out of the stall, staring intently at me.

John's expression is grim.

"Dad," I say. "I'm going to need Sean's phone number."

He practically preens about that. It seems all is forgiven, no, it's that he's practically delighted about the new horse, since it means I'll have to call Sean. But even though Dad has his number, I can't bring myself to call him right away. I know I shouldn't wait, but my fingers just won't listen. *After the ride home*, I tell myself. As if it will be much easier with a few thousand miles between us.

My best friend Mirdza thinks I'm crazy to drive all the way to England and Ireland for races, but the races in Latvia are neither lucrative nor challenging. I attended university in London and grew to love England during that time. My British friends don't understand why I moved back home.

But Latvia will always be my home. Latvian hills are mostly covered in forests, and we pass hundreds of miles of forest to reach Zasa parish, which was where I promised myself I'd call. The crisp clear air, the bright blue skies, and the long drive down to our beautiful, old, cobbled-together home help to calm my nerves. Only, I put it off again—it's

too early to call. The reception's not great. I'll wait until we're home. As we get closer and closer to Daugavpils, I get more and more nervous.

We finally pull onto the long driveway after another long night of driving. I slept a handful of hours while John and Dad drove, so I'm far less exhausted than I could be. Still, it takes its toll.

As we approach the homestead, everything looks exactly the same as when we left. Our sprawling home's still painted bright red with contrasting white window frames. The wooden siding looks well kept and the silhouette made by the sharp angles on the window frames and protruding turrets form the backdrop to some of my first memories as a child. Gambling-induced debt notwithstanding, my dad has managed the home quite well. Even if it hasn't been updated in thirty years, at least it's been well maintained.

A few hundred yards away, our main stable practically shines. It's built in the prettiest spot on our entire farm, framed by impressive old trees, and set back from the main road. My family has always loved their horses more than almost anything else. I came by it honestly.

In fact, I snuck away to sleep in the stables dozens of times as a child. That foundational love of horses has never changed, not for me anyway. The barn's painted a bright white and repainted every two years without fail. My mom's parents offered all sorts of lavish things as wedding gifts when she married my dad, but all she wanted was a new stable.

Each of the box stalls are 16 feet by 16 feet, a full six feet larger than the standard, and the sliding doors still work seamlessly, even almost forty years later. The only thing we've really had to redo are the drainage lines. Oh, and we had to install new pavers on the floors. My grandparents gave me money for that for my twenty-first birth-

day. It makes cleaning up after our beautiful horses much more convenient, and it was exactly what I wanted.

I'm close enough now that I can see the enormous enclosed arena behind the stable, too. That was initially created by my paternal grandfather, Ivanov, and it's been renovated several times. It makes winter training possible, although I'd have made it a few hundred yards bigger if I designed it myself. I suppose even then, cost was a factor. Our family has always cared more about horses than money, but it takes money to buy supplies and pay for labor.

Thinking about money reminds me of what I have to do. After I get Five Times Fast and Obsidian Devil unloaded and released in pastures to graze, I trudge back to the house and pull out my phone. I'm not sure how long I've been staring at it when Dad notices me standing like a statue.

"We should have just sold the farm, mīlu." After his initial shock over my irresponsible purchase, Dad didn't even scold me. He knows the loan is his fault, and he knows it shouldn't be my job to fix it. But we've waited too long to sell it now—it's either pay the first portion of the balloon note, or lose it to the bank.

We both know I have to call him. My hand shakes where I'm holding the phone.

"I love Liepašeta as much as you do," he says, "but losing it won't be the end. We can find another farm. Build another barn. Keep on living."

His words are hollow, though. He and I both know that begging for Sean's help is our only play.

"Do you think Rickets lured me in and convinced me to buy Obsidian Devil so we'd default on the loan?" I've been wondering that the entire way home.

Dad sighs. "He's very good at sensing people's weaknesses. It's his superpower."

Strangely, I don't regret buying Obsidian, even knowing

it may have been a setup. He would've beaten Five if I'd been riding him. "I still think that in the long run, he was a good investment, even if it plays into Ricket's filthy hands. We can race him, we can breed him, and we could end up with an entire line of winners."

"But we don't have time to race him before the money's due." Dad's eyes are sad.

"Man zēl, Papa." It's true. As much as I hate the idea. I thrust the phone at my dad. "You dial and hit talk. Then hand it to me."

He does as I ask, and while the phone rings, my pulse pounds in my ears. What am I going to say? How will I—

"Hello?"

He answered. I wasn't sure whether he would, since mine is an unknown number to him.

"Hello?" he asks again.

"It's me," I say. "And the thing is. . ."

"Let's talk about it in person," Sean says. "I'm in Latvia."

"What?" I splutter. "You'll—I don't—"

"I'm opening a branch here," he says. "We can get lunch. I'll come by and pick you up."

"No, not lunch. This isn't a date—"

"You need money," he says. "I think that's at least worth a lunch."

I grit my teeth. "Alright." It feels like I was kicked in the stomach. He's *in Latvia*? Why? What's he doing here?

"I'll be by the house around noon."

"Uh-huh," I say. And then I hang up.

4

"And?" Dad asks. "What did he say?"

"We're meeting for lunch." I frown. "Did you know he was here? Did he tell you he's opening an office nearby?"

"Not exactly." But Dad won't meet my eyes. And that means he knew.

Suddenly I'm shaking. How could my dad conspire with my ex? He was around after we broke up. When I fell apart. "Now I'm stuck going to lunch with him."

Dad's grin makes me want to punch him.

I'm distracted, though, which is lucky for Dad. John's striding toward me, his eyes flashing, his lips compressed.

What reason does he have to be angry? It's a brisk, beautiful Latvian fall. There's no snow on the ground yet, but I can feel it coming. Soon. Maybe a month more before we're blanketed. But for now, the weather's glorious.

"That *creature* you bought should be shot."

Is he talking about Obsidian? "I turned him out. What's there to complain about?"

"He's loose." John's hands clench. "He sailed over the fence and now he's racing around the stables, wreaking

havoc. No one can catch him, and all the other horses are freaking out. It'll be a miracle if none of them are injured."

I can hardly believe what he's saying. Obsidian cleared a five-foot fence on his own? Without a rider encouraging him? "You decided, with all that going on, to come over here and yell at me?"

"No one else can touch him," he says. "He's perfectly behaved around you and demonic for everyone else."

"Dad, I'll be back." I take off at a jog for our stables. I hope he'll calm down when he sees me. Because if he breaks his leg or eats something bad and colics. . . My quarter million euro gamble will be even more idiotic than before.

I love horses, but sometimes it feels like they're just looking for ways to kill themselves. I can't actually be the only one who can handle him. I have a vet practice to manage. I can't be at the barn around the clock.

As I get closer to the crime scene, I hear a sound like someone's whamming a sledgehammer into a metal wall. "What's going on in there?" I call out.

The sound immediately stops.

It goes entirely silent, except for a huffing and puffing behind me. To my surprise, John's coming up fast, wheezing like he's just finishing a footrace. When we reach the stable, no humans seem to be around, which is baffling, because wouldn't some of the grooms be trying to catch the loose stallion?

The second I round the turn and head down the main breezeway, heads pop out of stalls. Nearly a dozen horses have their heads hanging over their stable doors. Each stall opens onto its own outdoor run, so my babies have come inside specifically to welcome me. They all love me, and it fills my heart with joy, usually. Right now, I don't have time to greet them.

Because the clanging sound starts again. At the back of

the barn I find the source, where Obsidian Devil appears to be trying to open a gate. While I'm standing and watching him, he starts to apply his mouth to the latch as if he's earnestly trying to break free.

Maybe John wasn't entirely wrong. He's been an angel for me the past two days of the trip, but apparently he's more devious than I thought. I grab a halter and hold up my hand. "Obsidian," I call. "It's me, Kristiana. I'm here. Everything's okay."

His nostrils flare. His eyes roll. But he hears my voice and stops whamming the metal door and trying to open the latch. He throws his head up over and over, his shimmering mane rippling.

I walk toward him slowly, my hands moving up and outward, showing him that I have a halter, and waiting to see whether he'll bolt. One of the most important things *not* to do with a horse who's spooked is chase it. Horses are prey, so they run when chased. And once you start after them, they see you as the predator no matter how well they know or love you.

"It's okay. I'm here," I say softly. "Everything's alright." It takes me a moment or two, but he lets me approach, and then he lets me halter him.

"See?" John asks ominously.

"I think he might need a ride around the farm so he can see where he is," I say. "Maybe that'll help him feel more comfortable here. It's a lot for a normal horse, coming to a new home, but I imagine it's even worse for him. He's highly intelligent and athletically gifted."

John scoffs. "And he's going in the six-foot stallion enclosure from now on."

I probably should have started him there, but he was behaving so well for me. "Fine."

Obsidian Devil lets me lead him to the crossties without any issues.

"Let's see if you can stand here," I say. "Has anyone ever trained you about how these work?" I shift so he can turn his head left and right to see the setup. Our crossties have three separate sections for working on horses all laid out in a row. Each of them is almost as big as a standard stall, with bars in between on which we've mounted clips and ties. I lead him in slowly, and then turn him around. Then I clip the straps to the side of his halter, left, then right.

"See? It's not bad. It helps keep you still while I saddle you. Alright?"

He tosses his head and stomps his front right foot.

"Normally stomping and pawing are considered rude," I say.

"Are you talking to him?" John's eyebrow is raised. "Because you sound kind of crazy."

"Oh," I say. "I'm sorry. Did you want me to head back to the house and let you take over?"

John frowns, but he doesn't mock me again.

"Alright, boy, we're going to use a bit of a different saddle today, a bigger saddle than we use for races. It lets me hold on a little better. I think you might enjoy a hack around the whole property—we have a few thousand acres. There are some fun jumps, and some big open fields you might love. What do you think?"

"You're going to take him out solo?" John looks sick about it. "Is that wise?"

"Did you want to ride with us?" I ask. "Really?"

"Horses get spooky when they go out alone, but if you think he'll be fine, then do whatever you want. It's not my neck."

"How about it?" I turn toward Obsidian. "Do you want to go out alone? Bob your head if you do."

Obsidian Devil tosses his head.

"Or would you rather I have John saddle someone up and bring them along?" I eye him, but he's motionless. "If

you want someone else to come along, toss your head again."

Obsidian doesn't move a hair.

"See?" I eye John. "If you want to go alone, just you and me, toss your head."

He throws his head into the air again.

John's lip curls. "You've gone insane. You actually think he's answering your questions? Horses throw their heads."

I'm not sure how much of what I'm saying Obsidian really understands, but for some reason, I don't feel afraid of taking him out. "I want to see what he can do, alright? I'm worried that if we take others along, he'll see it as a race, and it won't be the nice, calm tour of our property that I have in mind."

"Or he'll get a whiff of wild hogs, freak out, throw you off, and break your back."

"I've never been thrown in my life," I say, "and I don't intend to break that streak today."

John shakes his head as he walks away.

"Don't worry, boy." I scratch behind Obsidian's ears. Most horses don't love it, but he seems to like it pretty well. "I trust you." I don't have my riding gloves, helmet, or proper riding boots, but that never stopped me as a child. "Are you ready to go explore?"

Obsidian tosses his head again.

As I tack him up, I do have a moment of panic that Obsidian might bolt or freak out on me. Horses going sideways in the crossties can be really harmful for them, and clearly everyone else has trouble managing him. But he stands calmly while I toss the saddle pad over his back, and he barely shifts a hoof while I tighten the saddle straps. He opens his mouth politely so I can place the bit when I put his bridle on. He never snaps, stomps or kicks.

He's a perfect gentleman.

I lead him out of the barn with no issues. I'm almost to

the indoor arena where I figured we'd warm up when he pulls hard, almost yanking the reins out of my hands. I'm worried he's trying to escape for a moment until I notice he's still standing near me calmly. He tosses his head in the direction of the open field behind the arena.

"It's cold, Obsidian. Really cold." I rub my arms. "I'm only wearing a jacket. We should at least warm up first, where there are walls to block the wind." He shifts and begins to walk slowly toward the stable we just left.

"No, we need to go the arena," I say. "It's over here. Once neither of us is cold, we can go out and—"

But he's stopped, and he's staring at the wall. There's an old coat hanging on a hook. I assume it belongs to one of the grooms, because it's not mine. I wrinkle my nose. "Are you wanting me to put on that stinky coat? I don't want to."

He paws the ground and whinnies. When he bumps my arm with his nose and rubs my hand with his face, I weaken. "Is that really what you're trying to do? Convince me to wear a coat?"

He tosses his head again.

Now I'm beginning to wonder whether I'm going crazy. Do I really think this horse is problem-solving my complaints and arguing with me about things? Maybe he's just sassy and tosses his head a lot.

"Okay, I'm going to get this coat." I stare at it for a moment without moving.

And he tosses his head again.

It feels like I'm starring in some live-action Disney movie. What's next? Squirrels cleaning my kitchen? Birds picking up debris from our walkway?

I finally close the gap between me and the barn and grab the heavy coat. It smells of sweat and dirt, but I slide my arms into it anyway. I really wish I had some gloves. My hands are going to freeze—but I doubt he'd stand stock

still while I jaunt into my house and change clothes. This is really the problem with my entire life. I never have time to prepare for anything. Everything happens in various states of emergency, leaving me scrambling with whatever I have on hand.

"I'm not pleased with you right now, sir. I mean, I love you, but I'm not happy. You could have just had some grass and taken a break in that pasture. I could have showered, and eaten something, and had a nap before I go on this horrible lunch date to beg my ex for money. It's your fault I even need money, by the way. But instead, we're going for a freezing ride, and I'll barely have time to shower before I have to face him."

I swear, Obsidian tilts his head and his eye swivels to focus on my face. I walk him out past the gate and close it behind us. I swing up on his back and for the first time, I'm actually riding the horse I just spent a fortune to acquire and have spent days now defending.

We walk briskly for a moment and trot for a bit longer, but at the slightest nudge, he takes off.

Riding him is like I imagine it feels to drive a Ferrari!

What was Finn complaining about? We make a big loop around the meadow behind our stable, and then I decide to take him a little farther. The four or five hundred acres closest to the house are forested with spruce, birch, and pine mostly, but we've cleared a path through it, and set up some jumps we use to train our hunt horses, including Five. I angle him toward the path, and he takes off.

He can really fly.

We approach the first jump, set up to mimic Becher's Brook in Liverpool, and I search for any sign of fear or nervousness, because this jump has a major ditch behind it, and it's tall. Almost five feet. I don't sense any, so I urge him forward. He leaps the fence with a foot to spare, and pulls his nose up almost immediately! It's the most effort-

less ride I've ever had over this fence, on one of the hardest jumps we have. We fly over the next few obstacles with the same energy and effortless ease. By the time we clear the last one, I'm so pleased that I lean forward to pat his neck.

"You were worth every penny. What an amazing jumper you are!"

He glances back at me, and I swear he's pleased with himself.

Five Times Fast is the best hunter I've ever raised. My mom's family gave me a filly when I was only five years old, and I grew up with her. We did quite well, and Five's her grandson. I have high hopes for him, but if I'm being honest, he's nothing to Obsidian.

"You could win it all, boy. Cheltenham, the Grand National, everything! You could change my life!" Buying him put me in major trouble, but somehow it felt like the most freeing thing, the most *Kristiana* thing I've done in months. If I can get past this balloon payment, forget just paying off the debt my father gambled us into, we could become a real, respected stable. We could put Latvia on the map.

And he's a stallion, so he could father a new line of jumpers. This might be the beginning we always needed. Then, maybe, Gustav would call *me, begging me* to breed my epic stallion to Grandma and Grandpa's mares.

I pull him up next to the brook and stop to see if he wants a drink. He's thirsty, so I let him take his fill, which is why we're still enough for me to feel the buzzing. I pull out my phone. Four missed calls from my dad. What could he want that's so urgent?

I text him. WHAT?

He texts back. SEAN'S HERE.

It's barely ten o'clock! Why would he show up so early?

"I hate this." I pat his neck again. He's warm and my hands are freezing. He glances back at me and his ears shift.

Horses always listen better than people, but this horse listens like none I've met before. "It feels like my dad's trying to sell me off."

He blinks. My horse actually blinks several times, like he's confused.

Maybe it'll be cathartic for me to talk about this. I certainly can't say it to my dad. He'd only feel worse. "Years ago, when I was just starting grad school in England, I met this perfect guy named Sean. He was handsome. He was smart. And his family had tons of money, though I didn't know that at the time. We dated for almost a year. It was a perfect romance. Calm and grounded, but also exciting and fresh. I thought he was going to propose one night, but instead. . .he broke up with me."

Obsidian walks in a circle, tossing his head in what looks like agitation.

"A break up is when the other person tells you they don't like you anymore, basically. Anyway, apparently his parents had found him a perfect little blue blood princess. It explained why, in the midst of all our perfection, I'd never met his family."

He's had a little break, so I ask him to go. I need to move again.

Obsidian obliges, racing through the trees on the roughly-kept path. The wind at my face calms me down some. But eventually we reach the fork in the path. I have to go right to reach Sean at the house. Or if I turn left, we head for another trail, full of new obstacles, and the place where the same stream cuts through the western side of our property.

I pull Obsidian up short.

"The worst part is that he told me that he and Clara, that perfect woman, got divorced. And now he wants to see me." My hands tighten on the reins. "I should just send him

packing. Or maybe use him to get a new loan, a better one, and *then* tell him off."

Obsidian whuffles.

"But." I almost can't say the words, even to a horse. "But I'm actually kind of. . .hopeful." There. I said it. I admitted that I'm actually excited to see Sean again, the guy who broke my heart. I've never really recovered, and no one else I've dated has even come close to him. And now he's here, and I hate myself for being excited.

"I hate how pathetic that makes me."

That's why I pull left.

Sean can wait for me for once.

We race again, clearing fallen logs, ditches, and fences. And finally, I haul on the reins and we stop. "I have to head back," I say. "But I don't want to." I sigh. "And I do want to. I'm a mess."

Obsidian neighs and paws at the riverbank, making a big muddy streak on the ground.

"Why can't I fall in love with a horse instead?" I think about how much time and effort have gone into horses in my life. How I just spent all my money on him. "Actually, if I hadn't bought you, I wouldn't need to see Sean at all. I don't know whether to blame you or thank you."

Obsidian lifts his head up high and angles his face back so I can see him. I lean forward and hug his big warm neck. "You'd never ditch me for some posh rich lady, right? I wish that, instead of a magnificent stallion, you were a human. Is that so wrong?"

A jolt runs through my body, starting at my hands where I'm touching Obsidian's neck and radiating outward. It zings through me and then rockets back in, like there's an explosion happening in every cell of my body. I'm flung upward in the air, and then I'm falling. Down, down, several feet down until I land with a splat in the mud.

46

Except I'm not really in the mud because I'm lying on something, something big. Not horse-big, but big to me.

I shake my head to clear it and look down to try and figure out what just happened.

I'm lying on a saddle.

My saddle.

Obsidian's gone, like he was just transported out of existence.

It's just me and this saddle.

Ermagosh.

Wait. The saddle's wrapped around a person, a very large, very masculine person, and my hands are resting on his very well shaped pectoral muscles. I scramble backward as quickly as I can from the saddle-wrapped man. At least he's as shocked as I am. He blinks over and over and over, these bright, golden-brown eyes that I'm staring at involuntarily.

My brain cannot seem to process the information my eyes are sending. Nothing I see makes any sense. The man underneath me has long black hair, and from what I can see, he's absolutely the most beautiful man I've ever seen in my life. Or at least, I think he is. There's a bridle obscuring part of his face. The man spits the bit out of his mouth and says in Russian, "What just happened?"

Luckily, I speak Russian, so I understand him. And now that I can see his face, I realize that I was right. High cheekbones. Sun-kissed golden skin. Pitch black hair. Wildly bright eyes. A curved, richly full mouth. Eyebrows like slashes of coal on a canvas. I need to stop staring and start making sense of what's going on.

I gather the facts in my overloaded brain. I was sitting on a horse. Then after touching the stallion's neck and wishing that he was a human, I'm suddenly sitting on the most gorgeous human I've ever seen. The answer seems clear.

I've obviously had a complete and total mental break.

The man doesn't exist.

I've either been thrown off my horse and I'm in a coma, or I'm still sitting on the horse's back and I'm imagining this whole thing. I decide to talk to my delusion in Russian in the hopes of convincing myself it's not real. "I think I've had a breakdown."

The beautiful man talks again, still in Russian. "Were you hurt?"

"Were you?" I ask. "I think I landed on you, whoever you are."

He shakes his head. "I'm fine. Better than fine. I've been stuck in my equine form for a very, very long time. It feels great to have two legs again."

This *must* be a dream.

Stuck as a horse?

I shake my head and blink rapidly, expecting him to disappear.

Being in a coma isn't ideal, but surely Dad will come looking for me. Or John. Or both of them, right? The last time something felt this surreal, the last time. . .was when I thought a horse intentionally threw a race for me. "Umm," I ask. "Are you. . .?" I can't quite bring myself to say it.

"Am I?" He quirks one eyebrow, and I swear, he could be posing for some kind of strange print ad in a magazine. He's that beautiful. Even though he looks a little dazed.

I clear my throat. "Are you. . . Obsidian Devil?" I wince as I say the words, because I could not possibly sound crazier.

"Of course not. My name's Aleksandr."

I breathe a heavy sigh of relief. So it really is some kind of delusion, or else I blacked out when Obsidian bolted and left me here, and this naked man. . .showed up and crawled under the saddle and. . .*What is going on?* "Why are you naked?"

He frowns. "I didn't have clothing on before I changed, obviously." He says it so matter-of-factly, like *I'm* the idiot for asking.

I swallow. "Right. Obviously."

"You're looking at me as if I'm insane, but you're the one who asked if I'm Obsidian Devil. That was never my name. It's just what those people kept calling me."

Those people.

As in.

It feels like my brain is swelling inside of my head. "You're saying that you're a horse."

"Well, not right now, clearly." He frowns.

His enormous, well-muscled shoulders shift, and my eyes track downward, ogling his beautifully sculpted chest. His unbelievable six pack. And then I find myself wondering what's beneath the saddle.

"How did you break the curse?" he asks. "Who are you that you *can*? And what took you so long?"

"The curse? What curse?" I'm not sure if I'm more concerned that I'm starting to engage with my hallucination, or that he seems to be talking about magic and shapeshifting.

"I helped you with your race because I thought you were different. I thought you might release me, so I could go home. I never even considered you might be able to *free* me."

"Free you? Home?" I scramble to my feet. "You can't leave. I just spent a fortune on you." I swallow. "I need you to be a horse. I need to win races. A lot of races." I've lost my mind. This horse wants me to release him, like he's a captured slave or something.

"I'm from Russia," he says. "My friends and I refused to help the Yurovsky and Kurakin families during the drought, and they cursed us. I only woke a year ago."

"You *woke*?"

49

"I was buried alive—in horse form—sometime in 1917."
His brow furrows. "I believe someone mentioned the year
as being twenty-something, now?"

"I. . ." I have no idea what to say to that.

"You needed money, and you got it in that race. Is that
not so?"

"Well, yes and no," I say. "I risked some of my money to
win more money, but then I spent almost all the money I
made when I bought you."

His frown deepens. "So because of me, you're still in
trouble."

I nod.

"That's frustrating." He stands up. And Oh. My. Word.

That phrase "hung like a horse" takes on an entirely
new meaning.

5

I stare for too long, but finally my brain engages, and I cover my own eyes with my hand.

"It's not my fault I'm naked." Aleksandr sounds annoyed.

"No, it's not," I say. "But I'm having trouble believing you're real."

"How could I *not* be real?" He blinks.

"I could have passed out. I could be dreaming."

Large hands reach out and grasp my forearms. A shiver races up my spine, and my entire body comes alive in a way it never has before. "I—what are you doing?"

His breath washes over my face and it's warm and smells earthy. "I'm real. Very, very real. And I'm grateful to you for breaking the curse. More grateful than you could possibly know."

"Okay." I can't really argue with him, not like this. He *feels* real, and he *sounds* real, and he *looks* real. "But I need you as a horse."

"But I'm not a horse. I'm a man."

"But I spent a fortune on a horse, and you can't just— what do you want to do now? Just leave for Russia?"

51

"Home." He nods.

"You won't have much of a home left," I say, "if you haven't been there since 1917. That's more than a hundred years." Can any of this actually be happening?

He looks concerned at the thought that his home may be gone. His shoulders slump a bit. I notice that he's not covered in goosebumps, in spite of being naked in the cold.

"Here." I slide out of the barn coat and hold it toward him. "Put this on, at least."

"I'm not cold." He crosses his arms, and I look down again involuntarily. He's not lying.

"Fine, but take it anyway."

This time, his expression looks smug. "Alright." He slides his arms into the coat, and thankfully it's long. Probably not quite long enough, but I'll take what I can get. It gives me somewhere to look that's safe.

"You need me to be a horse again, but I need to go home." His lips flatten into a hard line.

If this is for real, if he's not a horse, how can I keep him? Oh, no. I just spent my life savings buying a horse who isn't a horse. I bought a *man*. Obviously I can't own a *man*.

I'm doomed.

I slide to the ground and sit cross-legged, my eyes staring at a clump of weeds.

"You need money, or you'll lose the farm."

My nostrils flare. "I can borrow money from my ex."

"But you still have to pay him back."

I nod.

"You need to borrow money because you spent yours buying me."

I turn my head to face him slowly. The sun is shining behind his head, but I can just make out his expression. He's seriously smart for someone who was a horse until two minutes ago. "I can't believe you're a man. I'm ruined."

52

"I'm not exactly a man," he says. "I'm a shifter with a horse form."

"You're saying that you've always—"

"Been able to shift into that same horse form?" He nods again.

"Do it now," I say. Because I won't believe it until I watch it with my own eyeballs.

He smiles smugly, and then. . .nothing happens. His face falls, his mouth flattening in frustration.

"What's wrong?" I ask. "Is it hard or painful?"

Aleksandr grimaces. "No, but for some reason. . ."

"What?"

"I can't seem to shift."

This is bad. "So you're stuck as a human now?"

"It would seem so," he says.

I flop back on the ground. This is *so* how my life goes. I mean, if something insane is going to happen, it's going to completely ruin everything.

"At this rate, Sean will write me off, too, and we really will lose the farm."

Oh, no.

Sean's still waiting for me.

"Kristiana." The way he says my name sends another shiver up my spine. I want to slide into it—the person I sound like I am when he says my name.

He clears his throat. "Kris."

I startle a bit, hearing him use my nickname.

"Isn't that also what they call you? Your father? Your trainer?"

I nod.

"You were the first human whose words I could understand." He's speaking in Russian, but I realize that I wasn't, not until he did.

I switch to Latvian. "I knew you were listening to me." I change to English. "Even back in Ireland."

He nods. "I can understand you in every language you speak, and then after hearing your first words in that tongue, I could suddenly understand everyone else as well. That was my first clue that you were different." He tilts his head.

The hair on my arms rises, and not just because I'm cold. I speak three languages fluently. Russian, thanks to my grade school studies and our housekeeper, Latvian because this is my homeland, and English thanks to my mother and my time at university and grad school.

"In most parts of the world, it's pretty rare to find someone who's truly trilingual. Not in Latvia, but in most other places. That makes it pretty strange that you can speak all three of the languages that I can."

"I couldn't speak English or Latvian before," he says. "It must be related to your connection to the curse."

"That makes no sense."

He shrugs. "Like it or not, you're somehow connected to all of this, clearly. So I'd like to propose a deal."

"A deal?"

"You can likely change me back into my horse form. At least, it makes sense that you should be able to, since you changed me into my human form."

"And?"

"Assuming you can, I'll help you win the money you spent on me. After that we're even, and you'll free me."

"As a human."

He nods. "I'll go home and figure out the rest from there."

Seems more than fair. He won't sire the line of horses I'd hoped for, but at least I won't have thrown a quarter million down a rat hole.

"I want one more thing." Why does he look nervous?

"What is it?" I ask.

54

"You'll teach me about the modern world and help me break the curse in any way possible."

Oh, no. Not so fast. *In any way possible?* "I'm not promising to do *anything*, but I'll try my best to do both. Since it's two more things you want, I need a promise from you in exchange."

"What kind of promise?"

"You'll stay in horse form as long as you're with me, and you'll behave the way a horse should. No more jumping fences and trampling people any time I'm not around."

His brow furrows. "How will I learn about the modern world if I'm always in horse form?"

I think for a moment. "You can spend the evenings as a human in our old barn. It's empty now, but it has living quarters we can clean up."

He smiles. "It's a deal."

Describing his smile as breathtaking feels. . .somehow incomplete. It transforms his already gorgeous face into a work of art.

"Okay."

He holds out his hand.

"What?"

"Don't humans usually shake their hands?" His hand is still extended. "I've seen them do it."

I finally take his hand, but this time, I'm prepared for the electric zing. It still surprises me when it happens.

"I'm Aleksandr Volkonsky," he says. "And you're Kristiana. . .?"

"Liepa," I say. "Does the name mean anything to you?"

He shakes his head. "But you're connected to all of this somehow. You must be."

What if he's wrong? What if I can't turn him back and forth into a horse? What if he's stuck as a human? I'll never get my money back, and I'll have some random guy following me around.

Not that I'd mind that *so* much. I realize that I'm still holding his hand and yank mine back. What's wrong with me? A horse turns into a man and tells me he's magical, and I what? Fangirl?

Am I really swooning because he has pretty eyes? I'm such an idiot.

"We should probably head back," he says. "You'll want to dispatch that stupid banker as quickly as possible."

"Sean." I smack my forehead. "I can't dispatch him. I need his help."

Aleksandr frowns. "Why, exactly?"

"Our first loan payment is due in two days, and I've only got half of what I need."

"I know, but why him?" His eyes narrow. "I don't like how he looks at you. You should take money from someone else."

I laugh. "I'm lucky he can help me at all. There aren't many people who can come up with that kind of money in two days." Actually. If he changes his mind. . . "I've made him wait too long."

"You need to change me back." He looks simultaneously scared and relieved. I suppose if he's been stuck as a horse for a while, he'd be used to it. He's probably also nervous about being stuck again. I hope I can manage to turn him, because explaining that I left with a horse and I'm returning with a naked man would not be easy.

"How should I even try this?" Now that I'm staring at him, everything feels weird. He's naked except for a coat, staring at me expectantly. The longer I look at him, the stranger the idea that he was cursed to be a horse sounds.

"Start the same way you changed me in the first place, maybe?"

"Like, put my hand on your neck and say I wish you were a horse?" I arch one eyebrow. "Can it really be that simple?"

"Things like this usually are," he says.

He's so matter-of-fact, like he's an everyday expert on curses and their operations. He did say he could shift himself before.

I can't believe any of this is happening, but I force myself to think back anyway. We were racing down the path, and I was feeling sorry for myself. I touched his neck, and I said something about how I wished he was a human. I reach my hand back toward him. I try not to think about how he's wearing nothing beneath. . . Oh! The borrowed coat.

"Maybe you better take this off. If this works, it'll be a little too small for you."

I swear, his smile's going to kill me. "Just a little." He slides the coat off and hands it to me. I try not to think about how very naked he is. I take the coat, slide my arms back inside it, and then reach back toward him. He holds his hand out toward mine. Again, his touch against my skin feels electric, like static current before you get zapped. I wonder if the hair on my head is standing on end.

"Okay, we're touching. Now. Maybe I say something like. . .I wish this big, naked man was a horse instead."

It should be difficult and complex and horrifyingly problematic for me to transform a man into a stallion, but the same jolt I felt before repeats—stronger than the feeling when we touch, but not dissimilar—and I watch as it happens this time. One moment he's standing in front of me, naked, and for a split second, he blurs, and then he's a horse.

I'm unchanged, and he's a tremendously large black stallion. He has the same vibrant golden eyes, and the same jet-black hair, er, mane, but he's most definitely *equine*, not *homo sapiens*.

I know it's still him, but I can't help it. I think of him as

Obsidian again. He looks at me with the exact same expression the man did before, as if to say, *Are you an idiot? Let's go.*

I sigh. "Did I just imagine that entire thing?" I start walking back down the path toward the abandoned saddle and bridle, which are now both covered in mud, and I shake my head. I use the stream to clean off the saddle and pad as well as I can and then I rummage around until I find some leaf-covered branches to blot them some.

Everything else is still muddy, including my boots, pants, and jacket. The borrowed coat looks even worse than before, which I hadn't thought possible.

Obsidian, er, Aleksandr, or whoever, whatever—my head is irretrievably confused. He stands completely still while I saddle him. I really hope the saddle doesn't bother him on the way back, what with the mud and debris.

And the being a human underneath his horse-shaped suit. If this isn't a dream, it's so strange I could never have imagined it as a legitimate reality.

I rinse the bridle in the stream, too, before placing the bit in his mouth and putting it all back together. I do it mostly without thinking, but once I'm finished, I pause to think. I know he's a person, not a horse. I mean, he is a horse, but he's not a normal horse. I don't want to carry the saddle back home several miles, so putting it on him made sense, but should I have bridled him? Can I really *ride* him?

I probably shouldn't.

It feels wrong, somehow.

He's not my pet. He's a human who's been cursed. On the other hand, he did mention staying here and racing with me until I've earned my money back. That does imply he's fine with me riding him, doesn't it?

Why didn't I think to ask about that part back when he could talk? Now that I'm thinking about how he can't talk, my head fills with questions I haven't yet asked.

"What do I call you, now?"

Obsidian tilts his head.

"It feels weird to call you Aleksandr, since I've been thinking of you as Obsidian. I mean, you're back to being a horse."

He snorts. I can tell he's trying to say, *I'm still me, man or horse.*

"Fine, so you're the same, but it still feels weird. Can I keep calling you Obsidian? If I just start calling you Aleksandr, people will think I've lost my mind."

Obsidian exhales loudly.

I'm taking that as a yes. I pull the coat on and grab his reins. I tug him along behind me as I start the long walk home. I'm sort of jogging to expedite things and also to keep warm, when Obsidian just stops. The reins tighten as I keep moving and he doesn't.

I glance backward at him. "What's going on? Are you okay?"

He tosses his head back toward the saddle. I didn't tighten it much, not nearly enough for a rider, but it shouldn't fall off.

I shift it a bit where it's skewed and start walking again.

He still won't budge.

"What?" I ask. "I'm sorry, but I don't speak horse. I get that you're mad, but I have no idea why or what about."

He steps toward me, bumps me with his nose and then tosses his head toward the saddle again.

"You want me to *ride* you?"

He bobs his head.

"You're saying yes?"

Again.

"Uh, well, if I'm being honest, it feels weird now." Actually, it feels kind of dirty somehow. "I'd rather not." I turn to walk along again, but he still won't so much as budge. I turn back around and sigh. "I don't want to, okay? I know you now, and not as a horse. I would never ride a person

like that." Images come to mind of riding the naked man from a few minutes ago, in the mud for some reason, and I shake my head to clear it.

Shame on you, Kris.

He picks up his left hoof and then puts it down one inch ahead of where it was. Then he does the same thing with his right hoof. He then does the same with his left and right rear hooves. He starts again with the front, inching ahead.

"You're going to move like a snail now?"

He bobs his head.

"Why?"

He snorts. He bumps my arm with his nose and huffs. Then he moves his hooves again, very, very slowly.

"Me? I'm slow? That's what you're saying?"

Head bob.

"I'll have you know that I was jogging, and I'm pretty fast, actually. I'm in good shape."

He tilts his head to one side, clearly unimpressed.

"Oh fine, if you insist." I tighten the saddle. "Now, don't blow out your belly. When horses do that to keep the saddle from being uncomfortable, it makes it loose. I could slide off and die."

He exhales gustily, and I pull the saddle a few inches tighter. I use a nearby tree stump to help slide my foot into the stirrup and swing what feels like fifty feet up to his back. "Fine, I'm on now, so let's go."

I don't have to tell him twice. He shoots off toward home, flying over each jump we pass on the way. I should feel guilty, but once we get moving, I don't.

I'm having too much fun.

That's why I'm beaming when we finally get back, zooming into the meadow just behind the arena. I pull Obsidian up short and lean over his neck. "Now, listen. No one else can know, because I'm struggling to believe this,

and I saw it with my own two eyes. And don't forget your promise to be on your best behavior, even to the grooms and stable boys. Got it?"

He bobs his head.

"No more leaping fences, or banging on the wall, or snapping at anyone, okay?"

He snorts and leans down to snag a late blooming dandelion. He's munching on that when I notice someone waving at us from near the stable.

I'd almost forgotten about Sean. Again.

I'm so muddy. Maybe he'll give me a pass on lunch.

"I'm going to hand you off to a groom, okay?" I urge him forward slowly. "They'll make sure you get cooled down and then put you in the stallion pasture."

He shakes his head. Not the bob I've grown accustomed to. A side-to-side shake.

"No? Do you want to be in a stall?"

Another head shake.

"What do you want?" He heads toward the house at a trot.

"Oh, no." I yank on the reins, but he ignores me. Until this moment, I didn't realize how much I relied on him to be compliant. "Obsidian, you need to be with the horses. I have to meet Sean without worrying about you." I pull him left, back toward the barn, but he throws his head up so the bit isn't really controlling him anymore.

Butthead.

Is he kidding? "You said you'd behave," I hiss. "You can't meet Sean. Listen, I'm stressed enough right now. I can't be riding a demon-horse, which you promised not to be."

He paws the ground.

"Kristiana?"

And now it's too late. Sean's spotted us, and he's angling toward us at a brisk-but-still-proper British walk.

"How was the ride?" My dad stops his approach a few

61

paces away. "It looks like. . ." He squints. "You didn't fall, did you?"

I roll my eyes. "I didn't fall, but we had an incident."

Dad blinks.

Sean scans me head to toe. "Other than the mud, are you alright?"

"I'm fine. I'll just go put Obsidian away, and I'll be right back."

Only, Obsidian's still being a bit of a jerk, and he won't go.

"Come on," I hiss. "Now."

"I thought you said he was an angel for her," Sean says. "I can't say I'm keen on her riding a horse that no one can control."

"It's fine," I say. "*We may not even have him very long.*" I squeeze my legs and press him forward.

"Wait, you may not keep him?" Sean asks. "I wish you'd told your dad that before we signed papers."

"Papers?"

Obsidian's ears perk up too.

"We had to list *something* as collateral other than the farm," Dad says. "And we needed to get it submitted today so we'd have funds in the next thirty-six hours."

"That's why I came early," Sean says. "I realized that if I met you for lunch, we might not get it processed in time."

"Wait." I can barely breathe. "You listed Obsidian Devil as collateral on the new loan?" I feel like I might explode on them in this moment.

"We only did paperwork today on a loan large enough for the first payment," Sean says. "Since he's worth a quarter of a million and you just bought him, the bill of sale was all we needed to prove it up with the underwriters. Easy peasy."

Well, he agreed to stick around to help me pay the

balance off, so he can't be too angry to have been treated like chattel.

Obsidian's looking around now, his head swiveling frantically. "What are you doing?" I whisper-hiss.

He snorts, as if that's a real response. Although, I suppose it's the best he can do right now.

"Are you sure you're alright?" Sean asks.

"Fine." I dig my heels into his side. "Totally fine."

Obsidian finally sees whatever it is he was looking for, and he dives forward. Toward the old barn.

"Where are you going?" Dad shouts after us.

"Um, Obsidian Devil needs to be in a place that's not surrounded by new horses."

"So you're taking him to the old barn?" Dad sounds confused.

We use it as a quarantine barn, so it's not entirely dilapidated, but it's not used much.

"It's fine." I wave my hand. But now we're far enough away that I can shout at the person I'm really angry with. "What in the world are you doing?"

Obsidian slides to a stop in front of the old barn. He tosses his head.

"What?"

He turns around and bumps my hand with his nose.

"I have no idea what you want."

He snorts loudly, and then he paws at the ground.

"Listen, we agreed that we would come back, and then you would go to the pasture while I showered and went to lunch with—"

The pawing finally has a shape.

I think he's trying to draw something.

A stick figure.

Oh, it's a man.

He wants me to shift him.

I slide off his back.

"Absolutely not," I say. "You have to stay a horse right now."

He swings his head back and forth violently.

"Listen, I have to go with Sean, and—"

He leaps in front of me and rears back.

Maybe he has something important to tell me. "You need to talk?"

He nods.

"Fine." I point at the barn. "But you will stay inside the entire time I'm gone. Swear it."

He snorts.

I guess that's as good as it gets for a horse. I place my hand on his neck again and say, "I want you to become a man."

I need to come up with a better phrase, because that feels dirty for some reason.

Just like before, he shifts, the saddle collapsing on top of him, and luckily blocking the parts I'm really, really not accustomed to seeing. I cover my eyes. "No, do not stand up yet."

I dart into the old barn and rush up the breezeway. It takes a moment, but I jog into the living quarters—Dad was right that they're filthy—and grab some old clothing from the grooms who lived here. They aren't stylish, but they're better than him being buck-naked. I run back out and thrust a pair of pants and a shirt at him. "Put these on."

"Who cares about—"

"Me," I say. "I care."

"Fine."

I turn around until he has time to put clothing on. "What in the world was all that about? I'm already late, and—"

"I'm coming with you," he says.

"Excuse me?" I spin around, my hands going to my hips.

He's fiddling with the button on his pants, and for some

reason that's somehow hotter. Maybe because it makes him seem more *real*. His waist's tapered and flat, his abs pronounced. The muscles in his arms bulge as he moves, and speaking of bulges, I'm shocked he was even able to get the pants on.

Kristiana. I mentally shake myself and force my eyes upward, which isn't much better. His chest is so perfectly muscled that he could earn extra money on the side modeling for cologne ads. "Focus," I mutter.

"On what?" His brow furrows. "An excuse?"

"Huh?"

"We'll need a reason for me to accompany you." He looks deadly earnest.

"You cannot come," I say. "Have I been unclear?"

His grin this time is practically demonic. "Try and stop me."

❧ 6 ❧

"You swore," I say. "You swore before I changed you that you would stay here."

"I did no such thing," Aleksandr says. "I didn't say a word." He slides his arms into the sleeves of the dirty old shirt I handed him and grimaces.

"But you snorted."

He arches one perfect eyebrow as he rolls up the sleeves so it's not as obvious that they're way too short.

I swear under my breath, because the jerk's right. He didn't actually say anything at all. I hate that he's right.

"Look, I'm in this bind because of you, Aleksandr. The least you can do is—"

"Call me Aleks," he says. "We're going to be around each other often. We may as well be friendly. And you may as well come up with an excuse for my presence now."

"An excuse?" I throw my hands up in the air. "There's nothing anyone will believe. I said you had to hide in the barn because I can't explain my horse being gone and some random man being here."

"I'm not a random man," he says. "I'm Aleksandr

66

Volkonsky, and you can't teach me about the current world if I can't even experience it."

He has a point. "But you did agree to staying here, whether you want to wiggle out of it or not. I'll find a way that's safe for me to show you how things have changed."

"Tell them I'm a new trainer," he says, ignoring me. "You can say that you hired me to work with Obsidian Devil." The corner of his mouth tilts upward. "I can pretend that I only speak Russian."

"For the love of—"

"I bet that stupid banker doesn't speak Russian."

"Sean's wicked smart," I say. "I wouldn't count on it."

He scowls when I say that, for some reason.

"There's absolutely no reason for you to come to this. It's going to be hard enough as it is."

"You only say that because you haven't seen how that man looks at you. He's not trustworthy, and—"

"Aleksandr Volkonsky."

He freezes, becoming suddenly serious.

"I need to shower and get changed." If I'm firm, he'll have to agree. He's out of place and totally backward for this time, and until an hour ago, he was a horse. If it comes to it, I'll just change him back. Then he'll have to stay put.

He stalks toward me, and I circle the main area in the barn, backing away from him until I bump up against the wooden barn wall. He looms over me, his gaze intent, his eyes dropping from my eyes to my mouth. "Now that I'm in human form, we can both shower and change into something better." He spares a disapproving glance for the clothing I tossed him.

"I don't have anything better than that for you right now, and—"

He presses a long, strong finger to my lips, and I freeze. My heart hammers against my chest. Every part of my body focuses in on that one spot. I can barely drag in a breath.

"Kristiana, you're currently the *only person* on earth who can control my shape, and until I ensure the curse is broken and I've regained my magic—"

His magic? I mean, what else would he call shape-shifting, I guess?

"—you will not leave my side."

I've always been quite small, but I've never felt it as keenly as I do in this moment. He could pick me up and carry me out of here, and he does need to learn about the world. It's changed a lot in the last hundred years. I just wish he'd be a little more patient.

Then again, patience doesn't look like his long suit.

As a horse trainer, I know one thing. Horses are larger than me. Much larger. They're also stronger. There's absolutely no way, if they start pulling on a halter, for instance, that I can beat them. So getting into a pulling match with them is a terrible idea. It just teaches them that they can beat me. When I'm lunging a recalcitrant horse, the way I win is to give, just a little, but keep them on the line so they're turning and moving when I say. I never get into a pulling match I can't win. This is starting to feel like that.

"Fine," I say, giving just a little. "You can come today, but you only speak Russian, and you will not interfere in any way. Not with the conversation, not with any deal we strike." I lift my eyebrows as if I'm not afraid of him. "And this time, I need *your word,* not just a snort you'll later dismiss."

"I need to keep you safe, so I won't promise not to interfere with anything." His self-satisfied smirk irritates me, badly.

I duck under his arm and march toward the exit.

Unfortunately, he follows me. Barefoot. Other than the fact that he's built like a Greek god, he looks and smells homeless. "We'll both be sneaking through the back door of my house, and you have to shower and wear some of my

brother's old clothes. They aren't exactly *fashionable*, but at least they won't be filthy or moth-eaten."

"Agreed." He doesn't ask about Gustav, and I'm relieved. I love my brother, but I don't like talking about him. It's too complicated.

In fact, he doesn't say a word as we sneak into the back of my home. He's so quiet that when I dart through the back door and shoot up the stairs to my room, I have to glance back a few times to make sure he's still following me.

And when I shoot through my door and into my bathroom, he's still on my heels. So when my dad calls my name.

. .

I yank the bathroom door shut and lock it.

"You haven't showered yet?" Dad asks. From my bedroom. His hand rattles the knob.

Aleks and I barely fit in the standing space in my tiny bathroom. His back's pressed up against the shower glass, and I'm standing right in front of the door. "Not yet," I say.

"Well, let me in so I'm not talking to a door."

I wince a bit as I reach past Aleksandr and through the shower door. It's hard, but I manage not to touch him at all in the process. I flip the knobs and water starts to pour out. "Sorry. Already getting in the shower."

"What took you so long?"

I twist and suck in my breath to sneak back past Aleksandr and into my spot in front of the door. For some reason, the pains I'm taking to avoid touching him are making him smirk. "I left Obsidian in the pasture behind the old barn. I think to keep him calm, we'll leave him out there for a while."

"Won't he be agitated since he's all alone?" Dad asks.

"He's a strange horse," I say. "I don't think he loves other horses much."

Aleksandr frowns, but he can suck it. He *is* strange.

"Alright, well, hurry up. Poor Sean has been waiting for a very long time."

"Not more than ten years, though," I mutter. "So the balance sheet is still pretty skewed."

"I heard that, young lady, and I hope you'll keep in mind that he's doing us a tremendous favor." As if it occurs to him that we need the favor *because of his mistake*, he stops talking. I hear his footfalls as he retreats.

Once I'm sure he's gone, I reach for the doorknob.

Aleksandr's hand circles my wrist. "What are you doing?"

I freeze. "Letting you out."

"I need to wash as well."

He must be kidding. "You can wait in my room while I shower." I point behind him. "Then when I'm done, I'll let you go."

"That sounds inefficient." His half smile does something strange to my insides.

"Shut up." I yank my hand free and crack the door open, making sure the coast is clear.

It is, so I wave him out and motion for him to stay in my bedroom while I sneak next door to Gustav's for some clothing. Luckily my brother's almost as tall as Aleksandr, so I think his clothes will mostly fit.

Unfortunately, he took most of his stylish things with him when he left, and it's been *years*. Aleksandr will have to make do with a pair of faded jeans and a bizarrely patterned button-down shirt. Anything at all is an upgrade from the abandoned barn clothes that're probably infested with moth eggs.

"Okay, I'll be out shortly." I duck into the bathroom and lock the door faster than I ever have before. Even with a locked door between us, I'm absurdly conscious of the fact that there's an enormous, stupidly hot man poking at things in my room while I'm in here.

Even Dad would be proud of how quickly I shower.

Of course, now I'm stuck waiting for Aleksandr. "I don't think you'll need to mess with anything," I say. "I left the water running. You just step in, and the water goes down the drain, here." I point.

When I turn back toward him, he's naked again. I shut my eyes, but I can feel the heat rising in my cheeks. "What on earth are you—"

"Being pragmatic here: you're going to see me like this over and over." It sounds an awful lot like he's chuckling. "You may as well get used to it."

I don't open my eyes again and use my hands to fumble my way toward the door. "There's soap in the shower. Okay, bye." I shut the door behind me, but he is *definitely* laughing.

If I spend a little too much time agonizing over outfits, well, it's because of Sean, not because of the crazy, demanding Russian guy who thinks he has magical powers.

And who can change into a horse. So, who knows?

I'm pulling a cable knit sweater over my head when the door from the bathroom opens.

And Aleksandr—in nothing but a towel—steps out, an appreciative smile on his face. "I thought I left you ample time to dress, but apparently you were waiting for me to emerge."

He has *got* to be kidding. My cheeks heat again, and I want to throw something at him. "You should have knocked."

"Before leaving the bathroom?" He has way too much confidence for a hundred-year-old man who was cursed and lost everything.

"I'm dressed, so it's fine." I smooth down the edges of the bottom of my sweater. "Why aren't you?"

"It's so steamy in there. I had to come out here, or I'll never dry." As if his mention of it somehow draws my eyes,

I notice that he's literally glistening. If I thought he looked good before, I had no idea.

Then I recognize the noise—the shower's still running. "You have to turn that off."

I jog toward the bathroom and push past him to shut it off. "Okay. Well, if you can get dressed now, then—"

He drops his towel.

I clap my hand over my eyes and exhale. "Just hurry."

To his credit, he does dress much more quickly this time. "I'm done."

I open my eyes slowly, like I don't quite trust him, but he looks much, much better than I would have thought possible. He used one of my hair bands to pull his hair back into a knot. He's wearing Gustav's clothes properly, and he left the top three buttons undone on the shirt. It makes no sense—I've seen him naked now over and over, but for some reason, the golden-brown skin that's exposed nearly takes my breath away.

When he catches me looking, he grins.

"Alright," I say in Russian. "Remember to stick to only Russian, and to butt out of my conversation. Got it?"

He shrugs.

It's not very reassuring in light of the last few hours, but I can't keep Sean waiting any longer. I reach for the knob, my hand pausing just in front of it. I'm trembling, and I need to get it together. I don't blame myself for being a mess. It's been a weird day. But I can't walk out there and convince anyone that we're a good investment, and that the farm will be in good hands, when I can't even grasp a door-knob properly.

"Let me." Aleksandr reaches around me and flings the door open. "Can't keep your savior waiting." He said it in Russian, like I asked, but I'm beginning to wonder if telling him to speak Russian was a mistake.

He sounds. . .too confident in Russian. "What *were* you in your past life?" I ask.

"My past life?" One eyebrow arches. "I've only had one life. The curse locked me into horse form and froze me underground."

I blink. "So you've been alive for the past hundred years, and just stuck underground?" How could he not be insane? *Is* he insane?

He shrugs. "You might liken it to sleeping. My personal magic kept me alive—preserved me in a sort of stasis. It's such that I have a very long life in any case, but I couldn't use it to free myself because of the curse."

I have so many questions about this curse, and who he was, and what's going on, but they're going to have to wait. Because Sean's standing at the bottom of the stairs, staring at me.

And then his eyes move past me to the very tall, very large man standing behind me. And they widen with alarm.

"Who are you?" Trust Sean not to even ask me—he always goes straight to the source. It's the height of rudeness for an aristocrat to use blunt questions. He always said it made his mother insane.

Aleksandr turns toward me, a questioning look on his face. Thank goodness he didn't immediately give himself away by responding to an English question.

"This is my new trainer," I say.

"Your what?" My dad's spluttering behind Sean.

I toss my head and walk around the corner and down the stairs. "Mirdza told me last week before we left that she'd heard of an amazing trainer, just in from Russia, who needed work. I told her we didn't have anything for him, but now that I know how much John hates Obsidian." I shrug. "I called her, and she dropped him off."

"She dropped him. . ." Dad looks around and frowns.

"When? I didn't even see her today. I don't see any bags, either. He just sort of. . .appeared."

So he did. But Dad can't possibly know how true his words are.

"Look, he's starving, so I hope you don't mind if he tags along?" I've reached the bottom of the stairs, Aleks on my heels, and Sean's forced to step back to make room for us.

Sean doesn't look pleased. "It might be better—"

"I'm starving," I say. "And he won't understand a word we say, anyway. Can we just go?"

I brush past him, and Aleksandr does the same thing. As I turn sideways to make room for opening the front door, I watch Sean's face. Emotions flash across it in quick succession: irritation, appraisal as he looks Aleks over, and then determination.

"Where did you want to eat?" Sean asks.

"How about sandwiches," I say. "There's a decent—"

"I just tried a place called SkovoroTka," Sean says. "It's not bad. It's a bit of a drive from here, but that gives us time to talk."

To talk. Why does that sound so ominous to me? "Oh." I swallow. "Okay." It helps that he named my favorite restaurant.

"I've actually been pleasantly surprised," he says. "Daugavpils is a nicer city than I realized."

"The only city in Latvia larger is Rīga," I say.

"I didn't realize how close it was to Russia," he says. "I guess that's why you speak Russian."

I shrug. "A lot of people around here speak Russian. Actually, most people in Latvia know three languages. It's just that not many of them know English."

Sean smiles. "I'm glad you do."

For years, I hoped that the next time I saw him, Sean would be fat, bald, and not nearly as good-looking as I remembered. Isn't karma supposed to make that happen

when someone leaves you, if you're a good person? I'm not sure whether it doesn't actually work that way, or whether I'm not a very good person for even wanting it to.

But it didn't happen here. That's for sure.

As we climb into his shiny BMW, I steal some glances at him. His blonde hair's as thick and wavy as ever. His cobalt blue eyes practically shine from his aristocratic face. His jacket's open, so I can see that he still has the faint line in his polo shirt between his pec muscles that shows he's fit, but not overly muscular. Bodybuilding is gauche if you're part of the British aristocracy, after all.

"Um, is your new trainer a little slow?" Sean's staring rather pointedly behind me.

At Aleksandr. He's just standing, staring at the door with a perplexed look on his face.

Because a hundred years ago, cars looked nothing like this. They probably more closely resembled a buggy. "Ah, hang on." I open my door and stand halfway up, hissing in Russian. "Grab the handle and get in. He thinks you're an idiot."

Aleks turns toward me slowly, clearly glaring. "Is it safe?" At least he's remembering to answer in Russian.

"Totally safe," I say. "There's a belt you can clip in place that will keep you even safer. Just follow my lead when you get inside."

He blinks, but he listens.

I move more slowly than I ever have at locating, and then at clipping, my seatbelt. Then I turn back toward him.

"Why is he coming again?" Sean asks.

"He was hungry," I say. "And he didn't want to stay at the house with my dad, who doesn't speak much Russian."

Sean frowns. "But I haven't seen you in years, and—"

"Make him shut up," Aleksandr says. "Or I will."

I turn around in my seat and pin him with my best stare. "And how exactly are you going to do that?"

75

He shrugs. "I'll kill him."

At first, I think he's kidding. Then I wish he was. "Are you—are you serious right now?"

"Then you wouldn't have to pay him back," he says. "It's a win for both of us."

"First of all, it does not work that way. I owe his company. But second, what do you stand to gain?" I ask.

"He annoys me."

"There will be no killing," I say. "I don't know what kind of person you were a hundred years ago, but while you're with me, you're the kind of person who never kills anyone." I glare at him for good measure. "Got it?"

His brow furrows. "So I'm weak."

We'll have to talk more about this later. "Just drive," I say in English. "He's as crazy as the horse I hired him to train, so hopefully that's a perfect fit."

Aleksandr huffs from the back seat, and I want to remind him that he's not supposed to be able to understand me, but I'm too worried that Sean will figure it out.

"Why *did* you buy that horse?" Sean asks. "You'd won the race. You could have paid that first payment yourself."

I've been dreading this question, so I should have known he'd lead with it. "I can't stand animals being abused, and the way Rickets was treating that stallion didn't sit right with me."

"You were willing to lose the farm over it?" Sean's voice is measured, almost nervous.

I turn to look out the window, because I can't face him while I say this. "I knew you'd keep that from happening."

Knew might be a bit strong. I *hoped* he wouldn't.

"So even though you said you didn't want to see me, you do trust me, at least a little bit."

"I guess I do."

When I turn toward him, Sean's beaming. "I'm glad you called."

"I still think we should kill him," Aleks mutters.

I ignore him. "It wasn't as bad as I thought it would be."

"It won't be bad at all," Sean says. "Your dad filled out all the paperwork already."

"Oh, I remember," I say.

"Were you truly upset that we used Obsidian Devil as collateral?" Sean asks. "Because I need your signature on the form."

I sigh. I can't very well tell him that Obsidian Devil is actually a *man* who was trapped in a horse form, and that using a human as collateral makes me squeamish. So instead, I try an angle that might make sense. "Dad's gambling is what put us in this mess," I say. "And I saved us with that race—a race where I beat Obsidian Devil and six other horses on a horse I raised and own."

"And then you spent the winnings buying another horse," Sean says. If his tone is a little judgmental, he's probably justified.

"I've never been the best at business," I say. "And I've always cared too much about horses. But now something that *I* own is being chained up to go down with the ship my dad sank on his own."

"Except it won't go down," Sean says. "I'll loan you enough in the next twenty-four hours to make that first payment, and then we'll get you an even better loan to repay the rest. Fair terms, flexibility, and no huge penalties."

I should just say thank you, but it sits wrong with me. Why should Sean have to fix all our problems? I needed him today, for the looming balloon note, but I can't really let him just walk in like my fairy godmother and wave his wand. Besides the fact that it feels wrong, then I'd *owe* him. "I really do appreciate the offer, and you clearly saved us today, but I think we'll figure something out for the balance of the note."

"I could buy your entire farm," Aleks says. "Just take me back to Russia, and I'll—"

"You'll what?" I spin around in my seat, tired of his incessant commentary. "You haven't been *home* in a hundred years. How exactly do you plan to buy my farm?" I roll my eyes. "Just be quiet and let the adults talk."

Aleksandr narrows his eyes at me, but he doesn't argue. Thankfully.

"What's he saying?" Sean asks. He looks genuinely perplexed, and I breathe a huge internal sigh of relief. Part of me was moderately worried he might know enough Russian to be dangerous.

"Oh, nothing important. He's incredibly bossy for someone who came here with absolutely nothing," I say. "He has a lot of feelings about food as well, apparently."

Sean blinks. "What does he want to eat?"

"Grass, mostly," I say.

Sean's brow furrows.

"I'm kidding," I say. "He's asking for borsch, of all things."

"They actually have that at SkovoroTka!" Sean says, smiling like an idiot and gesturing like he's eating soup. "Yes, they do!"

Aleksandr tilts his head and widens his eyes. I know just what he's thinking, and it's rude. It's not Sean's fault for believing our lie that Aleks only speaks Russian.

"You can't kill him," I say. "He's not an idiot—he's being nice."

"He thinks I'm an impoverished imbecile," Aleks says. "And I hate him."

"You are poor," I say, "and that may not be the only thing he's right about."

He glowers, but at least he doesn't argue.

It allows me to turn back toward Sean and say, "He's delighted."

Sean raises one eyebrow. "He doesn't *look* very pleased, but maybe Russians are just like that?"

Finally we've reached the restaurant. I try to look at it as I might if I'd been alive in the early 1900s. The exterior was meticulously designed to make it look old—plaster hand applied over exposed brick that I'm quite sure was installed exactly as it is. But to Aleks? It might look like it's falling down.

At least the styling of the letters on the sign and the patio with the outdoor tables set up is all breathtakingly beautiful. There are individual tables underneath the tents, with large oil heaters allocated to each one. The red awnings from the tents bring out the red of the brick, and beautiful trees installed in between each third tent tie all of it together with a sort of old-world charm.

Aleks, strangely I'm discovering, isn't saying a word. He's simply absorbing everything around us.

"Do you think he'll be alright?" Sean whispers.

"What does that mean?" I ask.

"Will he embarrass us?" He frowns. "I like this place. I want to be able to come back while I'm setting up the office in Daugavpils."

"Oh, I'm sure he'll be fine."

Only, I'm not sure. Not at all. Now that Sean has asked the question, it's all I can think about. Will he embarrass me? What might he do or say?

The second we reach the front, a woman greets us at the door. "Welcome," she says in Latvian. "Table for three?" She's tall, which Latvians often are. We pride ourselves on having the tallest women in Europe, although I kind of buck that trend by being stupidly short. But she's also finely boned, with great cheekbones and blonde hair. She's really quite pretty.

I nod. "Three."

"Right this way," she says.

"Can we sit outside?" Sean asks in English.

She pauses, clearly not understanding him. "Did he say 'outside'?" She says the last word in English. We all have to take it at school, but most Latvians don't retain much. Recognition finally dawns, and she turns to me, still speaking in Latvian. "Your boyfriend wants to sit outside, no?"

"He's not her boyfriend," Aleks says in Russian.

This whole thing is not off to a great start, and if Sean is following at all, he'll realize that Aleks at least understands Latvian.

"I'm sorry," I say. "Sean." I nod at him. "He only speaks English." Then I nod at Aleks. "And he only speaks Russian."

"Ah!" Her pretty blue eyes light up, and she turns on Aleks like she's starving and he's a loaf of fresh rye bread. "I speak Russian. I grew up speaking Russian, actually."

I should have known. I mean, most people here speak at least a little.

"It's rare that we have such handsome Russians come to Daugavpils." She's practically eating him with her eyes.

"This woman," Aleks says. "She's going to bring us food?" He pins me with a stare. "Because all she seems to do is talk."

Her face falls and she looks down at her feet. "Of course I'll bring you food. Right this way." She hastily leads us to a tent-covered table, and then ducks around the corner.

"You embarrassed her," I say. "That was rude."

"How was it rude?" Aleks asks. "She's a servant girl. She should be serving, not talking."

I can't stop my eyes from rolling. "She's not a servant. She's a waitress."

"You compensate her for bringing you food, no?" Aleks asks.

"I mean, yes, but—"

He cocks one eyebrow. "Servant."

"What's he saying?" Sean asks.

I'm almost to the point that I want Aleks to just kill me. "Nothing," I say. "Nothing that matters, anyway."

"Call me crazy, but I think our waitress might actually *like* him," Sean says, eyeing Aleks like he'd inspect an orangutan at the zoo.

"Oh, she does," I say. "But Aleks wasn't very nice. I was scolding him for it."

"*He* doesn't like *her?*" Sean snorts. "That's ridiculous. A poor trainer who emigrated here for work and is living in your old barn quarters thinks he's too good for a gainfully-employed waitress?"

Put that way, he does seem insane. But he thinks he's important and that he has magic. I mean, he *can* shift into a horse. Or at least, with my help he can.

"Listen," I say. "It was really nice of you to ask me to lunch, but I'm a little confused to be honest."

"What's confusing?" Sean asks.

"Well, you dumped me, remember? And now, suddenly, out of the blue, you just turn up again?"

He presses his palms flat against the table, and swallows. "It's not out of the blue." He sighs. "I was never happy with Clara. She was a terrible match, and I never should have married her, but I wanted to make my parents happy." He meets my eyes. "I've missed you every day since we broke up."

"Could have fooled me," I mutter, looking down at the menu.

"Kris, I divorced Clara a few years ago, but it never occurred to me that I might have a chance with you. That's the only reason I didn't reach out sooner. My dad had a heart attack a year ago, and it made me think about how

little time we all have, and how little control we have over that."

This is getting really intense, and I'm very aware that Aleks is listening to every word. "Sean, I'm so happy you're willing to help us out, and I think it's really serendipitous you're opening an office here, but—"

"Oh, it's not luck that I'm expanding here. After your dad told me about his gambling debt, I decided I should have a reason to be here. That way my dad can't argue with me about how often I come out."

"Really?" That makes me even more uncomfortable. He's expanding to Latvia as an excuse. . .to see me?

"Kris, I can see you're uncomfortable, but listen. I didn't get as far as I have by giving people things for free," he says.

"Didn't you get where you are because your family was rich?"

Sean shrugs. "That's not wrong, but I've grown the net worth of the business by nearly fifty percent in the last five years."

His words sink in. He doesn't give people things for free. "What do you want, then?" A feeling of doom steals over me.

He doesn't hesitate to tell me. "A second chance," he says. "I want you to spend time with me."

Something about the way he phrased it makes me uncomfortable. "You're *buying* my time?" Doesn't that kind of make me a hooker?

He smirks. "It's not like that. I'm saying that if you want me to hand over all this money double quick, under advantageous terms, I want you to agree to give me another chance, a chance I know that I don't deserve."

"Like, four dates?"

"Four?" He grins. "Do you think I can win you back in just four dates?"

I shake my head. "Not a chance."

"Then I need more. Let's say twenty."

"*Twenty?*" I ask. "You're kidding, right?"

"How many do you think saving your family farm is worth?" he asks.

"I'm only accepting that first loan," I say. "And I'll definitely pay you back, so it's not like I'm saying you should give me a million euros for a few dates. I'm just saying you should loan me a quarter million for them."

"Twelve," he says. "Twelve dates between now and when the next balloon note would have been due."

That's three months. One date a week for three months. It's not unreasonable. "Fine."

"Absolutely not," Aleks says. "This man pretends to save you, but he's trying to *buy* you."

"You said you'd stay out of it," I say. "So honor your promise, and shut up."

The waitress returns with menus. "I brought one in Russian." She winks at Aleks.

"Would he be considered handsome?" Sean asks. "In Latvia, I mean?"

I'm pretty sure that Aleksandr's good-looking literally everywhere, but I don't say that. I bite my lip and look at him and say, "No, I wouldn't say that he is."

Sean looks relieved.

"Which of them is your boyfriend?" the waitress asks me in Latvian.

"Neither one," I say.

"But the Russian one?" She wiggles her eyebrows.

"He was horribly rude to you," I say. "You should just ignore him."

She giggles. "I kind of like it."

Why in the world do women want things that are bad for them? "Trust me. He's not a very good person."

"The woman belongs to me," Aleks says suddenly. "Until our meal is ready, go away and stop bothering her."

For heaven's sake. The poor waitress' eyes widen dramatically, and her lower lip wobbles.

"I don't belong to anyone," I snap.

Sean, apparently oblivious to all of the back and forth, says, "Are we ready to order?"

I help him place an order for a few different things, including the traditional grey peas and bacon, and skābu kāpostu zupa—our common but delicious cabbage soup, and then I order borsch for Aleks. I have no idea whether he likes it.

Actually, I rather hope he hates it.

"This doesn't count as one of them," Sean says.

"Excuse me?"

"Our lunch today." He looks pointedly at Aleks. "It isn't one of our dates, because your strange Russian trainer tagged along."

I can't help but smile. "Sure," I say. "I agree."

"I'm going to win you back in the next three months," Sean says. "Just wait."

"No, he won't," Aleks says. "Because I bet I kill him inside of a month."

This conversation alone might do me in.

I know one thing for sure: I absolutely have to figure out how to control this stupid horse-man, or I'm going to lose my mind long before Sean has any hope of changing it.

I survive the lunch, barely. Sean didn't want to pay for Aleks' meal, but he didn't want *me* to have to pay for it, so eventually, when it was clear that Aleks had no money, he paid for everything.

And miraculously, Aleks stuck to Russian the entire time, so that was a success. Sort of.

But when Sean drops us off—he thankfully has a meeting later and is in a rush—Dad's waiting outside on the front porch.

He does not look pleased.

"Mirdza's here," he says.

Blast. I knew she taught lessons on Tuesdays. Why didn't I find a spare second to call her?

Oh, I know. Because I've been plagued by Aleks since the second we arrived back home.

I told Dad she brought Aleks here, but she had no idea about the lie.

"Where is she?" I try my best not to wince. Dad sounds mad, but maybe it's not what I think. If I've learned anything in my more than thirty years of life, it's never to make things worse for myself.

Wait, watch, and observe. Only then, react.

"She's here." Mirdza's grimacing when she steps around the edge of the door and waves. "This must be Aleksandr." She forces a half smile.

"He only speaks Russian," I say quickly.

"Why would you lie? Mirdza doesn't know who he is or anything about him." Dad frowns.

I can't really blame him, but I'm scrambling for a better lie and coming up short.

From the corner of my eye, I notice movement and turn toward it. Anything to distract them and buy me a bit of time to think.

John's striding toward the house from the barn, and he looks ticked. He's not even close yet when he shouts, "You hired a new trainer?"

Why do bad things always converge at the same time and place?

"I bet my life savings on the Champion Chase at Down Royal, and I *won*, and then I spent my winnings on a horse no one else wanted. You're both upset. I get it." I put my hands on my hips. The one thing I learned from my American grandparents is that the best defense is a good offense. "But guess what? They're *my* winnings. And I hired a trainer for my new horse who's willing to work for just room and board." I spin on my heel to face my dad again. "And let me remind you. I had to have lunch with my ex-boyfriend today because we needed money to pay a debt that you incurred." I fold my arms underneath my chest and huff.

John gulps.

Dad looks at his feet.

Mirdza's eyes light up like things just got interesting.

"Later," I mouth to her.

She nods.

"I'll call," I mouth again.

Then I stomp up the stairs before the guys unwind enough to realize that I didn't answer a single question or explain my lie in any way.

The anger wasn't feigned, I realize, as my booted feet hit the wooden steps. I'm kind of livid. Yes, I'm lying about where Aleks came from, but I'm not doing it for a bad reason.

I worked for a decade to repay my student debt and then save enough for a down payment on a horse hospital. And I had to risk my entire life savings to try and save Dad from himself. I won, and then I did something that was probably stupid. I bought a horse who turned out *not to be a horse at all*, and now my ex-boyfriend is back saying things I wish he'd said a decade ago, and I'm tired of dealing with all of it.

All. Of. It.

When I turn to slam my bedroom door behind me, Aleks is standing there, staring at me. I guess with all my stomping, I didn't even notice his enormous footfalls right behind me.

And of course he had to follow me up here. He's certainly not going to try and talk to Dad—whose Russian is broken at best—or Mirdza, since she doesn't know the story.

And John clearly hates him.

Even so, I find myself annoyed with him, too. "What?" I ask.

"You're a little bit scary," he says.

I roll my eyes, and then I lean around the corner and peer down the stairwell. It looks like John and Dad didn't follow me, so that's progress. Now to think of something I can tell them.

"Why did you yell?" he asks.

I yank him into my bedroom again. It's becoming a dangerous habit—or maybe what makes me nervous is that

a small part of me *likes* the feel of dragging him inside my space. "You can't stay here," I clarify. "As soon as we're done talking, you have to go back to the barn and be a stallion again."

"I have a lot to learn about the modern world," he says. "I need more time as a man."

Something about the way he says *man* makes my knees tremble. I swallow. "Listen, mister, part of paying me back is keeping from blowing my cover. My family can't know that you're some kind of maniacal magician who's a hundred years old and turns into a horse."

"I'm not a magician," he says.

I need to find out exactly who and what he is before I take any more risks on him. I point at my desk chair. "Sit."

He actually listens, to my utter shock, dropping into the seat, but sitting just as ramrod-straight and regal as he did through all of dinner. He has the kind of posture that looks like it was drilled into him by a crazed governess.

"Tell me who you are, and why you got cursed. I need to know what I'm dealing with. I'm going to talk to my dad and try to figure out how we might be related, but I need to know what questions to ask."

Aleks stretches his arm out, dropping one hand to the top of my desk, and drums his fingers. "There were five of us with powers. I don't know why, and I'm not sure how long it had been that way."

"Five what?" I ask.

"Families," he says. "Five families that could work magic."

"Okay," I say. "All Russian families?"

He nods. "Sort of. My father told me it dated back to Genghis Kahn's time. There are only a few words in Russian that take their meaning from the Mongolian language, but money, horse, customs, and trade are among them. That man swept through with his mounted troops

and conquered all of Russia. We remained oppressed for more than two hundred years." He sighs heavily. "But after all that time, the people were desperate to be free. They began to pray to any God that would listen for help."

"Any God that would listen?"

Aleks shrugs. "I'm just telling you what I was taught. In order to free our people from the Mongolian rule, the locals began to make sacrifices. Some were small, ranging from widows giving up their bread to wealthy families releasing sheep or goats into the wild. Eventually, larger sacrifices were made, possibly dark ones. It's pretty unclear what exactly happened, but one thing we know is that something answered.

"Five families were gifted with powers. They became the ruling families in the region, after vanquishing the Mongols. My family, the Volkonsky family, received the gift of dominion over the earth."

Dominion over the earth? What does that even mean? "And you could shift into a horse. Is that part of it?"

"I assume they were connected, but shifting hasn't ever been easy," he says. "The process itself is simple enough and painless as well, but in order to master it, you must first conquer your skills with your element—for me, earth, as I mentioned."

"Okay," I say. "And you did?"

The line of his mouth is flat.

"I mean, I'm assuming you did, but who knows? You can't seem to shift without me, so. . ."

"As I said, that's because of the curse."

"Tell me about the curse, then," I say.

His eyes flash. "I don't know many details. The entire region of Russia was in the middle of a terrible drought. My friends and I had been working together to keep our lands and people safe—fed. But when the Yurovsky and the

Kurakin families came and demanded that we save their people too?" He shrugs. "We declined."

"Wait, there was a famine, but you could still feed your people?"

"I control the earth," he says. "As I mentioned. The Khilkovs mastered wind, and the Romanovs mastered water. There wasn't much of it to be had, but between the three of us, we were able to use everything at our disposal to grow enough crops for our provinces."

"The Romanovs?" I pause. "That name sounds familiar."

"The Czars of Russia?" He rolls his eyes. "I should hope so."

"Right. Duh." History wasn't really my favorite subject —ever.

"After we refused them, Mikhail Kurakin told me he'd destroy us. We didn't worry about it much." He frowns. "I suppose we should have."

"Wait, you refused to help them?" I blink. "You said Kurakin was one of the other magical families. If their people were also starving, why didn't you help them?"

Aleks stares at me.

"Were their people starving?"

"I can't save the whole world," he says. "No matter how much magic I have. Trying to do so would only have resulted in me failing my own people."

"But there were only five magical families. You were helping two of them, and when the others came to ask for help, you what? Sent them packing?"

"Sometimes you have to sacrifice something you care about in order to save what really matters."

"So that's what you did? You sacrificed the other two families and all the people they ruled, to save your friends and their people?"

He scowls. "They took revenge on me for that decision. One day, while I was already stretched thin, my magic

failed me, and then everything went black. Only a very powerful hex could rob me of my magic and then my consciousness like that."

"So you have no idea what happened?" I ask. "You could have eaten bad mushrooms or something, and—"

"I didn't eat anything bad." His mouth is a flat line. "In all my life, my magic never once failed me. Not until that day, and while I was unconscious, I could also sense their magic—lightning and fire."

"Then how did you free yourself?"

"I didn't," he says. "I simply awoke a year or so ago, trembling, and I heard a loud sound. I was encased in dirt on all sides."

"You were buried alive?"

"In my equine form. I'm not sure whether it was because of my elemental magic, or whether I was placed underground by those who cursed me, but I was buried."

"You were some kind of noble—"

"We were called Horse Lords by those who served us," he says.

Horse Lords? It sounds ridiculous, but it doesn't feel like the right time to laugh. "Okay."

"I was captured shortly after I flailed my way free, and then treated like an actual beast." He sneers. "Then that disgusting human won me in a bet, apparently. I never understood what he was saying until I met you and could suddenly understand him, but I always knew it was vile."

"You have no idea how they cursed you, or what the terms are?"

"Only that it happened in nineteen seventeen."

"Wait, wasn't that the beginning of the Russian Revolution?"

He straightens, his eyes intent. "Something important happened that year? Something you've studied and recall more than one hundred years later?"

"I think that's around when the entire royal family was murdered. The Romanovs, right?"

I've never seen anyone look quite as stricken as Aleks looks right now. "Nicholas?" He goes utterly still. "What about Alexei?"

"Is he the sickly one?"

Fury flashes across his face. "Is that what they said about him?"

"Um, look, I'm not trying to upset you." For a moment, it feels as if time has stopped. For me, this is ancient history, but he sounds like he knew the Czar's son quite well.

"This must be related," he says. "I need to locate a reliable source of information and research the details. Surely some things must have been recorded."

"I mean, I think a lot of it was," I say. "But we have the internet for that kind of thing now."

"The internet?" Aleks frowns.

"Oh, boy."

"You need to teach me," he says. "Where can we study this internet?"

I suppress my laugh. "You can do it anywhere you have service, but listen." I glance around my room. "You can't stay here, and there's no internet in the old barn. I still need to concoct some kind of lie to tell my dad and John, and Mirdza. She's my best friend, and she's here a lot. She teaches horseback lessons on our older and retired horses to kids who live in Daugavpils."

"But Kristiana, I *need* to study this internet *immediately*," he says, for all the world sounding like a melodramatic teenager. "How else will I discover my enemies?"

"Okay, but the internet, as with most records kept by people, always has an angle. You can't really trust anything you read."

"I can't trust it?" He looks absolutely shocked. "If the

internet is an unreliable source, then I demand we find a reliable one."

"I hate to tell you this, but history is always written by the victors, and it seems like that wasn't you." I pull out my laptop, and open it up. A few quick taps and it's booted up, and a few moments later, I've pulled up a webpage. "Okay, it seems that the Romanov family wasn't killed until 1918. Whoops. Off by a year."

Aleks still looks as if someone struck him between the eyes.

"Are you alright?"

"I will be." He motions for me to slide over. "I have a lot of things to search up."

"No, you don't search them *up*," I say. "You search for things like this—" Over the next hour, I try to show him as much as I can about how the internet works, and how to construct a decently successful search.

He spends the time asking me more questions than any preschooler could ever come up with, and practicing making the roundest eyes I've ever seen.

A rap at my door distracts me from the rabbit hole I've fallen into. "Yes?" I call. "Who is it?"

"It's me," my dad says. "We need to talk."

I may still suspect that Aleksandr may not be a very good person, especially by today's standards, but hunched over my laptop, typing in words with his index fingers, he doesn't look like much of a threat. "I'll be right out." I drop a hand on Aleks' shoulder.

He startles.

I drop my voice to a whisper. "I need to talk to my dad. I'm going to tell him I met you in Ireland, and that you begged me to let you come work for us. You found a ride out here. If anyone presses, speak quickly in Russian. Dad knows basics but is easily flustered if you use large words or speak rapidly. Got it?"

He shrugs. "Whatever."

"No, not whatever." I glare. "This is my life, and I need my dad and trainer and best friend to believe me when I tell them things. I never lie, but this is a weird situation. You didn't cause it, I guess, but I had less to do with it than you did."

"You're doing it for my good as well," he says. "I understand."

"Kris?" Dad's sounding less understanding.

"Coming."

"Keep searching," I say. "Maybe something will stand out to you that means nothing to me."

"Right." He turns back to the computer.

And I square my shoulders and exit, bracing myself to face the father I'm going to try to placate with even more lies. "Hey there."

"I know you're upset, and I know this mess is my fault," he says. "But why did you tell me that Mirdza sent that man to us?"

We aren't really much on small talk, the Liepas.

I sigh. "It felt easier, okay? I knew if I could just say that someone we knew vouched for him, you'd be fine. But—"

"But no one knows him at all. He's some kind of bizarre stranger who's sitting in your bedroom right now, wearing Gustav's clothing."

He's not wrong about that. "Look, Dad, all of this happened really fast. I had a lot of decisions to make, and after seeing Rickets shout at Smithers over Obsidian Devil, when Finn told me about a Russian trainer who was a friend of a friend and asked if I had heard of any work at all, I told him yes."

"But why didn't you just tell me that it was Finn who knew him?"

"Because Finn doesn't really know him personally, and

also, you hate Finn." I'm improvising, but I think it's true.

"I do not." But Dad's protest isn't very emphatic.

"You hated that he got me back into racing, and you hate that we've kept in touch all these years."

"But, you, well." He huffs. "The point is, we can't have some strange man spending time in your bedroom." He tosses his head at my doorway. "Especially not right now."

"Right now?" Fury pulses through me. "You mean, because Sean's around? And having Aleks in my bedroom might wreck that and ruin our chances of having him fix the mess you made?"

"You used to love him," Dad says. "Do you really hate him, now?"

"I don't know what I feel, but you haven't left me much choice, have you?"

"I'm sorry," he says. "I'll say it a hundred more times if it will help. I never should have gambled and certainly not against Rickets. But it's in the past, and I can't change it. What I don't want to do is have you keep making the same type of rash decisions and wind up like me."

That's a little bit irritating, coming from him. "I have some things to go over with Aleks—ideas I had about some training techniques. Once we're done, I'll rush him down to the old barn so we aren't being inappropriate. Okay?"

Only, once I get Dad to leave us alone, Aleks has no intention of leaving.

"I have far too much to learn," he says, never looking up from the computer. He sure adapted fast for an old geezer.

"You have to get your butt down to the barn," I say. "I have to feed Obsidian Devil dinner, and if you aren't there, eating hay, someone's going to notice. And how am I going to explain that my big black demon horse who's worth a quarter of a million euros is just *gone*?"

He finally looks away from the screen. His gorgeous

95

golden eyes search my face. "But I'm coming back later to learn more."

"You can't stay in my room all night long, poking around on the internet."

The corner of his mouth curls upward. His eyes track up my body and stop at my eyes. "Why not?" he asks slowly.

Is he serious? The little thrill that runs up my spine tells me that he may be out of the loop, but he's not past his expiration date. "I sleep here," I say. "You have to go to the barn and stay there, like I said."

"I had two allies," he says softly. "Among the five families, three of us were aligned. The Romanovs, my family—the Volkonskys—and the Khilkovs."

"You were earth. The Romanovs were water. I don't remember what the Khilkovs' magic was."

"Wind," he says. "We were all descended from Prince Riurik, who was really the only rightful ruler of the Russian people."

"Okay," I say.

"According to your internet, all of the families descended from him were destroyed in this revolution that took place. But the two families who opposed us were not destroyed."

"They weren't?"

"The Yurovsky family, who controlled lightning, which we later began calling electricity, and the Kurakins, who mastered flame, had powers very well suited to warfare. . .and revolutions." He pauses, but I can tell he's not done. "I think, after they cursed us, they reconfigured the entire government. And I think that somehow, they're still alive and well."

"Wait, the same two men who cursed you?"

He shrugs. "Their powers don't grant them longer life—but I imagine that was part of the curse. Had they just

96

wanted us dead, they'd have killed me, not buried me underground. They may yet be alive, their lives extended by stealing my power."

He really is from a whole world I know nothing about.

"Kris, they won't be pleased to discover that I'm free."

"Do you think they already know? I don't know much about curses, but if they put a hex on you, wouldn't they sense when it disappeared?"

"I'm not sure it has. I still can't use my magic." He shrugs. "I really don't know what they know. That may be the most concerning part of all this."

"If they know you're free, what will they do?"

"What do you think?" His eyes meet mine and hold my gaze calmly, steadily. "They'll try to trap me again, or if they can't, they'll kill me."

"That's bad."

He grins maniacally. "Not at all. They'll be much easier to destroy if they come to me first."

"There will be no destroying of any kind while you're living with me." His words and tone—the manic glee with which he said they'd be easier to destroy—make me very nervous.

I always distrust men.

Conversely, I always instinctively trust horses.

This guy came to me as a horse, so I loved and trusted him. But now that I'm seeing him as a man, I'm wondering if that was all a big mistake.

"Some people deserve to be destroyed."

I arch an eyebrow as if acting imperious will counteract the shiver that just ran up my spine.

"You can't do any destroying right now," I remind him. "You can't even turn yourself into a horse without my help."

My door swings open, my dad blinking furiously. "Turn yourself into what?"

I can't believe my dad just barged into my room. I'm

not a kid—we may not agree on my 'hiring' of Aleks—but I deserve my privacy. "Will you be taking my door off the hinges next?" I ask.

"We have a big problem," Dad says, his eyes alarmingly wide.

"What?" I ask.

"Obsidian Devil is *gone*."

❧ 8 ☙

Of all the stupid things to have to do, we spend the next hour pretending to look for a horse who's standing right next to me. It takes a lot of maneuvering, but we're finally able to send my dad and John and all the stable hands to the far end of the farm.

Once we're alone, I say, "It's time to change you back, big guy."

"Not yet," he says. "I haven't had time yet to try using my magic."

"You've had hours," I say.

"But to truly test it, I need a strong connection to the earth."

"As in, you need to touch the dirt?" I can't help being skeptical.

He crouches down on the ground, his hands sinking deep into the rich loamy soil of the Liepa land. His eyes close almost involuntarily, and he shudders.

In spite of myself, I lean forward, holding my breath and rocking up on my toes. What exactly can he *do* with earth powers? Can he. . .make things grow? Could he make

a mountain or a hill spring up out of the ground? Can he cause earthquakes?

Because if he busts up my land, or worse, wrecks my barn? I am going to be very, very displeased.

After a very anxious moment passes, and then another drags by as well, my excitement and my nervousness both fizzle.

"Listen," I say. "It's not that I'm not sympathetic to your plight." I know he can literally change into a horse, but part of me is beginning to wonder if he may be confused or making the other stuff up. I mean, *earth* powers? "But you need to appear as a horse, mister, and soon, or my dad's going to call Sean and—"

After ignoring me for more than five minutes, he straightens. "Fine."

Luckily, it's pretty easy to change him back into a horse. Although, now that he has clothing that fits, he *insists* on removing it before we shift him, and I'm really starting to feel uneasy about all the nudity. If he were old and hunch-backed, or if he just wasn't quite so. . .delicious. . .I might not feel so strange about it. But a weird kind of naughty-giddy thrill runs up my body every time I think about it, and when he starts to strip, it's like my entire mind goes blank.

I don't want to avert my eyes, which is how I know I need to, obviously. But once he's standing in front of me, a few simple words and voilà. He's equine again.

And that's when I realize how strange it is to halter someone I know isn't a horse. He stands there, patiently, not even so much as twitching while I halter him, but I'm very aware he's not an animal.

Sneaking him back into the barn while everyone else is searching in the woods is a little harder than the shift—he is ginormous and black, after all. Eventually we manage, but by then, I'm plenty annoyed.

"I told you that you couldn't stay in my room all night, searching things on the web." I swat Obsidian on his rump without thinking. . .and then realize that I probably shouldn't be doing that kind of thing anymore.

It definitely feels weird.

My cheeks heat up.

"Sorry," I mumble lamely. "But look, you need to listen to me, or people are going to find out, and then it's pitch-forks and torches, alright? It may have always been some-thing you could do, but in the present day, people do *not* change into horses. Ever. Got it?"

He tilts his huge, gorgeous head, as if to accuse me—he *did* turn into a man because I'd been lamenting that horses couldn't be men, after all. But I meant it hypothetically. "If you can't follow my rules, we won't have time for you to learn about the present. Got it?"

He tosses his head.

"I know you're a prince lord duke or whatever, but here, you're just a horse."

He snorts.

"And more importantly, if you want to walk on two legs again any time soon, you better make me believe you're going to listen to me."

He glares at me momentarily, which is a little discon-certing. I've never seen a horse actually glare in my entire life—side eye? Sure. Irritation? Definitely. But actually glar-ing, with flared nostrils and a narrowed eye?

Although now that I think about it. . .

Didn't he do that before I bought him? How did I ever think he was a real horse? He's been bizarre from the start.

"How about this?"

His nostrils flare, but he's listening.

"You stay in equine form all day, and let everyone see me working with you. Then I'll tell them that Aleksandr has a unique training method. It's proprietary and requires

total privacy. I'll come change you in the evening, and you can spend your nights doing research. I'll let you borrow my phone to boost the internet out here." Now I'm just talking to myself, really.

He has no idea what most of that means, but he'll pick it up fast, if the speed with which he was pecking at the keys on my laptop earlier is any indication.

He inhales deeply, and then bobs his head.

"Great. So I'll duck out for now, but I'll be back later."

He doesn't look or sound very pleased.

"Pawing at the stall floor is bad manners, Obsidian." He doesn't stop. But he doesn't start screaming or trying to undo the latch either.

As I walk back to the house, I think about how boring it would be to be stuck as a horse all day long, just standing around. Maybe I can get him a television out here or something. I wonder if I could extend the WiFi with a booster. . .

The major flaw in my plan doesn't hit me until the next day.

If I don't want to sit beside him while he's searching, and I'm certainly not doing that all night, I have to leave my phone out here. With him.

I'm not the kind of person who can't be parted from her phone, but I'm not exactly keen to allow him to be the first person to receive all my texts and calls, either. He's figuring things out alarmingly quickly, and the last thing I need is to have him answering my calls when Sean rings, and telling him who knows what.

Just having a man answer my phone would be problematic enough, but having Aleks answer? After that miserable lunch fiasco? Hard pass.

"You have a message," he says. He sounds so nonchalant, I should have known.

He's never mentioned when I had a message before.

I haven't even seen the name on the screen, but I know it's from Sean.

DATE TOMORROW? I HAVE TO HEAD HOME FOR A FEW DAYS AFTER THAT.

I snatch the phone from the rough-hewn desk we've cleared off in the corner of the living space above the barn. SURE.

"I'll bring you some books in the morning," I say. "I'm going to need my phone tomorrow night."

"That man isn't trustworthy," Aleks says.

I roll my eyes. "As if you're any better, Mr. Destroy Them."

"I am." He frowns. "In every way. I haven't run away, although I could at any point in my human form. I'm here, learning about the world slowly on your terms, and masquerading as your pet, just as we agreed I would." His expression is pretty sour, but I guess I don't blame him. "All so that you can repay the bank before you lose your collateral."

"But you don't have your powers back, and you have to figure out exactly what happened before you head out to confront your enemies," I say. "So it's not like I'm really in your way."

Reminding him of all the things he doesn't know only worsens his mood. He's practically scowling at me when he says, "I should come along when you go to dinner."

I can't help my barking laugh—it's not ladylike at all. "Thanks for the offer, but absolutely not."

He arches one eyebrow, and I can totally see him as an imperious lord, used to always getting his way. "I *will* come along."

I shake my head slowly. Words alone don't seem to be doing the trick. "You will not."

He folds his arms and glares. "You may be the key to reversing the curse and regaining my magic. Your safety is

my top priority currently, other than information gathering. I will accompany you until I'm positive this idiot can keep you safe."

I laugh again, but this time it's less aggressive, thankfully. "As if you could keep me safe. You don't even know how to call 911. I think I'll take my chances on my billionaire ex who owns a bank."

"Billionaire?" I can tell he's filing the word away to research. "He looks weak. Whether he owns a bank or not, I doubt he could prevent any attackers from harming you."

"Oh, for the love." I point at the barn stall. "You will wait here while I go on my date—this date, and any other that I set up. I'm quite capable of defending *myself*, and—"

He moves so fast, I'm utterly shocked when he leaps up and approaches me. His leg sweeps under mine, and his arms catch me before I hit the floor. "You were saying?"

I kick my feet back under me and shove him, hard. "I mistakenly assumed you weren't a threat." I drag a hand through my hair, pulling it away from my eyes. "I won't do that again." He's not the only one who can glare. "But try that again, buster, and you'll wind up with a black eye and sore balls."

"Sore. . . What?"

"Never mind."

He reaches for me again, and I'm ready. I wasn't lying. The second his hand touches my skin, I say, "I wish you were a horse."

I can't help my smirk as he rips through the clothing that looked so nice on him, and a huge black stallion takes form in front of me.

I hadn't thought about the fact that we were standing on the second floor—in my rather old and shoddily built barn apartment.

The floorboards creak as he shifts.

I press my hand to his flank and practically shout, "I wish you were a man."

And then in a blink, a very large, very naked, very angry man is standing next to me. "Are you trying to kill us both? Or just destroy this ramshackle excuse for a barn?"

I'm not sure whether I'm trembling because he's so very naked, and so very beautiful, and he smells so very intoxicating, or whether it's because I'm relieved that we didn't both crash into the horse stall below. It would not have been a fun trip to take.

"I'm sorry. I clearly wasn't thinking."

"Now I really need to come with you," he says.

I bolt past him, shoot down the stairs, and jog out the door without another word.

I'll deal with his insistence that he come along tomorrow.

Because there's no way my surly, infuriatingly strong, cursed magician man is coming with me on another date.

Absolutely no way.

R iding Obsidian Devil continues to be the best part of every single day. He moves like no horse I've ever ridden, and I guess that makes sense. Because he's not a real horse.

We sail over a four and a half foot jump, and he turns just where I signal. "Yes, exactly like that." I pat his neck. It's gotten easier to treat him like a horse when he's a horse, but I have found myself talking to Five a little more like he's a human without thinking.

Which isn't really that abnormal for me, anyway.

"I wonder how high you can actually jump."

Obsidian Devil tosses his head.

"I don't want to hurt you, of course."

He snorts.

"And it's not strictly necessary for us to test your limits. I mean, the races I do are more about speed and consistency. Some of the jumps are hard, technically, but it's the addition of the extra horses jockeying for a place that make them really difficult."

He jogs forward, pulling on the bit. I take it he's game to try a few higher jumps.

I call one of the grooms over to move the jump up another six inches. "This is five feet," I whisper. "It's the highest I've—"

Before I can even tell him that we'll take it in six-inch increments, he takes off, and we're moving toward a very steep jump without the right positioning. I consider ripping his mouth off. It's super rude to take off when I haven't told him to go.

But we're more of a partnership than a rider and mount. I decide to let him decide whether he can make it and simply let him move.

He sails over it with at least another six inches to spare.

The poor groom's mouth is dangling open.

"Eduards, why don't you take it up another notch?"

He nods, his eyes wide. After he shifts it, he doesn't bother walking toward the edge of the ring. He wants a front row seat, apparently.

"This time, how about you wait for me to tell you—"

But again, he just takes off.

"Hey, that's really rude." I gather up my reins, but just barely, before we're swinging around, heading for the wooden bars. "Whoa, there."

He doesn't seem to be listening to me at all when his shoulders bunch, and we sail over the five and a half foot jump.

Easily.

And now I'm wondering if we should try six feet. Because it really feels like he could do it, no problem.

Eduards might be having a mini-stroke. He's staring at us wide-eyed.

I mean, it has been fun, and he did clear it with room. "How about—"

"What on earth are you doing?" John asks. "That horse cost more than my home, and you're just turning him and

shooting him toward taller and taller jumps and hoping he clears them?"

I close my mouth with a snap.

"Where's his moronic trainer with the strange methods? He sleeps all day most days, and I never see him working with the horse, so at the very least, he should be out here telling you to stop instead of leaving me to deal with it."

Actually, I came out here with the intention of wearing Obsidian out enough that he'd forget about my date in a few hours. I'm planning to accidentally leave him in his stall. Somehow, Aleks always makes me lose my focus, and now it seems like Obsidian's just as dangerous.

"You raise a good point. I'll go work him on the flat."

Eduards actually looks pretty disappointed, but at least Obsidian doesn't fight with me when I wheel him around and head for the outdoor arena. It's cold, but at least the sun is shining. Just before we head out, I zip my coat up the rest of the way.

And then I work him as hard as I feel comfortable doing. Somehow, as I'm tacking him down, it almost feels like I worked harder than he did. My arms are tired. My back is sore. My thighs, which never get sore because of how often I ride, are a little shaky.

"Alright, boy. Let's get you back to your stall."

My plan doesn't work as well as I might have hoped. He's definitely not too distracted, tired, or absentminded when I go to put him away. We're about two feet away from the door to his stall when he sets his feet.

I tug.

He doesn't budge.

"Come on, Obsidian."

He glares at me and tosses his head, and I nearly drop the lead line. "Hey. None of that. Let's go."

He shakes his head slowly back and forth.

I grit my teeth. "You have to go into your stall, and then

I'll come shift you later." I glance at the window. "We have to keep you as a horse all day, like always. Fair is fair."

He paws at the ground and eyes me pointedly, as if to say, *Don't forget. You have to come back out.*

"I have a farm call to make, and then I need to shower, but I will come back." It's not exactly a lie. I just said *later*, not exactly when. Things with Sean are complicated enough without having an ancient, awkward Russian bouncer following me around.

I'm actually sort of proud of myself when I leave him in his stall. We may have gotten off to a bumpy start, but I'm learning to manage Obsidian the same way I learned to manage horses when I was just getting started. One misstep at a time.

Sure, I give on things like that first day, when he demanded to come. I give because I don't have a choice—I can't win a pulling match. But I outsmart him later, and that's what matters. That's what he'll remember.

Luckily, my farm call ends up being minor. A mare ripped a chunk off her heel. Horses stuck in stalls do all kinds of dumb things. That makes me think about Obsidian, and I almost feel bad. But then I remember that he thinks I need him to protect me. What a laughable thought. Once I bandage the mare, I head right back home. I have plenty of time to shower and get ready. The thought of an actual date with Sean, without a crazy horse shifter in tow, has my stomach doing tiny flip-flops.

Actually, in some ways, the craziness with Aleksandr or Obsidian—I really don't know what to call him in my head —has kept me from getting too anxious about the whole Sean thing. When you're dealing with a curse, possible magic, and a horse-man who needs to escape to fight the people who probably killed the Romanovs. . .well, it puts my little loan issues into perspective.

Sean is, as ever, right on time, pulling up in his black

sedan right at seven p.m. And if I hear a stallion screaming in the background, well, I ignore it.

"You look even more beautiful than you did back in school," Sean says.

It's nice that he appreciates the time I spent. I almost never curl my hair, and I'm lucky if I find time to swipe mascara on my eyelashes. Putting on eye shadow and concealer makes me feel like I'm Cinderella preparing for a ball.

And he noticed.

"I thought maybe we'd get something a little nicer tonight." Sean smiles.

"Discovered Gubernators, did you?" I pause. "Or wait, Cafe Imbir?" The beauty of living in Latvia is that, even though Daugavpils is considered to be a large town, by comparison to, say, London, or really anywhere else Sean has ever been, it's small. There just aren't that many places to eat.

He smiles. "I was thinking Art Hub."

I'm impressed. Art Hub isn't that easy to find, and usually only locals like it. "Someone has been doing his homework."

"I went there for lunch yesterday, and I thought, this is a place Kris would like."

He's not wrong. I do like it. It's a little pricey, but heaven knows Sean wouldn't care. "Great. Let's go there."

Of course, when we get there, they've lost his reservation. It *is* Latvia, after all. Nothing ever runs smoothly. Sean looks nearly apoplectic.

"It's fine," I say, placing my hand on his forearm.

"We can offer you seats on the patio," the attendant's saying.

"The patio? It's thirty-nine degrees outside." Sean's eyes are flashing, and his forearm muscles are clenched tight.

"They have nice gas heaters." I point. "I actually like the patio, especially when it's cold."

Sean relaxes visibly when I say that. "Really?"

I haven't actually tried it, but there are three or four other couples sitting out there already, and they don't look miserable. The heaters have bright red elements that seem to be humming away.

"Alright. We'll try it," he finally says.

I'm a little nervous they're going to spit in our food, so I specifically look for things that don't have a thick sauce, like the filet.

"How's the macaroni—"

I grab Sean's hand. "Their fish is also excellent. Every variety I've tried."

His brow furrows, but he follows my lead.

Luckily, the patio isn't bad at all. It's warm enough that my breath doesn't even puff out in a cloud. "See?" I ask as the waiter leaves. "This is nice. And there are fewer people, so it's cozier."

Which is absolutely true, all the way through dinner. We've just ordered dessert when it becomes false. Because an enormous black horse gallops to a stop about eight inches away from us, his nostrils flaring, his sides heaving, his eyes wild.

"Is that—?" Sean stands up, his hands splayed outward. "Is that your horse?"

I sigh. "Obsidian *Devil*, how on earth did you get loose?"

"And how did he find you? We're almost a twenty-minute drive *by car* from your house." Sean looks poleaxed.

I would agree with him—except we're only half a mile away from the place we came for lunch, and Aleks was paying close attention to the surrounding area that day. Most of the decent restaurants are in the same vicinity in Daugavpils.

Stupid blighter got lucky. "What on earth are you doing here?" Obsidian glares at *me,* like this whole mess is somehow my fault.

I guess my plan to tell him I forgot wasn't, perhaps, the best one. I wonder how he opened the stall door from the inside. "I should probably take him home."

Except I'm wearing a dress. And a fairly thin, relatively fancy coat, knowing I'd spend most of the night in a car and a heated restaurant. My hand is literally itching to slap Aleks right now. Whether he wanted to come on my date or not, that's my decision to make, not his.

Sean blinks. "I mean, how would you even get him home? We don't have a halter." He waves the waiter down, which isn't hard. Every single person on the patio is standing up, staring slack-jawed at the fabulously beautiful horse who's simply standing in front of me.

Until he neighs louder and longer than I've ever heard him neigh. It's almost like a battle cry, if I'm being honest.

And he's staring right at Sean when he does it.

"I know it's crazy," Sean says, "but I feel like that horse doesn't like me."

Obsidian snorts and manages to literally blow snot on Sean.

I'm thinking it's not all in his head.

Sean's grimacing and using his napkin to try and wipe it off when people start to pour out of the door that leads to the inside of the restaurant.

A man with a shocking amount of white hair seems to be in charge. "Don't worry," he says. "We've called the police, and animal control is on their way."

Oh, no. That's bad. Very, very bad. Latvia is full of bureaucracy, and none of it is easy to navigate. If he's taken in, it would be very bad. I'm not sure how long it would take me to recover him, or how many people he might permanently maim in the process.

They might just decide to put him down.

"You're such an idiot, Obsidian. Animal control?" I slide out of my heels and button my coat up tightly. "I swear, you're going to pay for this later."

"What?" Sean's looking at me like I've lost my mind.

"I can't let animal control take him," I whisper. "I'm going to ride him home."

"Without a bridle?" Sean's eyes are wild. "You cannot possibly do that. As your boyfriend, I strongly advise against that decision. And as your financial backer, I forbid it."

"Well, that's too bad." I hop the rail, and Obsidian helpfully lowers his front left leg so his stupidly high back isn't impossible for me to reach. I hear an alarming rip coming from something on the back of my dress when I swing up onto his back, and the skirt of my already not-very-long dress slides alarmingly high on my thighs, but I'm short on options. At least I'm wearing undies. "Because this feels like my only option at the moment."

Other than killing Obsidian.

Actually, watching Sean's face makes me wonder if that's a better call.

"This isn't some Disney movie, Kris," he says. "The insane horse isn't going to be an angel for you. You're very likely to break your neck." He's about to come over the railing after me, and that might be worse than animal control catching us, judging by the set of Obsidian's mouth and the way he's pawing at the ground.

"Sean, trust me. I don't know that many things, but one thing I do know is horses."

"And the way home?" He looks a little frantic. "Stay by the roads. I'll pay the check and follow you home, at least. Okay?"

"I've got to beat animal control," I say.

As if that's his cue, Obsidian Devil wheels around,

barely waiting for me to grab a fistful of mane before he springs away. I would kick him, but seeing as I'm bareback, barefoot, and not even wearing pants, it's all I can do not to fall off.

That doesn't keep me from rattling off a string of the worst profanities I know in all three languages in which I'm fluent. "You are the single worst person I've ever met," I say. "And when we get home, you're getting nothing but gruel until you die."

He snorts and speeds up.

"You better slow down, or I'll have you made into dog food. Or glue!" I slap his neck. "That's a real thing they do, you know. Turn horses into glue."

Luckily, he's been running the whole way here, it seems, and at least he's warm. All the energy I have to exert keeps me from freezing too much as well. But I do want to strangle him—every single step of the way home.

When we reach the barn, Sean's already there, and he looks so conflicted it's almost funny. It's like relief and fury are warring inside of him, and they're evenly matched. It's a little offensive, when I think about it. I'm probably the most talented rider he's ever met. I've never been unseated from any horse, ever. But this particular horse knows I'm on his back, wants me there—apparently—and was actively trying to make sure I wouldn't fall. I wasn't in any danger.

Other than the one argument we had about which bridge to take to cross the Daugava River. He won, of course. He can't use words, but he can just *go* wherever he thinks is best. It's not like I have a bit, a whip, or spurs to support my side of the argument.

"You're alive." As conflicted as he may look, he sounds nothing but relieved.

"I am definitely alive, and I'm furious with this idiotic stallion." I have to remind myself that Sean has no idea he's a person, or that I was as safe as I knew I was. "I'm freez-

ing, too. So I hate to do this, but I have to deal with him. Is there any chance you can head home and let me?"

Sean's face actually looks hurt, but he doesn't argue with me. After dealing with Obsidian lately, I'm beginning to really appreciate the strong sense of pride governing Sean. It's ironic, because it used to annoy me. "I took the liberty of bringing you warm clothing," he says. "I'll set it inside the barn, and then I'll go. But please call and let me know when you've safely installed him in the barn and are back inside."

He's slow as molasses at leaving, but I guess I can't fault him for that. He brought not only clothes, but socks and boots as well, bless him. And I'm guessing my high heels are already in my house. Dad must be as upset as Sean. I'm surprised he and John aren't out here, yelling at me.

As if he can read my mind, Sean turns. "I told your father that you have your phone, which I assume is still true, and that you'd call him and John if you wanted them around."

Everyone thinking that Obsidian only likes me is actually helping me, for once. "Right, of course. I do." I pat the strap of my shoulder bag, thanking my lucky stars again that I wore my crossbody purse. "I am sorry. Our next date will be better, I promise."

"I thought it was going pretty well until. . ." Sean trails off. "I know you like that horse, but I vote for racing him once, hopefully winning, and selling him afterward, either way. Actually, a claiming race might be—"

"I'll deal with it," I say. "We won't have him for long." Now that we're not moving, the cold air's stinging my skin. "I'll call you soon, I promise."

"I'm glad you made it back," Sean says. "But I mean it. Sell him off—even if it's a huge loss. I'll figure things out from our end. That horse is crazy, and I don't want you dealing with him any more."

Obsidian starts to trot toward him, and I yank on his mane as hard as I can. He acts like he can't even feel it.

Sean seems to recognize that he's not safe, and luckily, he begins to jog toward his car.

"Knock it off," I hiss, "or I'll change you right here. Then you can see how Sean feels about you being a man. I wonder who else he might tell."

Obsidian finally stops.

Once Sean's out of sight, I slide down from Obsidian's back. The ground's an awfully long way down, and it hurts when my bare feet hit the already icy gravel. I can't help whimpering.

Obsidian's head whips around so fast, he practically knocks me over. His big, warm mouth nuzzles around, as if he's trying to figure out whether I'm alright. "It just hurt my feet," I say. "And I'm absolutely freezing."

He throws his head toward the barn.

"Oh, I don't think so." I glance around, checking to see whether anyone else is within our circle of visibility. When I don't see a soul, I throw a hand up on his side and shift him.

Then I turn and run for the barn while he reorients from the shift. I'm half-inclined to throw the barn door closed and let him freeze outside while I change, but I end up settling for a head start.

By the time he finally gets upstairs, I'm already changed into the sturdy pants and work boots Sean brought, and Aleks is wearing pants, at least.

His eyes are just as bright in human form as they were as a horse. "You lied."

I shake my head. "I was going to come back later—I never said exactly when. In fact, I was pretty clear that I didn't want you to come."

"You aren't safe with him—"

Fury bubbles up inside of me, and I thrust a pointing

finger right at him, jabbing him in the chest. "You don't get to decide that. You're a crazy, ancient horse-man! You can't even keep yourself safe, much less me."

He freezes then, his bare chest heaving, his mouth dangling open just a bit. His eyes are hurt, and I realize that he hadn't really thought about it from that perspective.

To hear him tell the story, he was a noble of some kind —a prince, he keeps insisting—and he owned quite a lot of property. He had loads of servants and a huge estate with a gigantic mansion. He had power, and he was magical. He had allies and enemies, and he was a fairly scary dude.

Now he's woken up and a hundred years are gone, and his friends are not around—some are dead—and he can't use his magic. He's trapped, really.

Defenseless.

Penniless.

Powerless.

It must hurt.

I actually feel a little bad for rubbing his face in it.

Then he repositions himself slightly, and I realize that after jabbing him with my finger, I didn't drop my hand. I've been doing all this thinking with one hand pressed against his bare chest.

His very muscular, very warm, very naked chest. My hand is trembling when I step away from him. "I'm sorry. I'm not trying to hurt your feelings."

"But you feel safer when I'm *not* around."

"And when I'm not riding bareback through the coun-tryside in the freezing air," I say. "Yes, that's true."

His very full, very expressive lips are pressed into a tight line. His eyes look hard.

"You aren't a prince here," I say softly. "You're just a man, stuck pretending to be a horse until I can extricate you from this mess. I really, really need you to start listening to me."

Even if it means he feels powerless and vulnerable? Because I hate the way he looks right now. I'd almost rather deal with the overbearing, insufferable Aleks than this one, the crushed, defeated one with the shadowed eyes.

"I require more clothing," he says. "All that's left, now that you shredded my other decent shirt yesterday, are ratty, dirty things left by who knows what kind of person who used to live here."

I sigh. "Fine. I'll take you shopping tomorrow night."

"So you don't have another date tomorrow?" He raises his eyebrows.

I'm not sure why that makes my stomach do a flip, but I squash that feeling immediately. "I don't. Sean will be gone for a few days."

His smile reminds me that I can't trust him. "That's good."

"No." I shake my head. "Sean's a good man, and I like seeing him. It's bad that he'll be gone."

"If you say so."

"I do." I drop my phone next to him and race down the stairs so fast that I forget I'm supposed to call Sean until I've reached the house.

"Dad," I call. "I need your phone. Mine is dead."

It's not entirely true, but it's not the biggest lie I've told today, either.

"Thank goodness you're alright. Is Obsidian Devil okay?" Dad's clearly been pacing in here—the carpet has a path worn across it.

"We're both fine. That horse is stupid, but he's healthy."

"Thank goodness for that," Dad says. "I don't know what we'd do if he really disappeared."

I'm not entirely sure he's right. The part of me that thinks Obsidian Devil is a threat to my future is growing a little each day.

❧ 10 ❧

I should have just dropped Aleks off with a fistful of cash.

He probably would have come home with bizarre tweed pants and lace up shirts made for renaissance festivals, but at least he wouldn't keep trying to drag me into the changing room with him.

"It would be so much faster if you'd just stand in here," he says. "It's not like you'll see something you don't see all the time."

The sales lady blushes.

And I want to sink into the plush carpet and die. "Aleks." If I could inject even one more speck of censure into my tone, I would do it. "Stop, please." I switch to Russian. "Or at least use another language when you say such outrageous things."

"Outrageous? Me?" He smiles this time, and I realize he's not clueless.

He's baiting me.

"Your boyfriend is really good looking," the woman says. "You should just go in there. I'll give you some space."

Oh. My. Word. "He's not my boyfriend," I say. "My boyfriend—"

"Don't say Sean's your boyfriend," Aleks says. "Or I'll—"

"You'll what?" I ask. "Just go in the dressing room again and put things on, one at a time. You can make decisions on your own, but if you *insist* on asking my opinion, you can come out, fully dressed, like every normal person on earth does."

"Or I'd be happy to go inside and give you my opinion," the twenty-something sales clerk offers. "I don't have a Sean. . ."

For the love. I open my mouth to tell her to buzz off, when Aleks' laugh shocks us both.

"No, thanks." He slams the door shut, just like that.

I eye the sales clerk. She's young, attractive, and she has a great figure. Why did he laugh? Probably some kind of chauvinistic prince thing that dates back to his hundred-year-old mentality. "Don't let him make you feel bad," I say. "He's really, really old. Way too old for you."

She shrugs. "I kind of like older men." She's still staring at the door. "And he doesn't look very old to me."

Why does every single woman seem to lose her mind around Aleks? He's hot, yes, but is he really *that* hot?

When Aleks opens the door, it hits me. Maybe because I've been thinking about it. Maybe because I'm trying to see him from her perspective. Mine is a little skewed. I mean, sure, I know he's good looking. I thought he was the day he shifted into a man.

But he was such a mess. Muddy. With a bridle on his face. I've never really *looked* at him, like I might if I just saw him on the street.

He's knock-you-to-your-knees, slap-your-mama, weep-and-cry-all-day gorgeous. He's tall. Muscular. And he has a face that would make an angel sob with envy.

And he doesn't so much as spare Miss Low Self-Esteem

a single glance. He stares right at me, and then he spins in a slow circle.

That reminds me that instead of staring at his face, I'm supposed to be evaluating the clothing. His shirt isn't buttoned all the way up, and I'm struggling not to stare at the top of his beautiful chest. You'd think by now I'd be used to it, but no dice. It's just inhumanly perfect.

Golden skin.

Smooth and silky.

Defined muscles everywhere I look.

Even the places I shouldn't be looking.

"What do you think?"

"It's fine," I say, proud of how normal my voice sounds. "Just like everything else has been."

"You said I have how much to spend?" He narrows his eyes.

"I have an employee discount," the sales clerk chirps. "Fifty percent off. I'll let you use it."

I want to groan. I mean, have some self-respect.

Although, when we're checking out, I'm kind of grateful she's so infatuated with him. I mean, I'm the one paying, after all. That fifty percent makes a huge difference. And with the way we seem to be going through clothes. . . So what if she writes her name with a heart over the i? I'll keep Adriana's number handy for the next time we need more clothes.

We walk outside and turn toward the parking lot. "Time to get back," I say. "Because—"

Aleks takes my hand in his, and to say the movement shocks me would be a huge understatement. I glance down at our hands as if I'm staring at an alien.

If aliens made my heart skip a beat. If aliens made me want to slow down and turn toward them. If aliens were warm, and strong, and unbelievably beautiful.

But this isn't okay. I'm supposed to be dating Sean, not fangirling over a crazy old Russian man.

"What are you doing?" I ask, stopping on the sidewalk.

"What do you mean?" He glances around. "I thought you said we had to head back. I was walking to your car."

It's hard, but I stiffen my hand and pull it away. "Why were you holding my hand?" I wiggle my newly freed fingers.

He gestures. "They're all doing it."

I notice two couples, one ahead of us and one who just passed us, both holding hands. "Oh. Well, they're 'together.'"

"We're together." He looks genuinely confused.

"It's something people do when they're *dating*," I say. "I could hold hands with Sean, but not with you."

He blinks. And then he frowns. "But I like it."

Maybe I should get checked out, because my heart is now racing like we're in Liverpool at Aintree, preparing for the Grand National. "That's not the point."

"It's not?"

I sigh. "Just, don't, okay?"

"You have a lot of rules," Aleks says. But he doesn't argue further, and he doesn't take my hand again.

I should not be disappointed by that.

I'm *not* disappointed by that.

"Is it against the rules for us to eat together?" He eyes the pizza place next to us, his nose lifting a bit, sniffing the air.

I doubt he's ever had pizza. I can't help wondering whether he'll like it or hate it. "I guess not," I say.

The beatific smile that spreads across his face almost makes me regret saying yes.

"But we need to hurry."

It turns out that he loves pizza. I should have known. Aleks seems to like almost all food—as a horse, and as a

man. He eats more than any man I've ever seen. But then again, as a horse, he's always moving. His energy is seemingly limitless, and he really should be spending most of his time grazing. Maybe he needs all the extra calories.

Plus, there's no telling how much energy he expends to shift. I picked up a wolf shifter book last night, hoping it might shed some light on this whole thing, but there was a lot more dirty sex and a lot less information about shifting than I expected.

That did not help me focus on what matters, which is not my knowledge that no matter what he's eating, it's not resulting in surplus calories. His body has no extra fat reserves that I've seen, in either form.

Kris. Focus.

"—buy anything for yourself. I'd be happy to stop somewhere else and help you find something you might like."

"I have clothes," I say flatly.

His face falls.

"And you have no idea what's stylish."

"True fashion transcends fads." He sounds utterly confident of that.

I suppose, thinking about what he chose in the store, that makes sense. He picked classic trousers, plain but well-made sweaters, and nicely tailored button-down shirts. They're things that would *almost* have worked a hundred years ago, and they absolutely look amazing on him now.

Though, a cow feed sack would look good on him—I know that from painfully personal experience.

"What I mean is that I don't need more clothing."

"You seemed to need more the other night." He narrows his eyes.

"On my date?" I laugh. "Generally speaking, guys want you to wear *less* on dates, not more."

"I don't care what guys want. You looked cold." He

straightens his shoulders. "I could help you find something flattering that still keeps you warm."

"Duly noted," I say. "But I think I'll pass."

By the time I've paid the check for dinner and we're ready to head home, it's already dark outside. The early sunset thing during the winter gets pretty depressing sometimes.

As I'm climbing into my car, Aleks asks, "Should I drive?"

I almost choke. "Um. No."

"When we went out to eat with Sean, he drove instead of you. It seems to be a cultural standard for the man to drive when a man and a woman go out." He points, and I notice two different cars, with the man driving in one, and climbing into the driver's seat in the other.

"First, you have to have something called a driver's license here. If you don't have one, they can do bad things to you. Seeing as you don't have so much as a photo identification, it's better if you don't drive. Also. You can't drive."

"But I can. I had the nicest car in two provinces. I quite enjoy driving."

"And your car probably topped out at twenty miles an hour," I say. "I think I'll be the one driving, thanks."

He shrugs. "If you insist."

"I really do." The rest of the drive home is rather entertaining, with Aleks asking me a dozen different questions about things he observed while we walked around.

"They really pull their pants down on purpose?" Aleks grimaces. "It's some kind of style?"

"It's not as common here as it is in other places," I say. "But yes, some of the younger kids do. Their underwear becomes part of their fashion. It's not that they can't afford pants that fit." That suggestion makes me laugh again just thinking about it.

I didn't realize how many things he would learn just by

being around people. "Maybe we should go out a little more often."

He perks up at that. "Really? I agree. I think we should go out a lot. Every day, even. We could go out to dinner. We could do more shopping, and—"

"More shopping?" I roll my eyes. "I'm not a *princess*. I'm not made of money. I can't go shopping very often, and certainly not like we did today. You need to take care of these clothes and make them last. Got it?"

He grins. "Understood."

I'm about to turn down the long country road that leads us home when I notice it. My dad's car, parked in front of the tiny clubhouse at the end of the drive.

It's not a bar. It's not a restaurant. It's a small clubhouse, rented out to private parties. Like women's knitting circles.

And gamblers.

My hands stiffen on the steering wheel, but I make a split second decision. I want to stop and march in there right now, but that's not wise. I'll drop Aleks at home and come back. That's the smart thing to do. Nothing good will come of a confrontation with my dad in the middle of a hand of cards with a crazy Russian man in tow.

"What's wrong?" The light and airy banter is gone. Somehow Aleks noticed my mood shift. It's going to be really hard to get rid of him now.

"Nothing," I say, forcing a smile. "Just thinking of where else we might go. Places that won't cost me a fortune." I glance his way. "Maybe a park. People-watching can teach you a lot."

He shakes his head. "No way."

"You don't like to people watch?"

Aleks puts a hand on my arm. "Stop the car, Kris. Right now."

"What?" I glance at him again. "Why would I do that?"

"Something's wrong. You're going to tell me what it is."
His voice is low and compelling.

I find myself pulling off on the shoulder and turning on
my hazard lights.

Why did I listen to him? Am I going crazy?

"What happened?" He's focused entirely on me, his eyes
practically boring into me. "Something back there upset
you, at that dark brick building."

He pays far too close attention. "It's nothing, really.
Don't worry about it."

"You stopped the car. If it was nothing, if I was overre-
acting, you'd have laughed me off."

I hate him.

"What is it?"

I sigh. "My dad has a gambling problem, and he swore
he wouldn't gamble any more, but that's where he goes."

"You saw his car?" He turns, as if he can somehow see
back there in the dark. He spins back around to face me,
clearly frustrated.

I nod.

"You stay here." He opens the car door and starts off
down the road.

"It's a half mile away," I say. "Aleks!"

He keeps walking.

I circle the car, close the door, and get back in. It takes
me thirty seconds to turn around, and by the time I reach
him, he's nearly to the clubhouse. "Stop walking so fast and
listen," I say. "My dad won't care what you say."

"I don't plan to talk to him."

Aleks is almost as unreasonable as my father. "Stop and
listen for a moment."

He does freeze, his broad shoulders turning just enough
that we can see one another's faces. "What?"

"You have no plan here. If you insist on staying with me,
at least wait in the car while I go see him."

He sets his jaw and shakes his head. "Try again."

"Fine. You can come in with me, but don't say anything. Okay?"

He sighs. "Fine."

I throw the car into a parking spot and climb out. My hands are shaking.

"You're upset. You should wait here and let me deal with it," Aleks says.

I shake my head this time. "No, I'll go. He's my dad."

"A lousy father," he mutters.

I don't have the strength to argue with him, or the desire really, but he's the only parent I have. "Just stand behind me, and try to look menacing." I regret using that word almost the second I say it. I wouldn't have described Aleks as menacing.

Until now.

He looks downright terrifying, if I'm being honest. He's never scared me, not as a horse and not as a man. But if I didn't know him? He's hugely tall. He's very Russian looking with his sharp features and black hair. And his eyes are grim. There's no other way to describe him.

The phrase he used that first day comes back to me. *They'll be much easier to destroy if they come to me first.*

To *destroy*.

That's not a normal thing to say, but it feels like it fits, in this moment. And I won't lie to myself and pretend I don't want someone scary at my back.

I've always hated that Dad gambles, but it wasn't until I was an adult that I realized how much it wrecks our lives. After losing so much—almost everything—why would he come here? He promised me not to gamble any more, and I'm already turning my life inside out to try and fix his mistake. But even so, I know the answer.

Gamblers think they're always just one hand away from

fixing everything. That's what gets them into the situation to begin with.

I'm angry.

And I'm scared.

The worst people in Daugavpils are likely to be inside. I inhale and exhale slowly, and then I grab the doorknob and yank.

Nothing happens.

Because it's locked tight.

Of course they wouldn't just leave it open. I'm an idiot.

But then Aleks is there, one hand removing mine from the door, and his other giant hand tightening on the knob.

"It's locked," I say.

The knob flies off, as if it was made of aluminum foil and not stainless steel. I splutter a bit—I can't help it.

"You wanted to go inside?"

A normal person can't do that. How could he yank that off? But there's no time to ask questions. The noise of the door being busted open attracts some attention.

And I realize, a little late, that my dad wasn't here to gamble. He wasn't here to break his promise to me. No, he was definitely brought here against his will. His car may have been driven here and parked outside, but I doubt he did that himself, either.

Because he's tied to a chair, clearly getting the crap beaten out of him.

And we've just walked into a very large gathering of men who are apparently quite angry at my father. I fumble for my phone, but the man who's closest to me knocks it away, and my entire purse along with it. They fly out of my hands and onto the floor.

The contents of my purse scatter outward, flying across the dirty tile at strange angles. My lip gloss spins toward the wall. A tampon lands right in front of the angry man who caused the mess. A hair tie flies into the air and lands

at my dad's feet. A handful of change clatters and chimes as it lands all over the floor around the group of men. A parking ticket I couldn't find for the life of me last week flutters to my feet.

And I count eight strange men in the room.

That's the only useful thing my brain was doing while I watched my personal effects spill out everywhere. Counting the number of men who are gathered around, the men whose plans we just interrupted. Eight men against me and one crazy old Russian guy.

The odds aren't very good.

The one useful thing in my purse other than my phone, which is underneath a chair three feet away, was a can of mace. And that spun across the floor and stopped in front of the boot of the tallest, scariest looking guy in the room.

"What's a little girl doing here?" the big man asks. "This is a meeting of men."

"She brought me," Aleks says.

He doesn't sound scared. I turn enough to see him. He doesn't *look* scared either. So either he's crazy, or he knows something I don't. Are the police coming? Does he have a death wish?

Maybe he's immune to bullets?

Then again, his mysterious earth powers are MIA, so I doubt that, even if he *was* immune to bullets, that's going to help us much.

Not that these guys look like they use guns. The big guy's brandishing a really long, really nasty looking dagger. He looks like he likes to slice things.

I hate those guys the worst.

Be honest and fight someone, or have the decency to end things quickly with a gun, right? What kind of person carves on another human with a blade for fun?

A sick one.

"Just let my dad go, and we'll all walk out of here," I say. "No reason to call the police or get nasty."

The big man laughs, but it's an ugly sound, like a pig with bronchitis. "No reason to call the cops. We agree."

"I doubt they'd like this, though." I point at my dad. "I get why you'd want to remind him, if he owes you money, but I think he's motivated."

"I'm past reminding," the big man says. "I'm really ticked off, actually."

"But he can't pay you back if he's dead," I say. "And neither can I."

"You are?" the big man asks.

"I'm his daughter, and I own a business. I'm a vet," I say. "I can make enough to repay you. How much does he owe?" I tamp down on my anger with my dad. Being mad at him won't help us, not right now. But I can channel it like I always do, to brace myself and hopefully survive this.

"You can't come up with sixty thousand euros," he says. "If you could have, he'd already have gotten it to me."

If I wasn't surrounded by terrifying men, who are all slowly moving closer, I'd close my eyes and whimper. Sixty thousand? Really? Maybe I should let them carve him up a little. "Actually, hand me the knife," I say. "I'll help."

The big man laughs, but he's also shaking his head. "I'm sorry, but your dad has exhausted his extensions. I have a reputation to uphold."

"That reputation is predicated on killing women?" Aleks sneers. "And old men?"

The big man's attention shifts away from me and my dad and falls squarely on the other alpha male in the room.

"Aleks, just leave. This isn't your problem."

The last thing I should be doing is dragging Aleksandr into this. He's had bad enough luck. My dad's gambling has nothing to do with him. And Aleks is right. Will they really kill me, too?

I doubt it.

If Aleks runs, maybe he can call the police. How can I send him that message without explicitly saying it?

"Just go." I say again. "It's not like you'd *call the authorities*. You're not the kind of person who would dial one-one-two." I glare at him and widen my eyes, tossing my head at the door.

"Oh, I don't think so," the big guy says. "You can't leave. Sorry. It's definitely your business now."

Instead of swearing, or muttering, or shaking like a normal person, Aleks smiles. "I'm glad to hear you say that."

Before I have time to argue, Aleks springs across the room and punches the guy.

In the throat.

The huge man collapses like a house of cards slammed by a toddler.

And the other men all start toward him, finally realizing the threat he poses. I can't do much to keep him alive, but I can tackle the guy closest to me. So I do, leaping on his back like a crazed monkey, scratching at his eyes and face.

Biting his ear.

That pisses him off royally, and he's reaching back around frantically when another guy grabs me and shakes me like a terrier shaking a rat. My teeth rattle. I'm convinced I can hear my brain squishing around in my skull.

I definitely see stars.

Not the good kind.

I cry out in pain. I'm not proud of it, but it's a fact.

Aleks hears me—somehow, in spite of the fact he's fighting like five guys. And he roars. He shoves people off him, and he throws someone through a window, and then he's here, his hands moving in something very near a blur, and he's the one grabbing me, and pulling me to his chest.

A force like static electricity rises up inside of me then, and a feeling like a bubble's bursting accompanies it, and then Aleks screams. The shout I called a roar before was like the bleating of a sheep compared to the howling of a wolf.

It's so loud that several of the men cover their ears.

And then the ground opens up. . .and they disappear.

I wish I could think of another way to explain it.

The literal floor in the crummy little clubhouse rips open, the earth splitting with terrifying creaks and cracks, and the men tumble into gaping, black holes.

They're just gone.

This time, Aleks' smile is positively satisfied. "It's back," he says. "My power's finally back."

"Please tell me those men aren't all dead," I rasp.

Aleks shrugs. "Who cares? They're terrible people. And who will ever find them again?"

I thought I was shaking before, but this time? I'm practically convulsing. "They can't be dead," I say. "You have to —" I splutter. "You can't kill them." My eyes are wide, my tone frantic. "Aleksandr, please listen to me. You can't murder people, not now. Not anymore."

His perfect, appallingly beautiful brow furrows. "But they were going to kill your dad." He points. "Remember?"

My dad's slumped in the chair, entirely unconscious. One eye's swollen to the size of an orange. The skin is a very dark brown, purple, and greenish orange. His lip's swollen and still bleeding profusely from a gash near the bottom left. His arm looks broken. And he's covered with bruises and cuts.

"They threatened you," Aleks says.

"We aren't like them," I say.

He chuckles. "We should be worse, don't you think? The only thing that scares roaches is a bigger threat. We have to be lions."

"I'm not sure that's right," I say.

"Kris." This time, it's Aleks' voice that's trembling. "They were going to kill you. I can't allow——"

I stand up, forcing every ounce of confidence I possess into my voice. "You have to bring them back up to the surface," I say. "Before they're dead."

Aleks meets my gaze, searching my face for something. "You're serious."

"I am." I nod. "Really, really serious."

He huffs. "Fine." He turns his hands, palms up.

Only, nothing happens.

"Why. . ." He swallows slowly and inhales, and then he crouches down low and presses his hands against the now *very* dirty, very broken up, floor. And still, nothing happens.

Aleks must have been listening every time I swore and saving all those new words for this. Latvian. English. Russian. It's a really impressive mix.

If eight men weren't currently suffocating underground, buried alive, I'd probably be impressed.

"Think back. How did you make it happen before?"

"I have no idea." He shakes his head. "The same way I always do."

"Did it feel like. . .like static electricity? Like a bubble popping?"

He turns toward me slowly, his eyes widening. "Yes. It did." He blinks. "How do you know that?" He steps toward me, his eyes utterly intent.

"Well, I, I mean. I guess——"

Before I can sound any dumber, his hand finds my arm, his fingers curling around my wrist. "I think I need you in order to use my magic."

As he says the words, I feel it again. The static buzz and then the popping sensation.

The ground erupts, belching the men outward, spewing them upward, and then leaving them sprawling and

134

crawling across the floor. Most of them are heaving, retching, groaning, coughing, and cursing.

One of them is utterly motionless.

The big man he hit in the throat.

But we don't have time to deal with that. Not now that they're all back. I drag Aleks across toward where my dad's still tied. "Can you get him free?"

Aleks flicks two fingers and the ropes fall off.

"Wait, how—"

"I can explain later," he says. "For now, I think we should go."

He's right.

I try to lift my dad, but it's hopeless. He's not a huge man, but I'm a tiny woman.

Of course Aleks scoops him up like he's a rag doll and carries him easily. "Keep up," he barks.

I do.

I'm nearly through the door when one of the men notices us. "You can't leave. We know where you live."

Aleks freezes, and spins on his heel. His smile is absolutely terrifying when he says, "I know you on a molecular level now." He tilts his head slightly. "You're *only* alive because *she* begged for your life. If you touch her, or her despicable father, or if you even think about touching them, I'll bury you so deep that no one will ever find your corpse again. And then I'll do the same thing to your family, your friends, and everyone who shows up at your funeral. Am I clear?"

The light isn't great, but it's good enough for me to see when the man wets his pants.

Aleks takes that as a yes.

When we reach the parking lot, I realize that we have my car and my dad's.

"Aleks," I say.

He turns to face me.

"How'd you like to drive?"

He's silent. "I think you should let me drive you home."

"I was thinking you could bring my dad's car."

"I'll come back for it."

"The farm's three miles away," I say.

He shrugs. "I'll come back for it."

I don't argue with him. I'm too tired.

He drives us home, quite well, actually. He picks my dad up carefully from the back seat and carries him inside. Then he turns to me quietly, and says, "Can you come closer?"

I take two steps until we're only inches away, and he places his hand on my shoulder. "I need your permission for this."

"For what?"

"I can heal your dad, if you want me to."

"Heal him?" The hope in my voice is absurd.

"He's badly injured, and when he wakes up, he'll know just how badly. My earth powers let me heal things—not entirely, but they can speed things along quite a bit." His eyes meet mine. "You get angry about things, though, and I want to make sure you're alright with it."

"Is there a cost?"

His smile's sad. "There's always a cost, but this time, the cost is something I can pay."

"What does that mean?"

"It just wears me out," he says. "It's alright, I swear. I recover quickly."

I study his face for a moment, sussing out whether his words are truthful. It feels like they are, but I'm tired, and I want to believe him. "Do it."

Another slight swell of energy, much smaller, and then the same popping sensation, and my dad gasps.

"He'll sleep through the night," Aleks whispers. "And wake up exhausted in the morning."

"Another cost?" I lift my eyebrows.

He shrugs. "That's just the nature of healing, but I guess you could say that."

I notice his arm isn't crooked, and the swelling in his eye's almost gone. It's still purple, but much less angry than before. "Thank you."

He bobs his head a bit, and disappears.

I shift my dad a little, then I use a rag to clean him off as well as I can on the sofa. I'm just finishing up when I hear an engine growling outside. My heart races, but it's Aleks. In my dad's car.

True to his word, he must have jogged the three miles back to collect it. That's when it occurs to me. . .without me there, if the men had gone after him, he'd have been powerless.

I race to the door.

But he looks perfectly fine. And he's carrying my purse. "I thought you'd want your phone and your other things. I can't say I got every single item, but I got everything I could still find."

It's a miracle he could find anything at all, after the floors opened up and spewed dirt and bodies out all over. "Thank you."

He doesn't touch me—I'm careful to take the bag without even so much as our fingers brushing—but somehow, having him here makes me feel better.

Safer.

"I'll head for the barn."

He doesn't even ask for my phone. I think that's what does it. Ever since we saw my dad's car, he's been perfect. It's been all about Aleks helping me. He hasn't argued. He hasn't complained. He hasn't done anything but support and help and heal.

And almost kill eight men.

He probably did kill one.

But they were bad people. If the police come looking for us, I guess we'll cross that road when we get there. I really hope it doesn't come to that. "Can you stay?"

He freezes.

"In the house, I mean?" I ask. My voice sounds small to me, for some reason. Nervous, maybe? "Sean's going out of town. I'm not sure when or if he's even here, and I thought maybe—"

"I'll stay."

He doesn't say anything else. He helps me move my dad to his room, and when I go, he follows me upstairs, but he doesn't try to come into my room. "Your brother's room is there, right?" He points.

I nod.

"I'll be in there. Shout if you need me."

Somehow, knowing he's there, I'm able to shower and go right to sleep.

12

I was worried the police might show up. Or worse, an even bigger group of gangsters. No matter what powers Aleks has, at some point there'll be too many people for him to handle.

Or he'll be exposed.

I'm not sure which would be worse. Either way, I can't have him killing people to protect my dad and me. That's really, really not his problem. I told him not to destroy people, and then he had to do it to keep me safe.

One thing I completely did *not* expect was to have a man in black trousers and a white shirt with a delivery logo on his lapel appear first thing the next morning, brandishing a letter.

"You've been served." He hands me a letter in a big brown envelope.

It's a lawsuit, against my dad, for sixty thousand euros and a lot of interest. Apparently the thugs also know a few lawyers. I'm not entirely sure that Dad's hastily scrawled IOU would be admissible in court, but it would cost money we don't even have to try and fight it.

And I know he owes the money.

What I don't know is how many other debts are going to keep coming my way. Dad can't seem to stop, and I can't live the rest of my life fighting off his creditors. If he can't keep away from gambling now, when will he ever?

Which means that, even with Sean's help, even if we win a bunch of races, it won't do any good. It's just a matter of time. I'm like a hamster in a wheel, running my fastest to try and save a farm that's doomed simply because it's in his name.

I think about what Aleks told me the very same day I found out he was a man, not a horse. He said that sometimes people have to sacrifice things they want for things they need. It hits me then, what I have to do. I want the farm. I've always wanted it. It brings me joy, it makes me feel safe, and it has been our family's legacy for countless generations.

But I *need* to be safe. I *need* to know that when I wake up in the morning, there won't be yet another axe poised above my neck. I *need* to take hold of my future myself.

And to do that, sacrifices must be made.

When my dad finally wakes up, I tell him my conclusion. "We have to sell Liepašeta."

His eyes widen and he straightens up, groaning. He rubs his eyes. "What are you talking about?"

"Do you not remember anything about last night?" I frown. I assumed that Aleks healing him meant that. . .but what if the beating damaged his brain? Is that even something Aleks could heal? I should have taken Dad to the hospital.

"I was sure they broke my arm," Dad says. He stretches and swivels his arm around and around at the shoulder. "I was hoping it was a dream."

"Dad," I say. "It wasn't a dream. It was a *nightmare*. You can't stop."

He doesn't ask me what I'm talking about. He doesn't

even try to defend himself, but I'm just as angry as if he did try.

I shove the paper at him. "They're suing you, but only because I stopped them from *killing* you last night."

He blinks repeatedly. "You what?"

"I saw your car," I say. "I thought you were gambling in there. You're lucky I had Aleks with me, or I'd have probably died along with you."

I've never seen my dad look as crushed as he does in that moment. I'm so angry that I don't even care. I have zero pity for him in this moment.

"I know Mom said it's like a disease. I know she said you can't help yourself." I shake my head. "I don't care. I can't deal with it anymore." Tears well up in my eyes and my throat closes off. I need to say the words, but I can't force them out.

"I'll get help," he says. "They have programs—"

I shake my head. "It's too late for that. We have to sell the farm," I say. "I'll take my half of whatever's left and buy a new place, but only in my name. Your creditors will take your half. I don't know where you'll live or what you'll do, and Dad? I don't actually care. For the first time since I turned eighteen, you won't be my problem anymore."

"You can't—"

"But I can," I say. "Mom saw to that when she left me her entire share of the farm, and because her parents had to finance the whole thing more than once, she owned fifty-one percent. Which means, as much as I hate to do it, I can force the sale."

Even saying the words feels like a betrayal. I don't mind betraying Dad—he's clearly had no problems betraying me—but Mom left her share to me so that I could keep the farm safe. She may not have been born to the Liepa family, but I think she loved the land more than Dad.

I wanted to leave it to my children.

But I may never have any if I stay on this path. It's time to change something. Before I can chicken out, I pick up the phone and call a realtor.

I barely have time to meet with both clients I had scheduled for the morning, ride Five, and ride Obsidian, before it's time to meet the agent. She's a friend of Mirdza's, and she's way less perky than I expected. Actually, she looks downright deadpan as we walk the property.

"You don't want to sell the house?" She frowns. "Just all this land?"

"I mean, I *can* sell the house if we have to," I say. "I know it's all one piece of property right now, but ideally, I'd like to split it out."

"That's a separate legal process," Anete says. "And it takes some time to do." She spins in a circle. "And with the way the property is set up, with the road where it is, and the driveways, the only thing that makes sense is splitting it here." She points.

"But that means I'd have to sell the stables." The thought of that hurts.

She explains her reasoning for a while longer, showing me the plat lines, and I can't really disagree.

"With the living areas, we can actually call the barn a residence. Or a business. Either one. It should make it a much more attractive prospect. Plus, you'd still have that other barn." She points at the ramshackle old barn.

"It only has twelve stalls," I say. And there's no way all our grooms would be able to stay in the miserable apartment upstairs.

I guess we wouldn't need them if we pared down to just twelve horses. In Latvia, you really need one stall per horse, because sometimes the weather is just awful.

"Here's the thing." I stop walking. "I grew up here, and for generations before me, Liepas have owned this land." I get a little choked up just thinking about it. "I'm not

talking about selling it lightly. I know it might be a process, to separate the house from the rest of the acreage. But the acreage is substantial, it's close to the second largest city in Latvia, and it's beautiful. I have no doubt someone will want it."

"I'm sure you're right." Her half smile's actually the friendliest thing I've seen from her. "But you need to know that it's a lot of work for me, to set up the split process, to help shepherd it through. I'll have to plead my case to the housing officials and the land committee. I won't do it unless you'll agree to the location I chose, and I really don't want to do all that, working on commission, and then not sell the land. You seem unsure, and that makes me nervous."

In that moment, I think about what I'm doing. I'd be making my dad sign off on splitting the property. Our ancestral land. And then I'd be putting the home and the old barn with nine acres or so of pastures in my name, and letting a stranger come in and buy the land all around us.

Liepašeta.

It breaks my heart.

But it's the only way to keep it safe—and at least we'll still have the house and the old barn. Plenty of people have just a handful of acres for their horses. So I have to pare things down a bit. Mirdza will be upset, because I won't be able to keep letting her teach lessons to the local kids. I'll have to adjust my future plans, but at least without a farm to keep offering as collateral, my dad won't be able to keep putting my life in jeopardy.

"I'm not going to be wishy-washy. Let's get it split. Transferred." I sigh. "And sold."

Her car's pulling away when stupid freaking Obsidian Devil hops the fence and comes running over. He tosses his head her direction and then stares at me expectantly. Obviously he wants to know who she is.

"I'm selling the farm." I sound more depressed than I meant to, but it's not like he'll care. "I can't keep letting Dad gamble, and if he doesn't own the farm anymore, he won't have anything to offer. I need everyone he knows to hear that he's broke."

The huge black demon horse leans his head against my shoulder. It's a gesture of comfort, and I take it, leaning right back against him. If a tear rolls down my cheek, well. I swipe it away immediately.

And then he stamps and paws the ground. It almost looks like he's pushing rocks at me, but I don't have the bandwidth to deal with it right now, so I ignore him.

"Your stupid horse is loose again," John says, eying Obsidian anxiously and a little aggressively. "How does he keep getting out?"

I smirk. "You were worried about me clearing five feet, remember? He cleared a seven-foot fence to get here."

John frowns. "No way. On his own? Without a rider encouraging him?"

I shrug. I don't really care whether he believes it. "What's up?"

"Are you selling up?"

"Yes."

"Will I still have a job?"

"Unless even more debts come out? Yes. I plan to fix up the old barn and keep it and the house."

He nods. "But just twelve stalls."

I think about the configuration. "If we add a lean-to on the side, we could add two or three more. And we'll have all the pastures on the east side."

"Sounds painful. We'll be down to, what? One groom?"

I sigh.

"You're too good for a father like that," John says. "I've stuck around for you, you know."

"We'd have crumbled way back if you'd left."

He chuckles. "You'd have figured something out. I know you've been floating my salary from your vet practice most months. But we finally have a winner."

I grunt. He has no idea Obsidian can understand him, or he'd never compliment him like that.

"You're racing in the King George?"

"I should," I say. "It's the last chance for real money before the end of the year, and a new balloon payment's due January one."

"I thought you had an extension—" He cuts off. "Isn't that why you're seeing that pompous—"

"Sean isn't pompous," I say. "He's a very good man, but all we've taken so far was a note for the extra money we needed to pay that first note. If we sell the property soon, and if we can scrounge up enough for the January payment, I'd rather not ask for more."

"Because you like him." John's voice is quiet.

Why couldn't he have been my dad? He's hard working. He's smart. He cares about me. I trust him. And he pays attention. "I'd like to argue with you, but you're right. The more he does, the harder it is for me to separate whether I feel gratitude or whether I really like him."

"That horse is the strangest creature I've ever seen." John's staring at Obsidian.

And I realize how unnaturally quiet he's been.

Because he's been listening.

None of this conversation is any of his business. I mean, he did agree to help me out until we've repaid the money I spent on saving him, but it's not like I'm going to make an actual person race or anything. I just need him to hold tight until I can earn the money to pay off the note to Sean's bank.

"If we can win some money at the King George, and if we can shave off the land and sell it. . ." I can't help wincing at that thought. "Then I'll pay the current balloon note off

entirely, repay Sean for the bridge loan we got, and I'll be in the clear."

"So I should go ahead and enroll him?"

I sigh. "I'm not sure." What excuse can I make to get out of racing him? "Who else is running? Do we know yet?"

"Five's ready," John says. "No matter who else is running."

Five? I assumed he meant Obsidian. I should have known John didn't want me to race on the crazy horse who just broke out of his pasture to come eavesdrop on my conversation. "Okay. Sign him up."

Obsidian whinnies loudly and then snorts.

John's staring at him in a very strange way. "I can see why you're always talking to him like he understands you. It's almost like he knows we just said we're enrolling Five Times Fast, and *he* wants to race instead."

And now, as if he *wants* John to figure out the truth, he tosses his head and stomps. Then he neighs again.

"He's clearly not ready," I say. "He's a wildcard, and I'm not like my dad. I don't bet on wildcards."

Obsidian makes a whuffling sound.

"Did you know," John says, "that your boyfriend has called me three times to make sure you're not racing on this lunatic? He's worried about you."

Obsidian takes issue with that, and begins pushing me toward the old barn with his nose.

"You can't herd me." I swat at him.

"It's not anywhere near dinnertime," John says. "What's he doing that for? It's almost like he jumped the fence and came over here to get you. But for what? Horses don't *do* that kind of thing."

"Who knows?" I ask. "You know what? Go ahead and sign Five up for the race."

Obsidian neighs again, even louder this time.

"Are you sure?" John asks.

I laugh. "He wants a lot of things he can't have."

"You must be kidding. You give him whatever he wants." John almost looks. . .jealous.

"Do you really hate him?" I tilt my head.

"Why do you let him push you around? You know horses are pack animals. The more you let him get away with, the worse he'll be. He thinks he's either the top of the herd, or you are, and you keep letting him best you. It's dangerous."

Obsidian bends his head toward the ground like he's about to graze, but instead he picks up one of the rocks he was pawing at with his teeth. He lifts his head and bumps my hand.

And then he drops a rock onto my palm.

It's pretty—a strange greenish color. But what the heck do I need a rock for? Is he trying to look even more insane to John? "Um. Thanks?" I tuck it in my pocket, hoping John won't ask. I have no idea what I'd tell him. A horse is handing me rocks, now?

Obsidian rubs his big, gorgeous black head against my arm, like a cat might do when it's happy. Or when it's marking its person.

"I've been training horses for my entire life," John says. "Mostly they're predictable, but sometimes they surprise me. But in more than sixty years, I've never encountered one that strange."

"Which is why I can't treat him like all the others."

"You want to race him at the King George."

I sigh. "I do. I'll admit it. But I feel like this is Five's year, and if we keep Obsidian out of the way, he can probably win it. He's predictable, willing, talented, and he doesn't scare me or anyone else."

"You could have Finn ride Obsidian again," John says.

Obsidian's nostrils flare and he coughs. Horses don't sound good when they cough.

Even John can tell that he's expressing his unhappiness with that idea. "I swear, I thought you were nuts at first, but he does act like he can understand us." He shakes his head. "It's. . .uncanny."

"I could ride him, and Finn could ride Five."

"It would be like a reversal of Down Royal." John harrumphs. "I suppose so. Should I call him and register them both?"

"If Finn agrees, sure. Let's see what happens when we both ride all out."

A few minutes around Obsidian—not behaving like a total nutjob—and John's ready to let me ride him? Interesting. As we walk back to the old barn, the grooms we pass now so accustomed to seeing Obsidian without a halter that they don't even react, I think about why he came over in the first place.

"I'm selling the land," I say. "I know you overheard and already know."

He snorts.

"I'm sure that's your way of saying I shouldn't do it, but I can't keep bailing my dad out. The only way I can make myself safe is to stop giving him rope to hang me with. We'll have to sell our family land—" I just can't seem to say that without choking up.

Without anyone to be brave for, this time, choking up turns into full-blown tears.

Obsidian isn't acting like a lunatic now. He's utterly still, his big horsey head pressing against my face. His huge, velvety soft lips nuzzle my cheek, and he sighs.

"I know—I'll stop. I'm sorry. It's just that." I hiccup. "My mom and I love this farm way more than my dad ever did. My mom wasn't even born to this family, but she loved it. The legacy. The history. The security of having land all around us."

Obsidian bumps my chin with his nose.

"I have to sell it, though. As long as my dad owns half of it, as long as I keep paying his debts off, he'll just keep gambling. If it has to go anyway, we may as well use the sale to pay for the big mistake he already made." I slap my forehead. "Two. Remember those guys from last night? They're suing us now, for the sixty grand. Dad signed some IOU paper, I guess."

I start for the old barn again, and Obsidian keeps up.

It's kind of strange having a conversation with someone who can't speak. But it's also sort of cathartic. Without being able to talk, he can't argue with me. He presses his head to my side again, and then paws at the ground.

"What?" I'm annoyed now. Why's he pawing so much today? When I follow the motion to what he's pawing at, it's more rocks. For the love. "Stop that."

He bends down again and picks them up, dropping two or three in my hand. They're nice-looking crystals, but since when do horses collect rocks? "Yeah, thanks."

I can only deal with one crazy thing at once, thank you very much. I drop them in my now very dirty pocket.

"Look, I know you want to help, and that's why you keep handing me rocks or whatever. But I'm not someone who knows anything about rocks or how to sell them. I know one thing—horses. So the best thing you can do is run your best at the King George." I stop right in front of the barn doors. "That *is* what you were saying, right? You want to race with me?"

Head bob.

"That would be great, if we can win. It's right around a hundred and fifty just for the first place purse. Then, of course, if we bet and win. . ." I think about Obsidian leaving, and I know he has to, but the thought makes me really sad. "We'd be more than halfway there—to you helping me win back what I spent on you." If I bet a decent amount, with two to one odds, I could get the other hundred grand.

Obsidian—er, Aleks—could leave on December twenty-seventh. That's really soon.

"If we're doing that chase in a few weeks," I say, "we need to get you in top shape. That means training every day, almost."

And we really need to figure out how to break this dumb curse so he doesn't need me around.

But I'm afraid by the time we do, I'll be the one who needs him. . .and I'll be out of luck. So I'm relieved when an urgent farm call comes in and I have an excuse to leave. "I'll change you later," I promise.

By then, I'll have some excuse to dart away. Because spending time with Aleks is only going to make it harder when he leaves.

❧ 13 ❧

For all her warnings and complaints, Anete's lawyer gets our property split in under two weeks. The notice that the house and the old barn and nearly ten acres of pasture have been separated from the other nearly two thousand acres arrives ten days before Christmas.

"You're really going to put it on the market?" Sean asks.

He drove up just as I was checking the mail. I had mentioned my plan, but I don't think he really thought I'd go through with it. "I am."

As if she could hear me, Anete messages me. LAWYER CALLED. HE SAID PAPERS ARE DONE. HIS COUSIN RUNS THE STAMPS OFFICE.

Well, that's kind of gross, but it's handy too, I guess. No wonder he did it fast. The next letter in the stack is the lawyer's bill. Of course.

I TOOK PHOTOS LAST WEEK. ARE YOU READY FOR ME TO LIST IT?

"Actually," I say. "The listing's about to go live."

"Whoa," Sean says. "Are you serious?"

"The holdup on the land transfer was the bank,

approving the note split, which they miraculously didn't contest, probably because they can now foreclose on both properties, and they'd be easier to sell this way. And of course, the government moves notoriously slowly, unless you know someone."

"Which it appears you do."

"Well, my lawyer did," I say. "I guess that's the same thing."

"You're sure you want to do this?" Sean's brow furrows. "You don't have to. I'll refinance the entire note—heck, I'll refinance it, and then if you give me a few months of token payments I can just write it off."

As appealing as it would be to wave a magic wand and make Dad's debt disappear, that's not how things work. Or, it's not how things *should* work. You can't just erase the bad things that happen and assume nothing will change.

Things always change, and I want to pay the price I *know*. Money's always cheaper than intangibles.

"I really appreciate the offer," I say. "But I think this is the only path that makes sense."

Sean frowns, which only makes his classic good looks more striking. He really should have posed for professional photos at some point. I'd call his look Business Mogul Meets Cologne Ad Model.

Of course, it's always the people who don't need money at all that are gifted with the looks that could pay the bills. The rest of us who would *love* to be paid to smile are out of luck. No one wants to photograph my snaggle tooth and unruly hair.

"If you change your mind. . ."

Sean has been the perfect man to date since showing up out of the blue. Almost too perfect. He's not overbearing or demanding. He comes whenever I have time. Other than business trips back to England—hardly avoidable since he

lives and runs a bank there—he's been very attentive as well.

It's literally everything I wanted—ten years ago.

Once, when I was young, I remember telling my mom what I wanted for my birthday. "A cake, and a bowl of ice cream. A pudding. And a box of candy. And a soda."

"Oh," she said with a broad smile. "You want a stomachache for your birthday."

I rolled my eyes and shook my head. I knew what I wanted, and her warnings wouldn't change it. I never did get the mountainous pile of refined sugar I wanted, and I complained about it pretty often. But now that I'm looking back, I wonder what would have happened if I had gotten it.

Because in college, if you asked me to tell you what my utmost dreams of the future were, I'd have described just what I have right now. An attentive man who's not embarrassed of me. Someone who supports me but never tells me what to do. Someone who's present and communicates about his schedule to make sure he's around when I need him, but who also takes care of his work and personal matters in a reliable way. He even has a title and social clout.

It's a pile of very refined sugar. Very, very refined, indeed.

Obsidian must have noticed the car, because he comes racing toward us so fast that his tail lifts straight up in the back, like the top arch of a rainbow, or the spray of water that shoots out of the hose when you first turn it on.

Unlike Sean, Aleks gives me no space. He doesn't respect the things I say. He shoves himself into every situation he feels might be dangerous, alarming, or even somewhat interesting. Whether he's a horse or a human, he's overbearing, interfering, and irritating.

And whenever he's not nearby, it feels like something's missing.

I hate that it's true, so the second the thought pops into my brain, I tear it to shreds, stomp on it, and light it on fire.

Obsidian's a half dozen feet away when Sean shrieks and hops to the side. I don't bother moving. I know he'll stop before running me over.

And he does. A few inches away, he slides in a dirt-spray-inducing stop, just in time. His head slams into my shoulder, but not hard enough to sting.

"Graceful, your royal highness," I say. "What in the world is going through that beefy brain of yours?"

"How does he keep getting out?" Sean asks. "You need better fences."

I shrug. "We stopped locking him into stalls or pastures last week. It's a waste of time and energy."

"So he just roams around like a stray dog?" Sean looks both alarmed and confused. "A quarter of a million dollar horse just. . .free ranges?"

"It seemed better than having him pull a ligament or snap a tendon trying to leap the seven-foot stallion fence again."

"Buying him was the worst mistake of your life," Sean says.

"Really?" I lift my eyebrows. "For a decade, I've thought it was dating you."

Obsidian starts to whuffle and cough, and I swear it sounds like the closest thing I've ever heard to a horse laughing.

"What's wrong with him?" Sean's a master of avoidance. I swear, he could change the subject while talking to the king himself. Instead of addressing my old hurt feelings, he'd rather talk about the elephant—er—black, human-like stallion in the room.

"Don't get me started." I glare at Obsidian and point, for all the world, just like I would with a dog. "You need to go back to your pasture. Now, please. I'm not going to tell you again."

He just tosses his gorgeous black head, his mane shining like a waterfall in full sun.

"That worked well," Sean says. "But at least he doesn't seem to be a threat to you, though God knows why not. He scares everyone else half to death."

"We did have a groom quit last week," I say. "He couldn't handle our free range stallion." I don't mention that it made my life easier. I'll have to figure out how to let three more go when we sell the land.

"I'm surprised he's not bothering the mares," Sean says.

Obsidian makes a choking sound, like he inhaled a carrot without chewing it well enough first.

"It's winter," I say. "None of them are in heat."

"Duh, sorry." For someone who's spent his life around horses off and on, Sean sure says dumb things sometimes.

It's not like I can really explain that Obsidian wouldn't have much interest in mares. That would sound even crazier than telling John I think the stallion understands me when I ask him questions.

I start to walk toward the pasture, hoping that once we reach it, Obsidian will stay put and not try to trail us on another date. "Where did you want to go for dinner?"

"Do you have time to get away? I know the King George hunt is. . .what?" He starts to count on his fingers, ticking off the days. "Less than ten days, right?"

"I think Five Times Fast and Obsidian Devil are both ready to run. I'm just bummed we'll have to drive on Christmas Eve and arrive on Christmas Day just to run on the 26th. Even if we leave a day early, I'll still be stuck spending Christmas in a hotel."

"Actually." Sean pulls something out of his pocket. "We

have seen one another a lot lately, but it seems like something's always getting in the way." He extends his hand, holding out an envelope. "I talked to your dad and to John. They said they can haul the horses." The look on his face is almost sly.

I take the papers, staring at them in confusion. "Haul the horses?" I'm not following.

"Fly out early and spend Christmas with me. Kempton Park is close to my estate, as you know, and—"

My brain goes blank. He's asking me to come *home* with him. In the eighteen months we dated, he never once took me home. I was the girl he was mildly embarrassed to be dating. The Latvian girl. The horse-obsessed breeder who raced her own horses.

Jockeys don't fraternize with owners.

They certainly don't fraternize with British nobility.

Especially the ones who own banks.

I've always known that, but now it feels like something has changed.

"Dad got sick," Sean reminds me. "It shouldn't have taken something like that for them to realize their priorities were wrong, but they want to meet you now. Truly."

His parents.

They want to meet me.

I'd be welcome at his fabulous estate as a guest. Or, that's what he's saying. In my wildest dreams, I never imagined this day would come, but here we are.

"Kristiana." Sean steps closer and reaches for my hand with his right, gently lifting my chin with his left. "You are what I want—you've always been what I want." His head drops toward mine.

In all the time we've spent together since he came back into my life, somehow we still haven't kissed. How have we not kissed?

At first, things kept interfering, but then as it went

longer and longer, it felt like the kiss had to be epic. Like, throw all the papers and the lamp off a desk, hurl me on top of it, and kiss the life out of me.

Or put on fabulous dresses, attend a ball, and dip me for all to see. Then plant one on me.

But in this moment, I realize that a kiss isn't about the perfect moment. It's about the perfect person. The one who makes your heart flutter. The one who will keep you safe no matter what. Sean's head lowers slowly toward mine.

Until Obsidian snorts and shoves him sideways.

Sean falls face first into the dirt. He flies back to his feet, eyes flashing, fists clenched. "I'm going to kill that horse."

"He's a horse, Sean."

"I hate him, Kris. I really, really hate him."

Obsidian, always as obnoxious as possible, leans toward me and starts to nuzzle my jaw. Then my neck. I shove him off. "Knock it off already."

Sean looks ready to pull out a revolver and challenge Obsidian Devil to a duel at dawn. But the never-ridiculous Sean brushes off his impeccably tailored clothing and straightens. "So, how about it? Ditch the horses with the guys and come with me."

Before I can even say a word, Obsidian grabs the tickets out of my hands and starts chewing. I yank them back, but they're already slobbery and mangled.

"I can't go with you." I want to go, but I can't even imagine my dad and John trying to handle Obsidian. "I wish I could, honestly I do. But after the King George, we can sell Obsidian and then—"

"I have a buyer, you know. It's Robbie Stanford, whose family owns Dover Stables. His favorite stallion just died. He's looking for a new sire for their chase horses, and he's willing to pay quite well. He offered us a quarter of a

million for High Flyer last month, but I know his budget is all the way up to three hundred thousand pounds."

That's. . .I can't believe he waited to tell me this kind of news. I figured he'd be pressuring me.

"He actually asked me about Obsidian Devil himself. I told him you've made great strides in the behavior department, which clearly isn't strictly true, but. . ."

After all his stupid fits, I'm honestly tempted to tell him I'll think about it. Obsidian could use a little fear. But it's someone's life—it's not some kind of game. "I can't sell him, Sean, not yet anyway."

"You've signed up for the King George, I know. But think about this. If you manage to defeat Five there, while riding this monster, it'll keep Five's handicap lower."

"For the Grand National." I realize he's right. "Which will make it more likely that he could win." If I won that, I wouldn't need to sell the land at all. I could pay off the note, the demands of the lawsuit, all of it. It should even cover my taxes on the Ireland winnings, the Grand National winnings, and maybe part of King George.

Maybe after I did that, Dad might transfer the farm to me outright. The Grand National's not until April, but. . . "The King George money could pay the next balloon payment."

"Kris, let me assume the loan and change the terms. At least let me do that."

I shake my head. "Not unless I have no other choice."

"You're so stubborn." He brushes a stray lock of my hair back and tucks it behind my ear. "It's one of the things I love about you." His eyes drop to my mouth again, and I realize he's going to kiss me.

Who cares about the perfect time or place?

Miraculously, Obsidian doesn't stop us this time. He paws at the ground and snorts, but he doesn't body check

Sean. He doesn't bite anyone. He's actually quite well behaved as Sean's lips finally meet mine.

The little zing that has always accompanied physical interaction with Sean is still there. His mouth slants over mine with an eager energy that I appreciate. He's always been so forthright and open with physical affection, so different than Brits usually are in social settings.

His right hand brushes against my cheek, caressing me openly, but then he finally lets me go. "If you can't come for Christmas, if you insist on driving out to England in the middle of the most wonderful holiday of the year, at least I'll have this memory to keep me smiling."

"I do want to go," I say. "It's just not a good time."

Thankfully Sean doesn't sulk—he never has. Obsidian must have believed I meant what I said when I left him in the old barn, because he doesn't crash our date. The time Sean and I spend together at dinner is even better than our second first kiss. If I spend a little too much time staring at the window, expecting a black horse head to appear, well, that's my fault. Or is it Obsidian's? His craziness is making me act nutty, too.

When Sean drops me off, I'm actually disappointed I didn't change my mind and agree to go. Clearly when he knows it matters, Obsidian can behave himself. Maybe he'd be fine for a few days in the trailer. He's not a big fan of John, but surely he'd behave around my dad.

But the second I reach the stairs in the house that lead up to my room, I see him through the picture window on the landing, rearing back and neighing loudly from the hill by the old barn. He didn't race over and ruin the end of my date, and he's not here now, screaming outside. But clearly he's ready for me to change him. The poor guy has spent more and more time searching the internet frantically for some kind of clue to exactly what happened to him and

why, and less and less time sleeping. It's not good for his brain.

He's starting to worry he won't be able to break the curse, and I don't blame him. I was starting to think maybe he didn't have magic at all before we realized he could use it when he was touching me. We've made no progress there, though, and it's not as if he can carry me around like I'm Thor's hammer. He'll either need to figure out how to access his magic without me, or learn to manage without it. Hiding in my barn is not much better than being buried underground. Aleks knows it, too.

My dad was no help at all when I asked him about it. He did remember there were some old stories about a witch or animal shifters of some kind, but he insisted they were in his grandmother's journals. Journals he has no idea how to find.

I change into something more comfortable than the dress I wore to dinner and slide my arms into a heavy coat, and then I jog out to the barn. Obsidian's pacing out front.

"You're trashing the ground there." I frown. "A dumb beast wouldn't know what he was doing, but you can *see it* with your own two eyes."

I point, and he heads inside. We've developed a method that works beautifully. He wanders into a stall, I reach my hand through the hay feeder space to change him, and I don't have to see anything I shouldn't in the process. His clothes are already hanging over the side wall of the stall, so it's really much less *personal* than it was at first.

The first words out of his mouth when he's human surprise me. "I absolutely hate that stupid British guy."

"You're lucky he didn't flog you."

"You will not fly out to spend Christmas with him."

My hand practically flies to my hip. "You have as much right to tell me where I can go and what I can do as you

had to shove him into the dirt." I wish I had a whip. I'd give him the flogging Sean didn't.

Aleks is always in a hurry. He never behaves in a slow and measured way like Sean does, but he's worse today. He's practically slamming his arms and legs into his pants and shirt. It's like he's angry with the clothes for not already being in place, for not effortlessly doing their jobs.

"He had that coming to him. Human or horse, that guy's no match for me."

"No match for you?" I roll my eyes. "He could buy you and sell you and buy you again." I realize as I say the words that I *did* actually buy him, so that joke came out kind of strange.

Aleks glares at me. "People shouldn't buy people."

"Usually it's a phrase that means someone is much better off than you. But in this case." I wave my hands at him. "I'm still not used to people who can be horses. Do you really blame me? It's not exactly normal."

Aleks storms out of the stall, his hands fisted at his side. "Call him, and make him come back."

"Come back?" I ask. "I thought you hated him."

"I do." He looks confused, as if *I'm* the one not making sense.

"Why do you want Sean to come back? You just said you hated him, so I'm understandably lost."

"I abhor him," he says. "But if I punch him, I'll feel better."

"You want me to call him and ask him to come over. . .so you can hit him?" It's like all men are secretly toddlers who are piloting adult suits. "Aleks, look. Sean's important to me, and you need to stop—"

He spins on his heel and grabs me with both hands, pulling me closer, his fingers tightening around my upper arms. "Important to you? How?"

Now it's my turn to ask, "How what?"

"Why do you even like him?"

I blink. "He's handsome. He's smart. He's rich. He's polite and he cares about me." What's *not* to like about Sean? "And he puts up with *you*, which means he has the patience of a saint."

"He's too polite." His eyes spark like the embers of a fire that are too hot to remain contained. "He's not handsome at all. And who cares if he's rich? Plenty of people are rich."

I laugh. "I'm not rich, and neither are you. Hardly anyone is truly rich, at least, not in the way Sean's rich."

"I am rich," he says. "I practically own an entire state in Russia."

"You *did* own an entire state, you mean. Now, as far as the world knows, you're dead. That means you own nothing."

Aleks' shoulders droop a bit. "How do you think I owned all of that in the first place?"

I try to shake his hands off, but it doesn't work. His grip merely tightens. "I don't know. You have earth powers. Maybe you grew and sold a lot of rutabagas?"

He rolls his eyes. "Rutabagas? No, look—"

I slam my hands outward, knocking his away from me. "No, you look. Sean's polite. You may say he's too polite, but I like that he lets me make my own decisions without interference."

"You like that, do you?" Aleks steps toward me, his dark eyes intent.

I back up.

He steps toward me again.

And I practically trot backward until my back hits the wall of the horse stall behind me.

Aleks grins. "You don't even know what you like. You *say* you like that he's polite, but you never look like *this* when he's around."

"Like what?" My voice comes out all breathy and unsure, and I hate it. I clear my throat. "Like what?" This time, at least I sound solid.

"Like you're. . ." He takes another step, and this time, his body's only inches from mine.

Heat radiates outward from him, like he has his own personal heater. I'm drawn to it, like a fragile, stupid moth.

My heart hammers in my chest, like it did when we burst into that room with the men holding my dad. Like it did when I was about to race in Ireland.

Like it wants to run away with him and never look back.

Aleks shifts until his broad chest brushes against mine, and an uncontrollable shiver starts from down in my feet and slides all the way up to my head.

My entire body trembles like a leaf in gusty wind.

He lifts one hand and brushes the tips of his fingers down the side of my face, slowly. His progress down my face and then across my shoulder is painfully slow, like he's enjoying the experience of torturing me.

And I can't seem to break away from it.

I'm not sure I even want to.

"You're *alive* when you're with me in a way you never are with him."

I hate Aleksandr in this moment, maybe more than I've ever hated anyone. Why does my body react to his every whim, his every shift? Why, when Sean is so perfectly offering me everything I ever wanted, am I thinking about *him* instead?

Aleks' head lowers by an inch. Then half an inch more.

I can't tear my eyes away from his perfectly sculpted jaw, square and dusted with black-as-pitch stubble. His golden skin practically shines. His breathtaking eyes sparkle with mischief.

His lips curve into a wry half-smile that I want to smack off his face.

"You don't really want to kiss that guy at all. And you don't want him to save your farm, either."

My words feel torn out of me. "I don't."

I hate that he's making me admit things I don't want to admit, not even to myself. I hate everything about him. How gorgeous he is as a horse. How devastatingly hot he is as a man.

I shove my hands against his chest, but no matter how hard I push, he doesn't shift, not even a hair.

"You want to kiss someone powerful." His eyes are completely confident. "You want to be with someone who knows exactly what he wants and who *takes* it." He slams one hand up against the stall behind my head and leans toward me until we're less than an inch away. His hot breath fans over my face when he says, softly, "You want someone who can bury a dozen men with the flip of his hand. The man you want to kiss is. . ."

"You," I whisper.

And then his lips slant downward over mine.

He's not gentle. He's not a bit polite.

His kiss is savage, just like the man himself. He possesses me, his mouth claiming mine and sealing it as his. His hand curls around my face, pulling me impossibly closer and pressing against me like he'll never get enough.

And it's still not close enough.

I whimper, and his other hand, his free hand, grabs my hip possessively. It's such an electric, bone-searingly intense embrace that I find myself hopping up toward him just to be closer.

His hand releases my hip and catches my body, wrapping under my leg to hold me against him. My legs both curl around his waist, and my hands wrap around his face, not letting him stop kissing me, even if he wanted to. I squeeze my legs tighter, begging him to somehow bring us

closer, still. His lips are hot, full, and commanding, just like he behaves all the time.

And then I think about the man himself, and everything I've seen, and what I want to do next, and I can't help moaning. He actually makes a sound that's dangerously close to a growl in response.

I should hate it.

He's so feral that it should scare me, but it doesn't. Instead, it ignites something inside of me I never knew was there in the first place. My hand reaches for the buttons on his shirt, fumbling, nervous and excited at the same time.

"Kris?" John's voice is like an early morning alarm. Grating, obnoxious, and unwelcome. I may have known him forever, but I want him to go away and never come back. "*Kristiana*."

His tone penetrates the fog in my brain, and I realize he must have come into the barn, seen me with Aleks, and *still* interrupted. Which means something significant must be wrong.

I slam my hands against Aleks' chest once, twice, and then a third time.

And he finally releases me.

His eyes are predatory when he looks around the room.

John doesn't bother hiding his dislike. He's been ranting almost since Aleks showed up that the man is a drunk who never spends a second training horses. John's said directly to Aleks that the fact that we're not paying him anything but room and board means that we're being cheated, badly. Of course, Aleks mostly pretended not to understand, but there's no love lost between them.

The judgment in his face in the moment I meet John's gaze stings.

It doesn't help that I have no idea what in the world came over me. Why would I kiss Aleksandr Volkonsky,

cursed horse shifter? The last thing I need is an ancient lunatic who can work magic only when he's touching me. I need to get this curse lifted, get the money I paid to *buy* him back so I can pay the loan I took out, and then get him gone.

I'm still not sure what magical things he can even do, other than healing people and sometimes burying them alive. He keeps asking to "practice," but the thought of following him around while he's touching me and moving dirt?

Now that I'm actually thinking about touching him, my thoughts turn inappropriate. Which is just another reason to avoid him as much as possible.

"What's wrong, John?" I force the words out and make myself focus on them.

John's eyes shift—worry replacing disapproval. "It's Five."

My heart sinks. "What happened?"

"I'm not sure," he says. "He must have done something in his stall, because he's dead lame on his front left. Luckily, I know a great vet."

14

Dad jokes sometimes that the only reason we can afford to breed and race horses is that I'm a vet. His point is that, it's not the horses that ruin you. It's paying for their care and treatment. It simultaneously pokes fun at both horse people and vets.

Dad likes jokes. Especially ones that make fun of me. Or horses.

The reality is that even vets can't really afford the idiocy of horses. No one can. But in this case, being lame isn't Five's fault. He didn't do anything stupid or goofy.

"You poor guy." I pat his neck. "Hopefully it'll blow in the next day or so."

"You think?" John asks. "Because—"

"Oh, there's no way he'll be able to race in a week," I say. "I wonder if we could transfer his entry fee."

"To whom?" John frowns. "I paid for him and the demon already."

"Isn't his name Obsidian Devil?" Aleks uses a very stilted, very irritating Russian accent when he speaks English around John. It's painful.

"I'm sorry, why do you care what I call him?" John asks. "He's a pain in the rear end, just like you. So, a demon."

"I was thinking," I interject forcefully, "that maybe we could try entering About Face in the hurdle." Five Times Fast's little brother isn't quite as promising as he was, but he's talented. He might win us a little prize money, and then Obsidian won't have to travel alone. He and I know that he won't act strangely traveling without another horse, but no one else will understand. We may as well take another horse that might actually serve a purpose.

"I can call in the morning and check," John says. "But who would ride him?"

"I can ride both," I say. "Different times."

"Duh," John says. "And I should've realized it was just an abscess, too."

"It's been a long few weeks," I say. "You probably need some time off."

"Says the woman who's forcing me to take a work trip during Christmas."

John loves Christmas. It's a popular holiday in Latvia—though we call it Ziemassvētki, which roughly translates to something a little closer to winter holiday or something along those lines. But we hang ornaments on trees, and we put little nativity scenes out everywhere. If our gifts aren't as involved or as extravagant as in the United States, or even in most of Europe, well, Latvia hasn't ever been a terribly affluent nation. We focus a little more on the religious components.

Even so, I wasn't shocked by the British celebrations when I was there for school. They weren't too different from my own. At least we celebrate the same day—not January seventh like the Russians do.

"You should go home," I say. "We can drop you off on our way, and I'm sure Dad and I can manage without you

for one hunt. In fact, Sean might be able to loan me a guy or two to help—"

"John's too important," Aleks says.

My jaw nearly dangles open. Is he really saying that he wants John to come with us?

"Not need men from Sean," Aleks says again.

His fake broken English is really bad. We may need to practice it. I understand the importance of slowly weaning him into understanding our conversations—after all, if we keep lying, the odds of us being caught just grow—but he needs to learn to be more convincing. He sounds like he's auditioning to play the role of a mob boss.

"For once, I agree with him." John's lip curls. "I hate that."

"Your family would love to see you," I say.

"And if I think you can spare me, I'll head out to say hello *after the race*. I'm definitely not leaving you with just this guy to help manage the big black crazy."

"Oh, Aleks can't go with us," I say.

John's expression of utter and complete exasperation is actually pretty hilarious. "He's the trainer, no? Or that's what he claims to be, but he's not going to attend the race for the horse he's training?"

"He's more about the method and the experiences," I say. "Not the actual race."

"He sounds like a new age snake oil salesman. The experience? What does that even mean?"

Aleks opens his mouth to tell John off, I'm sure, but my long time family friend was speaking way too fast for anyone to believe a new student of English might understand.

"Well, I've wrapped Five. I think it's time to go to bed." I fake a yawn.

John and Aleks both yawn too, and that has me yawning for real. Yawns are stupid. One day, we'll discover the truth

behind why we do it and how they spread, and it's definitely something strange and possibly magical. I mean, if Aleks can suck people into the ground. . .maybe yawns are some kind of glitch in the fabric of our world that we all just collectively ignore.

"I'm heading back to the house."

"I walk you," Aleks says.

John lunges forward and grabs his arm. "Oh, no you don't, lover boy. You can stay right here with me while the pretty lady heads home. I'll let you go once she's safe."

Aleks shoots me a pointed look that says, *Get me out of here, before you have to watch me rip his arm off and feed it to him.*

But really, I know he's a little scared of John. The old trainer's like a second father to me, and I'd kill Aleks if he did anything harmful. Which means for once, Aleksandr is the one in trouble. He should be begging for my help.

Plus, John's right. Lover boy should stay there while I get some sleep. So I abandon him with nothing more than a little wave. "Night."

Aleks' jaw drops as I walk away.

I realize, as I reach my room, that it's the first night he hasn't had access to the internet while in his human form. I finally got the internet to extend out to the barn so I don't have to leave him my phone, but I didn't take a laptop or an iPad or anything out there.

He's going to be so bored. Maybe he'll actually sleep for once, instead of staying up all night like a vampire.

For some reason, that thought makes me smile. I've never been someone who thought vampires were hot. Sucking blood? Deadly cold skin? Hard pass. But now I have a supernatural creature in my barn.

And he's pressing me against the wall and kissing me.

I refuse to think about what might have happened if John hadn't come to tell me the terrible news about Five. I

mean, abscesses aren't that bad, but it's awful timing. The abscess. Not John saving me from myself. That was excellent timing. Practically miraculous.

Aleks is hot, sure. He's commanding. He has powers. And he is a man who is also a horse, which is kind of what I was begging the universe to give me. But he's not the good things about a horse—patient, submissive, and supportive.

No, he makes me feel things. Too many things. And he's always pushing to get his way. He argues. He digs. He presses. When I disagree, he jumps ridiculously tall fences and chases me down, forcing my hand.

Buying him was the worst mistake I've ever made.

I can't regret helping free a person from being stuck in the form of a horse forever, and I know it sucks he was cursed and all, but there's not much more I can do. Once I have the money to repay the loan I took out from Sean to pay that first balloon payment, once I don't need him as collateral, I'll kick him out and be done with the whole mess.

Until then, I just need to focus on what matters.

Which is *not* kissing him. Not wrecking my future with Sean, which is looking brighter by the day, and not throwing away everything I want for one hot moment of rippling abs and burning skin. Of course, now I'm thinking of touching the body I've seen way too many times. A body I can absolutely envision any second of the day.

I shake my head and stand up to change into pajamas.

And practically have a heart attack.

Because Aleksandr waves at me through my second floor window.

"What on earth are you doing?"

"I used to be great at climbing trees," he practically shouts. "Turns out, it's harder when you're much heavier. I think this branch might break. Can you let me in?"

For the love of all that's—I'm going to kill him. Or

maybe I'll just let him fall and break his neck, and then it's not my fault. "You are not coming inside my room." I fold my arms. "Go back to the barn."

"You forgot to give me a laptop," he says. "I have stuff to do."

I think about closing my curtains.

But knowing him, he'll just crash through the window and ruin everything.

I snatch my iPad off my desk and stomp to the window. Then I slide the glass open an inch and a half and poke the end of my iPad outside.

"Are you serious?" He scowls. "What if I drop it when I'm falling to my death?"

"You'll have a split second to pity me. I'll have gotten rid of a real nuisance, but I'll be out one very expensive piece of technology."

Aleks' mouth turns upward on the right side. "A nuisance?" I hate how confident he is. A normal guy would be a mass of insecurities. "You did seem *bothered* earlier. Maybe there's been a translation discrepancy." Which is ridiculous. He's as fluent as I am.

I try not to think about all the ways in which we're bizarrely connected. It just makes me feel bad for sending him away so severely, but I really can't afford to let him in my *bedroom*. He's practically irresistible in a dirty, run-down, spider-infested barn. What on earth would happen if he came in my warm, cozy, clean bedroom right now?

My panties would set on fire. That's what.

"You have to go." I wiggle the iPad a bit. "You have five seconds before I rescind my offer. "Five. Four."

He reaches for the iPad, but then at the last second, his hand shifts and shoves the window open. Before I can even object, he's hopping through the opening and into my room, along with a blast of frosty winter air.

"Thanks." He hasn't even touched the iPad, which is now dangling from my fingers.

"Did you lie?" I ask. "Did you even come here because you couldn't get online?"

He grabs the iPad and tosses it back on my desk. "You know why I came here." He steps toward me, his eyes scanning my face.

"No." I shake my head, and this time, I'm not going to back up like a rabbit fleeing a fox. "No, we are not doing that again."

"That?" His smile widens. "Why not? *That* was one of the best things I've ever done. And I have a lot of ideas for ways to improve that I can only practice with your help."

"NO," I say as emphatically as I can manage. I pull out my I'm-an-unhappy-horse-trainer voice and really put some energy behind it. "Aleks, you have to go."

"Say that again," he practically purrs.

"No," I say.

He laughs. "Not 'no.' Say *my name* again."

I choke. "The door is there." I duck sideways and point.

He ignores me, forcing me to do what I swore I wouldn't.

I back up. And he stalks me again, kicking my heart into high gear. After just a few steps, my butt hits the top of my nightstand—it really sucks to be so small sometimes—and there's nowhere else to go. "You're a Neanderthal," I say.

He blinks. "I'm not sure what that is. Is good or bad?"

"I don't want you here," I say.

"Your cheeks are flushed. Your pupils are dilated. Your breathing is heavy." His eyes drop to my lips. "My research tells me that means you *are* interested."

"Or scared," I say. "It's a fear response."

He laughs again, and this time, something pools deep inside of me at the sound.

"Stop," I say. "Get out."

"You're protesting too much," he says.

"No, in this day and age, protesting a lot literally means *get the hell out.*"

He pauses for a second, and the first note of uncertainty I've seen enters his tone. "You want to kiss me."

I'm getting nowhere lying about that. "I do."

His grin is back.

"But no matter what kind of reaction my body may have around you, my *brain* makes the decisions for my life, and you're not part of my future."

He freezes at that, and then he blinks.

"Sean wants to—"

He swears under his breath. "Not that guy, again."

"Yes," I say. "That guy. Again. He and I were in love before and—"

"You don't love him now," he practically roars. "And if you so much as—"

"As what? If I so much as do *what*? Kiss him? Fall for him? Marry him?" I ball my hand into a fist and punch Aleks as hard as I can in the midsection.

Which is a big mistake.

My hand feels like I just hit a brick wall.

"Ow."

"Why did you do that?" He sighs. "Kristiana, Sean isn't right for you. He's—"

"Oh, I know. You've said."

"It's not just that he's small and weak and lets you push him around. He's going to let you sell your family land."

"I told him to let me," I say. "It's my decision."

"You can't sell it." Aleks says that like he knows anything about my life or this modern world.

"You know who says things like that? Dramatic things? Absolutes, like, 'you *can't* sell it'?" I point. "Nobility. Entitled, rich brats. People who have never lived in the real

world. Because people like me? People who understand how things work and what life is about?" I shrug.

"You think I don't know how the world works?" His eyes flash.

"Maybe you did, but your world and my world aren't the same." It hits me then, what might get through to him. "You're the one who convinced me to sell it."

"I did no such thing," he says.

"You said that we have to sacrifice what we want for what we need, sometimes. You said you couldn't help save all those people because if you did, you might lose your ability to protect your people."

A muscle in Aleks' jaw pops. "My dad helped those two families, you know. He stepped in and helped them when they asked, when I was just a boy. And then, when he was weakened from helping with their favor, one of Russia's enemies killed him."

There's true pain in his face, and I realize that I'm throwing his words back at him, but it's not the win I wanted. It just reminded him of an old pain.

"The difference between your situation and mine? You have friends who want to help you *not* make the sacrifice. You have other options. You're just doing this to protect your pride, and if I've learned anything in my life, it's that pride serves no one. It just ruins lives and leads us to make bad decisions."

Fury rises inside of me. "You don't know anything about my life. I'm sorry about your dad—but do you think I wanted my mother to die? Did I want my dad to fall into a bottle and start gambling all the time, just to feel alive? I didn't want any of it, but that's what I got. My brother might have held things here together, but he hated our life even more than I did, so he left. Ran away to America and never looked back."

"They may have failed you, but you have options," Aleksandr says. "You should let other people help you."

"I told Sean he can't give me money or buy my land for one very important reason."

Aleks raises his eyebrows expectantly.

"Because we aren't equal right now," I say. "It's not that he's hugely rich and I'm poor. I've never been caught up on that. Before, when we were in school, he had everything, but at least I had my farm. I had intelligence and health and plans for the future. He left me, even then. He wanted our relationship to work less than I did, clearly. But now he's back, saying he never got over me, and I'm excited to hear that. But I'm in trouble. My dad's put the family farm in peril, and if I let him save me? What am I then? A Disney princess?" My lip curls, and my head shakes, and my hands tighten into fists at my side. "I will *never* be a Disney princess. I'm more than that. I work hard, and I do whatever it takes to fight for my happy ending."

"You aren't weak because you let someone else help," he says. "And Sean's not the only one who can help."

"Oh? Who else did you have in mind? You?"

He shrugs.

"Do you really think you can help me?"

"Of course I do."

"You have no money." I hold up one finger. "You have no identification or paperwork." Then another. "No home." I throw up all my fingers and wiggle them. "You can't control your magic, and we've located absolutely zero answers about your curse, your family, or your friends. You pick fights. You push me around. Aleks, I'm not trying to hurt you, but you bring nothing to the table other than trouble. What am I missing?"

He did save my dad's life, and mine, and he is the key to winning the purse at the King George in a few days. I'm too mad to acknowledge any of that, though.

"Probably most importantly, you never listen to me, not to anything I say. You think you know better than I do, but you don't know anything about my life or the modern world. You don't fit in. You have no place here, and that's why you have nothing to offer me. So please, please just go back to the barn and leave me alone."

To my surprise, after staring at me for a moment, he listens. He heads back out the window and disappears into the night. He didn't even bother taking my iPad with him.

15

About Face may be several years behind Five Times Fast, but he's still fun to ride. We clear the course I set up to mimic the upcoming hurdle with plenty of energy and focus. I pat his neck. "Nice work, boy. Really nice."

The prize money for the novice hurdle isn't quite as good as the champion chase, but at least I won't need to pay Finn. I can ride About Face and Obsidian myself. My dad won't be pleased, but he hasn't griped or sniped at all, not since Aleks had to save us from his latest issues.

After I'm done with About Face, I pass him off to a groom and saddle Obsidian up. Aleks may be upset at me, but at least when he's in his horse form, he behaves. Obsidian takes every single fence beautifully, in sync with me in every way. I'm not sure I've been on a horse that was more ready for a race than he is.

Why can't the man be half as perfect as the horse?

It's a little hard for me, as we ride back toward the main farm. "This will all be gone soon," I say. "I mean. Relatively soon."

Obsidian slows to a walk and turns his head back to look at me.

"I hope it's gone," I say. "The more I think about it, selling it really is the only way. But I'm going to miss it a lot, too. I mean, I grew up riding around in all these woods and hills."

When he stops entirely, I slide off his back. I walk toward the edge of the cleared path. Obsidian stays close, so close we're touching. It's nice, actually, because his huge body blocks the wind, and as always, heat rolls off of him, keeping me warm.

I breathe in and out, trying to find gratitude for the time I had with Liepašeta, so I'm not wallowing in sorrow that she'll soon belong to someone else instead.

Obsidian paws at the ground, at another pile of rocks he's found.

"What?" I ask. "I know you're obsessed with rocks, but I don't care about them. I left the ones you found before in that green bucket in the old barn. If they were on the path, I'd clear them for you. I don't want them bruising your feet, but these are way over here, by the trees."

I glance down at them. It's a large pile of green rocks, dozens and dozens of them. Some of them are actually pretty sparkly in a bizarre way. I mean, they're strange rocks. They kind of look like limestone or something, but then there are huge chunks of what looks almost like green glass stuck on the limestone in blobs. And there are also chunks of orangey and yellow resin-looking rock as well.

"They're kind of cool, really," I say. "But look, you don't need rocks, and neither do I. You're not twelve. You're too old for rock collections."

He snorts and turns away from me.

I feel like I'm ruining all his hopes and dreams, especially after my rude assessment of his future last night. "I know I was kind of harsh yesterday, and I know since you

woke up, life has sucked. I can't even imagine how hard it must be to lose everything you knew and everyone you loved. But you have to face reality. You and I can't find anything on this curse. No one has come to attack you, and it's not very clear whether you'll ever be able to shift or access your magic again, at least not without holding my hand."

He bumps my shoulder playfully and trots along ahead of me.

"No," I say. "As I mentioned yesterday, you can't hold my hand forever. I have to think about my future, and so do you. Realistically. You and I don't work. I can't adopt you like a dog—some homeless Russian man who can't accept that his glory days are past."

He stops moving, his eyes looking somehow more hurt while in a horse head than they did even as a man.

"Once we win this race, I'm going to have enough to pay the next balloon note. I won't have paid Sean back yet, but I doubt he'll notify anyone that my collateral went missing. I've given it a lot of thought, and I think it'll be time for you to go."

He's utterly and completely still, like midnight over a lake, like an onyx statue in a museum, like the beginning of an exam in a difficult class. No movement. No snorting or pawing. No reaction at all.

I hope that means he's processing what I've said.

"Let's head back," I say.

He doesn't argue, but he also doesn't walk close to me, not anymore.

Great. Now the horse and the man are both pouting.

I'm honestly, deep in my bones, trying to do the right thing, so no matter how bad I feel about hurting his feelings, no matter how uncomfortable it makes me, I don't take any of my words back. It'll be best for both of us if we can go our

separate ways. Fairy tales aren't all they're cracked up to be. I mean, powers and shifting and whatnot exists, but so do curses and being buried in the earth and stuck as a horse forever.

I like things safe, simple, and predictable. I want that life back.

But when I go to bed that night, I think about Aleks' face when I shifted him back to human and left a laptop on the dirty old table. He stared at me like I'd given up.

Like I quit.

Liepas aren't quitters. We just know when we've already lost. I need to explain that to him. I need to make sure he understands that what I'm doing is what's best for both of us. I wish I didn't care, but I know that I won't be able to sleep until I have cleared that up.

Only, when I get to the barn, he's not there.

I wander around a bit. I call for him over and over, and I wait for an hour before falling asleep, my head on my arms, slumped over the table.

A strange noise wakes me up, but once my mind clears from sleep, I can't for the life of me recall what the noise was. I stretch, check to confirm there's still no sign of Aleks, and reluctantly return to my bedroom. I hope he's alright, but at the end of the day, he's a grown man. If he's decided he can go where he wants without telling me about it, well, that's what I told him to do, isn't it?

The next day goes almost the same way. Aleks is back, but he doesn't offer an explanation as to where he was, so I don't tell him I even know he was gone. I shift him into Obsidian, we do a light workout—no jumps today. I want him to rest for the race—and then later in the day, I shift him back into a man. This time, I change him before I even go to do my house calls. He may as well have some normal daylight hours as a human. Especially if he's about to be human full time.

When I return a few hours later to check on him, he's gone again.

I know it's for the best, but it hurts a little bit. It's probably because he felt like a baby bird to me when we first met. He hadn't been in the world for so long, and he needed my guidance so much, and now he doesn't seem to need me at all.

He's learned to fly.

The next day goes almost the same way, and then it's time to leave. John and my dad are much more stressed about the whole thing than I am. I'm legitimately worried about Eduards, as John grills him about what he needs to do for the horses while we're gone.

"It's fine," I say eventually. "Eduards has been doing this for years. He knows as much as you do."

John's fits almost make up for Obsidian Devil's abnormally calm behavior. He doesn't snort, paw, whinny, or snap at anyone. And he lets John load him into the trailer.

"He's like a different horse," John says.

We work for months, no, more like years to truly 'break' a horse. A broke horse is a *good* thing. It means they're calm, they trust their rider, and they want to please you. It means you can rely on them to behave the way that you order them to behave. It makes them safe, and it makes them valuable.

Humans, unlike horses, shouldn't be broken. They need spirit, and resolve, and confidence. They need to have faith in their own decisions and their own desires. Looking at the way Obsidian is behaving? John and my dad think it's a miracle, but. . .

I worry that I broke him.

I meant well, at least. I was trying to help us both live the best lives we could. I keep telling myself that, all the way to England. We're a full day early, thanks to my unease. I just drive, and drive, and drive.

I decide to text Sean. I'M SURE YOU'RE BUSY. IT IS CHRISTMAS EVE. BUT WE'RE HERE, EARLY.

I don't have to wait more than ten seconds. COME SEE ME. One second later, he texts again. ACTUALLY, I'LL COME GET YOU.

I laugh. I NEED TO GET OBSIDIAN AND ABOUT FACE OUT ON THE TRACK TO ACCLIMATE THEM. GIVE ME THREE HOURS.

SEE YOU THEN.

I should have asked for five hours. I could've taken a nap, and maybe these bags under my eyes wouldn't have looked so awful. Oh, well. Done is done.

Obsidian, of course, is perfect when we go out. He dives forward a bit, and we're a little out of sync, but the other horses and the people milling around don't spook him. It's nice to have a horse who isn't the usual jumpy mess that herd animals always are in new, chaotic places.

About Face is another story. He's athletic and lean like Five, and he's tall too, but he's never been to a race, and he's jumpy as a kangaroo in a dingo conservatory. Luckily, I haven't forgotten how to manage a real horse, and we work until his spook's gone. The sun has set already—so early— when I put About Face away and prepare to leave.

Dad and John have already headed for the tavern a half block down the way. It's close enough to our hotel that they can just walk home. They left as soon as I finished with About Face. It's been a long few days—I don't blame them.

But I'm the only one around when Obsidian neighs and kicks the stall.

"What?" I ask.

He tosses his head.

"Is something wrong?"

He screams.

Horse screams are awful, and one of the grooms comes running over.

183

"He's fine," I say. "I'm going to close up his stall, though. I think he needs less stimulation."

"Sure," the man says.

Once the door's closed, I change him, holding up a saddle pad to preserve some semblance of decency. "What?"

"I need to stay human for a while."

"You're kidding me." I glance around. "You need to stay a horse, here. It's critical."

He frowns. "You can close the stall. Who'll go against your command?"

"My dad, for one," I say.

"He's with John. They'll both be drunk inside of an hour."

I roll my eyes. "Why do you need to be human?"

"Didn't you say I have to get used to it?" He glances sideways. "I've got some things to do."

"Like what?" I put a hand on my hip.

"You've made it clear you're not interested," he says. "But there are other women here." He arches one eyebrow. "They might feel differently."

I'm sure they will. For some reason, a strong flash of irritation pulses through me. For the past few weeks, he's been rude to every single female he meets other than me. Now he's moved on and wants to hook up with someone? Men are disgusting pigs. "Fine. Do whatever you want, but make sure Dad and John don't see you."

I spin around on my heel, leaving him to freeze to death, naked, in the stall. It would serve him right if he did.

"Hey."

I don't turn back when I respond. "What?"

"At least bring me some clothes."

This time, I can't help it. I pivot on my heel. "I'm sorry. I didn't realize you'd require clothing for a booty call while you were here. I'm fresh out of men's clubbing attire."

He's suppressing a smile, I can tell. I hate that I didn't stop my outburst. "I brought a bag. It's in the back of the trailer, under the tack. If you would just go get it, you can drop it into the stall and be on your way."

"After telling the grooms not to come into your stall no matter what, I guess?"

"Yes, after that."

I'm fuming by the time I finally lug his enormous bag—what's in there, rocks?—all the way to the racing stable and chuck it at his feet. "Have fun."

I hate how amused he looks as I snarl and leave. I can't stop thinking about it as I get ready to meet Sean and his family, but I really need to. I have to focus. Meeting his family's a big deal. I need to put my best foot forward. I didn't even get this far last time.

His parents rejected me without once meeting me.

If I'd planned to meet them today, I'd have agonized over what I would wear for hours and hours. As it is, I slide into my nicest pair of riding breeches—no holes at all and only one tiny stain just below the knee that my boots will cover—and a button-down white shirt. It's plain, but that's who I am.

Plain, but hard working.

And if they hate it, well, I guess that'll be the end of that.

I unhitch the truck from the trailer and climb inside, bracing myself to follow my phone's GPS to Sean's family's ancestral home. It's only six miles away. I could practically run there. I guess I'd never realized quite how close he lived to Kempton Park.

The racetrack's located on the west side of London, out in the suburbs a bit, but the whole area's pretty consistently full of people and businesses. Compared to Latvia, it looks like urban sprawl. Of course, having completed uni here, it's not as stressful to navigate as it was when I first came.

But then, from one minute to the next, the surrounding area transforms. It's like a huge park springs up in the middle of the city, and as I turn into the drive the GPS tells me to take, there's nothing but a blanket of trees, from fragrant Leland cypress, to horse chestnuts with their bizarrely spikey conker seeds still clinging to branches here and there, to towering oaks that look naked and bare against the winter landscape.

As I approach the estate, it's clear that someone has taken great care to cultivate plants that thrive even in the winter. No snow blankets the ground yet, thankfully for our race in two days, and the winter rye grass they must have planted is bright green, in carefully manicured rows. I wonder how many people must work here full time on the grounds to keep things—

And then my mind goes blank, because Sean's house comes into view.

Calling it a house seems inadequate somehow, like comparing a pair of Steve Madden pumps to a pair of Valentinos. It's utterly absurd. I *knew* that Sean McDermott was heir to the Earldom of Coventry, but I had no idea what the home that went with that title would look like.

I remember Sean describing it to me when we were in school. I told him about my home—the bright shutters, the long porch, an American-style home in Latvia. It had begun simply, but when Mom moved in, she changed a lot of little things to make it look like the houses she was used to back in the United States.

Sean told me about his house a few weeks into dating, saying it was old, out-of-date, and that while his mother would say it was neo-classical, designed by the late and great Charles Parker in the mid-seventeenth century, he wished that he could level it and build something that wasn't overlarge and drafty.

I had, stupidly, pictured a plantation-style home with tall ceilings and a lot of windows. I thought it might be twice the size of my family's home, or even three times that size.

I was very, very wrong.

This place would absolutely work as the setting of any regency-era romance television series, right down to the terribly tall windows every fifteen feet along the front and the carefully manicured hedges. The circular drive's paved now, but I can imagine how it looked for the past few centuries, with dukes, earls, and princes circling round in their carriages. The home's made up entirely of white and grey stone, three stories high, lined with so many picture windows that I finally stop counting.

I'm spinning out a little bit, made worse when a man in a ridiculously formal tuxedo comes to take the keys to my truck the second I shift into park. He just shot out of the two vast, double doors. Is he a butler? A driver?

Another man is standing at the top of the stairs, also in a tuxedo. How many people work for Sean? This is so much worse than I expected.

"Wait," Sean says. He's beaming at me as he jogs down the front steps. Thankfully, he's not wearing a tuxedo or even a suit. Just his normal slacks and a polo shirt with a wool coat on top and a nice, billowy grey scarf blowing behind him. He could be on the cover of *Horse and Rider* or *Town and Country* without shifting a single hair. "Mother's arguing with Ursula again. We'll just head down to the stables for a moment while they argue about the cheese soufflé."

He had me at stables.

When he smiles that broad smile of his, I can't help grinning back. "The stables?"

"I knew you'd want to see them right away." He pauses. "I hope they'll meet with your approval."

A little thrill runs through me at the thought that he wants me to approve. . .because he wants me to consider this as a possible future home.

When we turn the corner, one of the most beautiful gates I've ever seen comes into view. It's made of some kind of black metal—titanium?—and it's shaped into a large arch, clearly made to mimic a horseshoe. The opening must be ten feet tall, easily tall enough for a horse with a rider to pass underneath, and it's probably two horses wide. Once we're close enough, I notice that it frames the view of the barn perfectly.

Of course, it's one of the most staggeringly stunning barns I've ever seen.

Even the house didn't take me aback like this does.

My stables back at home are top of the line—I still thank my grandparents at least twice a year for their generous gift, because nothing makes me happier than knowing our horses are safe and well cared for. Plus, well-designed stables decrease my workload by a metric ton. It's one of the reasons that selling them makes me feel so sick.

Even so, as we walk toward the massive stables at the edge of the property, I can't help feeling a little envious. I forced myself to memorize all the strange British names for things before we left, so I know this is called the "Argan Estate." At home, we just name our homes after our family surname. Liepa becomes Liepašeta. But in England, they have more names than we have poor relatives.

Sean McDermott's father, James McDermott, is the Earl of Coventry, Lord of Argan Manor, Lord of the Hampersmill Estate in Sussex, and owner of the Forsythe House in London. Having a London house when their family estate is already so close probably seems bizarre now, but I suppose it would have been a long ride to make on horseback every day during the Season a billion years ago when they bought or inherited all these places.

The stables are made of the same white and grey stone used for the main house, so clearly this was either created to match or built at the same time. It's not three stories high, but it's easily twenty feet tall, which leaves plenty of room for a hayloft. As we stride easily inside, I peer back and forth, poleaxed.

There's no hayloft. Of course not. Instead, there's a very high, planked wood ceiling. Instead of being covered in cobwebs like our barn perpetually is, it has the most pristine, most beautiful light fixtures I've ever laid eyes upon. Blown glass orbs, cascading crystals that catch and scatter the light, and against the walls, huge fans that I imagine really circulate a lot of air when the summer heat hits.

In the center of the aisle, there's a life-sized bronze statue of a horse and rider, clearing a beautifully arranged floral obstacle. It's tall, but the width is what shocks me the most. They had to make the hall—nearly twenty-five feet across—into dead space, just to make sure there's room on either side of the statue for horses to easily move around.

I've never seen such a shocking waste of barn space in my life, but it's visually stunning, and that was clearly the goal. The stalls, instead of forming rows as they usually do, are shaped into giant wedges that open around the statue. They look massive, with narrow, eight-foot fronts, widening to thirty or forty feet across the back.

"If you have a horse that's supposed to be on stall rest, what do you do? Those stalls are far too big."

Sean's grin is diabolical. "I should have known you'd be thinking of the logistics. Mom's very impressed that you're a practicing large animal vet."

"I doubt she'd be as impressed if she knew that half of my calls involve sticking my arm up a horse's—" Sean's face looks so alarmed that I cut off mid-sentence.

"When we do meet my parents. . ."

"Less talk about oiling colicking horses?"

He swallows. "Or, you know what? Talk about it all you like. It's the side of horses they've always ignored, but it's real and it matters."

He's trying.

I'll give him that.

"It's fine. I'll be much more circumspect around your parents, I promise."

"And about the stalls, we only have these ten that are configured this way, and we use them for our prize horses, mostly. Then when guests come to visit, they can ooh and aah about the beauty of our stables." He waves for me to follow him.

After we round the bend, there are three more rows of stalls—the typical twelve by twelve stalls—with plenty of horses in those as well. The floors are made of interlocking brick. The walls, ceilings, and floors are all so clean I would eat off of them. They must have a professional cleaning staff just for the stable. All the walls and trim are a combination of dark-stained hardwood and shiny, bright chrome. I've been so distracted by the appearance that I almost forgot the part that matters.

"How many stalls do you have?"

"Forty-six," he says. "But we only have eighteen horses here right now."

"No one's paying much attention to it now that you're not riding?"

He frowns. "How do you know I'm not riding?"

His parents aren't here. No one I know is, either. I decide to be bold, and I slide my hand through his. Then I lift it up. "No calluses."

He rolls his eyes. "I wear gloves."

"Even so, you'd have some here if you rode more than once a week." I stroke the tips of his fingers.

He freezes in place. "I knew bringing you here was the

right move. You brighten the entire estate." His eyes are wistful. Yearning.

It's enough to distract me, even from the perfection of the stables.

"The real question is," he says softly, his eyes intent, "will you, Kristiana Liepa, ever in your life——"

My heart starts to race in my chest. What's this *real* question he's about to ask? It feels significant.

"——ever leave this stable, now that I've brought you here? Because even if they don't work out the drama with the cheese soufflés, I swear, my mom always manages to put together an amazing menu for Christmas Eve."

Why do I feel relieved that he didn't propose? Probably because it would have been way too early. Of course he wouldn't do that! I haven't met his parents. We've only just kissed again this time around.

"Of course," I say. "I'm actually starving. This stable isn't going anywhere. I can traipse back and poke around more later."

"Just promise me this," he says.

"What?"

"You won't steal any of my horses." He's grinning.

"I can't make any promises I may not keep."

The conversation stays easy and light the entire walk back to the house. It's much farther than the distance separating my house from my babies, but I suppose it's something you can get used to. A little extra exercise isn't so bad.

I hope we haven't kept his mother and father waiting. All the flirtatious joking about staying in the barn aside, I really want them to like me. If they're already annoyed at how late I am when we walk through those doors, it would be a real shame.

Before we can even walk up the steps, a bright red sports car roars down the private drive. It's a beautiful car, but it almost looks like it's trying too hard. The shaping

around the front headlights reminds me of huge nostrils or something. "Who's that?" I ask. "Were you expecting someone else?" For a split second, I'm terribly nervous he's invited more than one girl.

But Sean's brow furrows. "No, and I don't think I know anyone who drives a McLaren 720. My friend Abbott was looking at one, but he bought a Ferrari instead."

Ah, to have such friends. I've never even heard of a McLaren, and I certainly don't know what the model numbers mean.

The car rolls to a stop in front of us, but the windows are tinted. Sean's squinting, and his butler, whose tuxedo actually has tails, I notice from here, comes sprinting out the front door as if he may be needed to take a bullet or something. The driver must have retired after taking my truck.

"Hello." He's huffing a bit, but as the car door opens, he bows to welcome the new guest. "And who might you be, sir?"

When the driver stands up, I realize that I know him.

His black hair is cut and combed differently than it was, and he's wearing what looks a lot like designer clothing, but the man who's smiling at Sean and me is definitely Aleksandr Volkonsky.

❧ 16 ❧

"What are you doing here?" I can't help hissing. I'm just so shocked. How did he even know where Sean lives?

"Your father gave me the address," Aleks says.

"He can speak English?" Sean glances between Aleks and me the same way I'd stare at my dad if I found out he was running a cabal of alien-worshipping masseuses.

Why *is* Aleks speaking English all of a sudden?

And then it hits me. I asked him the question in English. I can't really be upset with him for responding in the same language that I initiated the conversation in.

"I learned," Aleks says. Then he smiles.

"How did you get a car?" I ask.

Aleks jingles the key fob. "Oh, this?"

"Isn't he working for board in the hopes of making a name for himself?" Sean asks. "John told me he was sitting this race out, because his training methods haven't been working well."

I practically choke.

Aleks' eyes widen, and then his lips twist.

This is not going well. But I really do want to know

where he got a car. I have a sneaking suspicion he buried the real owner six feet under. Or knowing Aleks, more. Ten. Fifteen feet. Ugh.

"Can someone tell me what's going on?" Sean asks. "I feel like we've stepped out of the real world and into some kind of twilight zone."

"Here you all are." A woman who must be in her early sixties but doesn't look a day over fifty steps out the front door and onto the top step. "Dinner's ready, and unlike me, soufflés aren't very forgiving."

"So you did get the cheese soufflé worked out," Sean says. "That's great."

The woman's gestures are smooth and fluid, and she looks entirely at ease. She's wearing a lovely grey business suit, and a string of black pearls with sensible black pumps.

She makes me look like a stable hand.

It's clear she's the lady of this gargantuan house. And if that wasn't enough to clue me in to her identity, she has the exact same sky blue eyes as Sean. "Well, it won't be made with Gruyere, but we have to be a little flexible with newer staff sometimes." The woman brushes her right hand over her absolutely perfectly coiffed hair, smoothing nonexistent flyaways toward her beautiful, dark bun.

"Mother, we'll be in shortly." Sean's voice is tight but firm.

As if she didn't hear him, she turns toward me and descends the stairs. "This must be Kristiana." She beams, and I can't tell whether it's forced or genuine. I suppose that's how you know if someone is quite practiced with their smiles. You can't really be sure either way. "I have heard nothing but your name for months, now."

"Come, Mother," Sean says.

"What?" she asks.

Sean smiles. "It's been far longer than that."

I'm sure they're exaggerating, but it's nice to hear all the

same. "You must be Sean's beautiful mother. It's a pleasure to finally meet you."

"The pleasure is entirely mine." She holds out her hand. "I hear your family hails from America."

"My mother's family," I say, "yes. My father's from Latvia—and we live there still."

"You don't say." Lady McDermott narrows her eyes at Sean. "You didn't mention that when you said you were opening a branch there."

He shrugs sheepishly—an expression I've never before seen on his face. "Well, it *did* make good business sense, too."

"Finding the right woman is the most important thing you'll ever do," Lady McDermott says. "I'm the last person who would argue with you for doing whatever it takes to succeed, there."

Aleks clears his throat.

"And who is this?" she asks.

"This is. . ." Sean pauses. "Actually, I can't recall his name. I usually just call him the crazy Russian trainer."

His mother's eyes widen and she turns toward me slowly. "He brought your car?"

I shake my head. "It's not my car." I'm actually legitimately worried that the constables will round the bend any moment, sirens blaring. "I'm not quite sure—"

"The last few months have been rough," Aleks says. His English accent sounds exactly like mine—American like my mother's was. "You see, we had some family. . ." He clears his throat. "Some family drama, you could say. My closest relative recently passed, leaving the paperwork in total disarray. Instead of coming to me as it should have, the family land, titles, estate, and businesses all. . .well, they *languished*."

"That's terrible," Lady McDermott says. "You should come inside. You can eat with us and tell us all about it."

"But what about the meal?" I ask. "Will there be enough food?"

She waves her hand at me airily. "Oh, yes. They always make another plate or two, just in case someone requests more or there's an issue with the existing food—a hair, too much salt, that sort of thing."

An extra plate or two? Who are these people?

"I'd love to join you for dinner. Thank you for extending the invite." For all the world, Aleksandr looks just like a vampire who recently secured a coveted invite into the home of someone delicious. It makes me *exceedingly* nervous.

"Actually," I say, "he was just dropping something off. He needs to get back and make sure our horse, Obsidian Devil, is doing fine for the race that's only two days away."

"I just saw him," Aleks says. "He looked perfect. And I do have to eat."

I scowl at him, but he just smiles.

"Sure," Sean says. "I'd love to hear more about this family drama as well, now we come to it." He also wants to know why Aleksandr can speak flawless English, I'm sure. Even geniuses couldn't pick it up that fast.

Which means that either Aleks lied to me about it, or we both lied to Sean.

I honestly don't know which one will upset poor Sean more. I feel sort of sick about it. I'd like defend myself because it's not like I'm lying because I want to. . .but then I think about how I kissed Aleks not too long ago and how much I enjoyed it.

That makes me hate myself and want to run away and hide.

"Thank you so much for welcoming me," Aleks says.

The second Sean's mother turns to go inside, Sean reaches to take my arm and lead me in behind her. All I want to do is kick Aleksandr as hard as I can, but I'm stuck

pretending like none of this is news to me, and I'm not worried that we're leading a criminal into Sean's gorgeous estate.

"I need to find the ladies' room," I say.

"Oh, of course." Sean points around the corner.

"Actually, I need to go too," Aleks says.

"To the ladies' room?" Sean smirks. Toddlers piloting adult suits, I swear.

"The washroom. Isn't that what the 'ladies' room' means?" I can't tell whether Aleks is genuinely confused, or whether he's acting. Either way, it pisses me off even more.

"Sure," Sean says. "But—"

Sean's mother has stopped as well. "There's another one just around—"

"I'll just follow her and wait until she's done," Aleks says.

Somehow, no one even acts like what he's saying is strange.

"Isaac will wait here and guide you to the dining room when you're ready," Lady McDermott says.

"Thank you," I say. "I'll just be a moment."

The second they're out of sight, I try to kick Aleks, but he dodges me with irritating ease.

"Someone's in a very bad mood," he says in English. And he's grinning.

Grinning.

Like this is all some kind of joke.

"Please tell me you didn't steal that car," I say in Latvian.

"I didn't steal that car," he says almost rotely. As if he's merely following my instructions. At least he isn't still speaking English.

I try to kick him again, but this time, instead of dodging me, he sidesteps and snags both my arms, encircling my wrists with his hands.

"Are you just saying that? Or is it actually true?"

"You told me to say I hadn't stolen it," he says. "You should make up your mind."

"Aleksandr Volkonsky," I say. "If I had any idea you would follow me—"

"I didn't follow you," he says. "Obviously. I didn't have this car yet when you left. I had to go and pick it up. It's not like it's hard to look up the residence of his eminence, Lord McDrivel."

I can't help spluttering. "First off, do not mock him."

"You mocked me when I said I was a prince." He looks utterly calm.

I try to shove him away, but his hands are stronger than metal cuffs. "The police could come to arrest you at any time. You have no idea what kind of evidence they have now, and you'll—"

"You're worried about me." He smiles. "DNA evidence. Is that the evidence you mean? Because that's actually what *got* me the car in the first place. If you'd taken the time to explain what kind of scientific advancements—"

"Aleks," I hiss. "Let me go. I need to get back to the dinner, and you need to go ditch that car somewhere."

His thumbs stroke the inside of my wrist in a shockingly intimate gesture I was not prepared to deal with. "I love that you're worried about me." His grin almost distracts me—combined with the fluttering sensations spreading through my body. . .I need to escape. Right now.

"Aleksandr. You're not listening to me."

"I didn't steal the car, alright? And I came here because I didn't want you to be stuck, alone, eating dinner with people who look at you as though you're spoiled meat."

"*Spoiled meat?*" I stomp on his foot—something he can't evade or sidestep.

He barely even flinches, and he doesn't let go of my hand.

"If you don't tell me what's going on right now—"

"You'll what?" He smiles. "You'll call the police? You'll tell Sean and his family that I can turn into a horse and that I actually am the same being as Obsidian Devil?"

My jaw drops open and dangles that way, idiotically.

"You told me that Sean was a better option for your future than I am, right? You said that he's a better man."

I blink.

He finally releases me and steps back a few inches. "He has money." He lifts one finger. "He's kind." He holds up another. "And he's refined." He lifts a third finger and waits expectantly.

"You have lost your mind."

"I'll explain how I got the car at dinner, and everything I say will be true. Or at least, mostly true."

"Family *drama*?" I ask.

"One of my relatives survived," he says. "That's the good news."

"Whoa, so there may be more horse men running around?" I ask.

"Well, he was an illegitimate cousin, but we did share half our DNA. I doubt he had any magical skill, but apparently it's enough for the Russian government."

"What are you talking about?"

"DNA is wonderful stuff. It turns out, after my half cousin's grandson passed away just over a year ago, leaving no heirs, the entire family estate just sat."

"You're kidding."

"I'll tell you the rest at dinner."

"But how—"

"You didn't think I spent the entire night for the last several weeks reading about movie stars and digging through the same tired articles speculating about the Russian Revolution, did you?"

It's like I don't know him at all. "I assumed you slept part of the time."

"Did you know horses can sleep in the pasture, day or night? Standing or lying down?" He shrugs. "I spent more time sleeping as a horse than anything else—which let me stay up all night as a human."

"We've been standing here far too long," I say. "We need to go."

"Yes, if we dally longer, Sean might suspect that something strange is going on between us." Aleks steps closer again.

I duck under his arm and practically sprint back to Isaac, who definitely noticed that something was off about the two of us, even though we spoke in a language he couldn't understand.

At least the dining room is close—just down a hall and to the left—and the first course is already prepared.

"I'm James." Sean's father stands when I arrive, Aleks on my heels. Lord McDermott is much shorter than I imagined he'd be—barely the same height as his stately wife —and quite stout. Sean must take all his looks from his mother's side.

"Lord James McDermott," Aleksandr says from behind me. "Earl of Coventry, Lord of the beautiful Argan Manor."

Even though I've been around him consistently for weeks and weeks now, it feels like I know nothing about him.

"I apologize profusely for crashing your dinner tonight." Aleks is still talking. Why's he talking? And in such *flawless* English? "I needed to bring Kris some news about the horse we're running in the King George, Obsidian Devil, and then your lovely wife invited me to stay."

"You're the unconventional Russian trainer," Lord McDermott says. "The one who has been dealing with

family drama?" When he smiles, he looks a lot more like Sean than I'd have thought possible.

"How did you learn English so quickly?" Sean asks. "Last I saw you, it was Russian or nothing."

Aleks' grin is a little sheepish. "I learned English as a child, but it was quite rusty, and I struggled quite a lot with the various accents. It was less that I learned it over the past six weeks, and more that I was able to brush it off and clean it up quickly by practicing with Kris every day."

"Every day?" Sean frowns.

"Darling," Lady McDermott says, "Why don't we all sit down. If we don't eat soon, the cook and I will both kill you." Lady McDermott's tone is light, and I'm sure she's trying to defuse the situation like all British nobility are trained to do, but when she glances my way. . .I can't argue with Aleks' assessment. She may not be arguing with her son about bringing me here, but I'm not sure that means she's really pleased he and I are dating.

I follow their lead, waiting for them to take their spots. Then I take the chair to the left of Sean. Aleks, unfortunately, takes the seat directly across from me.

No matter. I'm not going to let him ruin tonight. Regardless of what he says or does, he's just the crazy Russian trainer we found to manage a difficult horse.

I focus instead on the food—the tiny ramekins in front of us have something that's perfectly golden inside. The argument-inducing cheese soufflés, I'm guessing.

Lady McDermott lifts her fork and looks around the table, her way of encouraging us to follow her lead, and I don't need much prompting. The soufflés are even better than I imagined they might be, but Sean's mother keeps talking about the noticeable lack of Gruyere.

It must be hard to live life with such high standards.

"Now, then," Lady McDermott finally says. "Aleksandr,

did you say your name is? Why don't you tell us about this family drama."

"I'm not sure what Kris has told you." He's staring at Sean.

Sean's eyes widen. "Nothing."

I swallow.

Aleks frowns, a reaction that I *know* is fake, and glances my way. "You didn't tell them why you're helping me? That your friend *begged* you to lend a hand? Without your help, I'd never have gotten here."

I wish he'd just say where *here* is. I should be happy he's adapting so well, but really, I'm just more annoyed by the minute. "Right," I say. "But I don't like to brag." I widen my eyes at him pointedly.

"A very commendable trait." Aleks turns back toward Sean. I wish it was because he wanted to spin a good story, but I'm terribly afraid it's because he likes to taunt him. "You see, I was a prince in Russia."

"You and half of Europe." Sean chuckles.

I take a sip of the very excellent wine Lady McDermott paired with the soufflés to stifle my unladylike snort.

"Sean McDermott," his mother says. "That's not how I taught you to behave."

"It's true, Mother, that there are quite a few displaced former-royals from Russia living in hovels across Europe, muttering about the good old days."

"Admittedly, my people have had a difficult run," Aleks says. "But back in 2007, many aristocrats were either regifted their estates by the government, crumbling and slovenly though they had become, or they bought them back. Such was the case with my relative, and he got lucky."

Now we're all listening.

I can't help finishing off my glass of wine. Luckily, the serving people notice and refill it right away.

"My family's property is rich with what you call crude oil reserves, among other things."

Sean drops his fork.

"A few years ago, my nearest relative died, leaving no heir. Or so the government thought."

"But?" Sean asks.

"With the help of a competent lawyer here in England, I was able to submit DNA evidence that proves that I'm the last heir to the Volkonsky family fortune—including the land that was regranted *and* the accumulated funds from the exportation of the oil they've been drilling for on it."

Is he kidding?

"The Russian government is in the process of transferring the property and estate back to me."

Back? I cough.

"Rather, of transferring it *to* me," he says. "As you can see, English still trips me up on occasion."

Of course, the truth is more ridiculous, so they've really got no choice but to accept this is legitimate. It's not like they're more likely to think that he speaks the same languages as me because I'm the one who broke his curse. Or, halfway broke the curse.

They're certainly not going to guess that he still can't use his powers or shift without being in physical contact with me, or that every time I touch him, I want to rip his clothes off.

I take another big swallow of wine. It's so good that it should be savored, but this isn't a savoring type of conversation.

"Will you be heading back to Russia right away, then?" Sean sounds almost absurdly hopeful.

Before Aleks even has a chance to answer, Lord McDermott asks, "It sounds like it's quite a windfall for you. Does it come with a house, did you say?"

Aleks' lips twist and he shrugs. "I believe there's an ancestral palace, though what shape it's in is anyone's guess. I hear it was used as a children's home. I'm not in a huge hurry to rush back. After all she's done to help me reclaim my birthright, I can't leave Kris while she needs me." He turns toward me and flashes a bright, warm smile.

I kick him under the table, and this time he can't dodge.

Infuriatingly, he still doesn't give any sign that he even felt it. I'm beginning to wonder whether he suffers from chronic insensitivity to pain.

"What a wild story," Lady McDermott says.

"It has been quite a week," he says. "But the bank that holds my late cousin's assets moves much faster than the government itself. They've already released control of his accounts to me."

"Oh?" Sean wipes his perfectly clean mouth with a napkin. "Is that how you bought that car?"

"Of course. Finally having the money to do whatever I need to do is a real relief." Aleks turns and looks pointedly at me. "Apparently women don't *like* you unless you're rich. I had no idea."

Sean is many things, but unintelligent is not one of them. It's very clear, from the flare of his nostrils, that he knows Aleksandr is referring to me. Somehow, stupid Aleks managed to insult me and infuriate Sean at the same time.

I want to stab him with my fork, but since I'm holding a spoon, and even if I had a fork, it would only make matters worse, I drink more wine. Since I weigh almost nothing and rarely drink, downing my second glass might have been too much. I feel a little lightheaded.

"Did Kristiana pay for this solicitor who handled all this for you?" Sean asks. "Were you imposing on her for a job *and* borrowing money from her as well?"

"Certainly not," Aleks says. "That would have been too

much." He lowers his voice and leans forward almost an imperceptible amount. "And as you know, she doesn't have any extra money to loan me even had she wanted to."

The conspiratorial smile he flashes at Sean makes my blood boil.

"Luckily," Aleks says, "I had in my possession a number of flawless stones—demantoid garnets, mostly—that collectors of rare stones will give their left arm to find. Have you ever heard of them?"

"Even though they're garnets, they're green," Lord McDermott says, "right? And they're usually found in Russia?"

Aleks smiles. "Exactly. They were given to me by my father, and to him from his father. We've kept them this entire time, knowing they would help us prove our claim. In fact, they're the exact type of stone that was prized by the Czars of Russia for almost a hundred years."

The stones he kept kicking at me on runs and in the pasture were green. Were they these garnets? Where did he get them from?

"You don't say," Lord McDermott says. "They're recognized by their horsetail inclusions, aren't they?"

Judging from his earnest expression, Aleksandr appears to actually like Sean's father, or perhaps he's just impressed by his knowledge. "They don't all have horsetail inclusions —it's not a requirement—but some of the more beautifully formed inclusions can raise the value of the stone, which runs contrary to the general rules for other gems, where any inclusions lower their worth."

"My dad's a bit of a rockhound," Sean says. "It's become more and more of an active hobby as he's gotten older, and now that he's retired, it really keeps him busy."

"I still come in to the bank every now and again," Lord McDermott says. "I'm not totally retired."

"More like every never and whenever." Lady McDer-

mott's eyes crinkle. "He spends all day out with the horses or inside poring over his rock collection."

"Speaking of rocks, do you still happen to have any of those demantoid garnets?" Lord McDermott asks. "I'd love to see them."

"I recently sold most of what I had, but I saved a few." He shifts a bit so he can reach his hand into his pocket, and then pulls it out and lays his palm flat.

In spite of myself, I can't help leaning forward.

"There were a few I couldn't bring myself to part with." He shifts and two large green stones roll toward me, sparkling in the light from the sconces set in the walls behind us.

"Whoa," Lord McDermott says, his cheeks coloring. "How large are those? It's extremely rare to see any over a few carats, isn't it?" He reaches toward Aleks' hand tentatively.

"Most of the stones are under a carat," Aleksandr says, his posture quite relaxed. "These are both just above two carats, and one is essentially flawless, while the other is full of the signature horsetail inclusions."

It's not lost on me that he's holding rare, Russian-discovered gemstones that have *horsetail* inclusions. It's a little strange, but I suppose now that I know the Russian czars were secretly magical horse shifters, it makes sense they'd appreciate gems that had something that looked like a horse's tail inside them.

It's hard, but I force myself not to reach over and snatch them from his hand. That would look strange to everyone here. Even from where I'm sitting, I can tell there's no way those are the same rocks he was kicking around back in Latvia.

So where did he get them? I can't ask him now, clearly, but I really want to know. I saw him the first time he

shifted, and there's no way he was hiding those gems anywhere on his person.

Lord McDermott studies the stones as if they're priceless, oohing and aahing over them enough that I worry Sean might shout at his own father. But eventually, the last course is served and Lady McDermott and Sean and I change the subject, ignoring Aleks' and Lord McDermott's fixation on rocks.

"But the alexandrite that's coming out of Sri Lanka and Brazil is fairly impressive," Lord McDermott says.

"There's no way it can compete with the pieces found in Russia," Aleks says. "After all, it was named for Czar Alexander—it was discovered there."

"I'm not sure," Lord McDermott says. "I recently heard—"

"Dad, even Aleksandr must be tired of hearing what you heard." Sean looks like he's getting a headache from gritting his teeth.

I know I am. "It's getting late," I say. "I probably better head back." Because if I have to hear one more thing about the difference in value between alexandrite and the stupid demantoid garnets? I'm going to throw a toddler-esque temper tantrum right here.

"I'm sure you'll have to be up early to find time on the track with the demon," Sean says.

"Yes," I say. "I will. I also know it's Christmas Eve, and I don't want to interfere with your family traditions." I'm not sure quite what the protocol is for me to leave a dinner party, but I can't wait all night to try and figure it out. I push away from the table and stand up.

And the men all shove to their feet as if that was some kind of command by a general. Lady McDermott, at least, stands slowly and calmly. "Sean, you need to drive her home. I think she's had a bit too much wine."

The room's spinning just a bit, but I'm sure it's not that

bad. It's probably from standing too quickly. "I'm fine." I grab my purse from the back of the chair and turn to head out the door.

And I stumble and practically eat their carpet.

Sean helps me to my feet, but by the time we reach the door, Aleksandr has taken my other arm. "I'll drive her. I haven't had a drop."

"That can't be—"

"I noticed," Lady McDermott says. "I almost asked you whether you don't drink for any particular reason."

Aleks shrugs. "Never been a big fan of anything but vodka, if I'm being honest. Drinking anything else always feels like a waste of time."

Sean's nose scrunches. "Vodka?" He shudders. "It burns like fire when you swallow it."

"That's how you know it's strong enough to do what it's supposed to do," Aleks says.

"A true Russian man." Lord McDermott claps Aleks on his shoulder with his left hand. He has circled around the table and holds out his other hand to Aleksandr. There's clearly something clasped inside of it. In order to take it, Aleks would have to let go of me. I wonder whether Lord McDermott is fumbly. . .or sly.

"You can keep that one," Aleks says. "Consider it a gift from a newly discovered Russian prince for another rock hound's collection."

"Oh, I couldn't possibly keep it," Lord McDermott says.

"I insist," Aleksandr says, tightening his hold on my arm.

"Then I should get you something in return!" Lord McDermott beams.

"Dad, another time, perhaps. Kris needs to get home." Sean tries to tug me away from Aleksandr, but it doesn't work.

Aleks begins to pull the other way.

I'm suddenly reminded of these horrible firecrackers my maternal grandfather used to bring over from America. Gustav loved them—a popper in the center with gunpowder in it, and a string coming out from either side. You'd tie each side to something, and when it was pulled apart? BANG.

I don't want to go bang.

"Stop," I say. "You can't both have an arm. I can totally just drive myself." I slur a little bit at the end, which is embarrassing.

Judging from Lady McDermott's face, I may not have been speaking English, either.

"It's silly for anyone but me to take her home," Aleks says. "We're going the same place, after all."

"No." I shake my arm again. "You're going to sleep in a stall, and I'm sleeping in a bed."

Sean laughs. "I imagine that even the strange Russian will sleep in a bed, sweetheart."

"I can take her from here," Aleks says. "In fact, I insist."

"She's my girlfriend, and I should take her home." Sean is glaring at Aleks, who is staring right back.

I hate everything about this. I try to stomp on both their feet, and only succeed in doing a partial version of the splits. There's also a kind of a ripping sound I don't want to think about too hard.

Things get a little bleary for a moment, and then I realize I'm being carried.

By Aleks. "Oh." My own voice sounds strange. A little airy and light. "You won."

When he chuckles, I feel the movement in his chest against my face.

"I like when you carry me."

I think he's smiling. "Me too."

"You're not taking me to sleep on shavings, right?"

"No, we're definitely going to the hotel. You need a bed."

"So do you, when you're not a horse."

"Shh," Aleks whispers. "Your wannabe boyfriend is following us, and even though we're speaking in Russian, I'm not sure what he may pick up."

"He can't speak a word of Russian." I laugh. "Not a word." I tap Aleksandr on the nose.

"Good heavens," Sean says. "She never drinks. I didn't even think to tell the waitstaff not to refill her wine glass."

Aleks freezes, and I blink and look around. We've reached the front door. "I really will take it from here."

Sean looks prepared to argue.

"Let's not make a scene," Aleks says. "No matter what I may say or do, you know it's you she came to see."

That calms Sean down, and he helps tuck me into the passenger side of Aleks' new car.

"This car is loud," I shout, once the engine roars to life.

"I'll call you tomorrow," Sean says as he closes the door.

I lean against the door and press my lips to the glass. Then I blow him a raspberry.

I thought he would think it was sweet, but Sean looks horrified.

"Just drive," I mumble.

Aleks obliges, speeding away from Argan Manor way, way too fast.

"My stomach does not like that," I say, closing and opening my eyes slowly.

"Hang in there, zaychonuk. I'll get you there soon."

"Rabbit? I'm not a rabbit." But I'm too tired to argue with him. Besides, I kind of like that word—zaychonuk. I've heard people use it, but no one ever has for me.

I think I drift off, because seconds later, the car's stopping. And a blink later, Aleksandr's opening the door. A

split second after that, I'm shoving my purse at him. "You get the key."

"The—what?"

"The key to the room. I can't find it." I practically dump the entire contents of my purse on the ground.

Aleks retrieves most of it, and, blessedly, finds my key. "But where do we take this?" He looks at the blank card with the hotel name written on it in befuddlement.

It makes me laugh.

"What's funny?"

"My room is number three oh five. On the third floor. Room five. I remember because that was the first three numbers in my phone number in college. Three oh five. But my phone wasn't on the third floor in college." I lean closer to him and blink a few times until I can focus. "It was on the fourth."

Aleks helps me reach the third floor, and he even figures out how to open the door, but then he tries to leave.

"Wait." I grab his lapels.

"I need to go back to the barn," he says. "I've been gone too long."

"No," I say, suddenly desperately sad at the thought that he won't be with me. "I need you to stay."

He blinks. "Stay?" He peers past me. "On that single bed?"

I shove his chest. His very solid, very nice chest. "You're not a horse right now. You should sleep on a bed, and I'm tired. Too tired to take you to the barn."

"I'll go there and sleep in the stall—I can make up something if someone shows up," he says. "I'll come back and grab you in the morning."

"No," I say.

"Trust me, zaychonuk, in the morning you'll remember how mad at me you are. You'll be glad I didn't stick around. Or I will. . ."

His words remind me that I *am* upset with him. "I cannot believe you just showed up like that—"

"You're not mad I came. You're upset that I'm not helpless anymore."

He makes no sense, and I'm still standing in the doorway. Alone. "Why would I want you to be helpless?" I sigh. "Either go or stay. Stop standing there, talking to me. My head hurts."

"You're wrong." Aleksandr leans toward me.

My heart races.

"You're scared at the thought of *being with* anyone, and when you thought of me as poor, when I was nothing but a lost mess, you could hold me at arm's length."

"I was telling you to come inside, so. . ." I duck inside and start to pull the door closed behind me. I have the sudden feeling like a predator's coming for me.

Aleksandr's hand slams against the doorframe, blocking my attempt to close it, and he inches closer to me still. "Now you don't have a reason to run, and that scares you most of all."

"I don't run away from people," I hiss. "Sean left me back then, for the record." All the woozy, warm feelings I had before are gone. Does that mean I'm suddenly sober?

"I've always said that he's a moron," Aleks says. "But that doesn't mean you aren't one, too."

Now he's really pissing me off. I open the door wide, so I can really lay into him. "You think you know everything, but you don't. Whether you have a car or not, you're still the same guy who didn't know coffee could be made from a tube, and—"

He scrunches his nose. "I still maintain it can't. What you believe passes for coffee these days is a travesty."

"You couldn't use a cell phone or even buckle your seatbelt."

"I learned all of that within twenty-four hours of being freed by you."

He's not wrong about that. I'm not exactly sure why I'm so mad, but I am. Spitting mad. "Just get out." I try to slam the door again, and almost mash his hand. Before, I wanted him to stay and he wanted to go. Now I want him to go, and he's blocking the door.

"I read something last week that I think you should hear. Anger is what they call a masking emotion." His smile makes his face so handsome it hurts me to look at it.

"Who cares?" I ask.

"It's always a cover for something else. So right now, you're angry with me to keep from thinking about what you really feel. Maybe you should think about that, zaychonuk."

I hate how much I like hearing him use a pet name for me. I hate how it makes me quiver inside. "Stop calling me that."

"You focus on you." His half smile is almost sexier than his full smile.

"It's not like you know what you want or how you feel."

"Oh, but I do."

"You can't even tell me why you really came tonight, Mr. Masking Emotions."

"Oh, but I can."

"Why? Do you really hate Sean that much? He's not that bad a guy, and I don't need your help. I'm a big girl."

He laughs then, throwing back his head and really making some noise. "That's rich." He eyes me from my toes to my head. "You're the smallest woman I know."

"Shut up," I say. "No matter what size I am, I don't need you to keep me safe."

"I didn't come tonight to keep you safe." His words are soft.

"Good, because—"

"I had things to do tonight, actually, but the thought of you spending the evening with Sean, or maybe even spending the night with him. . ." That same muscle in his jaw works, and he inhales sharply. "I picked up my car early, and skipped out on a meeting I should have taken, because I wanted to kill him, but I figured making him look bad might be a decent alternative."

"Well, that backfired," I say.

"Oh?"

"Because I like Sean more than ever after the way he acted tonight. And I dislike you more than ever, too."

His eyes flash. "Well, you know what they say."

"Who's they?" I hate this new Aleks. I miss the one who was a ball of never-ending questions.

"Love and hate aren't opposites." His voice drops just a hair. "There's only a razor-thin line between them."

"Well then I must practically love you," I say. "Because I can't think of anyone I hate more."

❧ 17 ❧

Aleksandr finally leaves, but when he does, he's smiling. Something about me saying I hated him made him *happy*. At least one thing hasn't changed.

He's still insane.

By the time I wake up, Sean's left me a few text messages. My truck is in the parking lot, and he left the keys with the front desk. He went by to check on Obsidian, but the attendants told him that they hadn't seen me and they had strict orders to leave his stall entirely alone.

The orders were from a crazy, rich Russian man.

Which means Aleksandr bribed them.

I wish it didn't, but it makes me like him more. He paid the grooms at Kempton Park to let me sleep in after I drank too much. If that's not a man worth his weight in gold, I don't know what is.

Even so, when I arrive, I'm irrationally angry with him again. He tries to talk to me about last night now that I'm totally sober, but it makes me feel twitchy and terse.

"Sean's a nice guy," Aleks finally admits.

215

I almost take the bait, but I can sense there's something more coming.

"Don't you think so?" He quirks one eyebrow.

"I think that you're trying to trick me," I say. "And I think that we need everyone around here to see Obsidian soon, or they're going to start to wonder whether he's real."

Aleksandr circles the stall toward me.

I back up just as fast.

"We still have some things to talk about," he says.

I notice shavings in his hair. That makes me think about him sleeping in here all night long, as a human. Instead of staying with me like I asked him to. . . And then I feel angry.

A masking emotion.

That makes me even more angry.

So the second he gets close enough, I change him. At this rate, even with his secret bag, he's not going to have any clothes left for very long. It's a good thing I changed him, though, because seconds later, Sean's tapping on the stall wall. "Kris? I brought breakfast."

I don't groan. I'm happy to see him.

"Let me get the halter on Obsidian first." And kick his shredded clothing into the corner, under shavings.

"Is everything okay? Is that demon acting up?"

Obsidian's pawing at the ground, agitated either by the sound of Sean's voice or by my quick change.

"Time to show them all what you've got," I whisper. Then I slide the halter over his nose and buckle it in place. "No more fits, alright? And no kicking or biting Sean, either."

"You're still talking to him like he understands you?" The smirk on Sean's face annoys me.

"Sometimes," I admit.

Obsidian Devil bumps me and slides his face right alongside mine, nuzzling my neck. With any other horse—

with Five, for instance—I'd think it was cute. I'd probably grin and rub his nose.

But knowing it's Aleks kind of weirds me out. If he did that as a person I'd be disgusted.

That's a lie.

The thought of Aleks nuzzling my neck with his mouth? It sends a big-time shiver up my spine and makes me want to bite my lip.

"Listen, I know you had no way of knowing he'd come by last night," Sean says. "But I hate that Russian guy."

"I know you do," I say. "But—"

"Just listen for a second," he says.

That's fair.

"I get why you hired him. John hates this horse." He glares. "I hate him, too. Actually, no one but you likes him, and then this guy shows up, and he's pathetic and he needs work and he's willing to help."

I open my mouth, but Sean presses a finger to it.

Obsidian bumps and rubs my face even more. I swat him away.

"You have a big heart, Kris. That's one of the things I love about you."

Obsidian snorts. It flings snot on my shoulder.

I shove him this time, hard.

"But I need you to really hear me this time. I know you like your projects, and I know you like to help people, but I mean this. I *hate* the idea of him working with you, for you, whatever, and it makes me uncomfortable. And now that he's rich? He doesn't need you."

"What are you saying?"

"Fire him," Sean says. "Or lay him off, or call it whatever you want. He clearly doesn't need your money, and you don't need him, either. You have me for whatever you need." He waves at Obsidian. "Besides. That horse will do anything for you."

"I'll think about it," I say.

Sean steps closer. "I know you. That means no. And I need you to say yes."

"But I—"

He does it again, pressing his hand to my mouth. "No buts." He smiles. "Say yes."

"I'll talk to him, and—"

"He's strange," Sean says. "And did you hear what he said last night? He said women only like men if they're *rich*. He was talking about you when he said that." His right hand balls into a fist. "He meant that you'd like him now that he's got money. He said it like it was the only thing keeping you with me instead of him. Tell me you got that subtext."

"I'm not an idiot," I say. "But I think this is more complicated than you're making it out to be. I wish you'd trust me to manage my own life and my own affairs."

"I do," Sean says. "But I also think that if we're going to be together again, we should respect the things that the other person needs." He leans in closer, his breath against my face. "I love you, Kris. I never stopped loving you, and I want you with me all the time. If you can't get rid of that guy, I might go nuts."

He's right. He's not issuing ultimatums. He's telling me how he feels, and I should be listening. In fact, what he's saying isn't even incongruent with what I'd already decided. Aleksandr needs to go—soon. I just wish I could explain exactly what was going on to Sean. Since it would put another person's life and future at risk, I still don't feel like I can.

"I hear what you're saying and I'm taking it seriously," I say. "I swear."

He smiles then, slowly. "Thank you. And I have something I brought for you, as well." He reaches in his pocket and pulls out a box.

My heart goes crazy. Is he. . .about to propose? The box isn't super small, but it's not huge, either. And how should I know what an engagement ring box looks like?

But when he opens it, he's not down on one knee. . .and it's a necklace. A diamond necklace, with a single, *huge* heart stone, set in white gold. The stone must be several carats, because it's bigger than the end of my thumb. "Merry Christmas," he says.

"I didn't bring anything for you," I say. "I was too busy planning for the hunt."

He shakes his head. "Of course you didn't." He stands, still holding out the necklace. "I hadn't planned anything this elaborate either, but Mother noticed you didn't really have any jewelry on. And I agreed with her that I should do something to change that."

It should make me giddy with joy. The guy I've been dating is giving me something stunning. Something that sends a clear signal that I matter to him.

Only, the way he said that kind of feels. . .judgmental. Like I was found lacking somehow, and they need to fix me up. Also, I was relieved that he didn't seem to care as much what his parents thought, but his back and forth with them isn't very reassuring.

"I told Mom I'd go pick something out right away, but it's Christmas Day, so obviously nothing's open. Dad actually suggested I use one of his special stones—he'd just had it set like this."

I'm not sure what to say about that. He brought me a necklace his dad had put in a pendant. . .for his mom?

"Do you like it?" Sean's still holding it out toward me.

I'm a horrible, rude troll. I grab the box and clutch it against my chest. "I love it," I say. "But the reason I don't wear much jewelry is that I'm always outside, getting dirty and muddy. What if I wore it and then I lost it?"

"Do you think you might? Even if you tuck it inside

your shirt?" He frowns. "Maybe you should just wear it for special occasions, then. In fact, Mom wanted to see if you could come for dinner again tonight. She's having a few people over—just extended family, really, and she'd love it if you could come, too."

"Oh," I say.

"Preferably without accompaniment, this time."

And now I feel like I'm being scolded. I didn't bring Aleks last time. I certainly didn't want him there. Sean and I should be on the same side, but instead, Aleksandr's like a wedge between us.

"For sure I'll come," I say. "And I won't bring anyone along, I promise."

As I say that, I remember with slight surprise that Obsidian hasn't made a peep in a little too long. I glance over my shoulder, and he's watching us. Intently. A little too intently.

Sean has no idea Aleksandr's here, and it feels almost. . .disloyal of me that I haven't told him. But if I do tell him, I put Aleksandr at risk. I have no idea whom he might tell, or what might snowball from that.

Ugh. Just, ugh.

"I'm really looking forward to spending Christmas Eve with you," he says. "Like the one we spent together years and years ago." He smiles. "Do you remember?"

Dad and Gustav had the flu back home, so I had to stay at school. At the last minute, Sean stayed, too. It was probably the nicest few days we shared in the entire time we were together. No one else was around, and he focused entirely on me.

"I do."

"I love you, Kris."

I inhale slowly, and as I exhale, I start to lean toward him. At least I can reassure him that I care about him too,

and that I'm in this. Sean relaxes as I soften, and I think he's about to kiss me.

When Obsidian bites his shoulder.

Sean balls up his fist, ready to sock Obsidian on the nose. I wouldn't blame him at all.

"He's just a horse, he's just a horse," he's chanting under his breath.

"But he shouldn't behave like that." I slap Obsidian Devil's neck as hard as I can. Unfortunately, I know just how little a slap from me really bothers him.

"I'm going to cast my vote that Aleksandr *and* the demon here both go." Sean scowls. "But—this should tell you how much I despise him—sack that trainer first."

Oh, the irony of him telling me that he wants them both gone.

"Noted," I say. "But for now, I ought to get him out there and get familiar with the course for tomorrow."

"Right." Sean straightens his shoulder and levels his best angry stare at Obsidian. "If you even *think* about acting around my sweet Kris the way you act around me?" He holds up one finger and points. "I'll bring a rifle and shoot you in the head. Don't think I won't. I'd gladly write her a check for a half million euros to buy your corpse, if I think that's what it'll take to keep her safe."

When I saw the movie *Tangled*, like all horse people, I kind of hated how they made the white horse into such a humanlike character. Horses have their own personalities—they don't need to be just like humans. But I swear, Obsidian's glaring at Sean in the exact same way that white horse glared at the thief guy.

"You better head out before you get bitten again," I say, and then I pointedly fasten the diamond pendant around my neck right in front of Obsidian. In case he's not getting the point, I want him to see that Sean and I are fine. I may not have officially called him my boyfriend, and I may not

have been able to bring myself to say 'I love you' back—yet —but we are doing really well.

There's no room for him to pry us apart as some kind of weird joke.

Once I'm done with the pendant, Obsidian starts pawing the ground of the stall until the shavings are gone, and then he keeps right on going, dragging his hoof across the rubber mats.

I ignore him.

He whinnies and whickers and tries nuzzling my arm.

I slap him.

He tosses his head when I try to bridle him, and snaps at my fingers to show me he's serious.

"I know you want me to change you back into human form. I know you want to talk to me." I pause. "But I don't want to hear what you have to say." I fume. "You came to my boyfriend's house last night because you were *jealous*. Not to help me, and not because you were worried about me. I remember what you said—you wrecked my night *for you*. You were being selfish. I'm delighted you've gotten your life back on track. I think it's great you've found some rocks, though I do want know where the heck they came from. I'm happy that, once again, your DNA has landed you in the top quarter of a percent of the world's wealthiest people or whatever. But I'm about done letting your whims wreck *my* life. Now that you're fine?"

I make a decision in that moment. One I can't come back from.

"I want you to leave after tomorrow's race."

It's a little hypocritical of me. I do know that.

I mean, I should send him home *today* if that's how I feel. Certainly, Sean would want me to if he knew Obsidian was Aleks, and that Aleks was Obsidian. If he knew the truth, I have no idea what he'd do to Aleks, but I know how he'd feel about them being the same being.

But with Five unable to race, well. I kind of need Obsidian's help to win so I can pay the next loan payment. I've scraped together all the money I could in the hopes I might avoid either selling the family farm or begging Sean for more money.

But once I've won tomorrow? Then he can go without damaging me.

Doesn't that mean I'm selfish too? Am I just as bad as I was accusing him of being?

The difference is that, as far as I know, one more day with me won't cause him harm. He knew that causing a disturbance with Sean would be damaging to me.

"If, once you get back to Russia, you figure something out about the curse, you can come back and talk to me about it. I'll be happy to do whatever I can do to help with that, even in the future." It's not like he doesn't know where I live.

His eyes flash, and he throws his head. He lets out an almost startling neigh.

Even so, I shake my head. "No. I'll change you tomorrow. You can yell at me then—after the race. You can plead your case, or whatever. I know you have money now. You even have a car. You don't need me anymore for any of those things, so I'm going to tell Sean I sold you to Aleks. The irony makes me laugh. And then I'm going to leave you here." I sigh. "No matter what you say."

He's still not happy, but Obsidian settles down after that and lets me lead him outside. I saddle him up, and when I'm about to swing onto his back, my phone rings.

It's my real estate agent.

Calling on Christmas Day.

"You've gotten an offer," she says.

"You're kidding. Has anyone even seen the property?"

"We've had two showings while you've been gone," she says. "It must be from one of them. And the offer is good.

It's actually ten percent *above* asking, which is almost unheard of right now. But there's one strange thing."

Of course there is. It *is* my life we're talking about. "What?"

"I'm not sure who the offer's from."

"I'm sorry?"

"It's through an intermediary. One of the terms of the offer is that you can't know anything about the buyer."

"But they'll become my *neighbor*," I say. "I'm keeping the house and the old barn, plus a few of the pastures. They'll be right across a fence line. Won't I eventually find out?"

"I think it's likely to be someone you don't like." She's quiet for a moment. "I mean, who else would keep it a secret?"

Sean might.

"Do you have any enemies?"

Rickets comes to mind immediately. If he keeps tabs on my dad, he might even have noticed that our land went up for sale. I'm sure he'd be delighted to lord it over my dad that he impoverished him. He might even put up a mansion a hundred yards from our house to rub Dad's face in it.

Ugh.

"I mean, not really," I lie.

I have no idea what to do about it.

It's probably Sean, right? He's the only person I know with money who might actually want to buy it.

"I'll forward the offer along to you for your review. The terms say you have seventy-two hours to decide."

"But it's Christmas. Surely it's seventy-two hours from, say, New Year's Day."

"It's all very strange, but I think you should strongly consider it. That's a lot of money, and the earnest money isn't bad, either. It's also not a contingent offer, which means if they, for some reason, can't come up with financing for the sales price, you can keep the deposit."

"Isn't that usually only a stipulation someone who knew they were good for the money would agree to?"

"Usually, yes."

I hang up.

And then I stand utterly still, staring at my shiny black boots until Obsidian bumps my hand.

I nearly drop my phone.

"Careful," I snap. "It's been a very weird day, and it only seems to be getting stranger."

The forecast called for a sunny, albeit cold, and clear weekend. While we're breezing the track, it starts to drizzle, and for some reason, I'm not even surprised.

❧ 18 ❧

Obsidian Devil lives up to his name, acting up badly when I refuse to turn him after our workout.

"I know you want to be human, but when I change you, you do things I can't deal with right now."

I think about how he carried me to my room. How he brushed my hair back gently. And how he made my heart flutter and my stomach flip flop.

That's the real reason I can't change him. It confuses me.

But his tantrum has my dad and John both worried.

"Do you think he'll injure his legs?" My dad's eyes are wide. "I've never heard him kick the stall that much. I'm worried he might break the wood."

"Sean said Aleksandr's here somewhere," John says. "Maybe he can calm him down."

I stifle my laugh.

"If we can't calm him down, we may need to sedate him," Dad says. "If we don't, he really might hurt himself."

He's taken to throwing himself against the wall of the stall, and the grooms are looking at us sideways. I know the

truth—even if he hurts himself, he can heal any injury that will heal on its own with time. Hopefully the moron won't do any real damage.

He's not a real horse, and therefore he has a little more sense, but I guess with men there's no way to know for sure. "Give me a moment."

When I duck back into the stall, he's waiting expectantly.

That's when I realize I don't have his bag—which is probably still in his new car—and if I change him now, he'll be standing there naked. Aside from the fact that he'll be awfully cold, I don't think it's a great idea for me either.

"I'm going to change you right now," I say.

Most people call it smiling when a horse throws its top lip up, baring its teeth. Some of them do it after getting molasses treats. It's definitely a funny image, and I get why they call it that.

But until that moment, I didn't know what a horse really looked like when it was smiling. It's like his whole body shivers, and his lips shake, and he looks undeniably pleased.

"You need clothes, first," I say reasonably.

He paws at the corner of the stall, and I shake my head. "Those are shredded."

But he's not unearthing his destroyed clothes. He's unburying his car key. I snatch it and dash past a surprised John and my dad.

"Where are you going?" John asks.

"And how'd you get him to stop flipping out?" Dad chases after me for a moment, but since he's pretty out of shape, I'm not surprised when he stops well before the parking lot.

It allows me to snag Aleksandr's bag without much trouble, and I have the whole walk back to think up some kind of plausible story.

"I'm going to need you both to leave," I say. "The thing is, Aleksandr has a strange way of doing things, and he didn't want you to know he was coming. He's meeting with some people, and he'll be leaving us soon. But he's also found a buyer for Obsidian. The whole thing could be wrapped up quickly."

I don't mention the offer on the farm. Hopefully, by tomorrow, we won't need it.

"Okay," John says.

"Why didn't you do this before?" Dad asks.

"It's a long story," I say. "But I need you two to buy some things. Strange things. Aleksandr says that when Obsidian really has a bad day, the only thing that works to calm him down is a couple of beers."

John and my dad exchange glances.

"And you know the treats I used to make? Those help, too." I've done some web searching, and I discovered that the ingredients for some homemade horse treats I learned at camp two decades back will be difficult to locate in the UK. Tracking the ingredients down should actually take them most of the day, given that it's Christmas Day and most places are closed.

Once I explain what I'm planning, they both calm down. My request that they spend the day traipsing halfway across London to find an imported variety of beer doesn't seem strange to them, apparently. Probably because they're horse people. That's kind of our thing—strange requests to mollify uber-expensive animals that are no longer necessary for anything essential, but that we love beyond all reason.

Once they leave, I gird up my logic and reason and prepare to duel with Aleksandr Volkonsky. I'm going to have to change him eventually. It may as well be quickly, right now, before I leave for another dinner at Sean's mansion.

I duck into the stall and observe my ancient magician.

He's standing totally still, and if a horse could make puppy eyes, well, he'd be making them. "Don't give me that. I don't believe it for a nanosecond." I arch one eyebrow. "I'm going to make you human for five minutes, and then you go right back. Don't even *think* about following me to Sean's house again."

He snorts.

"Is that a yes?" I glare. "Bob your head, or I'm going right back out this door."

He exhales. And then he bobs his head.

"Fine. Now, behave when I change you, and don't make me regret this."

I walk toward him and place my hand on his neck. "I want you to be human again," I say simply.

It still amazes me that it's all it takes. Obviously it's because it's really *his power,* not mine, and I'm just somehow able to release what he can already do. Even so, it's miraculous.

Which is why I watch for too long and end up with an eyeful.

It's not because I *wanted* to see anything.

I turn away too late, but at least I'm quick about it when I do.

"You don't have to turn around," he says boldly. "I'm not shy."

"That's the problem," I practically hiss. "You're not nearly shy enough. I have a boyfriend—"

"Oh, I don't think so. I've heard you dance around the word. And I've heard him say 'I love you' a few times without a response from you. If I'm not mistaken, the two of you haven't—"

I throw my hand out, palm toward him. "Stop."

"Look, I need to explain a few things." He clears his throat. "I have clothes on, now. You can turn around."

I do, but I really shouldn't have. "Trousers are not the

same as clothes," I say as grumpily as I can muster. But I don't turn back around. I can't help staring as much as I can. After all, starting tomorrow, I won't be able to see all that rich, golden skin. Those rippling muscles. The swollen shoulders and burly arms.

I don't even have any photos of him. The thought makes me kind of sad, but taking any now would be beyond obvious.

He clears his throat again. "You okay?"

I snap my eyes up to meet his. "Your time is ticking."

"Ah, yes." He snorts, and it sounds just like when Obsidian does it. "First off, I just want to say that, while you are angry with me for things like biting your dumb wannabe boyfriend, consider the things I *could* have done and didn't."

"What are you saying?"

"I was in horse form, but I was standing right next to you. I could have leaned against your arm, and while we were in contact, I could have sucked him down into the earth, for instance."

My jaw drops.

"I didn't do that," he says. "Nor did I use my powers to prematurely age him."

I blink.

"We haven't really gone over what I can do, but I can accelerate the growth process of things like plants. . .and people. It's tied to my ability to heal, but it also means I could have done some real damage. I'd like you to at least *acknowledge* that I exercised some restraint."

I think about the men he buried alive, and I want to argue that leaving a huge bruise on Sean's arm isn't really exercising restraint, but to him? I think it actually may have been. "Fine," I say. "Now, what else?"

"You asked, sort of, how I got the stones."

I shrug.

"Care to follow me outside?" He throws up his hands. "I'll be quick. I know, you have a date tonight, and I wouldn't dream of interfering."

When I arch one eyebrow, he grins sheepishly.

"Not again, anyway."

I gesture for the door, and then I follow him out.

We don't go far—a few dozen yards past the parking lot. Then he stops, glances around, and satisfied that no one is close, he hunches down toward the ground. Then he reaches his hand back toward me.

"What?"

He rolls his eyes. "I have to be touching you."

"Is this some kind of trick?"

He shakes his head. "Not at all. I promise."

I shuffle just close enough for our fingers to touch, and then I stop.

He compresses his lips but doesn't argue. His fingers take mine, and then he turns toward the ground.

He swears under his breath, and then he exhales gustily. "You know, anywhere else on earth would be better for this demonstration. I'm not sure whether it's the vast number of people who have lived here for so long that they picked it clean, or whether it's just not a great area for gems, but it feels like there's nothing valuable here for *miles and miles*."

"What are we doing?"

He turns his eyes heavenward. "Give me another moment."

I shift a bit closer, and he clamps down on my fingers and digs his free hand into the sloppy dirt. It's not exactly the best time to be out here, given the recent rain.

"There." He heaves out a breath he'd been holding and stands, his hand totally covered in mud. He's beaming, for some reason.

I drop my hand from his. "What am I looking at, exactly?"

"Stupid England and its incessant rain." He walks toward the closest building and hunts around until he finds a spigot. Then he rinses his hand, revealing something amazing.

A glistening piece of amber.

"And it's not just that." There are two people walking a horse about twenty feet away, but once they're past, he holds out his hand again, motioning for me to take it.

"It's been much more than five minutes," I say.

"I didn't agree to that time limit," he says.

"Are you kidding me right now?" I'm so mad I could punch him.

He frowns. "I mean, I did bob my head, but if I could have spoken, I'd have said I needed ten to fifteen at least."

"Just do it." I offer my hand.

He takes it immediately.

And I pretend I feel *nothing* when he touches me. No rush of adrenaline that makes my heart soar. No butterflies chasing one another around in my stomach. No sinking sensation deep down at the bottom of my belly that makes me want to drag him closer and kiss him. Hard.

None of that.

"Okay, now watch."

Yes, I should watch. That will keep me from staring at his gorgeous mouth. At his—oh. He is doing something. I focus on the rough-hewn amber, marveling as he reshapes it effortlessly in front of me.

"Part of my power is that I can sense the inside of the stones and gems. So in addition to pulling them to me from most anywhere as long as it's not *too* far away, I can also shape them, removing the imperfections and faceting the edges."

He hands me a stunning, fiery reddish-orange stone, faceted and sparkling in the rare burst of sunlight. In the

very center, there's the fossil of a tiny butterfly, caught in the prime of its life and frozen in time forever.

"If we were anywhere but this sorry lump of rock they call Britain, I'd give you something decent." He sighs. "But listen, I found those demantoid garnets on your land, and—"

I shake my head. "They're yours. I'd never have found them. Don't even think about feeling guilty. You even tried to talk to me about them, and I shut you down."

"Kris." His voice is different than I'm used to hearing. Gruffer, maybe? Rough around the edges.

I turn to meet his eyes. "What?"

"Sean likes you. I believe that he truly does, in his way. But he has parents who are very involved, and no matter what you do, no matter what you say or how you change, you'll never be what they want you to be. They'll always be there, making you feel bad about yourself."

I shake my head. "Aleks, this is—"

"Come with me to Russia, zaychonuk," he says. "I have no parents to tell you what to do, and from what I can tell, my old home is still palatial, but it's a huge pile of moldering rock. You can remodel it however you want, or we can level it and build something new. I don't care what colors or materials you pick, or how big it is, or how many stalls you put in the barn I'll build for you."

My throat closes off. My eyes well with tears. Even though I know this isn't real, it still affects me.

He's saying he'll give me anything and everything I could ever want.

But I'd be like that butterfly. I know the real reason he wants me to leave with him—it's not that he can't look away from me like I can't keep my eyes off of him.

It's because I'm the only way he can use his stupid magic.

Without me, he can't do any of the things he wants to do.

Which means I'll always be the thing he needs, but not the thing he wants. At least I know Sean wants me.

"Aleksandr," I say. "I can't."

His eyes fall, then. "Why not? Do you really prefer him to me? Is it because of the past? Or because I'm Russian? Because I'm a horse?"

"I can't do this," I say. "I told you what I want, and I haven't changed my mind."

"You really want me to leave tomorrow?"

"I know we haven't cracked the curse, but I need to live my life, and it's time you face the truth. You're going to have to live yours. . .without your magical powers. Trust me when I say, it may be harder, but you'll get used to it. It's still worth living."

He swallows slowly and nods his head, his eyes deep and intense. "Okay."

He doesn't fight me when I turn him back into a horse. I almost wish he would, because this quiet enduring thing he's doing is almost the worst thing he's done yet.

The tiny group of extended family Sean said his mom invited? Yeah, it's like twenty people.

I suppose I can't blame her. I mean, it *is* Christmas, but it drags on and on, and I find myself wishing over and over that I had someone for whom I could pretend I was drunk. Then they could toss me over their shoulder and carry me out of here.

All the guests compliment me on my necklace, and I realize that Sean or his father or both have told them it was his gift to me.

Several of them say things like, "Oh, how lovely for you."

Or, "You must be so delighted to have something so valuable."

Like I'm a puppy with a blinged-up collar, and I should be eternally grateful for the largesse of the McDermotts.

The whole thing starts to piss me off.

I know it's probably not something I'll have to deal with forever, and I'm sure if Sean heard it, he'd shut them down. But it annoys me all the same.

Finally, about an hour after I really needed to leave to

get enough sleep for tomorrow's race, I make my way to Sean's side and tap his arm. "I called an Uber. I need to head out front to meet it."

His eyes widen. "An Uber?" He laughs. "You're so funny, all the time."

"I really did," I say.

His aunt's eyes dart sideways toward Sean in horror.

In for a penny, in for a pound. "I really do need to go, or I'll get charged an extra fee for making them wait. Then I might not be able to make my credit card bill payment this month." I widen my eyes, compress my lips, and meet the aunt's gaze solemnly, as if she might commiserate with me.

The sad thing is that, while I'm hamming it up, I didn't need to stretch to come up with that. I doubt they even fully comprehend what I'm saying, and I'm quite sure his aunt has never taken an Uber in her life. Actually, I doubt Sean has either. I've heard him mention that he has a driver.

"I'll see you in the morning?" Before he can argue with me, I'm darting out the door and shooting toward the front entrance.

Down the hall, their butler's arguing with my Uber driver. It doesn't appear to be going well.

"I assure you, *sir*, that no one in this residence would dream of—"

"Hey there." I wave. "Thanks for getting here so fast."

I almost make it into the back of the Kia Sedona before Sean hurtles through the front doors. I suppress my groan.

"Really, Sean, I'm fine. I'll see you tomorrow."

"I can drive you," he says. "Or—"

"If you suggest that your driver take me home," I say, "I might scream."

At least Sean knows his limits. He doesn't argue anymore. He just waves goodbye.

And I spend the entire ride back to Kempton Park

thinking about how different we are. Though, that may not be the biggest issue. I mean, Aleksandr is *Russian*, he's about a gazillion years older than I am, and he can turn into a horse. I doubt we could be more different.

But I haven't been put in the same situations with him. We've never dated, and he only likes me because he wants to take me home in his pocket and pull me out whenever things go wrong.

It's hard to remember that, sometimes.

Like all night long, when I dream of long, hard rides and sweating skin. I wake up feeling very exhausted and remarkably bothered.

I'm proud of myself for not showing any of that when I reach the stables. Without a mention about last night or the drama or my doubts, I saddle Obsidian Devil calmly and walk him out to the birdcage so we'll be there for the build-up, parade, and regirthing. Finn's there with a large horse I've seen at least once before, and he's having trouble keeping him still.

Racehorses aren't known for being calm on the ground, but I'm worried he might run over Finn before he even swings up into the saddle.

I flog my brain to try and place whose mount it is. "Is that—"

"Flaming Shot," he says. "I rode him last season, in the Champion Hurdle, at Cheltenham."

"Ah, right. The day before the Cup."

Finn nods. As we approach, his large grey whinnies a loud *Hello*. Obsidian snorts and paws at the ground.

"Are you going to be able to control your boy?" Finn shakes his head a bit.

It's a little bit ironic he's asking, since Obsidian is standing utterly calm and his horse is throwing a fit.

"I don't envy you the ride today," Finn continues, "if I'm

being honest. I hate riding stallions for hunts, but he's the worst I've ever had to deal with."

I shrug and run a hand over his nose. "There are just eight horses in today's race. Plus, I've had him almost two months. He'll be a totally different horse this time, trust me."

"They're saying it'll be a tight race. My mum's here and she put a fiver on both of us to win." He laughs. "She said she'll buy me ice cream to cheer me up if I lose."

"Your own mum's betting against you." I whistle. "That must hurt."

"I told her you were the only horse here that might take me."

I shiver. "But ice cream? It's forty degrees and wet outside. I hate to be the one to tell you this, but there's something wrong with your mom, Finn."

He shrugs. "That's why, no matter how much I liked you back when you were in school, we never would have worked. You just don't have the same passion for ice cream that McGees do."

Finn's just being ridiculous. There's no way he ever liked me back then. Before I can mock him for teasing me, Flaming Shot shifts and starts to veer sideways, so Finn walks him in a big circle. I take a moment to check out our competition, now that we're nose-to-nose.

Brigadier General, a large bay gelding, is actually favored to win, but I heard that Flaming Shot was ranked just behind him. I can see why they favor Brigadier, but he doesn't do well on heavy ground. If I remember right from last year, Flaming Shot will have the edge on him there. Leggy horses tend to run better in the sloppy races. Heavy weights like Brigadier General sink too much with each stride. He may have recently picked up both the Sodexo Gold and the Betvictor, but this will be his first significant challenge.

Brigadier's jockey is mean as a badger. I try never to talk to Rex McComb. It seems fitting that Rickets would have hired him as one of his permanent stable jockeys. Brigadier's only seven, just like Five Times Fast. He's shiny and sleek and if I wasn't racing against him, I'd put a fiver on him. Except if I won, it would mean that Rickets won. That's extra incentive for me to try hard, as if I needed any more.

Apex, a chestnut gelding with three white socks and a blaze, keeps tossing his head and shying, and I wonder whether Paddy Farland can handle him. He won the King George last year on Apex, so they'll be a hard pair to beat, but Apex looks off today. Or maybe that's just wishful thinking.

Down On My Luck is a leggy, dappled roan, but I've seen him run before and although they look strange, his gangly legs work just fine, especially when the ground's soggy like today. It's a lucky draw for a mudlark like him, especially since the weather was supposed to be sunny and dry. His jockey, Anthony Felt, knows what he's doing, and his trainer has been talking for months about his improvement this season.

Stay Behind Me is a write in, and other than feeling like the patchy looking sorrel is a little out of his element, I don't know much about him. The owner—Hertzman Farms —was a major player for years, but I thought they'd kind of given up on steeplechase in favor of flat. Maybe they're reprioritizing.

In It To Win It and Earl Grey are here again. Now I know that Earl Grey starts out quick but isn't a stayer, so I'm not worried. In It To Win It did quite well last time, coming in third place, but was always a length behind Five and me. I'm not too worried about either of them facing off against Obsidian Devil at full throttle. I haven't heard from Patrick, In It To Win It's owner, since I

smoked his horse at Down Royal, so I didn't even know he'd be here.

I feel a little guilty about that. I should've reached out to him, since I beat him, but I've been too busy.

Someone makes whistling sounds, and I turn to see Sean standing on the sidelines, waving. I smile at him, and he blows me a kiss.

Obsidian bumps my arm. I turn to face him, and he's shining like onyx. I try to see him as I did the very first time, lining up for the race at Down Royal, except this time, he's my horse. I'm riding him as his owner. The other jockeys and owners are looking at him, well-behaved, massive, powerful, and shiny, and they're thinking, "that gorgeous monster's going to destroy my horse!"

A rush of exhilaration pumps through me. For the very first time in my life, I'm absolutely sure I'll win. When I bet every last euro I had on Obsidian, I didn't feel sick like I did at Down Royal.

I felt confident.

So even though he's been a pain, and even though I'm both sad and relieved that he's leaving, at least we'll have this race to look back on.

I look around for my dad and finally spot him coming from the direction of the betting booth. At least I know he didn't have much to wager, and I'm pretty sure he bet on the winner this time.

When it's time to regirth, I don't even bother tightening the straps. All horses breathe in to make sure they have some extra room in their girth when you put on the saddle. A tight saddle's uncomfortable, after all. Eventually, they let it out and the saddle can be tightened. Obsidian knows a loose saddle might hurt me, so he never does that. I've never had to retighten it, not once.

Finn snorts at me. "Not even gonna check it, huh? He's just the perfect horse for you every time? Doesn't

240

even try for a little more comfortable ride?" He rolls his eyes.

"Stop. I already re-tightened it," I lie. "Can't fault me for getting ready a bit early on an important day like today."

Finn pats Flaming Shot's neck. At least he seems less frenetic than he was earlier. "Your horses are always well behaved, I'll give you that. Even the maniac you bought."

After the regirth, we mount up and walk in a circle. This time, Obsidian stands completely still, like he's carved from granite.

"What's your secret?" Finn asks. "Why do they always love you so much?"

I shrug. "I use carrot-scented shampoo."

Obsidian snorts.

"I roll in manure?" I smile. "And for my coup d'état, I have fingernails, so I give the best butt scratches."

Finn wrinkles his nose. "I know you're kidding, but there must be something," he says. "Butterscotch? Coffee? Peppermint-flavored beer? What do you give them that makes them love you so?"

Obsidian bares his teeth at Finn and shifts sideways. Flaming Shot practically bounces away, almost unseating my friend. "Even now, it's like he's mad at me for giving you a hard time." Finn shakes his head. "I still feel like that horse threw the race at Down Royal so you could win." He waves at me with one hand, shifting the reins a bit and startling Flaming Shot. "I know that sounds crazy, so you don't need to mock me, alright?"

Luckily, before I have time to say much else, they call for the tape.

It's still drizzling, just like it was at the Grand National when Mom raced. And when Mom died from her fall.

I'm usually uneasy when it's raining because of that, but today I feel as solid as I've ever felt. My horse is a partner,

not a liability, and I know he's got the skill and power to win.

We all shift in an unruly mass toward the tape, the jockeys barely containing our horses, our hearts hammering almost as much as theirs.

We're all ready to go.

The ground's heavy, and chunks of it fly up from the horses' hooves as we trot ahead. My hands are clammy in my gloves, and I shudder. Now that we've come down to it, even knowing I'm on Obsidian, even knowing it's not Aintree and I'm not my mother, part of me wants to back out, to turn Obsidian around and trot him right off the track.

He glances back and whinnies at me, as if to say, *I'm here. You're not alone.*

Strangely, it helps.

I breathe in and out deeply. The tape drops and we're off. I rise to posting easily, and Obsidian's familiar, pounding run calms my staccato heartbeat.

I hold Obsidian back and he tugs, trying to surge forward, but I want to see the other horses—how they run, how they move, and the way they maneuver. The only chance to do that is to be behind them on the first jump. It's a plain fence that's straight, no ditch. Obsidian's literally chomping at the bit, but he listens to me and hangs back.

Flaming Shot pulls ahead quickly, with Brigadier General less than a length behind him. Down On My Luck and Apex are neck and neck just behind, with In It to Win it and Earl Grey just barely ahead of us. Apex pulls left, and Brigadier holds back before the jump, almost like he dreads the fences. Obsidian sails over the obstacle, his hooves not even brushing the spruce branches laid out on top, not that very many are still in place by the time we finally clear it.

As we come up on the open ditch, our second jump, I

let Obsidian go. He flies over it and tears up the turf, chunks of sod pelting the ground behind us, one of them even flying forward to hit my helmet. We pass In It To Win It and Earl Grey before we reach the third jump, which we take going into a right curve. Kempton's a right-turning triangle track, and I worry for a moment that Obsidian took the jump too fast. But his stride doesn't falter, and we swing tightly around the curve, passing Apex and pulling even with Down On My Luck. He runs alongside Down for a moment, but just after the fourth fence, we pull ahead of him, too.

Only Flaming Shot and Brigadier General are ahead of us as we sail over the second open ditch. I pull back on Obsidian a bit and we cruise along, gaining very slowly on the two frontrunners.

I watch them carefully as we approach. Flaming Shot's sailing over his jumps, barely brushing the top of the sixth fence. Finn's a talented rider, probably even better than I am, and Flaming Shot's clearly in his element, running on boggy ground.

I glance up around the curve. After the sixth, there's a long straight. "This is our window. Let's do this."

Obsidian's hooves are churning already, but when I urge him to speed up, he shoots ahead like a rocket, plowing past Brigadier General, who shies right as we pass him. We pull up neck-and-neck with Flaming Shot as we go over the seventh jump. Obsidian bobs his head at Finn, who startles at being acknowledged by a horse, but he regains his focus and turns back to the course and his mount. We pound along, staying neck-and-neck through fences eight and nine and into the open stretch that follows.

I glance at Finn for a moment. If there was anyone I could ever tell, anyone who would believe me and keep his mouth shut, it's him. I meet his eye once, and then I ask Obsidian to make his move. As fast as we've been going all

along, I've never really asked Obsidian to pull out all the stops. We sail over the tenth fence, and I swear we're defying gravity over the first open ditch in the second circuit.

I glance behind us just before the next jump, and I see that we're five or six lengths ahead, and Brigadier trails Flaming Shot by almost as much. This race was supposed to be a close one, but we've blown the other grade one horses, including last year's champion, out of the water. It's a good thing Obsidian isn't going to the Grand National, because today's race will earn him a steep handicap.

Thankfully, it'll also earn me a big pile of money.

All we have to do is maintain our monstrous lead through the end. Only, Obsidian stumbles. I very nearly topple over his ears, barely hanging on.

"What was that?" I gasp.

Obsidian rights himself, never really stopping, but slowing alarmingly before he picks up speed again.

I don't dare look back, but I can *hear* how close the other riders have drawn. We're still going to pull it off, but then he stumbles again, this time harder, like there's something wrong with his front right hoof.

I was already nervous, so I was holding on tighter than usual. That means I don't come close to falling, but it's happened too near the finish line. Finn passed us just after the second stumble, and we don't have time to recover.

We lose to Flaming Shot by a nose.

In the two months I've had him, I've never felt Obsidian stumble like that. In fact, I didn't think he could.

While everyone cheers and shouts for Finn and Flaming Shot, I hop off Obsidian immediately. "Are you alright?" I stare him in the eyes.

He bobs his head.

"Are you sure?"

He tosses his head toward the stands.

I turn to look where he's pointing, but my dad and Sean aren't there. Actually, I don't see anyone I recognize. "Did something happen?"

He bobs his head.

But, what?

I won't know until I manage to get him alone and I can change him. Ugh, what a mess.

It hits me then, how bad it really is.

I was counting on the prize money. I needed it, not only to repay the balloon note, but to pay taxes on the winnings I used to buy Obsidian Devil. And on top of that, I bet every single euro I had left.

And I just lost all of that, too.

I'm dead broke, and I'm sure my dad is as well.

At this point, I'm out of options. I'm going to have to sell all the land and just pray that our new neighbor isn't the villain I worry he might be.

Maybe it's Sean. I've always thought that might be a possibility. But as I ponder that chance, for some reason, it doesn't make me feel any better.

It makes me feel worse.

And I don't want to explore what that means, but I'm terribly afraid it's because I've just realized that my only option may be the one I don't want.

20

Sean doesn't even seem upset.

"Hey, look, you took a horse no one could control and almost made him a champion." He winces, hearing how that sounds. "It wasn't on you. I think there's something wrong with his leg, maybe. And that insane trainer wasn't even there. I looked everywhere. Maybe he's drunk and passed out, I don't know."

"Sean—"

He holds up a hand. "No, it's fine. I'll stop talking about it. Not the time."

"It's hard to believe that just happened," I say. "I mean, we had it."

"Please don't worry about it. And on the bright side, I bet I can get the bank to release him as collateral, now." He winks.

As if it would take more than a simple call from him at any point.

"Have you thought about selling him to my friend? I still think we could make that work. Maybe not for quite as much, though, maybe we still could. It's not like he wants to run him—he wants to use him as a stud for his program,

and clearly the horse can clear a fence. Plus, he loves black as a color."

It's like he can't stop talking. Does he think it'll cheer me up? It's just depressing me more.

"Sean," I say quietly. "It's fine. I'll be alright."

Luckily, my dad and John show up to distract him. The three of them are like drunk frat boys, encouraging each other, and I'm kind of sick of hearing it. None of them really *get* it, and I still feel like Obsidian has something to tell me.

But when I look down, I have a new text from my real estate agent. She's checking in, again, to see if I've made a decision about the deal.

It's the day after Christmas, but I don't blame her. The offer is time sensitive, and it's a lot of money. As soon as I get Obsidian into his stall, I pick up my phone and call her. It's not like I could change him right now, anyway. Literally anyone could walk through that stall at any moment. It's too risky.

She picks up on the third ring.

And I tell her we'll take the offer.

"I need it to close as soon as it possibly can," I say.

Between the taxes on the sale of the land—which will be brutal—and on my winnings from Down Royal to two different countries, I'm not going to have much left over, but I should still be able to repay Sean and the balloon note, and then all this will be behind me. If I'm lucky, I'll have a bit left to replenish my business account from the hits it's taken recently.

Obsidian begins pacing, and I know he wants me to change him, but I can't. Not yet. "I'm sorry," I say. "We just lost a big, high profile race, and there's no telling who might come in here, and no plausible reason to tell them why you're not here."

As predicted, Sean's head pops over the edge of the stall

less than five minutes later. "I know you need to clean up, regroup, whatever. But since you're close, I want to see you, obviously."

Before I can even open my mouth, he plows ahead.

"Let me take you to dinner. You've been amazing, putting up with my house, my parents, and the worst parts of my life. Let me remind you what the good parts are."

It's the smart thing to do.

It's really the only thing to do. Even if I don't think he's the guy for me, I don't think I can afford to upset him right now. Which. . .what does that make me? Am I a prostitute? Oh, no. I am. Am I?

I nod numbly. "Sure."

"Text me when you're ready, and I'll be right over."

My dad and John come by to cheerlead as well, but I send them away just as quickly. And then, between what seems like one moment and the next, things become quiet. The horses have mostly been led away or fed their dinner and left for the night.

When Obsidian bumps my shoulder, I nod. "Yeah, it's time." I'm frankly surprised he wasn't making himself much more obnoxious.

This time, when I change him, I have clothing already waiting. He changes without any fuss or jokes. When I turn to face him, he's fully dressed and wearing the long wool overcoat I found in the boot of his car.

"What happened?" I ask.

He shrugs. "I thought at the time that maybe someone had tampered with the track, but that was crazy. I guess I just stumbled."

"Not to mention, it was our second time around. If someone had done something dicey, we'd have noticed on that first pass."

I'd been thinking about it, too. Wet weather is danger-ous, and the faster you're moving, the less control you have.

I'm sure for someone like Obsidian, someone powerful and talented and strong, that's a hard thing to admit, even to yourself.

"I'm just glad you're alright," I lie.

"You're disappointed," he says. "I'm sorry about that. I feel really bad—I know you needed that money."

I shrug. "It's fine. Sean will take care of it." I hate myself for saying that, but it's the right thing to do. Other than staying close to me to have access to his powers, he has no reason to want me.

I'm poor.

I'm not young or fresh.

I'm average looking.

And I'm not that smart.

Plus I owe a bundle of money, to pretty much everyone, and I'm about to lose my family land.

For a split second, I contemplate calling my brother again. I dismiss it right away. Even if he changed his mind, which seems really unlikely, help from him would be worse than help from Sean. If I can't let my, well, almost my boyfriend, pay my debt, how could I let the brother who abandoned us do it? No, we'll still have the house, the old barn, and a few small pastures. It's enough.

"I owe you an apology," Aleks says. "After we lost, instead of trying to barge my way over and force you to do something, I sat back and listened for a moment."

This should be interesting.

"And when I started doing that, it made me think. I know this sounds idiotic, but for the first time since meeting you, I thought back to the moment we met, at a race like this one, and I thought about what that was like for you. What you gave up for me, to save me, and then how your sacrifice became even worse when you found out I wasn't really a horse at all."

It's taken him eight weeks to get there, but I'm glad

that he's learning to think about things from another person's viewpoint. That's some real, adult behavior. He may be over a hundred, but he hasn't really acted very mature.

Until now.

"I'm sorry, Kristiana. I'm sorry for further wrecking a life that was already hard. I'm sorry for being another burden to you. I'm sorry for interfering with your relationship with—" He chokes up here, and clears his throat. "With your relationship." He coughs again.

"It's fine—"

"No," he says. "It's not fine. For my entire life, I've seen what I wanted, and then I've taken it. End of story. Except, with you, I don't want the story to end." He freezes then, and he shakes his head. "What I mean is, I don't want to hurt you. Not any more than I already have." He shuffles a bit, and looks down at his hands. It may be the first time I've seen him look nervous. "I guess what I'm trying to say is that I'm sorry for everything, and I'll do as you asked and leave, and I hope that one day, you'll forgive me."

It's one of the nicest apologies I've ever heard, and it makes me feel a little better. "It's been a rough few weeks, but very few of my difficulties were caused by you, and almost none of them were caused on purpose."

"I think Sean will move past it, for what it's worth," he says. "Once I'm gone, I doubt he'll look back much on what I've done. He doesn't seem to be that kind of guy."

He's not. I'm lucky about that, at least. "You're right, and now it's my turn."

"Turn?" Aleks' brow furrows. "For what?"

"You made a very nice apology. Now you have to listen to my answer."

"Your—you don't have to give me an—"

I reach out and take his hand. "I forgive you, Aleksandr Volkonsky. I forgive you for being rude, for being pushy, for

biting people, and for arguing with me all the time. I forgive you for costing me a quarter million to save, and then for losing that race with a stumble. I forgive you for that, and for anything and everything else. All that you've done, and all that you will do."

A weird sort of shivery, twitchy, buzzy kind of sensation begins, starting at the base of my back, and traveling up my body and down at the same time, and then exploding out my extremities. My entire body bows, and then constricts, and I cry out and collapse against the shavings piled up in the stall.

And then the insane feeling is just. . .gone.

"Kris," Aleks says. "Are you alright?" He crouches next to me, but before he can touch me, he freezes. His eyes widen. His mouth drops open, and he inhales, slowly.

"What?" I force myself into a seated position and look around. The lights are still on outside. No one else is crying out or making a sound. Even the horses on either side of us seem calm enough, judging by the lack of pawing, neighing, or whinnying.

"It's gone," Aleks says. "For the first time since that night when everything went black in 1917, the curse is gone, and I sense my powers."

I just lost a race—with the highest stakes I've ever had —and now I'm out of options.

So why does what just happened upset me more than that?

The answer's horrifying, but in this moment, I have to face the truth. I'm desperate for Aleksandr to stay. Had he needed me to use his powers, he would have pressed to stick around. He probably would have continued trying to convince me to go with him to Russia, too. Because he needed me.

He. Needed. Me.

Without me, he didn't have access to his magic.

He felt vulnerable. He was afraid. He has enemies that could come for him at any time, and he wanted me around in case they showed. I knew all of that, but at the same time, I also thought maybe we shared something special, a bond.

"That's good news," I force myself to say. "Isn't it?"

He swallows slowly, his eyes intent on my face. "Is it?"

"Of course," I say. "I was going to send you away either way, but now you don't even need my help anymore."

He nods. "It's true that I don't."

"You can go home, and I can too. Neither of us need to worry, or fret, or stress."

"Aren't you the least bit curious *why* the curse suddenly just. . .lifted?" Aleks glances around the stall. "I mean, two months of riding and shifting and intermittent instances of me using my power, and nothing. And then today? Bam."

It is kind of strange. "Maybe it was on some kind of bizarro timer. Or it could have been linked to some kind of life force, like a tree? And someone cut it down."

"At that moment?" He looks unconvinced.

"Does it really matter?" I ask. "Why?"

He stares at me.

"I mean, it's not like you want to stay with me now, right?" I hate myself for asking. The wobble in my voice is even worse than the words. It feels like even a kindergartner would be able to tell that I'm *hoping* he'll say yes. Desperately hoping that he still wants me now, even though he doesn't need me.

I hate myself for it.

"Kristiana." His voice is low, and it does something to me. The same thing it always does.

Heat in my stomach. Butterflies in my chest. My heart beating wildly. "Yeah?"

"You told me yourself." The corner of his full lips turns up. "You said I had to go, as soon as the race was past."

But I thought we'd win, I want to cry out. *I thought I'd be better without you. I thought I'd be relieved to watch you walk away.*

I never imagined it would feel like this. I never thought I'd be centimeters—no, millimeters—from collapsing in a heap and completely losing it.

But that's my answer. The answer I hoped I wouldn't find, but I kind of knew was there. The brilliant, powerful, absurdly handsome horse shifter was always far too good for me, and now he doesn't need me at all.

And he's going to do exactly what I made him swear to do.

He's going to leave me.

And he's not the one who's broken.

It's me.

It was me all along.

❧ 21 ❧

Just as they said they would, the buyer remains anonymous from start to finish. They provide the earnest money. They have a third party sign on their behalf, and now all that remains is for me to show up and sign for myself. My dad insists on going with me, even though we had the entire property transferred into my name.

"I'm going for moral support," he says.

But I know it's because he's worried this buyer will be there, ready to attack or mock or do who knows what, and he doesn't want me to be alone if that happens.

Since it's probably his fault if the person does something.

I spent a lot of time hoping it was Sean, which is ridiculous because I've basically been avoiding him since we left Kempton Park. It was almost necessary, actually. Even after all his pressure to let Aleksandr go and sell Obsidian, he was upset about how I handled it.

"I don't understand how you could just *decide* he had laminitis and sell him off like that," he said. "For pennies. *To the guy you laid off.*"

"It wasn't pennies," I countered.

"Did you feel guilty about letting him go?" He sighed. "He was rich, Kris. If he wanted that stallion, he could have paid for him."

Aleks did offer to repay me for the money I spent on buying him, but that felt. . .wrong somehow. I made all the decisions I made, and I just couldn't take it.

I did get some prize money for the races on both About Face, who won second place as well, and for Obsidian. Second place is called reserve champion. The purse isn't as big, but it's not nothing. It's just not enough to make much of a difference.

Which is why I specifically had to ask Sean to remove Obsidian Devil as collateral. . .since I didn't have him anymore. I had to fabricate the sale papers showing that I sold him for twenty grand. Two hundred and fifty to twenty in two months is pretty brutal, and maybe I shouldn't have had the sale made out to Aleksandr Volkonsky, but it just seemed easier. That way, no one could appear later, claiming that they were short one stallion.

"It's just. . .it's going to be hard to justify the huge loss, since he was jumping like a kangaroo at that race," he said. "A race that was broadcast internationally. He didn't look like he was close to laminitis."

The whole thing with Obsidian Devil was set up to make me a loser from the start, but at least I'm finally through with all that.

"Don't get me wrong," Sean finally said. "I'm delighted he's gone, along with that snake of a trainer, but my friend would have paid so much for him—even just as a stud. That money would've helped you a lot, I'm sure."

But the real reason he was upset was that I wouldn't take money from him, either.

"I know you spent all your funds on that race—you

were so sure you'd win." He shook his head. "It wasn't prudent."

I really thought it was, but turns out, like always, Sean was right.

Now that I'm standing in front of the door to the title company, my hope has reached a fever pitch. The only person who could have bought this land that might be good for me is Sean.

And at the same time, if he did that, I'm really stuck.

Because if he's such a good person that he'd do that for me in spite of me telling him not to? If he knows me well enough to know I'd always insist that he not help, while secretly hoping that he would? Well, it's substantial evidence of his love, for one. And beyond that, it shows how solid he is in his belief that he and I belong together.

Meanwhile, I grow more unsteady about a future with him every day.

When Aleks left, I thought his memory would fade. But every horse I ride reminds me he's not Obsidian. Even Five is no substitute. And every time I see a dark-haired, broad-shouldered man, my heart leaps.

None of them are him, of course.

He was only here while he needed me. It makes sense. A prince with magical powers who can shift into the most gorgeous stallion I've ever seen? And he even managed to regain his land and wealth?

We're not evenly matched.

We never were.

In fact, when I think about it, I still wonder why Sean likes me. He offers to give me the money for the loans and taxes daily. He's done that since the beginning. And if I asked him to, he'd pay the current buyer double just to cancel the contract, and then he'd pay off the note.

I know he would.

But now my time has come, and there's no stay of

execution waiting for me. Sean's not there with a big smile and a check in his hand. Even though I'm here to sign the final papers, there's still absolutely no evidence of who that buyer really is.

Fine. I also kind of hoped that maybe my brother Gustav would come through at the last minute. Or that my grandparents would have checked in and noticed that I was struggling. But, no. Nothing like that. The buyer stays anonymous, and my land and my stables are all gone, with the swirl of a pen.

None of it matters as much as I thought it would. Even selling most of my horses, and helping my dear friend Mirdza find another barn at which to teach, and cleaning up the old barn for the horses we're keeping. None of it hurts as much as the ache that's become omnipresent.

The ache from Aleks being gone.

After Sean left me so many years ago, I vowed that I'd never stand by and watch as someone I loved abandoned me. If I ever felt about someone the way I'd felt about Sean, I swore I would burn the world down to keep them by my side.

But the way I feel about Aleks, the way I mourn his absence, the way I pine for his memory, and the way I dream of the future I wish we'd had is like a torch compared to the candle I held for Sean.

And still, I let him go.

Why?

I didn't confess my feelings. I didn't beg him to take me. I was too stupid to agree to go with him when I still had a compelling reason. Maybe, given enough time, he'd have fallen for me.

Probably not, but who knows? "You see ugly girls with hot guys all the time, right?"

My dad frowns. "Are you talking to me?"

"No," I say. "I was talking to Mirdza."

"Oh. She's here?" He spins around, examining every inch of the office we're sitting in, waiting for copies of the final papers.

"Dad." I roll my eyes. "I'm kidding. Yes, I was talking to you."

"About ugly guys?" He opens his mouth to say something and then closes it again. "I don't understand."

"No." I drop my head on my hands. "Not ugly guys," I mumble. "Ugly girls."

"What girls are you talking about?"

"Never mind," I say.

That's sort of my mantra over the next few weeks. I work through my backlog of teeth floats, lameness checks, vaccinations, Coggins tests, and wolf-teeth removals, working harder than I ever have as a vet. And when I'm not growing my formerly flailing veterinary practice, I'm working with John on Five Times Fast.

"He's really come a long way since the time off with his abscess," John says. "I think he has a real shot."

Not that it really matters anymore. A million pounds would be amazing if we won, but even if I got it, I have no idea who I'd even petition about buying our land back. I focus on working and training every second I can, because when I'm not doing those things, I'm usually crying.

One dreary day in early March, Sean surprises me by just stopping by. I went from seeing him a few times a week before Christmas to just once a week since. It's been hard enough to force my smiles and make small talk just the one time.

Today's visit wasn't on the calendar.

I pull About Face up short. "Hey. What are you doing here? Did I forget something?"

He shakes his head. "No, I just decided to drop by."

"Oh." About Face dances sideways, and I tighten my

reins, reminding him to stand still. The young ones always have too much energy for their own good.

"This will only take a minute. Are you almost done?"

"Done?"

"On the horse?"

I pat the big sorrel's neck. "This is Five's brother, About Face. Remember?"

Sean blinks. "Oh. Okay."

He's never cared as much as I do about horses, but I thought he'd recall my star pony's little brother. Especially since he saw me take reserve—second place—on the hurdle with About Face the day after my epic fail on Obsidian.

"To answer your question, I can cool him down now. Give me ten minutes."

"I'll wait by that big tree near the barn."

We stopped calling it the 'old barn,' because now it's our only barn. I wonder about the reason for his visit the entire time I'm cooling About Face down. When I hand him off to John, I've narrowed the possibilities down to two.

He's either proposing, or he's dumping me.

You don't propose out of the blue like this. . .by saying "it'll only take a minute." Right?

So, maybe I've narrowed it down to one.

When I reach the big tree, I'm a little tense. "What's going on?" That sounds a little more aggressive than I intended, but I can't change that now.

Sean stands up and turns to face me, rubbing his gloved hands down the front of his slacks to smooth the wrinkles.

"Are you alright? Are your parents?"

He runs a hand over his face. "No, nothing like that. We're all fine. I'm sorry for being so cryptic."

"Okay."

He points at the barn. "It's super windy. Want to talk inside?"

I do not want to chat with him where Aleks pushed me against the wall and kissed me, but I can't tell him that, so I just say, "Uh, sure."

After we duck inside, I shove back all the memories that I usually pause to appreciate.

Sean looks edgy. Nervous. Even worse than me. "I need to get back for a meeting, but I just woke up today and had to see you."

"What?"

He turns so that we're staring right at one another. It's super strange.

"I always need to see you."

I swallow. "You're standing in front of me."

"No, what I mean is, every single day, I have this burning desire to see you. I. . .yearn. . .for you. Is that the right word? Maybe. Seeing you brings me joy. It makes me happy, and I know that might sound pathetic, but it's true."

A proposal? Is that actually happening?

"And I realized, as I looked at my calendar, that it feels like you don't care whether you see me or not. You schedule me in, like you'd set up your hair appointment, or a visit to see the dentist."

Oh. It's a break up after all.

"I want to ask you something, Kris, and I need an honest answer." He drops down on one knee. And he pulls a box from the inside pocket of his beautiful wool jacket.

He flips the box open. It's a gorgeous, deep blue sapphire—huge of course—with very large, very sparkly diamonds set on either side.

"If you hate this ring, you can pick anything you want. A dozen rings. I don't care."

I have no idea what to say.

"My question is this. Do you long to see me? Ever? And if so, then will you just marry me already?" His eyes look full to the brim with sorrow, not hopeful and excited. He

sighs, then, long and slow. "And Kris, if you don't long to see me, then let me go."

It's the weirdest, and quite possibly the saddest, proposal of all time.

I open my mouth to talk, but he cuts me off. Again.

"I know this might seem strange." He stands up, but he's still holding the box open. "I should explain. I know it's my fault we're in this spot. When I was younger, I let my parents dictate to me—pick the 'right' girl for me. I was too stupid to see that they had no idea what would make me happy. I was too weak to fight for you, then. But I've come to the conclusion that I can fight anyone and everyone in the world for you. . .except you."

Sean has always been very, very bright. And what he says hits me as exceptionally profound.

That's what I've been doing.

I've been fighting myself for him, trying to force myself to love him.

But it will never work, because I love Aleksandr.

"I'm sorry," I say. "I think you're right. I think the feelings I have for you are leftovers." I sigh. "If what we had then wasn't so special, neither of us would want to find it again so badly." I reach forward and gently close the box. "But I think we're both fighting too hard for something that isn't ever going to be the same."

Sean looks like he wants to argue with me. Maybe he wants to tell me that he's not fighting, and that being with me again is easy. But he's pragmatic enough to know that he has his answer, even if it's not the one he wants.

He hops up and hugs me abruptly, holding me tighter and longer than he ever has. And when he pulls back, a single tear rolls down his cheek.

Then he gets in his car and leaves.

It's such a *British* breakup. That thought makes me laugh, and then I start to cry. Because I should love him. It

would be so easy! Even if his family's annoying and even if we fight over where to live or how many children to have, life with Sean would be effortless, relatively speaking. He's supportive, and kind, and sensible, and he works hard.

But I can't change how I feel.

And what I want is a bullheaded, supercilious, brash, powerful, breathtakingly handsome Russian shapeshifter.

Who doesn't happen to want me.

And that's why I can't stop crying.

Certified letters are never good news.

In fact, I can't think of a single time in my entire life I've gotten a certified letter that wasn't *bad* news.

I've had more than my share of bad news the past twelve months, and I'm not keen on dealing with anything else. I stare at the letter addressed to Kristiana Liepa for way too long without opening it. But finally I march into my dad's bedroom, where he's still asleep, and poke him awake.

"Dad."

"What?" He sits up and rubs his eyes.

"Be honest."

He blinks. "About what?"

"Did you gamble again? Is someone else suing me for the house?"

He splutters. "Mīlu, what are you saying?"

"This." I thrust the letter at him.

He rubs his eyes and squints. "Who's it from?"

"A law office in England." Which is why I'm so suspi-

cious. He and John spent a lot of time 'out' when we were there a few months back. Could he have snuck off?

"Don't you think it's more likely that it has to do with Sean?"

"Why would Sean send me a certified letter?"

He shrugs. "I can't even afford to hire a lawyer, but even if I could, I've been good. I swear."

"Will you open it for me?"

Dad meets my eye. "Are you sure you want me to? What if it *is* from Sean? It could be personal."

"Like his bank suing me for selling Obsidian Devil?" It's honestly the only thing I can think of that might come to me from there. I looked it up—they can come after me personally for losses on assets pledged as collateral. I just didn't think they could do it now that we've paid off the note.

But who knows?

My English is decent, but it's much harder when I'm reading it instead of speaking. Plus, when half the words are bizarre legal ones based in Latin roots? The laws are confusing enough to make me nervous.

My hands shake as I open the letter.

But it's not from Sean.

It's from Aleksandr.

Or, his lawyer, anyway.

"Dear Ms. Liepa," I read. "Enclosed please find the documents required to deed the nineteen hundred and eleven acre tract of land and large horse barn adjacent to your homestead back into your name." I almost drop the letter.

"What?" Dad stands up, dragging half his blankets off the bed in the process.

"My client, one Aleksandr Volkonsky, has purchased the land on your behalf. It took some time to process the deed, given that he's a Russian citizen, but he wished us to

transfer it back into your name at the earliest possible date. Should you have questions or concerns, you may contact me, or you may reach out to my client directly at your convenience."

I can't believe what I'm seeing.

For all those weeks, I suspected that Sean might have bought my land, and that there may be some kind of giant surprise waiting for me. He certainly offered to do it often enough.

But Aleksandr knew me well enough to know I wouldn't accept money—and he just bullheadedly, brashly, *rudely* bought it in secret.

And then gifted it back to me.

I can't accept a gift like this, of course. Now, more than any other time in my life, I have a burning desire to win the Grand National so that I can repay him.

I'd need to do that in person, obviously, which means I'd need to travel to Russia and see him, face-to-face.

I buckle down over the weeks that remain, working harder than ever. I've never been more determined to win a race in my life, even if it is the one race that scares me more than any other.

My mother was determined to be the first woman to win the Grand National, many years ago. We all went to cheer her on. And we all saw when she lost her balance, fell, and struck the support beam on the Canal Turn.

She died in the hospital, two days later.

And I've never been able to make myself actually race in the Grand National. A woman did win a few years back, but I still think Mom would be proud of me for conquering her demons and mine. At least, I'm proud when I call up and register and when I put my check in the mail, with a shaking hand, to run the hardest course in the Grade One steeplechase circuit.

My desire to win that prize and take it to Aleksandr

carries me all the way to Liverpool, but looking at the track, all the fear comes back. I have three days to get used to being here, to breeze the course, and to shore up my confidence before I'm due to race.

I spend the first night drinking far, far too much.

Which makes me think about the last time I was drunk. Aleksandr got me back to the hotel room. It makes perfect sense for me to call him, now. But how can I? I don't have his phone number. Does he even have a phone number?

Something in the recesses of my brain surfaces.

That lawyer's letter. It said if I had questions, I could reach his client directly. At the time, I wondered if it was some kind of message. Was Aleksandr asking me to call him?

Of course he was.

How did I miss that before? I was an idiot.

I call the barn and talk to Eduards. With a little bit of explanation, he combs through the house and finds that stupid letter. And then he reads me the numbers. It takes a few tries, but I finally get it written on my arm, and then I dial it.

The numbers are weird. Like, to call Latvia, it's 371, but to call Russia, it's just one number. Seven. Like calling America. One. Why does England, which is just as fancy as America and Russia, maybe fancier, have *two* numbers? Forty-four? None of it makes any sense.

But when I get a voicemail—it is the middle of the night, isn't it? I start to talk.

"Aleksandr! It's me. You know me. I can change you into a horse. And you gave me an orange rock. With a dead butterfly. Anyway, I'm about to race, and then I'll be rich, and I'll come give you your money. Or if I'm not rich, I'll probably be dead."

That thought makes me sad, so I start to cry.

And I can't seem to stop crying.

Because he left me. And now I'm here, but he's not. "I almost wish you could just stumble again, because now I have to ride Five, and I love him, and I think he's great, but a lot of horses are great, and there are *so many* of them in the Grand National, that I could totally get jostled. I mean, I've never fallen off a horse before, but everyone does something for the first time."

Something hits me then.

"Like this. It's my first time calling you, and from a hotel phone, too. I had to press a lot of things to dial out, and I think the receptionist is mad at me, because she called me room eight-oh-one, and not even by my name." I swear under my breath. "Oh, no. I think calling from a hotel's really expensive." I swear again. "I should have used my cell phone, but it's roaming maybe so that costs a lot, too. And I have to save my money to pay you back. Bollocks. I should hang up."

And then I do.

Once I've told him how I feel, I realize how tired I am, and I curl up around my phone and go to sleep.

❧ 23 ❧

The next morning, there's a tapping at my door.

"Go away," I mumble. I groggily check my phone to see the time. "I don't have to be up for another hour."

The tapping continues.

I'm going to kill whatever housekeeper won't leave off and let me sleep off my hangover. John and Dad said they'd feed Five. But the tapping's so bad that I can't sleep through it.

Actually, it's transformed into something more like banging at this point. I shove myself up in bed, realize my hair's sticking out several inches away from my head in multiple directions, and decide I don't care. Nor does it matter that I'm wearing a ratty old shirt that Aleksandr ripped in one change or another, and that I sewed up again. Very badly. He took all his nice clothes when he left, and it's all I've got to remind me of him.

Well, this shirt and a lump of amber.

Not exactly very impressive mementos of our time together, but you work with what you have.

"I don't know who you are," I mutter, "but you're currently wrecking my morning at seven a.m., and I am not pleased." I slide the chain off the track and flip the lock. "I haven't gotten truly drunk in a very, very long time, and if you have a problem with my Frankenstein-inspired nightshirt, you can—" I whip the door open with a snarl, and freeze.

Aleksandr Volkonsky's standing in front of my door, wearing black pants and a charcoal sweater. His hair's grown out a little longer again—long enough to fall across his face again—but it doesn't quite block his flashing golden eyes. "Are you comparing my shirt to Dr. Frankenstein? Or to his monster?" He lifts both his eyebrows. "Because the doctor was just sad, but I feel like the monster was misunderstood."

I haven't even read the book, so I have no idea what I was saying. And I have no idea what he's doing here. Part of me thinks this is all some kind of dream.

"Are you going to invite me in, zaychonuk?"

I think about my trashed hotel room and shake my head. "No. I'm not."

"That's pretty rude. An old friend shows up, a friend you haven't seen in months, and whom you've barely called, and—"

"Barely called?" Why is my voice so high-pitched and squeaky? I force it down. "When did I call you?"

Aleksandr's head tilts sideways. "You called me last night. You don't remember?"

Last night's a big old blur. . .but I probe it, hard.

And I vaguely remember crying, and. . . Did I call Eduards? I close my eyes and wonder whether, instead of a dream, this could possibly be a nightmare. I open just one eye.

Nope.

Sinfully handsome Russian prince, still standing there.

"About that." I wince. "The thing is, I had a *lot* to drink last night, and—"

"Kris."

I can't meet his eyes. "I really didn't mean whatever I said."

"No?" His voice is so querulous, and I can't help myself. I look up.

"No," I say. "Not a word of it."

He leans against the doorframe, his face both cocky and curious at the very same time. "What exactly are you imagining you might have said?"

I swallow. "I always say things like that when I'm drunk. I mean, I haven't been drunk much—"

"You were drunk on Christmas Eve," he says.

I roll my eyes. "Barely. I mean, too drunk to drive, but not *really* drunk. Not so much that I don't recall what I said."

"What do you usually say to men when you're drunk?" He leans toward me a bit. It's too much, too early.

I know how I look in the morning, and I can see how he looks, and they're not a match. Adonis and a hedge witch do not fit. "The point is that, whatever I *did* say, it wasn't true."

"Even if you said you loved me?" I didn't realize someone could swagger with their tone, but now I know, and it's dangerous.

Also, I want to crawl behind the door and die. Did I really drunk call him and tell him I loved him? I'm a walking cliché. "Especially that."

He bites his lip to keep from beaming. "I knew it."

"Wait." I'm so lost. "Knew what?"

"You barely said anything at all, other than warning me that you were worried you might *die* if you rode Five Times Fast in the Grand National instead of me."

I roll my eyes. "It's not that I really think I might die. It's just that—"

"I looked it up." All the mockery in his tone and expression is gone. He frowns. "Your mother passed away, after a fall in the Grand National."

My nod's tight.

"I'm so sorry. You never mentioned it before."

I shrug.

"So I'm here." He reaches for my hand.

I shy back, scooting away from him as fast as I can without losing sight of him. There's no telling what he might do if I'm not watching. "I don't need comforting. It happened a long time ago."

He uses my retreat to advance through the door, shutting it behind him with an evil gleam in his eye. "But you've never raced in the Grand National before. I looked that up, too."

"You managed to dig up a lot of information for someone who spent all night on a redeye flight." The more I think about it, the more confused I get. "Wait, I called you really late."

He smirks. "They have internet on airplanes, you know, and you're kind of stuck on there with nothing else to do."

"They had a flight from Russia in the middle of the night?" I cross my arms.

He shrugs.

"Well, I'm sorry you flew all the way here, but I'm just fine, and I really don't need any help."

"I'm glad you're fine." He glances around the room, and then casually, almost too casually, says, "I don't see Sean here lending a hand."

"So there are some things you couldn't find the answers to on the internet." I can't help my self-satisfied grin.

A muscle in his jaw pulses in a very satisfying way. "Is he

here as your boyfriend? I mean, I assume he is, somewhere."

I look down at my feet. "Not as my boyfriend."

"So you're getting married?" Something about his choked tone has my eyes shooting upward. And for the first time, his confidence looks shaken.

"No," I say.

"You *already are* married?" Now he looks stricken.

"We broke up," I whisper.

"You. . ."

And then he's crashing into me, his arms wrapping around my waist and crushing me to him. Once our bodies are in contact from our knees all the way upward, one hand lifts my chin, and his mouth claims mine.

He's not a gentle, considerate kisser.

Aleksandr Volkonsky only knows one way to act: he possesses, takes, and conquers.

And it's glorious. Kissing him, being claimed by him, is every single thing I remembered. His body's so large, so strong, and so unyielding that I melt against him. He pulls back for a moment, and then another, simply breathing next to me. Staring at my face.

Until I whimper.

And he practically snarls. "Not being near you has been torture." His voice is ragged. "Even when I played my last card, nothing."

"Your last. . ." Realization dawns. "Do you mean the land?"

"The land that you were desperate to save." He exhales, his breath warming my entire body and heating me up in places I didn't realize I had gone cold. "The land you didn't want someone else to give you."

"Because I wanted *you* to give it to me," I whisper.

And he kisses me again, even more passionately than before. His hands drag upward, from my lower back to my

shoulders, bringing me closer, closer, and impossibly closer still, until I can't tell where he stops and I begin.

Somehow, it's still not close enough.

It might never be enough.

"The worst thing about leaving," he breathes against my ear, "was knowing that *he* was right here with you. By your side. But I knew I couldn't win you by simply taking what I wanted. No, like breaking a horse—you had to come to me."

And my drunk call? That's what he was waiting for? "I should've gotten hammered long before last night."

"Oh, yes," he says. "You should have."

"I'm glad you flew all night," I say. "I've missed you for a very long time. Since the day you left."

"But you sent me away." He blinks, his grip on my shoulders loosening. "You made me go."

"Because you didn't really want me," I say. "As soon as you didn't *need* me to let you use your magic, you stopped fighting about taking me with you."

His eyebrows draw together, making a tiny number eleven above his nose. "No, that's not it."

"Why did you leave, then?"

"That day, when I stumbled?" He releases me entirely and drops to a seat on the edge of my bed. He closes his eyes. "I thought they were there. I was certain of it. The ground became terribly hot beneath my hooves, and I turned to look at the stands, and I saw Mikhail. That's why I stumbled. The second time, I saw Boris. You weren't physically touching me, thanks to the saddle, your boots, and your gloves. I couldn't have done a thing to keep you safe—I was powerless and vulnerable."

"Wait, Mikhail and Boris? Is that—"

"Boris Yurovsky and Mikhail Kurakin," he says. "I'd been waiting for them to find me since the day I woke up, but the day had finally come. When they didn't come after

me initially, I panicked a bit. What if they waited until it was just me and you? What if I couldn't keep you safe? I had no idea how many of them there were."

"Did they find you?" I can't believe I sent him away to deal with that alone.

"When the curse was broken that very day, I saw it as a sign. I needed to get away from you and deal with my past. I needed to be clear of all that before I could risk being with you." He shakes his head. "You'd been through enough."

"And?"

He shrugs. "I must've been mistaken. If there's one thing they'd surely take note of, it was me moving back into my ancestral home. If it really was them, if they're still alive, they'd have come for me. They never did."

"It's been months, now." A shiver shoots up my spine, but not a good one. An ominous one.

"Even once I was back in Russia, I couldn't find the Romanovs or the Khilkovs, either. I searched every lead I could find." He shrugs. "I'm sorry I stayed away so long—I needed to make sure you'd be safe with me. And I thought I'd give you time to realize that you cared for me."

"I knew that all along."

"I've been terrified that my desire to keep you safe might have made enough space for that stupid British moron to squeeze in."

"I didn't have enough room in my heart for anyone but you." I clap my hand over my mouth.

But it's too late. Aleks has never smiled quite this big. Not once. "Say it again."

"You."

"Ha." He stands up and begins to advance on me again. "Did I mention that I love seeing you wearing nothing but my shirt?"

The inside of my stomach drops out. My body begins to

tremble, and I back up, slowly. "What did you want me to say, exactly?" I bat my eyes at him, wondering if it's actually cute or whether I look idiotic.

"You said you felt a certain way about me." His sideways grin is cockier than I've ever seen it.

"Why don't you tell me how *you* feel, and then we'll see what I want to say in return?"

"Kristiana Liepa," he says, "from the moment you climbed up on me and rode me—"

"That sounds really dirty."

"Oh, I should hope so."

I roll my eyes. "Start over."

He laughs. "Fine. From the moment I set my horsey eye on you that day at Down Royal until today, I have felt almost exactly the same. There's no one else in the world I'd rather be with, and that's why I was already in England when I got your message—I had lost patience with waiting on you, and I was going to be here for your race."

He was already here?

I was out drinking, wallowing, thinking about racing on the track where my mom died alone, and wishing he was here with me, and he was already here?

"We're both idiots," I say.

"But we both figured it out, in the end." His eyes darken a bit, and his gaze intensifies. "When you're willing to do absolutely anything for someone, when you're willing to kill anyone—"

"*Kill* anyone?" I can't help giggling. "You're really bad at this. You shouldn't talk about killing people when you're supposed to be telling me you love me."

"Who says?" He frowns. "I think it would be sexy, knowing you'd do anything for me."

"I wouldn't kill someone for you," I say.

His mouth drops open. "No?"

I shrug. "And I won't ever have to." It's my turn to

275

smile. "I think that's what I love most about you, Aleksandr Volkonsky. You may be old, and you may be pushy, and you may sometimes act like a horse's rear end, but when it matters, I know you'll literally bury people alive to keep me safe, and that's a very good feeling."

This time, he does *not* release me for any reason.

24

Aleks really wasn't kidding when he said he came to make sure I felt as safe as I possibly could. Apparently that includes bribing officials to allow us to change our farm's entry from Five Times Fast. . .to Obsidian Devil.

"But I sold him." I'm still staring at the slip that says I'm riding Obsidian Devil in the Grand National tomorrow. "I mean, I have papers that say I did."

He shrugs. "I guess you bought him back."

"Sean will know something's up," I say.

Aleks lifts one eyebrow. "Is that going to be a problem?"

I shrug. "Probably not. I mean, I suppose he could also believe I bought you back again."

"Is he here?"

"No idea," I say. "I haven't talked to him since we broke up—I mean, we weren't officially *together*, but you know."

"Actually, breakups and whatnot are pretty modern," he says. "In my time, your parents kind of pointed and said, 'you're marrying her,' and you just did it."

I have trouble believing that. "Are you serious?"

"I mean, they'd point and they'd say that. The 'just did it' part might have been a stretch, even then."

"Did they ever tell you to marry someone?"

"My parents died when I was eleven," he says. "So, no."

How did I not know that? "I have a lot of things to learn about you, old man."

He scowls at me. "Keep calling me that, and we'll see how much I share."

"I guess we will see," I say, "because I have no intention of giving up my favorite nickname. No one else in the world knows how old you really are."

"True enough," he says.

"I hope you've stayed in decent shape—have you spent any time as a horse lately? We're running the biggest race in the entire circuit tomorrow, so you'd better be ready."

"I spent some time as a horse," he says. "I'm sure we'll do fine."

"Assuming you don't trip and fall and ruin everything again," I tease.

"Yes, assuming that." He reaches his hand into his pocket. "But even if you don't win the purse, trust me when I say, you can buy and do anything you want from here on out." He pulls his hand out, and he's clearly holding something. He shakes his hand a little, clearly telling me to hold mine out, too.

"What?" I extend my hand and flip my palm over.

"Here."

He drops an entire handful of gemstones onto my palm. Deep red, a gorgeous, cerulean blue, a rich, vibrant green, and several enormous diamonds. I can barely believe I'm staring at them.

"I couldn't have your nicest gemstone be a gift from *that guy.*"

"Oh, please. My nicest—"

I also write contemporary romance and women's fiction under B. E. Baker.

The Finding Home Series:

Finding Faith (1)

Finding Cupid (2)

Finding Spring (3)

Finding Liberty (4)

Finding Holly (5)

Finding Home (6)

Finding Balance (7)

Finding Peace (8)

The Finding Home Series Boxset Books 1-3

The Finding Home Series Boxset Books 4-6

The Birch Creek Ranch Series:

The Bequest

The Vow

The Ranch

The Retreat

The Reboot

Children's Picture Book

Yuck! What's for Dinner?

ALSO BY BRIDGET E. BAKER

The Magical Misfits Series:

Mates: Minerva (1)

Mates: Xander (2)

The Birthright Series:

Displaced (1)

unForgiven (2)

Disillusioned (3)

misUnderstood (4)

Disavowed (5)

unRepentant (6)

Destroyed (7)

The Birthright Series Collection, Books 1-3

The Anchored Series:

Anchored (1)

Adrift (2)

Awoken (3)

Capsized (4)

The Sins of Our Ancestors Series:

Marked (1)

Suppressed (2)

Redeemed (3)

Renounced (4)

Reclaimed (5) a novella!

A stand alone YA romantic suspense:

Already Gone

ABOUT THE AUTHOR

Bridget's a lawyer, but does as little legal work as possible. She has five kids and soooo many animals that she loses count. There are for sure horses, dogs, cats, rabbits, and so many chickens. Animals are her great love, after the hubby, the kids, and the books.

She makes cookies waaaaay too often and believes they should be their own food group. In a (possibly misguided) attempt at balancing the scales, she kickboxes daily. So if you don't like her books, maybe don't tell her in person.

Bridget is active on social media, and has a facebook group she comments in often. (Her husband even gets on there sometimes.) Please feel free to join her there: https://www.facebook.com/groups/750807222376182

She also gives a free book to everyone who joins her newsletter at www.BridgetEBakerWrites.com